Robert Derry is in his fifties<s>,</s> <s>a</s>
Consultant, living in Somerset, England<s>,</s>
University before moving to London, w<s>here he</s>
London, the location of his first novel - '<s>The</s> <s>W</s>aterman - published by
Austin Macauley Publishers Ltd in 2021. He is an avid supporter of
Aston Villa Football Club, who hail from his hometown of
Birmingham, England and of the NFL, following the Green Bay
Packers, from a distance. He is married to Tina with two grown-up
children and two troublesome cats.

THE BROTHERS

"O earth, O Sea, cover not thou their blood."

ROBERT DERRY

To / Jo

Hope you like it

[signature]

The Brothers is a work of fiction, based on historical fact. All names or characters, businesses or places, events, or incidents, are based on contemporary sources, primarily the accounts of Thomas Clarkson and Granville Sharp, though some scenes are of course entirely fictitious. Some names – of people and companies – and dates have been changed to suit the plot and/or to preserve anonymity, however, as far as possible I have stuck to the timing of events as they unfolded according to official records and memoirs.

Conversations between my main protagonists and certain characters, including John Newton, John Wesley, various Members of Parliament including Pitt and Wilberforce, and slave traders including Tobin and Pinney, are often based on actual tracts and transcripts written by or attributed to them in their lifetimes, so as to properly represent their views and their place in history. Although the settings for the meetings are entirely fictitious and the conversations completely imagined, in many cases, their words are not.

IN MEMORY OF THE MILLIONS OF AFRICAN LIVES THAT WERE STOLEN, THEIR NAMES LOST TO HISTORY, BEFORE AND SINCE THE ABOLITIONIST CAUSE WAS WON, AND TO THE TWELVE WHO DEDICATED THEIR LIVES TO BRING ABOUT AN END TO THE TRADE.

Book subtitle quote – *'O Earth O Sea Cover Not Thou Their Blood'* – John Wesley

CHAPTER ONE

"The merchants of Bristol, tho' very rich, are not like the merchants of London; the latter may be said to vie with Princes of the Earth; whereas the former, being rais'd by good fortune, and prizes taken in the wars, from masters of ships and blunt tars, have inbib'd the manners of those rough gentlemen so strongly, that they transmit it to their descendants, only with a little more of the sordid than is generally to be found among British sailors."

Daniel Defoe – A Tour through the whole island of Great Britain (Ed. 1742)

Bristol in the latter years of the eighteenth century was a city on the edge. In less than one hundred years it had been transformed from an unremarkable stage-post on a westbound pilgrim's journey into a bustling and thriving port. By then its burgeoning population had burst forth across the remnants of its southern walls to lay claim to the surrounding countryside in the name of progress, as the port of Bristol took its place amongst the most prominent in all of England.

Teetering tiers of ramshackle houses peered into every passing cart as an endless line of draymen coaxed and cursed their weary packhorses along each cramped and cobbled street. The waggons creaked and groaned in protest, as each weaved its way ever closer to the quayside and the repellent river, whose stink was overwhelming to the untrained nose. The stench of every human and inhuman waste came together in that short stretch of waterway, the fall-out from a rapidly expanding city and its ravenous populace. In between the hulls of a hundred or more seabound vessels, a flotilla of discarded garbage so obscured the water beneath, that a newly arrived visitor could have easily mistaken it for some exotic carpet and stepped unwittingly onto its surface.

Not that anyone would have done so and lived to tell the tale.

An armada of ships and boats knocked and barged at the quayside to block the way of anyone curious enough to want to cross; their mooring ropes locked in monstrous coils amongst the filth and slime, as if primed to strike out at the unwary. In the early morning light, a forest of masts stretched skywards, their long shadows reaching across the docks like fingers, to fan the stone frontage of the Custom House on the other side of the stunted waterway and to signal the start of another day's trading.

Stacked high on the quayside, waiting patiently for the weary labourers to emerge from the drinking dens and flophouses that filled the dark forbidding back streets of Bristol, sat a line of bricks, and worked stone; the carefully measured ballast of several ships that would soon set sail for Africa and then onwards, to what many still called 'the New World'. Further on, dull figures sloped from boat to shore and back again, unloading and loading their goods under the watchful eye of stewards and Agents, who were carefully taking stock of each delivery before entrusting them to the crew. Only then would they begin the arduous task of onboarding the vast array of barrels and boxes, in readiness for another unforgiving voyage.

This was the scene that greeted the Reverend Thomas Clarkson as he cantered past the New Rooms at Broad Mead to meet with his nemesis. In a city such as this, a stranger could easily go unnoticed for weeks on end, quietly slipping into its shadows to evade detection, if that was his wont, but not this man. This man was striking in his stature, and although his pallid complexion and unremarkable face were not his calling card, his strident frame always ensured that he was never quickly forgotten. That and his unkempt mop of red hair, which refused to let him become lost in any crowded city, not least one where strangers were advised never to walk unaccompanied.

Any wish that he may have had to keep a low profile in the west of England was therefore doomed from the start, but preserving his anonymity was not his primary purpose on that damp April day in the year of our Lord 1787.

The red-headed Reverend was intent on causing a stir and the merchants of Bristol were firmly in his sights, but it would be an untruth to claim that his arrival that morning was an entirely fearless one. Even with God on his side, Thomas Clarkson knew that the venture on which he was about to embark was a dangerous one for any man, even for a man of the cloth. What he was about to do would strike at the very heart of capitalism, it would take the sword of justice to the very heartbeat of the nation's flourishing Empire in an attempt to uncouple a vital link in the ever-expanding chain of free commerce.

The Trade.

-ooo-

Thomas Clarkson was born in Wisbech in Norfolk in April 1760, at which time millions of enslaved Africans had already been forced to make the hazardous journey across the Atlantic Ocean, where a short and savage life in servitude awaited them. As the second son of an Anglican minister, a long and comfortable life of service in some East Anglian backwater beckoned him. In spite of his father's untimely death, when he was just eleven years old, he had excelled at his local grammar school under his doting mother's watchful eye and was soon propelled towards Cambridge University and a life of academic and theological contemplation.

That was until he decided to enter a competition.

A Latin competition to be precise, The Vice-Chancellor's annual prize awarded to the student who could write the best, most comprehensive and compelling rationale as to whether or not it was acceptable for one man to enslave another.

Or to give it its proper Latin title, '*Anne liceat invitos in servitutem dare.*'

Needless to say, after many months of research and many nights spent poring over faded manuscripts and obscure letters by the light of his late father's lantern, he had won the competition and returned to Cambridge in 1785 to receive his prize and to read his essay out loud, in Latin, to a variety of assembled honoured guests and dignitaries.

Most of the men gathered there that day saw the competition as little more than an academic exercise, one that might give rise to some lively conversation around the candlelit dinner tables of the local landed gentry, but which would soon slip from the collective memory once winter had loosened its grip and the Fenlands had begun to thaw. A nice diversion, an interesting conversation piece, but not a suitable topic for polite company and so, one best debated late into the night in the billiard room or drawing room of their fine Georgian houses, accompanied by a suitably rich bottle of rum and a measure of finest Virginian tobacco.

Yet for the young Thomas Clarkson, something had been awakened in him during those months of study that would not leave him, however hard he tried to look forward to his assigned career in the clergy as the newly appointed Deacon at Winchester. A sturdy hand had clutched at his conscience and refused to let it go, tugging at him like a carp that is caught on an angler's line, pulling him ever further into a river that had already begun to flood. As he mounted his horse and headed south that day, along the old Cambridge Road towards London, he had no idea what awaited him, nor how his life was about to be changed forever in one single cataclysmic moment.

His research had exposed him to the dreadful facts, and they had rendered him a tortured man. As a young man, growing up in blissful ignorance of the world and all its evils, he had been completely unprepared for the dreadful reality of human trafficking, a scourge that he now knew beyond all doubt lay at the heart of his beloved country's commercial revolution.

During the daytime his newly acquired knowledge had left him with an uneasy feeling, not unlike nausea, but at night he would find rest hard to come by. Sometimes he could not even close his eyes for fear of unrelenting nightmares, and the first light of day would often be creeping into his room before, completely exhausted, he was finally able to sleep. But it was often a fitful slumber into which he sank.

For months he had argued aloud with himself, and with anyone else that had the misfortune to cross his path, that someone should take on the task of bringing these outrages to an end once and for all. As the months turned into a year, he had become increasingly dismayed that no eighteenth-century Saint George had charged onto the scene, lance in hand and shield aloft, to slay the European dragon that was continuing to strike terror into the beating heart of the African continent. His daily walks in the local woods had been intended to clear his mind. But whilst the fresh air may have been good for his constitution, the solitude that he had felt in those moments failed to rid him of the rising sense of dread, at the thought that no one was ever going to step forward to shield those souls from the vicious assault of the slave trade.

If anything, the situation seemed to be getting worse by the year. In correspondence with a whole raft of leading industrialists, merchants, and politicians, it had become clear to him that London, as well as many of Britain's western ports, were now flourishing off the back of triangular trade as it had become known. A plethora of manufactured goods such as guns, worked metal, linen and cotton garments were shipped to Africa, where they were used to barter for the slaves. In turn, the captives were then shipped to the colonies across the Atlantic, where they were sold or traded for sugar, cocoa, and tobacco.

Finally, these raw materials were then returned to England to feed the insatiable and increasingly varied appetites of a rapidly expanding English audience. And in the slaving ports of England, each one had long since taken full advantage of the new opportunities that The Trade had to offer. As a result, the local merchant classes had become the proud owners of sugar refineries, chocolate processing plants and cigarette factories, embracing the chance to turn opportunity into profit in full knowledge of The Trade that supplied them.

When it came to The Trade, they put their consciences to one side and invested with relish.

He would always be able to recall the moment when the realisation dawned that it was he who was to take on the might of Empire, in an attempt to rid the world of the curse of slavery. In fact, it was an unchanging tale that he would tell over and over again as the years went by, and never once would he take credit for the act or its consequences; he would always lay all the glory for that squarely at the feet of God.

On the second day of a two-day journey down from Cambridge to London, he had set out early on horseback from his humble lodgings in Royston, quite unprepared for the revelation that was about to befall him. It was a pleasant morning on the cusp of summer, and the field hands were already out in the meadows, standing watch over cattle that had wandered down to the river's edge for watering. As he passed through hamlet after hamlet, he had bid good morning to several cheery villagers as he would often do, some of whom may even have recognised him from previous expeditions to the capital. He was quite unmistakable in his outward appearance, his six-foot frame bedecked in black from head to foot and his flaming red hair on display even beneath his black felt hat, which sprawled over his kerchief atop his flowing tailcoat like a ginger ruff from a former age.

As he arrived at Wadesmill the church clock perched high above his head struck noon. He had made better time than was usual and so dismounted to give his faithful horse some time to recover and whilst it did, he walked for a while, lost in thought. After a few hundred yards he came across a grassy bank overlooking the peaceful water and decided that it would make a comfortable spot for lunch. The inn had prepared some thickly cut bread and sliced cheese and as his horse stomped off to graze and to take his fill of the fresh cold stream, Thomas Clarkson was struck all at once by a sudden realisation that was to be the defining moment of his life.

It hit him like a thunderbolt from a clear blue sky. A lightning strike that scorched his soul and branded the cause that would become his life's work onto his very being.

"It is I," he announced to himself, for there was no one else who could have heard it. "I am the one that must do it. I am the only one that can do it." Immediately, he whistled for his horse, but to no avail and instead he was forced to trot down to the edge of the River Rib, where the beast of burden had set its mind to settle for the day. A tug on the reins was met with a remorseful whinny, as the black stallion made his feelings on the matter clear, but the clergyman was not to be denied, and within minutes the rider was back in his well-worn saddle and cantering into the distance towards the fabled city, which was still half a day's ride away.

As he bore down on London he was becoming ever more frantic at the thought of the many tasks that lay ahead. A plan was already beginning to form in his mathematical mind, one that he had expressed in part to his Quaker friends, both in writing and in person over recent months. He knew only too well that overturning years of history was something that he could not hope to effect alone, nor was it something that could be brought to heel overnight, but the sudden need for urgency was now pressing on his heart, which was thumping like a blacksmith's anvil in his chest. He knew only too well that every minute wasted was another life lost, and although he was well aware that his efforts would take many years, if not decades, before he could hope to win a final victory, he was not a man to be put off a mission once he had accepted it for his own.

He knew that he was not the first to speak out against The Trade; many had gone before him, but it seemed that the world was not listening. His essay, which he hoped would soon be in print and so readily available to place before the most influential men in England, would only add to the reams of literature that was already stacked up against the whole sordid business. The Quakers had taken a moral stand against it over one hundred years before, and as a result no

Quaker in the country would dare to take another man, woman, or child into their household as their slave, for fear of expulsion from their community.

Even the foreign members of The Society of Friends who had become established in the colonies of the New World, were set fair against The Trade and all that it stood for. As recently as June 1783, just four years earlier, three hundred of their number had submitted a petition to Parliament opposing the vile trade in their fellow man and despite its predictable rejection, they had since organised their own committee dedicated to pursuing the cause to its natural conclusion. But no one with the authority to intervene at the highest level of British society was then prepared to listen to the ramblings of these extremists, who they saw as intent on bringing the country to its knees for the sake of a few inconsequential foreigners. Most of the established order that filled the Parliamentary ranks of Whigs and Tories, viewed these hard working and pious people as religious fanatics, and as Quakers were not permitted to stand for Parliament, there would never be an opportunity for them to bring down slavery from the inside.

The Great North Road remained bereft of carts to block his route and Clarkson was thankful for that small mercy as he trotted on in the trail of a London-bound stagecoach. The heavy dust that swirled up around him in its wake was less welcome though, irritating his eyes and throat, but he paid it no mind. In his head he was already three or four thousand miles away, at the Guinea Coast or on the island of St Kitts, far from England's rugged shore on the other side of the vast Atlantic Ocean.

The accounts that he'd had the misfortune to read, in all of their gruesome detail, had all the hallmarks of evil fantasy. Yet in the months that had passed since his essay had been submitted, he'd come to believe them all to be the truth, and in that truth the fire of his convictions had been stoked until he could take it no more. For a time, he had tried his best to convince himself that the stories he'd read and heard were exaggerations, like the tales of two-headed beasts in the age of discovery under Good Queen Bess. But the more he read, the more the accounts of several independent eyewitnesses corroborated each other, often exceeding the last in their horror and depravation, until he came to the only conclusion that any sane and intelligent man could.

It was all true.

And if it was all true, then in the name of God, it had to be stopped.

Unbeknownst to Clarkson, just fifty miles or so to the south, the chief co-agitators in his future cause were already hard at work, defending the rights of disenfranchised Africans who had found themselves marooned on the streets of England, and endeavouring every day to disturb the privileged sensitivities of England's ruling classes. For too long, the clergy, the landed gentry, the aristocracy, and the Parliamentarians, as well as the public at large, had lived in blissful ignorance of the crimes that were being perpetrated in their name under the thin disguise of wealth, progress, and the propagation of the Gospel. In the last twenty years of the eighteenth century, a tidal wave of information was about to test the social consciences of ten million Britons, in a flood of propaganda of biblical proportions.

The movement was waiting for its champion, and however unwitting or unlikely in both looks and stature that activist would be, his moment had finally arrived.

CHAPTER TWO

"When I entered the city I entered it with an undaunted spirit, determined that no labour should make me shrink, no danger nor even persecution deter me from my pursuit."

The Reverend Thomas Clarkson, The History of The Abolition of the African Slave Trade

His rooms at the lodging house on Park Street in the heart of Bristol were comfortable yet sparse, but that was of no consequence to him. He had all that he needed, and as the newly constructed Georgian building was situated just a short walk up the steep hill from the docks, he was happy just to be where the main thrust of his business would be conducted. After stabling his horse in livery at the bottom of the hill, Clarkson had decided to retire early for the night, having made short work of a dubious looking meat pie served with boiled potatoes and local greens. As he ate, he was fully conscious that his days would soon be busy and fraught with danger, the form of which he could not yet hope to comprehend.

He had arranged to meet a Walter Chandler, a prominent local member of The Society of Friends, in The African House, a coffee shop that was conveniently situated on Prince Street just a few hundred yards away. The next morning, as he strode out as keen as mustard to start his undertaking, he followed his landlord's advice and hailed a ferry to take him the short trip across the river Frome. In so doing, he avoided a long diversion to cross at Traitor's Bridge, which would have made him late for his appointment. Thomas Clarkson did not hold with any form of tardiness and lateness was chief amongst those sins. He hated being late for anything and would always rather arrive at his destination half an hour before his time, rather than to suffer the embarrassment of having to make his excuses.

As it turned out, he need not have worried, as the appointed time came and went in his own company. Just as he was beginning to wonder if he himself had got his dates wrong and was contemplating a return to his rooms to check his correspondence, a flustered gentleman burst in from the cobbled street outside.

"Welcome Mr Chandler" the proprietor called out, saving Clarkson the need to ask for an introduction. "The usual Sir?"

"That would be most kind Bennett," the plainly dressed gentleman responded, his eyes searching furtively around the room, but Clarkson saved him the trouble and raised his hand in greeting, to which the Quaker smiled cheerily and squeezed through the small gathering of merchants and Agents, until close enough to offer a firm and welcoming handshake. "Welcome to Bristol Thomas. I trust that you had a safe and pleasant journey?"

"Uneventful" remarked Clarkson with a knowing smile, at which Chandler nodded in return, fully aware of the dangers that a lone traveller faced on the highways and byways of England in the late 1780s. "It is a fair city, not at all what I had expected, and the streets and houses so tightly packed that it's hard to believe that a bustling port sits just beyond the square."

"It is that" Chandler replied, nodding his thanks to the shopkeeper who had just delivered his steaming mug of sweet black coffee and a second cup of tea for his companion. "Queen Square is very grand indeed," he said, gesturing with his forefinger in the general direction of the beautiful buildings that had only recently been erected to the rear of Prince Street. "Many of the merchants that we are concerned with have their homes in that neighbourhood, so that they can be close to their ships and their livelihoods, though some have now moved up to the new developments in Clifton."

"So I understand" Clarkson answered, grateful that he had a native son of this strange city to provide him with some much-needed counsel.

"There's something in this week's journal that might pique your interest," his guide announced, keen to show his value as he rifled through the pages of a large broadsheet newspaper and thrust it across the table. "I only had it brought to my attention this morning. Sadly, it is not uncommon in these parts to see this kind of thing every now and again, though it is frowned upon by many of our more enlightened residents."

The pages of *Felix Farley's Bristol Journal* were crammed with articles and advertisements for goods and offers, but there amongst the tightly pressed typeface, the subject of Chandler's disgust was all too obvious; a roughly drawn cartoon of a black boy stood out from the condensed lines of text and the Reverend Clarkson could not hide his dismay as its meaning quickly dawned on him.

Bristol, 10th April 1787: RUN AWAY from his Master, a small slender Negroe, about 10 years of age, answers to the name of Jim. Whosoever gives notice to the Bristol post-master so that the said Negroe may be had again, shall have two Guineas Reward.

"I have no words" muttered Clarkson, pushing it away. "It is barbaric, and I am determined to have it stopped. No man has the right to own another. It is unchristian. His 'master' does not even have the gumption to include his own name in it."

"It is widely known in this locale to whom he 'belongs'" said Chandler, his emphasis landing rather too heavily on the last word.

Even in his disgust, Clarkson could not help but notice that one or two heads had turned in their direction. Their long clay pipes hanging limply from their pursed lips, billows of tobacco smoke gathering into grey clouds that nestled in between the roughly hewn beams above their heads. It put Clarkson in mind of a threatening storm that was close to bursting down on them from the ornate plasterwork ceiling, and he smiled to himself at the irony of it.

All of them were well dressed, in large ornate tailcoats with finely embroidered waistcoats and elegant brass buttons by the dozen. Their breeches were tailored from the finest linen with long and gartered plain stockings and kerchiefs of silk about their necks, none of which could detract from their tri-cornered hats which shaded their eyes from view. The clothes of gentlemen, yet their weather-beaten hands, lined with the scars of a hard life of labour, gave away their true lineage and though most chose to sit in silence, the quiet conversations that now drifted from each corner of the uneven room told quite a different tale.

Chandler caught his line of sight and with a nod, acknowledged his nervousness at speaking too openly on this their first meeting. "I suspect that you would like a tour of our town?" he asked, quite certain that Clarkson's response would be one of enthusiastic agreement. "You are lucky my friend, the day is set fair, so I'd suggest that we finish our drinks and walk the harbour, then up to the heights of Clifton from whence you will see the great vista of our glorious port."

Clarkson nodded in approval, and they spoke no more of their true intentions, instead engaging in some minor small talk until they each fell silent, much to the disappointment of the surrounding clientele. Thomas Clarkson was not known for inane conversation. He was not comfortable or even interested in the latest fashions or in the gossip of the day and found it difficult to partake in the usual after dinner exchange that was so often expected of him. However, should the line of conversation turn back to more serious matters he would happily speak up, often intervening as another guest held court and if he disagreed with them, to correct them in mid flow. Some did not like him for these traits, others called him brusque in his manners, several may well have thought him rude, but that was not his concern. He stood up for the truth wherever he was able, and the truth often weighed heavily upon his shoulders and sometimes, on his soul.

The facts were all that mattered to him. He could not bear idle gossip; it was a waste of breath.

The coffee house sat adjacent to the relatively new and very grand Queen Square in the heart of the city and once they were outside in the warm sunshine, they found that they were not in need of their coats, such was the clement weather. Thomas Clarkson had flung his across his arm, and dispensed with his hat, which he used instead as a makeshift fan to ward off the pungent smell that had started to rise around them as they closed in on the harbour.

"Yes, it does get rather tiresome" said Chandler, seeing that his newfound friend had turned his nose up in disgust. "One does get used to it, after a time, but it's worse in the summer and so we will have to put up with it for a few months yet."

They walked across the diagonal of Queen Square and Thomas was soon struck by the beautiful architecture that faced them from all four sides. The four story buildings, that had sprung up thirty years or more before in a very precise plan, were impressive in their grandeur with ample panelled doors of red, blue, and green, surrounded by a host of regimented sash windows on every level. The highest of the floors was consistently smaller than the rest as was the new style, the windows half the size, where he suspected an army of servants would have their rooms.

They emerged on the corner of King Street where the taverns and inns that were home to Bristol's nocturnal life were to be found, and walked along The Back, which bordered the busy River Avon and the docks. As they emerged from behind the closely packed buildings Clarkson caught sight of the thicket of masts for the first time and the revealed scene took him completely by surprise. Although he knew full well where the port lay, its abrupt appearance in the flood of morning sunlight proved an unexpected delight for a man who'd been raised amongst the flat and featureless countryside of East Anglia. The two of them walked on in silence, Clarkson content to drink in the sounds of the seafarers, fully absorbed in the prospect that was now playing out before him.

The dockside was alive with activity, and he found it impossible to make a count of the number of ships that were moored there, where they competed for every inch of available space. Dockers jumped from ship to ship to make a short cut for their errands, hollering to each other to gain the attention of a porter or Agent, as each vessel was prepared for its next voyage or relieved of the cargo from its last. Wooden cranes swung about their heads, their long ropes swaying in the calm as the weight of the ballast swung this way and that, a guiding hand carefully coaxing the bricks and blocks down to the dockside with apparent ease. Elsewhere a chain of men slung sacks from one to another in a long line across the gangplanks, that traversed the gap between the land and the water, not once dropping a load or misjudging a catch, like a well-orchestrated symphony in sweat and muscle.

Men clad in black and grey barked out their orders to willing underlings who ran from ship to shore and back again, in turn yelling their commands to every burly or wiry labourer, who waited attentively for orders that were never long in coming. No one stood idle; each man knew and performed his duties with strength and precision, as if their lives depended on the swift completion of their allotted tasks.

"It goes like clockwork" remarked Clarkson, in awe of the organisation and speed with which the scene before him unfolded. "Who are the men with the boards?" he asked, noting the way that each ship seemed to have at least one prominent steward who was clearly in charge of proceedings.

"The Agents," Chandler explained. "Each venture has one. They oversee the whole operation and make sure that all goods are properly loaded or offloaded, then stored away ready for transporting. They count it all on and off the ship, they make certain that there is no thievery and that their investors are not robbed of their portions. Every penny is accounted for, every last farthing."

Clarkson nodded in appreciation, recognising the skill, commitment and organisation that must go into every voyage, and noting the role of these industrious men who had their work cut out to ensure that nothing was lost to pilfer or bribery. They walked on a short way until the old bridge came into view, its rickety houses perched high above the water putting Thomas Clarkson in mind of its architectural cousin in London. As they made their way across the tight and narrow street, the two of them continued to talk and without the risk of eavesdroppers, they were able now to be more candid in their views.

"I came upon an account by James Ramsay, an Anglican minister, that made me ashamed to be an Englishman" recalled

Clarkson. "The horrors that he speaks of are so outrageous that on first reading them I doubted their authenticity, but I am now certain that they offer a true representation of the life of a slave in our colonies."

Chandler nodded gravely, confirming that he too had read the tract and was of the same view. "Wesley has also preached on that very subject around these parts and I myself have heard him talk of it."

"I never knew that humanity could be so depraved, or sink to such depths of immorality, but it seems that when it comes to The Trade, the white man's cruelty knows no bounds. I would like to meet with John Wesley whilst I am here" announced Clarkson. "Do you think that might be possible? I hear that he has only recently built a new chapel in Bristol."

"Yes" Chandler confirmed, "the New Rooms, as they are called, on Horsefair, not a ten-minute walk from the bridge we just crossed. I'm sure that a meeting could be arranged, but it might be even better for you to hear him speak, he is a fine orator and an inspiration to us all."

They wandered further down Redcliffe Street, so deep in conversation that Reverend Clarkson did not notice the ornate but spireless stone church of St. Mary Redcliffe until they were almost upon it, its red stone exterior dominating the rise in the land to their left.

"It was struck by lightning in 1446 and its spire has never been replaced," said Chandler, pointing out the tower and its stunted spire, "but it's where many of the merchants come to worship on Sundays, several of the leading families in The Trade have their own pews there, I believe." The hypocrisy in their public show of piety was not lost on the Reverend and he made a mental note to offload that sentiment to the first representative of any such family that he should meet over the coming days.

From there, they turned down Guinea Street, named in honour of the western coast of Africa on which the city's wealth had been founded and then towards the floating dock where several ocean-going vessels were being made ready for their voyage.

"A marvel of ingenuity" exclaimed Chandler as they closed in on the system of locks and dry docks that made up the Wapping site. Clarkson was surprised to see that they had walked in a complete circle, doubling back on themselves to pass the church, such that they were now looking back across the river to the rear of the Queen Square buildings. It was indeed an impressive sight to behold. A collection of dry docks, where ships stood free of the water to be repaired of the damage inflicted in distant storms, lay right next to the floating docks where ships were lowered into the river in time with the tide, to begin their arduous journey to a distant land.

"Which ones are the slavers' ships?" the Reverend asked, quite unable to determine the difference between the various boats that were lined up like a military fleet. Schooners and sloops contended with the numerous packet boats that offered transit upstream to Gloucester up to the river's navigable limits in Worcestershire, or down the coastline of Devon to Bideford and beyond, transporting people and goods for affordable fares. But it was the slavers that dominated and commanded most attention through their size, shape, and obvious intent.

"There are three docked at present" his guide informed him, pointing out each one in turn. "The Prince, The Pilgrim, and The Pearl. And one that is getting ready to sail very soon" he announced pointing away to his right, where a shabby looking crew were readying themselves to leave at a moment's notice. "I can't quite make out the name" he admitted, squinting in a vain attempt to enhance his failing vision.

"The Brothers" Clarkson informed him somewhat despondently, reading the familial name from the ship's stern, painted in red and black ink beneath the semi-naked figure of a mermaid. "So, there can be no doubting where that one is headed as soon as it is made ready."

"Which won't be too much longer if Captain Howlett has his way."

Both Chandler and Clarkson had not seen the man crouched on his haunches to the side of the vessel and as they both turned in time to look, they each thought the very same thing, as they regarded the sorry wretch of a man with pitying eyes. His clothes were almost rags, his feet bare and about his head he wore a red piece of cloth like a bandana. Another man joined him, followed by a third, both equally haggard and in clear need of refreshment after a long morning's work readying the ship for the high seas.

"Do you all belong to The Brothers?" Clarkson enquired, his unsolicited question taking them a little by surprise. When all three looked up and two nodded in unison, the Reverend decided to make further use of this unexpected opportunity to garner some information in support of his fledgling investigations. "From what I have heard it is a tiresome trade for a sailor, are you not afraid to put to sea on such a venture?"

For a moment no one spoke up, but Clarkson was comfortable with the silence, taking the chance to run his eyes over the ship, admiring its expert craftsmanship. A modest line of cannon poked their snouts out from above the deck line, each circular barrel standing ready in case of conflict, and further below a line of smaller portholes with their square covers raised up on iron hinges hinted at another purpose. At the prow of the ship, the bowsprit pointed over towards the Mendip Hills to the south, the forecastle also armed with swivel guns, from which point the foremast stretched high above their heads, its rigging set and its sails stored away. To the rear stepped the decks at the half and quarter points where the mizzenmast rose out of the poop deck and between the two, the main mast took centre stage. Clarkson had to shield his eyes in the low morning sunshine to properly make out the platform of the crow's nest, which marked the highest point of the ship's navigation system, above which the British flag was already unfurled and flapping like a landed fish gasping for breath on the bank.

Clarkson was so engrossed in his visual survey, that when the taller of the three finally broke the silence from amidship, he regarded all three men in turn to see who it was that had spoken, but what the melancholy sailor had to say strongly suggested that he was resigned to his fate.

"If it is to be my lot to die in Africa, then I must and if it is not then I will return here someday," he pronounced, rather theatrically. "If it is my lot to live a while longer, then I may as well live aboard this ship than anywhere else, but unless the Captain can find some more men, then we will be staying here for a while longer yet."

"Why, is there no crew to be had then?" Clarkson asked hoping to add more meat to the bone that he had been thrown. "Is it not a well-paid profession for young men like yourselves?"

Two of the three laughed at the suggestion, the other one just spat on the deck in disgust, and it was he that finally spoke up to put the stranger in his place. "Firstly, it's no profession for the likes of us. There's no apprenticeship to be gained and scant skills to be learned, other than how to survive the heat and disease, and the meagre rations."

"And as for the pay," the youngest one added, as he busied himself checking that the folded sails were all well secured, "what you're promised is never what you get. On my last voyage, I didn't see half of what I was told I'd be getting. They just said I was lucky to still have my life."

"And that Captain Howlett is a cruel devil" the first one snarled unprompted, now leaning over the gunnel to inspect his inquisitor up close. "The whole crew put ashore the last time out, we'd had enough of his ways. If he's not ordering the cargo to be whipped then he's taking it out on us, any excuse to bring out the cat o' nine tails, he takes it, and we get it."

"The cargo?" Clarkson probed, almost certain that he knew what the man meant by it, and that his answer wouldn't be to his own liking. "I assume that by that you don't mean the goods that are being loaded at the quayside?"

"The slaves" the seaman sniggered and spat at the stranger's obvious ignorance. "They's not regarded as men, they's not human, how else could anyone do this job? They's cargo that's all. No more than the ballast that we stow aboard to keep us afloat, but worth a lot more to the Slavers than what we takes with us to Africa or brings back from the Islands."

"So how will he find his men then?" asked Clarkson, deciding against arguing the point on this occasion, knowing full well that it would be futile and that to do so might reveal his true purpose. Better that they think of him as an interested bystander on a sightseeing trip, or even as a potential investor out for a stroll in the morning sunlight, than that they should have any inkling of his true intent. Clarkson kept up the pretence with another tame enquiry. "If no one will sail under him, how will he find a willing and able crew?"

The three of them guffawed at that, and Clarkson did not begrudge them their mirth, even if it was at his expense. It was a price worth paying for this first hand intelligence and he waited patiently for their answer, even smiling to himself, and glancing across at Chandler to see if he was sharing in the joke. He wasn't, but he remained attentive, clearly making his own mental notes as the seamen spun their yarns.

"He won't find a 'willing' crew, and they may not be 'able', but he'll find a crew by the morning, you can count on it" the taller one said sombrely. "He'll be down Marsh Street tonight with his First Mate and between the two of them, they'll find a bunch of desperate degenerates who'll be ready to join us by first light. Most of them won't know what's hit them 'til we turn out of the estuary and by then it'll be too late for any of 'em that's had a change of heart."

None of them may have known what irony was, but all three managed to force an ironic smile anyway, and as Clarkson slipped them all a penny for a final pint of Bristol's finest before they set sail, each went back to his work and bid the strangers a reluctant good day. A remarkably informative end to a potentially difficult encounter, is how the Reverend would describe it when he wrote up his diary beneath the faint light of a candle later that evening.

From there, the two of them sauntered through the small shipyard of Sydenham Teast, a local shipwright that co-owned the

Duke of York and The Brothers and had recently fitted out The Hector for yet another slaving venture. Clarkson was delighted to be able to observe the skeleton of a slaving snow "upon the sticks", its newly formed and carefully crafted ribs bared like the carcass of a whale before them. As an orchestra of craftsmen toiled and tapped away in its belly, the sound of hammering resonated around the excavated chamber in which the hull was resting, like music in a concert hall. It was hard to make out the ship's orientation without the usual nautical paraphernalia, but sensing his confusion, Chandler pointed out that they were looking at the stern. The curvature of its American oak keel swept beneath the emerging boat, where more carpenters were busy cladding an inner skin of shaped English elm to its graceful frame. The sweet scent of freshly shaved wood was everywhere, being forcibly shed like an outer skin, as the timbers were shaped and smoothed to sit snugly inside and both men could not help but stand and admire the ingenuity that was on show.

"It is a thing of beauty" exclaimed Clarkson, but his sad countenance did not sit well with his words. "To think that such an elegant creation as that will soon become a beast to devour a nation."

"Not without a devil at its helm it won't" said Chandler, his eyes scanning the length of the ship until they reached its lowest point where several carpenters were hard at work securing planed timber planks into position. "You see there?" he asked of his new-found friend whilst pointing into the belly of the ship's frame. "There, where they are securing the platform above the bilge line. Regard it well, for it shall never seem so clean as that again, not once it's seen its first commission at the Coast".

"The bilge line?" asked Clarkson, bemused. "I see no line, is that a nautical term?"

"Apologies Thomas, I forgot that you have not yet earned your sea legs!" said Chandler with a chuckle. "Yes, it is indeed. It is the line that marks the lowest accessible point of the boat, below which all of the wastewater from the journey comes to rest. It does no harm, it acts as ballast on the high seas as it accumulates, but it can get to proper stinking on these ships, though that's not a seemly topic for two gentlemen on a day like this."

"Do not spare my feelings on the matter Walter please," pleaded Clarkson, "pray tell, I want to know all there is to know about this evil trade, leave nothing out and add nothing in. The whole truth if you please."

And so, his Quaker friend did exactly that, and gave him chapter and verse, explaining how all of the human waste that wasn't tossed overboard on the journey found its way down there by the natural way of things, as excrement, urine, blood, vomit, and sea water, all combined to seep down through the gaps in the decks and settled down there in the dark in an ugly noxious soup. "I did say it wouldn't be pleasant on the ear", said Chandler apologetically as Clarkson turned up his nose in disdain.

"Is there nowhere on board for men to attend to their toilet in dignity?" asked Clarkson, his naivety showing him to be a real novice when it came to the realities of the sea. "Nowhere, more private?"

"For the officers, yes, in the form of chamber pots, that get despatched into the sea at morning and evening, a duty that usually falls to be cabin boys as the lowest of all the crew", said Chandler. "For the crew themselves there is a space at the prow of the ship where all ablutions are simply washed away on the waves, which is far healthier all round if you ask me. But for the slaves, alas no, they may use the 'necessary tubs' when they have freedom to move around, but mostly they must do their business where they lay and wait until morning to be washed down with buckets of sea water, which the crew delight in showering upon them. And all of that water eventually finds its way down there, where it stays until it is pumped out again on arrival in port."

As they hailed a passing ferry and left the construction site behind, Clarkson felt sick to his stomach, though he did his best to put all thought of it out of his mind. The slaving vessels were everywhere, though in truth there may have been but seven in port that day. On that day, there were twice as many already out at sea, waiting at the Guinea Coast, or busy in that very moment selling their cargoes to the highest bidder on the other side of the Atlantic, whilst several more were in various stages of construction.

The path up to the heights of Clifton was a strenuous one, in part traversed by wooden steps and in others by rough and narrow pathways that took them from the streets below, through copse and meadow, up to the very edge of the Downs. From there it was possible to survey the whole of the city, looking down upon the docks and waterways of the Frome and Avon and on to the recent development at Queen Square close to where the waters' meet. Clarkson counted the number of masts that stood out from the disarray of the ramshackle city, but it was impossible to pick out the slavers from the tangle of other vessels that jostled for a berth at the crowded quaysides. To his right, the newly constructed crescents gave the city an appearance of nearby Bath, each semi-circular stretch of town houses built to take maximum advantage of the view below and as result, he was sure that they would command the highest rents from those who were lucky enough to lodge there.

"Beautiful isn't it?" asked his companion, though it wasn't really a question. There was no denying the natural and unnatural beauty of the fantastic panorama that was laid out before them and as Clarkson had now sufficiently recovered from the exertions of the climb, he agreed wholeheartedly with the sentiment.

"It is quite breath taking" he panted, "in both its aspect and its effect."

"Yes, it was quite a climb wasn't it," laughed the Quaker noticing Clarkson's breathlessness, and immediately promising that it would be "easier on the way down." After pointing out all of the major landmarks from the church of St. Mary Redcliffe at the western edge to the Floating Dock in the east and everything in between, he suggested that they should take the 'long route back," skirting the edge of the Downs and then heading down the hill towards College Green and the city's impressive cathedral.

The day had already run away with them, but before adjourning to their rooms to dress for dinner, it occurred to Chandler to show his guest one more sight. So, they made their way down Park Street to pass by St. Marks Churchyard and crossed by the small footbridge over the River Frome, until they reached the shop fronts of Clare Street.

They were now a block or two away from Queen Square again and after making a dog's leg at Broad Quay, the Reverend was surprised to find himself in a place where a clergyman should never be seen, or if needs must, only under the cover of darkness. The infamous drinking dens of Marsh Street. The sheer number of public houses and one-room drinking haunts was quite staggering, and as they wandered along in the relative quiet of a weekday afternoon, Thomas was shocked to count upwards of forty establishments in a mere one-hundred-and-fifty-yard run. The Lamb and Anchor, the Blue Ball, the Ship and Castle, the Three Sugar Loaves, the Three Legs of Man, the Fortune of War, and the Britannia, all hinted at the city's trading links and he would write all of their names down in his memoirs later that night. Only then would he begin to hatch the plan that would take a few days to come together and a few weeks to put into action.

But for now, he'd had enough for one day.

It had been a tiring tour and as he was still recovering from the excesses of his gruelling journey west, he decided to cut their circuit short. Chandler bade his newfound friend a good afternoon and agreed to meet him later for dinner at the inn closest to his lodgings, together with a mysterious contact with whom Clarkson was yet to become acquainted. Chandler assured him that he would not be disappointed and at that, they parted company, for a few hours at least.

-OOO-

"May I introduce you to William Thompson of the infamous Seven Stars Inn."

Clarkson found himself in the company of a heavy-set man in his mid-to-late thirties, his not unpleasant face beset with the scars of a labouring life, but his grey-green eyes betraying an intelligent undertone that, in his experience, was a rare find in an uneducated man.

"Delighted to make your acquaintance" said the Reverend, reaching out his hand and imparting his name and title. At the very mention of his calling, Thomas was well used to witnessing a sudden change in mood, even a rapid withdrawal of the hand as the recipient realised that he was talking with a man of the cloth. However, on this occasion there was no such reaction. Instead, the handshake was firm, but friendly and he immediately found himself warming to the thought of spending an evening in conversation with this man. There was something about him that exuded confidence, a righteousness that was rarely to be found amongst the labouring classes, especially someone that spent most of his life serving beers and spirits to those who had settled for life at the bottom of the barrel.

"Same here," Thompson replied, his eyes never leaving Clarkson's, but there was no judgement there, at least not directed at the Anglican minister's faith. "You can call me Thompson, most do, though I'll also answer to Bill. I'm not a religious man myself," he admitted, as if it was something that he felt needed to be understood from the very start. "Never read the Bible, or even been to church since I was a boy, but I've listened to the street preachers hereabouts and I like that Wesley. He's got a lot of good things to say, especially about our common cause."

It was clear that the man had been prepared by Chandler, and it wasn't long before their conversation turned to The Trade and Bristol's part in it. They each ordered a portion of mutton stew and with their tankards full to the brim with a dark local ale, Clarkson began to quiz his informant, to glean from him every ounce of pertinent knowledge that he possessed.

"The Stars is a bit off the beaten track when it comes to The Trade" the publican explained. "It's down off Temple Street, near to the derelict Church of St Thomas."

"Just a street over from Redcliffe Street, where we walked this morning," added Chandler by way of explanation. "Just across the bridge, only five minutes or so beyond the turning."

"We don't get too many of the ship's Captains or Agents coming by," Thompson continued, "and when they do, we don't pay them much mind. It suits me that way, I don't hold with what they are about at nights, it makes me shiver at the thought of it."

Clarkson looked to Chandler and then back to Thompson, as if to check their understanding before voicing his own. "You mean how they go about finding the crews for their voyages?" He was met with knowing smiles from both men, and a nod from Thompson, which encouraged Clarkson to continue. "We spoke with some of the crew from The Brothers this morning, they were very open with us. It was very clear from their disclosures that the Captain will be out this very night, with that singular purpose in mind."

"Yes, I have heard the same," Thompson confirmed. "There are a few ships lining up to leave soon, The Brothers being the first, but The Pilgrim won't be far behind her. They will be seeking out the debtors on Marsh Street tonight, that's for sure, and by the morrow they'll be on their way to the Guinea Coast with them on deck or asleep below, it's all to the same end."

"The debtors?" Clarkson asked bemused. "What relevance does their financial situation have to their selection? I assumed that they would just be drunkards, incapable of fighting off their kidnappers and then carried aboard in a state of intemperance?"

"It's a nasty trick that the landlords play," Chandler explained with a knowing frown.

"Well, some of them anyway" the innkeeper added, keen to let it be known that present company should be excepted. "Not all of us are so compliant, but there's many on Marsh Street who are more than happy to help their old shipmates out. Many of them were once in The Trade themselves, some of them even rose to the rank of Captain or First Mate."

"And they ply these men with intoxicating liquor?" probed Clarkson.

"They target some men, the desperate ones. The young and stupid ones," Thompson went on for the benefit of his inquisitor, "especially the out-of-towners, the bloody fools. Sometimes they plies them for weeks on end. They befriends them, lets them build up a hefty debt that they cannot hope to repay, and then they lets the Captains know where to find them."

"So, it's all pre-arranged?" Clarkson asked, surprised to learn that the acquisition of the crew was not just some random act, carried out on a single night.

"Yes, almost always" Thompson confirmed. "The innkeepers get a tidy sum for supplying the information and the poor inebriated souls, finding themselves so weighed down in arrears and facing gaol if they don't immediately cough up, that they cannot resist the temptation to make good on their debt by throwing their lot in with the next venture. And to make sure that they don't change their minds, the whole thing is always a last-minute endeavour, with the ship usually setting sail the very next day. If it doesn't, due to the weather or some other delay, then it's not unknown for the assembled crew to be locked below decks for a couple of days, at least until the vessel is out on the high seas, when they've no hope of a safe return by any other means than the slaver on which they find themselves."

"Do things never turn violent?"

"Yes, sometimes," he said, "but then it's just a drunken brawl in the eyes of the Magistrate, and it's always those that are down-and-out on their luck, that end up in the drunk tank or in the cells. It's rarely the fine Captains, but if it is then they can always call on their shipping magnate's lawyers to get them out of any such scrapes. And if the crew turn violent when out at sea," he continued, "then there's always enough strong men on hand, to show them the error of their ways."

Their food had arrived, and each sizeable bowl was filled to the brim with chunks of fatty meat and a generous portion of potatoes, with a large hunk of bread to soak up the dark brown juices that threatened to spill over the sides and onto the table. It was piping hot and as each of them tucked greedily into the fayre, the conversation took a back seat for a few minutes as they took their fill. Clarkson's mind did not stop turning though, the new facts churning over like water over a millwheel, as he honed his strategy that would eventually fan the flames of public condemnation over the slave trade and all its machinations.

"And yet so many seem to go back out again," he declared quizzically, as if trying to get into the minds of the sailors who seemed incapable of turning their backs on The Trade. "If they are so unwilling to go in the first place, why do they let themselves be caught for it a second time?"

"It's a good question Reverend," Thompson admitted, gulping down a large swig of the frothy beer. "One that I have pondered on myself. I have wondered why they don't just make themselves scarce on their return, and I suspect that each has his own reasons for that, but they are poor wretches all of them and drink can seem to be a man's best friend in times of trouble. Those that do return, and they are often few and far between, try to stay away from their old hangouts, but it is hard for them to find employ elsewhere, and so they are often tempted back by the promise of a share in the riches that come to some of the most successful ventures. They come to lodge at The Stars for a while, as my reputation for fair treatment is well known about the town, and if they really must go back, then I try to find them a berth under one of the less evil bastards!"

"What happens to those that don't make it back?" asked Clarkson somewhat naively, "do they stay in the colonies or make their escape some other way?"

Thompson looked across to Chandler, almost in disbelief at the stupidity of the question, giving a sideways flick of his head towards the newest member of their party as if to say, '*who is this jester that you have me spending my evening with, does he know nothing of the world*'?

"They die" he answered bluntly, as if the fact were obvious to anyone who knew anything about the true nature of the slave trade. "They are often so weak, so malnourished and so defeated, that on arrival in those shores they just succumb to the heat or to local ailments and expire. Almost half of the crew on every venture, as a rule, don't ever make it home."

Clarkson was taken aback by this revelation; he had truly not known of this. He had thought that his whole concern was with the plight of the slaves and here he was, being told by his 'man in the know', that the crew themselves were also victims in this dreadful undertaking. "I thought they provided a steady stream of conscripts to His Majesty's Navy?" he said. "I thought they were able seamen who once they had become experienced on the high seas were then ready recruits to serve under the flag against the French or the Dutch, or whichever imperialist state takes up arms against us?"

"Who told you that?" laughed Thompson. "Don't worry, you're not the first that has believed it! No, the Navy wouldn't take slave crews if they were offered 'em on a silver platter. They're too unruly, too unmanageable, and so underfed that they often refer to themselves as the 'white slaves', as they fare little better and often worse than those who are chained below decks."

Chandler shook his head now, having heard the same thing himself a hundred times before, and always from the mouths of those whose only interest was to defend The Trade and all it stood for. "The whole idea of the Navy reserve is a myth" said the Quaker. "None of its true. Never was neither."

Clarkson was incredulous and looked from one back to the other as if asking to be enlightened further. He felt like a fool. He had journeyed to Bristol, so full of his own importance and self-confident in his own accumulated understanding, and yet it now appeared that he knew nothing of the true workings of the foul and odious business that he was so opposed to. "So how do they usually die?" he asked, "is it sickness, drowning, are they killed in fights or brawls?"

"There are many reasons," answered Thompson. "Disease, yes, especially if they have to stay in the Tropics for long. Sometimes the slaves manage to revolt and so a few of them get themselves killed in putting it down, sometimes by blade or by musket, but also at the bare hands of a desperate captive. But mostly, I'm afraid to say, they are killed at the Captain's behest or by his First Mate whose treatment of slave and crew are not so different. In fact, they often see their crew as being more expendable than the slaves, as at least the slaves can be sold at a good price when they get where they are going. The men that sail the ship needs paying when they get home, but that's only if they're still breathing."

Clarkson was dumbstruck and the look on his face told his companions that he was momentarily lost for words.

"You look shocked Reverend" the innkeeper observed with a wry smile, a little pleased that his knowledge had left his up-country cousin feeling not so well informed after all.

"We did hear just today that this Captain Howlett is a scoundrel," Clarkson recounted, "but I could never have imagined the depths to which he might sink."

"Yes, he's one of the worst we have in Bristol" said Thompson, "but there are worse. I hear that some of the Liverpool Captains are devils. There is only one in this port that is not worthy of a hanging and that is Captain Frazer, lately of The Emilia, but as for the rest..." He didn't bother to finish his sentence. The disgusted expression on his face said it all.

The very mention of the rapidly expanding northern port and their pre-eminent role in the rise of slavery, put Clarkson in mind of The Zong expedition which, under the control of Captain Luke Collingwood, had seen one hundred and thirty-two sick and dying slaves murdered, in order to claim the losses on the ship's insurance at thirty pounds sterling per head. His friend and ally, Granville Sharp, had set about trying to get the said Captain convicted for murder in a flagship London trial, but had failed in his efforts in the highest court in the land. The facts of the case were truly sobering and although the initial trial in Jamaica had found in favour of the owner James Gregson, the insurance company was bailed out when the outcome was overturned on appeal. Yet to the horror of the Abolitionist cause, the whole case turned on the designation of the poor slaves as simply 'chattels or goods' – the ship's cargo – and was therefore under the complete control of the Captain. The 'Zong massacre' as it had become known in the years that had passed since that terrible day, had seen seventeen of the crew die of sickness plus a further fifty of the four hundred and seventy slaves that had been packed into its hold. And then the Captain had made his decision to throw the weakest of the remaining slaves overboard, claiming in his defence that the four hundred and twenty gallons of water that he had on board was not enough to sustain the remaining crew and cargo. His real motivation had been to ensure that the venture remained profitable, as the insurance policy covered owners for losses that had come about due to the "perils of the sea," and not to death through disease. He had planned to sell the remaining healthy slaves at their destination and then to claim for those that were murdered on the ship's insurance, which like all other forms of international trade was taken out in advance to cover the loss of goods in-transit.

"I know Granville Sharp personally," Clarkson informed them both "and he was furious at the outcome. He told me, that on his return from the trial that Justice John Lee, who presided over the case, had point blank refused to take up the criminal charges and was disgusted with Sharp for bringing them. 'What is this claim that human people have been thrown overboard?' he had said. 'Blacks are goods and property; it is madness to accuse these well serving and honourable men of murder'. The case was doomed to fail from the start as Lee had held shares himself in several slaving ventures out of Liverpool and London. So, he was never going to find against them."

"Can we ever win this fight?" asked Chandler gloomily, "there are so many forces stacked against us. Even the British Government and the Peerage it would seem."

"Not unless you can change the views of a nation towards The Trade in human beings," said Thompson. "And until the slaves are viewed as human beings by the great and the good of our land, then no, there's no way that we can win."

"The Quakers are set against it," Clarkson countered.

"The Quakers are seen as nutcases and fanatics," scoffed Thompson, "no offence Chandler."

"None taken" snorted the Quaker, laughing heartily at the rebuke that was all too commonplace. "I know some personally, who are indeed nutcases."

"Why it's less than a hundred years since we were burning them at the stake up there on Brandon Hill," said Thompson, pointing towards the window. "It was only the crowning of King James that brought it all to a sudden stop, but even now they are regarded as crackpots hereabouts. It wouldn't take much to encourage another round of Quaker bashing, I can tell you, and attempting to get The Trade abolished might just be the spark that sets the fires ablaze again."

It was a sombre thought, but the Reverend Thomas Clarkson was not to be put off what he saw as his destiny quite so easily. A plan was starting to form in his head, but at that moment, he wasn't yet prepared to share it. "We need to try a different tack," was all that he would say, "one that can swing the views of the people in our favour. One that cuts through their prejudice so that they can see this evil trade for what it really is." He wiped up the dregs of the gravy with his last remaining crust of bread and placed his knife and spoon into his empty bowl, then sat back in his chair as if in contemplation and grinned widely. It wasn't an expression that he was known for, and it didn't sit well, but the embers of an idea were starting to burn brightly in his head, and, with the help of Mr Thompson, he would soon be able to put his plans into action. "When can we meet again?" he asked directly of his new and only publican friend.

"Come to The Stars" he replied, "tomorrow night at seven."

"I can't make it tomorrow," Chandler interceded, "we have a committee meeting at Broadmead."

"No matter," Clarkson said, quite happy to go it alone and seemingly unafraid for his safety. "I can find my way to you from the instructions given, it's not too far and I am very keen to see your humble inn for myself."

"It is agreed then" said Thompson, scraping back his chair against the wooden floorboards as he stood up to leave, and leaving his coin upon the tabletop, added, "I bid thee both a very restful night."

When he had been gone for a few minutes and the risk of being overheard had passed, Clarkson couldn't help but ask his Quaker friend if Thompson was to be taken at his word, an action that he would later be ashamed to call his own.

"He's as strong an Abolitionist as you will ever meet," assured Chandler, "though his reasons may differ from ours, as I doubt that he has ever read a word of the Good Book. It was his brother you see, died at the Captain's hands on his first slaving voyage when he was just sixteen. From his base south of the river, he does his best to help where he can, without running afoul of the Slavers, and he has been very useful to me in my efforts as I am sure he will be to you also."

"I see," said Clarkson, nodding thoughtfully. "That is as good a reason as any I would say and one that will hold fast to a man's hatred 'til his dying day."

CHAPTER THREE

"Regard not money. All that a man hath will he give for his life? Whatever you lose, lose not your soul: nothing can countervail that loss. Immediately quit the horrid trade: at all events, be an honest man"

John Wesley, Thoughts upon Slavery

The snow was almost ready and the ship's husband, as the Agents were known locally, was full of confidence that this latest venture would be a successful one. Profits could never be guaranteed as several recent voyages could testify, but he had never yet been found wanting when it came to the financials. He believed wholeheartedly that good preparation was the key to good fortune, and he was determined that his latest undertaking would not be the exception that proved his golden rule.

Horatio Mullins, or Hal to those that knew him well, was in his own humble opinion the best Agent in Bristol having spent the whole of his working life in The Trade. As a young cabin boy, he'd been the sole survivor of a slaves' revolt, when he'd witnessed the murder of every crew member including his own uncle, Captain Holliday. His own life was spared, and on returning to Bristol he'd been apprenticed to one of the city's most reputable shipping magnates and had never looked back, working six days a week to ensure the continuance of The Trade in sworn vengeance for the death of his shipmates. He knew the vagaries of their dirty business inside out and despised the religious maniacs who were intent on bringing his lucrative lifestyle to a premature end. He had married well, the daughter of a prominent Bristol sugar merchant who had taken his fancy at a very young age, and his four well-bred daughters were now considered to be a fine match for any son of a local landed family.

It seemed to Hal that the number of capable Agents in Bristol was on the wane as these same prominent houses that had amassed their fortunes in The Trade, no longer saw it as a path to riches for their own sons. He didn't take it personally though, so long as they continued to invest. Indeed, their reticence had simply left the way open for the few Agents that remained, and Hal had not hesitated to step into the breach. At that very moment he was signatory to six ventures and the invested Agent in four more, all at various stages of completion, and there was a healthy pipeline too with several still in discussion.

That he had personally visited some of the Winward and Leeward Islands in his youth had contributed to every well-informed speculation in his portfolio, choosing only the most profitable plantations for his own investments. He knew several of the planters personally, and so was well aware of their habits and methods and had always steered clear of those that had a liking for rum or other vices that could cloud their judgement. It was true that his wife had brought with her an ample dowry, which he had put to immediate use after their marriage, building them an impressive home on the outskirts of the city. The money had also funded comfortable offices in Queen Square, and so he could usually guarantee that his name would be sought out whenever any of the other Agents were assembling a venture. Having him on the rolls was often the deciding factor in persuading others to come on board, and so he was always able to negotiate a healthy slice of the profits in return for his signature. Although Liverpool had now begun to take full advantage of its more favourable north westerly position, closer to the rapidly industrialising north and its growing network of canals, there was still enough business to go around, and the small pool of Bristol Agents remained as keen as ever.

His admission to the Bristol Society of Slaving Ventures had never been in any doubt, and as soon as he'd come of age he was immediately sworn in, joining the other one hundred and fifty active members whose hands were firmly on the tiller of Bristol's economic powerhouse. The Society was a closed group of like-minded merchants, whose lofty aim was the propagation and continuation of The Trade for the benefit of the people of Bristol, and for themselves of course. They considered themselves to be the singularly most important band of brothers the city had ever known and had been personally affronted by the recent swathe of unwanted publicity from within the ranks of the Quaker community, who were becoming an ever more irksome thorn in their side. In his younger years he had been heavily involved in the faction that had tried to put a stop to their blasphemous preaching. Yet despite the arsonists' fires that had sprung up in their plain meeting houses, and bloody beatings that had mysteriously befallen the most vocal of their ministers, their number had somehow survived to flourish in the Kingswood area of Bristol, and more recently right in the heart of his beloved city.

The Brothers had proven its worth as a sturdy and reliable ship, having already completed several voyages along the triangular route, bringing in profits on almost every trip in a steady if not spectacular track record. Eventually, he had been forced to close the book on her latest voyage, as to continue to take monies from prospective investors would have only gone to dilute the final share of profits for the rest, including himself. His primary clients, many of whom he now counted as his personal friends, were expecting a healthy dividend, and so protecting their interests was of paramount importance.

"Never shit where you sleep" was one of his favourite sayings and although he tried to keep such colourful language for the docks, and not for the drawing room, his wife did occasionally have to chide him whenever he slipped up and used such a turn of phrase at home. He was always careful not to, as in spite of his less than salubrious upbringing, his social life now moved in more genteel circles and consequently, he had two very different reputations to uphold; but his preference would always be for the docks.

The ship was almost ready for the next high tide and although he'd been informed of some last-minute complications with the crew, he was assured it was nothing to concern himself with. He had full confidence that the Captain and his First Mate were able to 'persuade' a rag tag collection of men from the sewers of Marsh Street to join them by the morning, as they always did whenever they needed to make up the numbers. Promises of untold riches usually did the trick, so desperate were these men to drag themselves out of the gutter, and if it meant that one or two of them turned out to be trouble – as they had found to their own cost on the last voyage - then the Captain and his trusty officers were well accustomed to dealing with that kind of thing. The sharks of the Atlantic were well fed from the sides of every slaver that ever set forth from the mouth of the Severn, and it was never just the cargo that paid the ultimate price for insubordination.

"Hal" hailed a voice from the shore. It was the Captain, no doubt come to check on his Agent's preparations ahead of a planned morning departure. He raised his hand in acknowledgement and pulling on the rigging to swing himself across the deck and onto the quayside, he was soon beside his skipper embracing him warmly and slapping his back in a hearty gesture of friendship. There was no disguising the manner of their business and any Bristolian would have known what they were about just by their looks. Their flamboyant clothes and officious mannerisms were their unmistakable trademark, and these two were no exception.

"Where are you to?" the rough Captain Howlett asked, his broad Bristolian tones evident as he spoke in contradiction of his fine garments and polished black buckled shoes. "I'd be keen to get abroad on the morrow's tide," he explained. "Is she ready for me?"

"She's ready" the Agent answered, "still waiting on the muskets from Birmingham, but I had a runner tell me this morning that they've arrived at the warehouse, so I've sent a couple of the lads across town to fetch them here."

"Better late than never, I suppose" the Captain snarled. "I got some work to do this night," he continued, "we're short of a few hands, but I'll have 'em ready, willing or not, before morning."

"I don't doubt that you will" Horatio laughed, knowing full well what the skipper would be doing that evening; the cider cellars and beer halls of Marsh Street would not know what had hit them between midnight and three in the morning. "We have a full manifest," he added getting back to business. "I am waiting for the last before we batten down the hatches. The usual stuff that should be good for trade on the Guinea Coast; two hundred of the muskets with balls and powder, as I said, good quality cotton and linen goods from the northern mills, though those rogues from Manchester have been pushing up the price. Copper pans and manilla bars; gin, whisky, rum. As I say, all the usual."

The Captain nodded in understanding, planning to return later in the day and only once the guns were packed, to review and sign the manifest in readiness for their departure. The more trusted members of his threadbare crew were primed and ready to sleep aboard the vessel, to stand guard overnight, with another surreptitiously situated onshore to watch over them. That way they'd all be ready and sober enough to raise the anchor as soon as the rest had been dragged from the cesspits of Marsh Street.

Horatio Mullins took one last look at the low-slung ship, its two and a half masts and modest size singling it out as a '*snow*', and like all the other slave ships, up close it was very distinct from the rest that were crammed in at Bristol's quaysides. All looked good, the ship was set to bursting with products that could be traded on the Guinea Coast for the increasingly expensive human commodity, that would then be sold at a premium on the other side of the ocean, so long as they could reach those distant shores without significant fatalities. The Captain was well versed in minimising such losses and would be quick to separate the sick from the healthy and to jettison those that threatened to eat away at his profits.

It was getting late; the sun was high in the sky and not yet falling through the rocks of the gorge to the west, and he had to attend upon the rest of the ship's investors, some of whom would be there in person, though some might simply choose to wait on his report. He went back aboard and hailed the boatswain, who was perched up high in the rigging checking that the stays were all secure, to let him know that he would be gone for at least two hours and not to expect him back any sooner than mid-afternoon.

As he walked back along the gangplank, the dandy Captain shouted a final warning for him to be on the lookout for petty thieves, who had been known to take a chance to steal a musket or two from a fully laden ship, if and when an opportunity presented itself. Once on dry land, he headed off towards the Merchant Hall on Broad Quay, a brisk ten-minute jaunt away by path and river, where he planned to take an early luncheon and to learn of any final matters which needed his attention, before finally signing and submitting the reams of paperwork at the nearby Custom House.

He disembarked from the ferry at the quayside paying his fare in coppers and after stopping for coffee and an ounce or two of tobacco, he arrived at the fine imposing building at just after noon, as measured by the large ornate clock that dominated the entrance lobby. He was early and so he idled away an hour in the company of other Agents who were always to be found in the vicinity until his time came. The venue was the haunt of Captains and seafarers of every shape, size, and stature and so it was not unusual to find it beset by money men at any time of the day, each hurrying to their next appointment, or back to the docks after concluding their business in the hall. Its grandeur was unparalleled amongst Bristol's newest and best architecture, and it was always a fine sight to any Agent as it marked the start of a new venture, with all of its hopes and expectations.

He climbed the grandest of staircases, overlooked by portraits and paintings of famous ships and their Captains, alongside the glories of Empire, and turned towards the open Guinea Room, where his invited guests were already gathered. It was a fairly small group in the end, but that would mean less debate and more time for pressing matters to be discussed, and so Horatio was excited at the prospect. His two main investors were in attendance as expected; Henry Webb former Captain of The Nevis Planter and Sydenham Teast, the fabled shipbuilder and Quaker, who had never allowed his religious leanings to get in the way of a good business deal. Finally, the ship's Captain was also there as expected, comfortably seated at the head of the table, a large ornate pipe already in full flow, the very size of which exuded wealth in spades.

"Welcome Hal" Henry boomed, "I trust that all is ready with our venture?"

"Yes" he confirmed, a little nervous to be in such esteemed company and well aware that all of their hopes hung on his fastidious preparation. "Yes" he repeated, far more confidently, "all is well, the guns have arrived and are being loaded as we speak. The rest of the manifest is all stacked and stored and ready for the tide."

"The paperwork is all ready for our perusal?" pressed the stern shipbuilder, staring out over small round wire spectacles that were the latest in London fashion.

"It is, I have it all here, ready for your signatures," the Agent confirmed, retrieving the scrolls from his satchel, and unrolling them onto the long table before them. He weighed down each corner with paperweights to stop the six feet length curling back up immediately that he let it go. "It's all in order," he added as if there was some doubt. "I declined a couple of last-minute enquiries from Pinney and Newton, I deemed them to be too late to throw in their lot now, especially as both turned me down in my initial enquiries."

"Quite right too" proclaimed Webb, "that Newton needs to decide whose side he's on! He was never one of us, he always sailed under Manesty out of Liverpool, and turned down at least one commission from the good merchants of Bristol if memory serves." He dismissed the name with a pursing of his lips and a sudden puff of air, an action that might have been a spit in less official company.

"And Penney gets more than his fair share of interests" added Teast, "he's only wanting to muscle in now because he and Tobin lost their shirts on their last outing. He's trying to recoup his losses by barging in on our arrangement."

The three of them laughed heartily at those men's expense; clearly there was no love lost between them and they were quick to pick over the bones of their latest misfortune. The Africa was lying at anchor in the mouth of the Avon and news had reached them that twenty-two members of the crew had not returned, some of them dead at the hands of a careless Captain and his cronies. Whilst none of the present company ever held any crew members in high regard, to lose almost three quarters of them at sea was nothing short of a scandal and suggested that they must have endured far greater losses than was yet widely known. At least the crew would not now need to be paid, something that the Captain probably had in mind when he'd put the last of them to the sword or to the sharks, though those events remained no more than a scurrilous rumour and one that they would not be responsible for spreading outside the confines of their own four walls.

"And what of our venture Captain Howlett?" the Bristolian Teast enquired, as the ship's skipper tended his recently refilled and lavishly carved pipe, its bulbous bowl closely resembling the sorrowful head of an African male. "Shall we discuss your strategy at sea, or do you have all that under your large and expensively proportioned hat?"

The two investors shared in the joke, but Hal limited himself to a smile, knowing how sensitive this particular Captain could be whenever his outward appearance was called into question. He had been known to slice a man in half for less, and Hal knew only too well that his extravagant hats were never to be ridiculed. This time, the

Captain seemed to be in a far more settled state of mind, as he leant back in his chair and smoked his pipe thoughtfully, winking at the Agent with whom he was well acquainted before finally revealing his hand.

"Thee must know me well enough be now" he said with a mischievous wrinkle of his purple nose, its unnatural colour betraying his penchant for rum. "I likes to pack 'em in, nice an' tight. If I can get 'em I'll take 'em, the hard part these days is can 'ee get 'em. There lies the rub for every Guineaman that drops anchor at the coast, where will they be and can 'ee strike a deal afore the next boat hollers 'land ho!'"

It was true, and more ships seemed to be returning to England with tales of woe than not.

Profits had fallen since the middle of the century and it was hard to see a way out of it, but every now and again a venture would make a tremendous profit and that was enough to keep the investors interested. The Society's corners had been full of whispers that investments in The Trade were no longer a 'sure thing', and so every owner was now keen to acquire a sensible Captain, one that fully understood the economics of the business and the implications of his every decision. Their very livelihood depended on it, and they could stand or fall with one reckless moment on the slaving coast or at the ports of Jamaica or in the Carolinas. There was no such thing as easy pickings anymore when it came to the African trade, though fortunately for them their investors fully understood that where there was nothing ventured, there would also be nothing gained.

"Timing is everything" Webb reminded the Captain, "getting it right can be the difference between success and failure. Get down to Guinea as quick as possible in full sail and take advantage of the tides, then don't waste any time in finding the cargo. It's imperative that the ship is loaded and sailing again within a month, no more, else you'll risk missing the harvest in the islands and then they won't want to take on any more mouths until the planting season is upon them again." The Captain nodded irritably, fully aware of the pressing need for speed on every venture and not all that willing to listen to an old sea dog, who had chosen long ago to hang up his hat in favour of a more genteel existence, rubbing shoulders with England's aristocracy. "What's your break even?" Webb asked him, unsure of what their Captain was planning. "How many slaves is enough for our ship, would you say?"

At that the three men glanced at each other as if deep in calculation, but it was clear that none of them wanted to speak up, in case their recommended fill might come back to bite them hard, if profits were lacking. In the end it was the Agent who made the first suggestion. "I'd say no less than three hundred if you can get them all in one place. If you're at two hundred and you have to go hunting upriver or down the coastline, then maybe two fifty, but if you can break three hundred then we should be in profit by some margin. Four would be a bonus."

"So long as you don't lose them in the middle passage of course" the retired sea Captain reminded them all. "The more you stow, the more 'll go!"

"That be easier said than done" the far-from-retired Captain snapped back. "Last time pickings were slim. There's too many slavers and not enough slaves these days, the crews often come to blows and last time out we had to scarper after one of ours killed two of theirs."

"Then keep your crew in order Captain" Webb instructed, "that's what we are paying you for."

"And don't pack them in too tight" the Agent added. "If the flux takes hold you'll lose half of them to sickness before you're across and half the crew besides."

"I'm more concerned about striking the right price" Sydenham Teast attested. He had been quiet until that moment but was now determined to have his say. "The prices for slaves on the first leg have been rising steadily this last ten years, as high as £20 for an adult male I hear, and according to these papers we've also had to pay a pretty penny for the guns. Was that really the best price that you could get Hal? They've had you at that, I tell you, you've had your tail pulled there."

"I drove them down by several pounds apiece" Horatio argued defensively. "I drove a hard bargain; I dropped our usual supplier in Bath Street because he wouldn't meet me halfway. It was the best price; the America's war has pushed up demand and it's outstripped the supply by a wide margin. It's the best I could get and better than most."

"Well, you'll need to drive a hard bargain with the Portuguese, Captain Howlett, that's for sure" said Webb, for the first time looking worried that this investment might yet prove to be a little riskier that he had hoped. "Two muskets at most for a healthy adult male I'd say, that should do it. We'll still be in healthy profit at that, so long as you can get a good deal for most of them on the other side."

They were all silent then, each grappling with their own concerns, the Captain blowing rings of tobacco into the air, whilst Webb and Teast regarded him warily, each beginning to doubt the wisdom of his appointment. But it was too late to change their minds, that ship had sailed.

"The negroes are getting wise to us" Webb added in a final word of warning. "They are well aware of what awaits them now, they know all about us and what our game is, so they'll be looking to run or jump at every opportunity. So, don't give them any. As soon as you begin to slave, let the netting be breast high fore and aft, and always keep them shackled and hand-bolted on deck to prevent them from rising and leaping overboard."

The Captain nodded, but he was clearly tired of being told how to do his job and the three other men could sense it, so they backed off. They had made their choice and they would have to live with it.

"Horatio, send for the quill and a round of rum, lets drink to this man's success." It was Webb who had called time on their small rebellion, and it was Webb who was the first to lay his mark upon the page. Then Teast added his and finally the Captain scratched a flamboyant swirling signature across his printed name. Finally, as the appointed Agent, Hal added his moniker to the approvals and taking the stick of red wax, he melted the end in the flames of a ready candle and pressed the seal of the Bristol Society of Slaving Ventures into the whole bloody mess.

Their fate was sealed, the deal was done.

They each raised a glass, brimming to the top with the sweet dark liquid, brought them together and as they had witnessed many times, said as one "to the venture." They refilled their glasses several times until the bottle was drained and, their thirst slated, then they stood and said their farewells, not to meet again in this purpose for another year or more, when the ship would return with its story to tell.

Of good or evil they had no way of knowing. It was now in the hands of God.

The next morning, Thomas had been delighted to make the acquaintance of Harry Gandy at breakfast, another who hailed from a Quaker family in Castle-Green and one who practised the law in Bristol. The two had been corresponding for weeks and he was well aware of Harry's history in The Trade, having already explained that he'd regretfully spent time at sea as a headstrong youth, before joining The Society of Friends, and was now very keen to make up for his earlier transgressions.

"Thomas Clarkson?" The Quaker had greeted him in the manner that had become the expected norm amongst the Friends, refusing the general custom of using his formal clerical title or even the usual 'Mr'. Such greetings were deemed to be inflammatory for the ego, attaching a higher level of importance to a person's station in life than was warranted in the eyes of God.

Harry would be his guide for the day and although the Reverend objected at his insistence on taking out a whole day from a lawyer's busy schedule to act as his chaperone, his resistance proved futile. As before, they had made a beeline for the docks, planning on making enquiries of any crew members that they happened upon, or others in authority who were willing to talk. It seemed that his presence had already caused quite a stir, and as they walked, Harry quickly recounted the tales that he had already heard, to whit a tall and imposing red-headed man in black.

"Oh, what a mysterious fellow I must sound" he chuckled at the very suggestion, surprised that news could travel so fast around a city of fifty thousand people.

When they arrived back at the docks, it proved surprisingly easy to get on board the ships. Indeed, they were invited to come on board The Pilgrim that still sat astride The Prince in the water, but The Pearl was now in dry dock with a suspected infestation of *toredo navalis*, the shipworm that thrived in tropical waters and was a constant problem for any ships that had spent too long at anchor there. A group of bare-chested men were hard at work, affixing a dull metal skin to the boat's underside, the clanking of wooden mallets on the copper plating resounded around the confined space like a stampede of hooves through a rocky canyon.

It wasn't exactly a welcoming committee, but as it turned out they were more than willing to talk, and Clarkson wanted to take full advantage of their good-natured outlook before the opportunity was lost. He had come prepared to 'lace a few palms with silver' if needs be, and so he wasn't slow to withdraw a full flask of finest rum from the inside of his tailcoat, offering it in turn to each member of the crew, none of whom had ever been known to decline a tot or two of their favourite tipple. It did the trick, and the sightseers were immediately ushered below deck, the Reverend careful not to crack his head on the challengingly low beams that ran along the length of the ship.

"Hair of the dog!" the first saluted as he raised the pewter flask to his lips, his first alcoholic drink since the Fortune of War had closed its doors at three o'clock that morning. "Good 'elth!" said the next in line, "Salut" the very next and so on, down the line. Even the cabin boy took a healthy quaff, not wanting to be left out; but then he coughed and almost choked in disgust, a reaction that had his soon-to-be shipmates falling about the deck in fits of hilarity, which was only stopped when Clarkson asked his first question.

The Reverend had not been 'below' before on a purpose-built slaving ship and so he took full advantage of the opportunity to survey the scene, taking the stairs beneath the quarter deck and into the galley from where a brick-built kiln dominated the space. They sat around the wooden capstan, the winch that would soon be turned to raise the heavy chain of the ship's anchor and regarded each other with a mix of curiosity and unease. Clarkson passed the flask around once more, and all but the cabin boy accepted the offer of another shot. When it was finally returned it was empty.

"How did you fare on your last voyage?" a leading question and he knew it. "Were you treated well? I have heard that it is not always the case on these ventures."

At first no one answered, as if daring each other to be the first to break the silence, but once it was broken there was no stopping them and Clarkson was unable to keep up with the sheer number of tales, that they were only too keen to tell.

"Wasn't too bad last time out," the tallest of them said, his silver blue eyes twinkling in the daylight.

"I've, I've, I've been on m-m-much worse," stammered another almost simultaneously.

"There's a slaver that's just come in, The Alfred I think it's called, where I heard that the Captain had two of the crew whipped to death and thrown overboard for insubordination," a fair-headed third man added.

"I have heard the same," said Gandy, motioning to Clarkson that they should check out the circumstances as soon as they were able. "That'll be Captain Robe, if I'm not mistaken."

"Why do you never make a complaint?" Clarkson asked naively, "to the ships owner's or to the local magistrates court?"

"There's no shortage of stories" the one with the silver-blue eyes added as he regarded the two of them with more than a hint of trepidation, knowing full well what would befall them if they were seen fraternising with the enemy. Especially the kind that liked to ask questions about The Trade. "But you'll never get anyone to testify against them lot, 'cos we knows that we can't win see, we'll just end up in the drink, with our throats cut, one dark night."

"Would none of you be willing to testify against these men?" Clarkson asked, glancing from one to the next, but his gaze returned to the tall blue-eyed sailor as the other two quickly shook their heads and turned their faces away. "Surely you must want to see them behind bars, after what they've done to you and your friends. Don't they deserve to see the scales of justice weighed against them? If their guilt could be proven beyond all doubt, would you not be willing to testify?"

"It's not about proving their guilt is it my red friend?" It was the Spanish looking man that was speaking now in an unfamiliar accent, and he seemed primed for a fight. "They are all guilty of something, they're all the same. All these men of money are all in it together, the lawyers, the magistrates, they have the thing sewn up and sealed between them. We don't have a chance."

It was as if some silent signal went off in that moment, as the crew stood to shepherd them out, scattering about the ship and leaving their visitors stranded below deck. Clarkson didn't hesitate to take the opportunity to complete his unannounced inspection and dipped down through the open metal grill to assess the cargo hold beneath, where several hundred slaves would soon be stowed. It was a shockingly small space, so much so that Clarkson was almost on his knees as he staggered about inside. Running in parallel down the full length of each side, a second platform was raised along its length upon whose timbers enslaved people would soon be chained, a seated few crammed into the middle beneath the grills to complete the ship's full compliment.

"How many human beings are forced between these walls?" asked Clarkson of no one in particular, his mind working overtime to compute an unfathomable number.

"Three or four hundred," a small childlike voice answered from somewhere in the gloom. "Sometimes more if trading is good. The Captain likes to pack them in as much as he can, I often thinks its full and still they keep on coming, sometimes for days. It's like fish in a barrel down here by the time they've finished, and then I has to crawl between them all, line by line, to ensure that the fetters are all well fastened. That's my main job, anyways. And woe betide me if I miss anything."

Clarkson turned with difficulty, to be greeted by the bewildered face of the cabin boy as he emerged from the darkest corner. He had snuck downstairs in an effort to avoid the angry directives of the First Mate, who was now bellowing out orders from above.

"How many voyages have you seen?" whispered Clarkson, keen not to give away his advantage.

"This will be my third," said the boy, "I'm not much looking forward to another, but there is no way out for me. The master fetched me from the poorhouse when I was eight and so I'm apprenticed to him for seven years."

"Are you treated well?" asked the Reverend, knowing full well that the answer was unlikely to be a pleasant one.

"I'm used to it," shrugged the boy. "The poor house was worse, and food's better on here, so long as it lasts. And I gets to see the world I suppose."

"Is the Captain not cruel?" said Clarkson, knowing now that their time was short and wanting to make the most of this unexpected chance to glean some more information from an eyewitness, albeit a very young one.

"Of course he is," the boy scowled, glancing over his shoulder, and motioning to leave. "He's brutal, but so was the beadle and so was the overseer in the workhouse. Life's cruel ain't it mister? I just got to take my chances where I can. That's what me old mam told me, before she died."

"Well, take this for your honesty," said Clarkson, slipping some copper coins into the boy's hand, as they made their way out into the morning sunshine. It wasn't much, but a few pennies might at least buy him a decent breakfast. The conversation left Thomas Clarkson feeling foolish, giving him a mental nudge as to the size of the task that lay ahead. He was left feeling quite embarrassed to think just how naïve he'd been to believe that he could walk right up to these people and come to their rescue.

"Don't be too downhearted," Harry piped up, offering Thomas his hand, and pulling him up the last two rungs to the deck. "It was never going to be easy, but there are others that may yet help us."

Thomas Clarkson did not share in his optimism and the prospect of interviewing even more of these waifs and strays that were masquerading as able seamen, filled him with trepidation. The Pilgrim was next in line and as they sauntered up close to the side of the ship and clambered aboard, a rotund and flustered face turned to greet them.

"Can I help you?" The accent was not an entirely local one and at first Clarkson could not place it, but his next sentence marked him out as a Welshman. "I'm the ship's Doctor," he said sheepishly, as if embarrassed by it. "Doctor Gardiner of The Pilgrim, but I'm about to put to sea aboard The Brothers."

"Thomas Clarkson," he declared, holding out his hand and gripping the Doctor's in a warm embrace. "Do I detect a Welsh accent good Doctor?" at which Gardiner offered a welcoming smile and a nod. "That's perfect. Can we talk?"

"Not sure that I should", he said with a mutinous wink. "I've been told to keep away from you! Your name is already doing the rounds; all the captains are putting out warnings to keep our distance!"

They sat at the dockside, perched on a pair of mooring bollards that were bolted securely to the quay, whilst Harry Gandy kept watch, wary that their interventions that morning may not have gone unnoticed by the merchants of his adopted city. When asked later that night why he had succumbed to a sudden onset of nerves, he couldn't quite say, but he had instinctively felt the need to be on the lookout, and so had left the two men to talk, and talk they did. In fact, they became so engrossed in each other's company that almost two hours passed and before departing, the Doctor had agreed to meet him at the Seven Stars, so that they could talk some more.

It transpired that the innkeeper Thompson was a mutual friend, one that had helped the Doctor in his efforts to find new pastures for more than one of his shipmates, those that had wanted to escape without trace from the clutches of the Captains and their mates. "No slaving vessel will leave port without a Doctor on board" the physician explained, "first and foremost to care for the crew who often fall victim to disease when they first visit the Tropics, but also for the captured slaves, whose sale value will diminish if their health visibly declines during transit. Their new owners don't want their assets to depreciate from one side of the Atlantic to the other." It was a sobering thought and not something that the Reverend had given the faintest consideration to before that moment.

"And how do you feel about this trade in your fellow man?" Clarkson asked bluntly, intending to provoke a reaction in his new business connection. For a moment Doctor Gardiner was quiet, as if trying to think of the right words to use, that would offer up some form of defence for his chosen occupation.

"There's never been a subject that demanded so loudly the interference of the legislature as that of the Slave Trade", he admitted, much to Clarkson's surprise. "But there are many in my profession, who think that they can do some good by taking off on these voyages, but most do it for the money." It was a frank admission and one that he was clearly not proud of. "So did I, to begin with. Like the others, I thought The Trade to be justified by God, and so I went along with it for a time, but the more that I see of this barbaric business, the more that I want out of it."

"Then why don't you get out of it?" asked Clarkson bemused.

"I come from lowly stock" he admitted. "My family had no spare money to pay for an education, and so, if I want medicine to be my profession then I need to raise my own funds to pay for it. I save some money towards it each time I take the Articles, but once I have enough put by, then I will wipe my hands clean of this detestable trade."

His motivation was not a topic on which he wished to linger, and so he changed the subject. "Did you hear of The Alfred, just come into port these last few days?"

"I heard that some members of the crew did not see home again."

"Indeed, and what of Mr Thomas, the surgeon's mate on board, a fine fellow who was on his first voyage and I pray that it might be his last." As Clarkson shook his head, Gardiner continued, giving the Reverend renewed hope that he mind soon find another witness for the cause. "He has been most cruelly treated by Captain Robe after he objected to the treatment of the slaves, but he is now most gravely ill and confined to his rooms."

"Is he here in Bristol? Can you take me to him?" Clarkson asked, keen to bring a case against this Captain to help raise public awareness of the inherent cruelty of The Trade. "He must have some stories to tell and if he has opposed the act of enslavement itself, then he could be a most useful informant."

"He resides not far from here, in the slums of Temple Back," the Doctor pointed out.

"Then let us make haste" the Reverend insisted, "there's not a moment to lose".

But the Doctor didn't move, his eyes locked in step with the Reverend's as if trying to speak without moving his lips. It took a moment or two for the penny to drop and as it did, Clarkson nodded sagely and reached for his purse.

"How much is your fee good Doctor," he asked, an intended edge of sarcasm in his tone.

"One guinea should be sufficient good Reverend."

"And very appropriate given the nature of my request," said Clarkson as he reluctantly handed over the substantial coin, but before relinquishing his grip he added one condition, his trust for this supposed man of honour now tainted beyond repair by this simple transaction. "This on the expectation that the man can be found and that he is still alive, and another to follow if and when he testifies."

"Done," said the Doctor with a knowing smile. "We can get most of the way there by river," he added, whistling across to a boatman on the opposite bank. The ferryman wasted no time in traversing the short distance from one side of the quay to the other and after Clarkson relieved Harry Gandy of his duties for the afternoon, the two men made their way upstream, travelling first along The Back and then right around the sharp bend in the River Avon, affording both men a sailor's view of the tightly packed city.

They disembarked at the counter slip stairs and emerged into a far less genteel neighbourhood than he had seen so far, not unlike Bermondsey or Deptford back in London. The houses crowded in on each other, each door so close to the next that it was hard to see where one timber-framed house ended and another began. The buildings leaned precariously forward across the lane and in its centre, a drainage channel flowed with the effluent of the overcrowded quarter, in which pigs squealed in alarm as their snouts scoured the muddy flow for pickings.

It wasn't long before the Doctor was knocking at the door of a down-at-heel lodging house. A bedraggled woman in a grey dress and shabby apron, that made her look far older than she probably was, bid them inside and Clarkson couldn't help but cover his mouth with his neck scarf to mask the overpowering odour that seemed to cling to every crevice.

"He's in the far room on the first floor" she croaked, "he's needing to see a Doctor, but he says that he doesn't have the coin."

"That's alright," said Gardiner. "I'm a Doctor, I will see he gets the care that he needs." It wasn't entirely true, but he was at least willing to try, and as they hauled themselves up the precarious staircase and turned into the tiny room, their eyes settled upon a motionless lump buried under a mound of mismatched rags.

"Mr Thomas?" the Doctor enquired, unsure if it was indeed the surgeon's mate that occupied the room. "It's Doctor Gardiner, lately of The Pilgrim, I've been sent to help you."

The shape stirred and groaned, turning over once then twice, before pushing himself up on his elbows to regard his visitors with sad mistrustful eyes. "Please don't make me go back again," he pleaded, "I can't go back again, not to Guinea, you can't make me."

"No one's going to make you go anywhere" the Doctor soothed in an attempt to calm him. "We are not sent from Captain Robe; we are here to make you well again."

"He's the Devil!" he screamed, "he's evil, he is. He killed my friend, whipped him within an inch of his life then threw him overboard and left him to drown and dine with the fishes. I'm not going back. I'm not." He was becoming distraught now, lines of sweat seeping forth from every pore and thrashing about so wildly that the two visitors were fearful that the bare wooden floor might soon give way beneath them.

"Please be calm Mr Thomas." Clarkson's calming voice seemed to do the trick for a moment or two, until the feverish seaman looked into his eyes and saw that it was a stranger at his bedside.

"Who are you?" he screeched, wincing through the pain. "Has he sent you? Have you come to take me back? I'm not going back, I'd rather die. I tried to die three times you know. I jumped overboard, but they dragged me back up, I wish they'd left me alone. I wish I'd drowned or been eaten by the sharks! It'd be all over now and I'd be at peace."

"No one is taking you back" Gardiner said, reaching into his bag and retrieving some powders, which he slipped into the nearby jug of murky water, before stirring it until he judged it to have been completely dissolved. "Here, drink this, it will make you feel better." He wasn't certain that it would, but it was worth a try and they both helped the man to sit up and pressed the mug to his grateful lips. As he did so, the cloths that passed for blankets slipped from his legs and Clarkson winced at the number of unsightly welts that covered them, wrapping around the sides of his thighs and calves to the hidden flesh beneath.

"You were whipped by this Captain Robe?" the Reverend asked.

"Aye" answered the former surgeon's mate, "and by his First Mate." He had recovered a bit of his composure now and was more collected as he started to tell more of his tale. "Whipped and held in chains until we put back into port, all because I made a fuss."

"What about?" asked Clarkson unwillingly, quite sure that he was not going to like the answer.

"He almost killed a freed slave called John Dean, in front of everyone" he stammered, "but first he manacled him to the deck, had him whipped and then poured boiling hot pitch upon his back." He stopped there, but it was not for effect, it was only to recover his nerve to be able to continue. "The poor fellow was living when I left him, but he was moaning and groaning so terribly, I can't forget the sight and the sound, and the smell of his burning flesh."

"Then there was another boy," he continued. "He was supposed to belong to the First Mate, they'd already made their selections from amongst the unwanted before we left the colonies, but he'd grown bored of him and so gave him over to the Captain to make an example of."

"And what became of him?" asked Clarkson, knowing already what the answer must be.

"After they'd had their fun with him, they threw him overboard, still alive, and claimed the loss on the insurance most likely," he said, "I think they call it jettison or some such thing."

"Yes, I know of it" Clarkson admitted sadly, recalling to his disdain the tale of The Zong.

"Please can you help me to get away?" the pathetic specimen of a man begged, recovering something of his old self. "I can't go back to that life, I just can't. Ask Dixon, ask Matthew Pyke or James Bulpin; they all saw what happened to me, and they had some of the same themselves. White slaves we called ourselves, 'white slaves' cos that's what we were. That's what we are."

"I know a man that can help," the Doctor answered, "he keeps the inn called the Seven Stars. You just need to get better now and rest up. I'm leaving you some ointment for your wounds. I'll put some on for you now, but you need to keep it up for the next few days, and I'll leave you these powders too. Keep drinking the water, and nothing else mind, it will help you to heal."

"Thank you, Doctor," Mr Thomas said, through his searing pain. "I know of Thompson at The Stars, he is a good man. If there's anything that I can do for you, when I'm better." Gardiner just nodded, but Clarkson could not resist the offer, and although he held back from revealing the full extent of his request, he left a window of possibility open for his return.

"There may be something that you can help us with" he smiled knowingly, "but you need to fully recover first and then we can talk some more. Where can I find these other men that you speak of; Pyke, Bulpin and Dixon? Are they still in port?" But Mr Thomas had slipped back into his delirium and no further sense could be had from him, though they sat at his bedside for a further fifteen minutes in the hope that he would come around.

Mr Thomas, the late surgeon's mate of the slaving vessel The Alfred, died three days later from an infection that permeated his wounds and left him with a fever that took his young life.

He was buried in an unmarked pauper's grave at Temple Church.

He was just twenty-two years old.

CHAPTER FOUR

"While I deplore the fact that the genuine friends of humanity, [those] who are not hoodwinked by prejudice or ignorance or blinded by self-interest, will find that slavery - in its essence - exists at home as well as abroad."

Captain Hugh Crow – Memoirs comprising a narrative of his life, 1830.

The Seven Stars peered out at him from the side of a narrow alleyway that ran down between the public house and the side of St Thomas's church. A street lantern marked the corner of the building, and it would soon receive the attentions of the lamplighter, who had already begun his rounds. The Reverend Thomas Clarkson arrived alone, having navigated his way back to the Temple quarter and then, following Thompson's simple instructions to the letter, he came upon it all at once. It was indeed easy to find, though he had felt uneasy from the moment he had first stepped out onto the bridge, wary of every stooping figure and every furtive glance from the people he passed and for the first time since his arrival in the West Country, he had felt horribly conspicuous. It wasn't a feeling that sat well with him in what he'd been told was a den of thieves.

For that reason, he had not hung around outside with the other vagabonds, but as with most inns, he found that he'd had to bow his head to get through the door. Once inside, his scalp had continued to brush up against the low ceiling, so much so, that he was relieved to be able take up a place at the bar, where he shook the familiar hand of the landlord who now looked right at home in his customary place. As Thompson welcomed him to his unassuming abode, the other bookends at either end of the bar regarded Clarkson with suspicion, but when he made eye contact they each looked away, choosing instead to consider the contents of their own pint pot as if the meaning of life lay within.

"You found us well enough then?" the barman said, asking the obvious question as he reached up to take down a tankard from the line of crooked square-ended nails above his head. As Clarkson nodded in response, the Landlord went on, "what can I get you, on the house?"

"That's very kind" Clarkson beamed, "I'll take a draught of your best ale please." The bookends sniggered at his east country accent, but when they looked to the owner for his sanction, he didn't share in the joke. Instead, he studiously watched as the pewter tankard filled up before him, taking care to ensure a full head had formed at the lip before he handed it over.

"To your good health" toasted the Reverend, and his soon-to-be informant nodded back, deciding then that the time was now right to introduce him to one of the two stooges that was seated on his right flank, as the other downed his pint and ambled off in the vague direction of the street.

"May I introduce you to James Arnold, ship's surgeon late of The Ruby, and a regular frequenter of my humble tavern." A gaunt visage greeted him; a middle-aged man of slender frame and face, who's facial features twitched nervously between left eye and upper lip, putting Clarkson in mind of a flickering candle that has burned down to its last inch of wick.

It would prove to be a good analogy, but Clarkson had not been expecting to be plunged headfirst into another interview and was ill prepared for it. After exchanging some pleasantries about the city and the temperate weather, he supped his drink in a greedy gulp that was not becoming of a clergyman and was surprised to see the jar refilled in an instant. In the end it was the Doctor that broke the silence, raising the subject that was at the forefront of all of their minds.

"I read an account of your newly formed movement in the local press," Arnold said, "I was quite impressed, though I'm not convinced that everyone is. It's time that someone spoke out, but you need to take great care in these parts. Your presence has been noted."

"Really? Well, I'm glad to hear it. I was rather fearful that it would fail to make even the most diligent of readers sit up and take notice," Clarkson replied, though in reality he wasn't the least bit surprised. He knew full well that it would cause a stir, but he wanted to downplay his influence until he became better acquainted with the evening's clientele. "By whom, may I ask?"

"The Slavers" he went on. "They have their spies everywhere in this city, even in here."

Clarkson looked around, to see who might be in earshot. The inn was so small that almost everyone could be so described, and none would have had to crane their necks to listen in on their conversation, had they had the mind to do so. "Are you recently returned from Africa or waiting on your next voyage?" he asked, trying to deflect attention from himself. "There are a few ships in port, I wondered if one of them was yours? I didn't see one named The Ruby, did you say?"

"No, she's gone up country" he informed him. "Sailed up the Irish Sea to Liverpool, picking up some crew and some ballast there, and getting fitted out for the next trip. I'll be heading up there shortly myself; I signed my Articles last week and so I am committed."

The Reverend could not yet work out whose side this man was on, as there had been no indication from the barman, who was now busying himself attaching a fresh barrel to satisfy the evening's demand for beer. Arnold raised his tankard to his lips and sank most of his draught in a single swig, before opening up some more as the ale started to loosen his tongue.

"It's a grim business" he confessed, "one that I've never been too proud to be part of."

"Then why do you continue to allow yourself to be so used?" asked Clarkson, rather more directly than he had intended and so, unsure of how the man might react, he readied himself for a rebuke that never came.

"Cruel necessity" the ship's surgeon remarked, finishing his drink, and raising his empty vessel into the air to indicate that he was ready for another. "On the last voyage under Captain Joseph Williams, damn his hide, we took on board one hundred and five slaves at the coast of Cameroon. Ninety-five survived the crossing to be sold at the island of Grenada."

"What happened to the rest?" It was the pertinent question and Arnold knew it was coming before the words had left his lips.

"Two of them were shot, when they resisted the order to go below," he recalled with a grimace. "One was scalded with hot fat as an example to the rest and left to fester in the hold. The Captain said that 'his death cries would act as a warning to the rest of them.'"

"Every time I talk to someone that has had some involvement in this damn trade, I hear of new atrocities" Clarkson lamented, as he listened attentively to another tale of terror. "And was the guilty man brought to account for his actions?"

"Of course not," said Arnold, surprised that the Reverend would be so clueless as to think that justice would have been dished out on board a slaving vessel by anyone other than the Captain himself. "The Captain wields ultimate power on board his ship Reverend, no one has any authority over him and even though such cruelties could be brought before the magistrates, or even to the Admiralty themselves, it'll be a very cold day in hell before we see such a thing as that."

"So, I am coming to realise," said Clarkson, sinking the last of his own pint and vigorously refusing the innkeeper's efforts to refill it. Though the next time he looked, it would be full once more.

"I keep a journal, on every voyage" Arnold admitted. "Most ship's surgeons do, but I don't only record what the Slavers want to see. I keep a record of 'everything' I see."

"Everything?" asked Clarkson intrigued at the sudden twist in the tale.

"Everything" Arnold confirmed, looking between the now attentive barman and the clergyman. "Of course, I have to submit them all with the official ship's log and all of the other records, but I'm not sure that anyone ever reads them. I've done four trips now and the contents have never varied that much. I've never been told to take a different tone, or not to include so much of the details, so I have just assumed that they don't care that it's all written down, in black and white, and so I will carry on doing it until I get told any different."

The obvious value of this potential evidence was not lost on the Reverend, and his appetite had been whetted. He had to see those records, but just as he was about to ask for permission to include them in his official reports, they were joined by a second member of the medical profession who, after apologising for his lateness insisted on a round of rum at his expense. The Reverend did his best to object, but the soon-to-be introduced Falconbridge was having none of it and before long, a generous shot of the sweet liquor was lined up before each of them.

"I was just telling your vicar here" Arnold slurred, "we all keep a log don't we Alexander."

Until that moment, Clarkson had been quite unaware of the new man's name and so, instead of correcting Arnold's mistaken use of his official clerical title, he allowed it to slide as Doctor Falconbridge confirmed that he too had always kept a detailed journal on every voyage.

"Without fail," he said, "It's essential to provide a record, the insurance companies always want to see them in case of any claims, and we can often get asked to give evidence if there is any recompense payable to the owners due to deterioration or loss."

Eating was just about the last thing that the three of them felt like doing in that moment, but as three generous plates of sausage and potatoes were placed before them, they felt obliged to tuck in, each hoping that it would at least help to soak up the alcohol. Given the several pints that they had already consumed, and the amount that was yet to come, it was probably for the best, but it only served to hasten the flow of information that was now coming thick and fast.

"The treatment of the poor slaves is contemptable," Arnold confessed.

"It's criminal," agreed Falconbridge as he spat a piece of gristle into his hand and dropped it to the floor where the resident Jack Russell wasted no time in snaffling it up.

"But nobody cares" they said almost in time with one another, as if it had been rehearsed. "Nobody cares" echoed Arnold, "and so it carries on, like it has for the last one hundred and fifty years and I have no doubt that it will be the same for the next one hundred and fifty, unless someone does something about it."

"That's exactly what I intend to do" announced Clarkson, his head held as high as the low ceiling would allow. "I am here to gather the evidence that is needed to challenge this evil trade, once and for all, but I can't do it alone. I need real evidence, and not just about the slaves either. I fear that too many people in our land, don't care much for the wellbeing of foreigners, least of all the blackamoors. So, I must gain their attention by other means, and I think that I know exactly how to do it. But I need your help with that."

"We're listening" the landlord said, taking the opportunity to speak for all three of them.

"From what I have heard and learned from you and others," he began, "the way that the crews are treated on these vessels is abhorrent, it's as if they are even more expendable than the slaves."

"Well, that's because they are" said Arnold, backing up what Clarkson had already been told by the absent Gardiner at the quayside. "They can always be replaced, in any port, any place around the route, there's always someone who's trying to get to the next stop or trying to run away from the last. And they are not needed on the final leg, a skeleton crew could sail the ship home, the vessels are so small, so if they're not on board for the homeward journey, well they're not on board."

"And if they're not on board," added Falconbridge, "then they don't need paying when they pull into port. Do you remember that scoundrel on board The Alexandria, Alexander?"

In an instant Clarkson understood that the two of them had sailed together aboard the coincidentally named ship, but he opted against making any further enquiries in the moment in favour of keeping their conversation on track. "And I bet that the investors are happy with that outcome" concluded Clarkson, beginning to understand the unforgiving rules of this particularly evil undertaking. "I need to gather as much evidence and find as many eyewitness testimonies as we can muster" Clarkson said enthusiastically, "and as quickly as possible. I can't sleep at night for worrying that every minute wasted is another life lost and another enslaved."

"It won't be easy," sighed Arnold. "The Slavers run this city and they will run down any man, woman or child that stands against their interests. They will stop at nothing, and I mean nothing, to keep us quiet, so getting crew members to testify against one of their Captains is going to be a hard trick to pull off, I can tell you."

"But will you testify against them?" asked Clarkson, more in hope than expectation.

For a moment they were silent, but then both men nodded, and the Reverend's eyes brimmed full of tears. He was not an emotional man, but in that moment, he was overcome by their willingness to stand with him and for the first time in days it left him with a real sense of hope.

"And I am sure of another too," slurred Falconbridge, "but you'll have to be quick! He's jumped ship to The Brothers from The Pilgrim - they offered him double his usual rate - and let's just say he has a need for some easy money right now! I'll get a message to him."

"I think I have met with him already, at the Quayside," smiled Clarkson, "and yes, he has already given me his word too and I must say, never have such simple words been more welcome to my ears!" he exclaimed, taking up his rum and downing it in one, something that he had witnessed others do many times before. But this was his first time, and his face brightened as the warm glow slid down his gullet, but he immediately regretted it, his cheeks beginning to shine in a reddish shade of purple. "And that's my last" he hiccupped.

"On that point," James Arnold said, "I cannot agree with you vicar." A rare moment of brotherhood followed, as the four of them laughed together, for what would be the first and only time in their brief association. *The Society for Effecting the Abolition of the Slave Trade* had three more members and the fight was well and truly on.

-ooo-

The drinking dens and crimping houses of Marsh Street had become dominated by an influx of Irish immigrants in recent years and many of the landlords and landladies, who tried and often failed to keep order in their establishments at night, had come across the Irish Sea from Cork and Dublin in the last thirty years or so.

Clarkson and Thompson had left the good Doctors with strict orders to head straight to their beds, whilst they made their first visit to the den of iniquity that was Marsh Street. Their mission was a simple one; to observe the behaviour of the Captains and First Mates as they patrolled the pubs in search of reluctant crews and to find victims who would be willing to testify against their mistreatment, so exposing the sordid nature of The Trade to public scrutiny.

The Reverend had been as good as his own word and that first shot had been his last. Another had not passed his lips that night, but he continued to drink water in similar sized glasses to give the impression that he was still drinking to excess. It was one way to blend in, if such a thing had been possible for him. His compatriot was made of sterner stuff and so he remained with a tankard in his hand for most of the evening, without ever seeming to be any the worse for wear, which was quite a feat considering the number of establishments they had now visited.

They had walked up and down the street with no particular route in mind, but the innkeeper took the lead in selecting each target, after giving due consideration for the ships that were in port and each Captain's favourite haunt. He seemed to know them all and was welcomed into each by the predominantly Irish owners, recognising one or two of the regulars inside with a handshake and a snarled local greeting, which Clarkson was quite unable to translate into his version of the English language. Each had accepted Clarkson without hesitation purely on Thompson's say so, and because of that and for that reason alone, the Reverend did not feel in any danger, in spite of the inebriated state that most were in. By 'the cut of their gib', as the local saying went, none of their number was sober enough to recall any of the finer details from the evening's conversation, and he strongly doubted that many would even remember his name come the morning.

For about an hour they had trawled the area, stopping in several places to get a feel for the place, listening into discussions or just on the lookout for likely candidates with whom to strike up a conversation. Some were willing to talk, others were not and chose instead to sit and drown their substantial sorrows alone. One or two were suspicious and threatened violence, others were emotional and easily upset, but most were the worse for wear having been drinking for hours, if not for days, and few were able to string together even the shortest of coherent sentences.

It was in The Star and Ball, a cramped and drab drinking den under the watchful eye of its fearsome landlady Martha Hunt, that they made their first breakthrough. At first the place had seemed empty, and the two men had planned to stay for only a short time, ordering their agreed drinks from the bar, at which point the Reverend received a queer look as the buxom serving girl handed over his shot of what she said was water. Then from out of the darkest corner of the room came a pitiful sigh, as a faint and weary outline peered out at them, barely noticeable in the meagre candlelight.

As the two of them looked and listened more intently, it became clear that he was singing a melancholy song to himself, an ode to the far-flung places of his youth or to a long-lost love. As Thompson looked at Clarkson they nodded in collusion, and wandered into the darkness, each withdrawing a rickety chair from beneath the table at which the man was slumped and sitting down to wait it out. It took a few moments before the man became fully aware that he had company, and a full minute before his eyes had focused enough on his uninvited guests to register their presence.

"Whatcha looking at?" the dishevelled drunkard growled at them. "Whatcha want?"

"You look like you could do with some company my friend?" Thompson said and the suggestion was not met with an immediate rebuff.

"I don't want to go" he wailed, as if he'd been waiting all night for an audience. "I don't want to go."

"Don't want to go where?" asked Clarkson intrigued, knowing only too well what the answer was going to be long before he spat it at them across the table.

"The Guinea Coast" he dribbled. "I signed it, but I didn't want to, they made me sign it, I never read it, nor did the others. Them's a mystery to most of 'em, they can't even read."

"The Articles of Agreement?" Thompson queried, knowing full well what he meant.

"The crew has to sign 'em," he said, looking straight at Clarkson and straight past him at the same time, his misaligned eyes failing to focus on either target. "They lays out what they gives us in food and pay and what they has to do. I signed 'em, but I didn't see 'em. I didn't know what I was signing. They never showed 'em me you see, they folds 'em like this, so's I couldn't see the papers" and he took a soggy cardboard beer mat and folded it into rectangles until the whole thing disintegrated into a sodden mess on the surface between them.

"When do you leave port?" Clarkson asked, hoping that he could seize on this opportunity to intervene in a clear injustice and so fit another piece into his puzzle.

"On the morning tide" the sailor whimpered.

"You're on The Brothers?" Clarkson asked in sudden realisation. They would have to act quickly. "What is your name my good fellow? And what is your position on the ship?"

"My name is Sheriff" he told them, giving only his surname. "I'm one of the ship's mates, one of the officers. I don't want to let them down."

"If you were misled," started Clarkson, "if you have been treated dishonestly, then they have no legal grounds to keep you to your word, for they have not been true to theirs."

"We've all been swindled" he cried. "I've been told that this Captain, that he's a rogue, a murderer some says. I hear that he's killed his crew before, when they won't do his bidding, or left 'em marooned in Africa or on some remote island. I've never been slaving before, I never wanted to, I don't want to now" he cried out, causing one or two heads to turn. They were being watched. That was clear.

"We won't let him have you" Clarkson promised. "I won't let him get away with it. Anyone that wants off that ship will be given the chance to do so, in the name of God I'll make it so." It was a rather extravagant promise to make in the circumstances and the Reverend found himself regretting it almost as soon as he'd spoken it out loud. Quite how he was going to keep his promise, he had no idea, and even Thompson was staring at him in some disbelief.

"But he has my mark, if I runs I'll be left to rot in Newgate gaol," he sobbed. "Starved to death at His Majesty's pleasure, that's what they said would happen to us if we ran, once we'd signed."

Thomas Clarkson could not stand idly by and see injustice done to another man, and so as he listened to this man's travesty, in his head he was already donning the armour of truth and picking up the shield of honour before the sword was in his hand. Though he had no doubt whatsoever that he would be putting himself in harm's way to help out a stranger, of whom he knew nothing, he was simply unable to help himself. The moral steam engine was stoking his boiler and his gears were beginning to grind.

"I will be at the quay in time for the morning tide," said Clarkson vehemently. "I will personally see to it, that you are not boarded when that boat sails."

-ooo-

The night had been a long one, one of the longest in Clarkson's relatively young life, but it had been most productive, and any doubts that he'd harboured as to the truth behind the tales had been well and truly vanquished. Account after account had been corroborated again and again, and although some reporters may have been a little circumspect with the truth, especially when it came to their own involvement, Clarkson was left with much to ponder as he began to put each snippet into order and to sort his ordered evidence into a list of charges.

The tale of The Thomas, long since returned from its trials abroad, was told and retold in almost every drinking den they had frequented and though Clarkson had expected the accounts to have varied in their retelling, they had not. Indeed, each time he'd heard of William Lines' murder at the hands of the Chief Mate, the details were astonishingly similar, as if the truth of it was far more horrific to the ear than any fiction could ever be. Then there was the story of The Alfred and the abhorrent abuse of the black sailor and freeman, John Dean, whose terrible treatment was also confirmed by a pub Landlord by the name of Donovan, who was only too eager to share all that he had heard from some of Dean's shipmates. They had seen for themselves the scars upon his back, the result of the hot pitch that had spread across it and the tearing of his flesh by the hot tongs that the Captain had wielded. He had even had the good fortune to come across James Bulpin, the very man that Mr Thomas had named from his death bed and from him he heard how Joseph Cunningham and Charles Horseler had each been beaten about the chest by the captain with a knotted rope that had killed Charles and left his shipmate severely wounded.

The litany of crimes against the purveyors of The Trade seemed endless, and Clarkson feared that he might lose track so numerous were they in number and so similar in their evildoing, but such a failing was not in his makeup.

CHAPTER FIVE

"It has been asserted, that the Slave Trade is a desirable employ, and a nursery for our seamen. Were this the case, sailors would be found as willing to offer themselves to this, as to any other traffic. But the direct contrary is the fact. Nothing is more difficult than to procure a sufficient number of hands for a Guinea voyage."

James Field Stanfield – Observations on a Voyage to the Coast of Africa

Clarkson arrived at the quayside not a moment too soon. The Brothers had already raised her hefty anchor, before leaving the shelter of the dock and her bulk was beginning to shift on the morning tide. She moved away from the edge at a snail's pace, in slow pursuit of the pilot that navigated their course out along the treacherous channel of the Avon, and he was forced to leap the few feet that now divided its starboard side from the shore. As he hit the deck, his tall frame cast a long and wiry shadow across the length of the boat, where the Captain stood with his mouth agape. Clarkson had made a graceful landing for a man of his stature, but as he did so, his eyes settled on a long iron chain that clanked against his leading foot. It ran the length of the midship, from the forecastle to the half deck and was twinned with another on the portside, similarly proportioned with the same sturdy links and heavy rings, upon which the slaves would soon be hung like a pair of demonic charm bracelets.

The crew had been busy with the sheets, raising the fore and aft sails, taking up the tension in pairs as they caught the wind, before securing each with the winch upon the rails. Almost to a man, they stood and stared, their eyes shifting from their Captain to the intruder and back again, like well-trained dogs, waiting on their master for the order to attack.

"And what is the meaning of this intrusion?" roared Captain Howlett. "On whose authority do you dare to board my vessel."

"On the King's authority!" Clarkson roared, the lie booming with conviction, in the certain knowledge that no one aboard that ship would be in any position to contradict him. "You have a man aboard this ship without proper licence. Where is Mr Sheriff?"

"You have no business with any member of my crew Sir" the Captain barked.

"I am making it my business," Clarkson snapped, "because a man's liberty is at stake."

"I am here" the mate cried out, emerging from below decks in response to the commotion, having clambered up through the bowels of the ship at the sound of his name.

"Do you know this villain?" the Captain sneered, "speak up man, or I'll have you flogged before we've passed the Pillars of Hercules."

"There will be no flogging here this morning" said the Reverend calmly, "this man is coming with me. You will set us down at the Hot Wells or I will see you in Newgate gaol this very day."

"It may have escaped your attention Sir," mocked the Captain, "but this ship has left port, which means that my authority is absolute. We will indeed see *you* to shore at Hot Wells, or we will cast you adrift in the channel and you can fend for yourself on the tide. You'll be halfway to the Emerald Isle by eventide."

Clarkson found that he was the only one on board that wasn't now laughing, with the exception of Mr Sheriff who was looking increasingly desperate, unsure of which corner he should be running to.

As their fun began to wane, all eyes turned to the only man whose name was not recorded on the ship's muster roll.

"Mr Sheriff!" the Captain's voice commanded. "Can you enlighten us as to this gentleman's purpose here today or are you as dumbstruck as the rest of us?"

"There is no need for that," Clarkson interceded. "I am the Reverend Thomas Clarkson, Deacon of Winchester and late of Wisbech, Norfolk, and I have come to rightfully return this man to shore. His articles are null and void, as are any others that were taken in ignorance of their substance. You have acquired your crew through lies, deception and skulduggery Sir, and no court in the land would find in your favour."

"There is no court at sea, but mine" spat the Captain through gritted teeth, furious that his authority was now being questioned on his own ship. "And I will have none of it, put this man in chains" he ordered pointing directly towards their unwanted guest, "and this one too." He meant for Mr Sheriff to join Clarkson in the same manacles, that had not been intended for use until the coast of Africa, but he didn't reckon on the Reverend Thomas Clarkson.

"I am a man of the cloth, Captain" he resolutely reminded him. "And I come clad in God's armour. No chains will hold me when my friends in Parliament hear of this outrage and you will be pursued under the full weight of the law until you are caught, tried, and sentenced in the harshest manner. My contacts here in Bristol know of my plans this day and, should I not return with Mr Sheriff by noon, they have been instructed to raise the alarm with the Lord of the Admiralty, who will no doubt send a force to be reckoned with to stop you before this little boat gets out of the estuary."

It was all a lie of course, but Clarkson was sure that on this occasion, God would forgive him for being a little liberal with the truth. It seemed to do the trick. The crew stopped dead in their tracks and on a reluctant intake of breath, the Captain ordered them to stand down.

"Take 'em ashore" he growled, sending his First Mate off to prepare the small, but seaworthy canoe, that would take them the short journey to the tiny quay at Hot Wells. "Get 'im out of my sight," he growled, his eyes fixed fast on Mr Sheriff, "before I hurl his wretched arse overboard meself."

It was a short trip. Not a word was exchanged, though the skinny mate who accompanied them seemed awestruck, as his shipmates rowed the small vessel like their lives depended on it. Clarkson could feel his shifty dark eyes bearing down on him, but he refused to return his stare, instead staring forlornly into the mid-distance as the bemused mate looked on. As Clarkson and Sheriff scrambled ashore, they each turned to watch The Brothers as it continued on its way, against the picturesque backdrop of the Avon Gorge. The small rowing boat beat the waves in steady pursuit, and as the seabound man at its stern tentatively held up his hand in an unexpected farewell, Clarkson sensed the sorrow in his gesture and said a silent prayer for the man, whose skeletal frame suggested that he may yet be blown overboard at the first hint of a gale.

"Thank 'ee" Mr Sheriff spluttered, his heart thumping hard in his chest. "I'd given up hope." Clarkson did not reply immediately. He couldn't quite believe what had just transpired, nor that he had been the sole architect of such an implausible rescue mission.

"I didn't think myself capable of such a thing" he finally admitted, visibly shaking as he thought about what could have happened. "If I'd planned it, I would never have done it. I must be more of a *Jack Adams* than I thought."

As a result of their jaunt downstream, they were now quite a distance to the west of the city and the absence of any other river traffic that morning had left them stranded, but they were finally able to hitch a ride on a goods ferry, which had been moored at the far end of the parade since their arrival and was now making its way back. They disembarked at Bristol Bridge and walked back through the narrow and cobbled streets to The Seven Stars, just as it was opening its doors to its regulars from the local market on Thomas Street.

"That's quite the tale" the landlord exclaimed as Clarkson recounted his morning's work. "I'd never have been so bold. Don't be vexing yourself further with it though Reverend, I'll take things from here" and he ushered Mr Sheriff to a quiet table of his own that was nestled in the far corner of the room, supplying him with a generous helping of pie and mash and a tankard of rough cider to keep him quiet. "That'll keep him happy for a while, 'til I work out what to do with him, but I've something else that you'll be wanting to see, come with me."

Clarkson followed the landlord around the back of the narrow bar and into a storeroom, whose only light was a small porthole fixed high into the sloping ceiling above. The room was full of bottles and barrels, mostly empty, together with a single roughly upholstered chair that had long seen better days.

"Wait here!" he instructed and returned to the bar, pulling up the trapdoor to the cellar and signalling to encourage someone up, a person that was clearly reluctant to comply. After a few more moments, Clarkson saw the black hair and dark features of a small black boy emerge into the dusky light, his white eyes wide with terror and his bottom lip trembling with fear.

"Oh, my good heavens" was all that Clarkson could think to say, as of all the sights that he'd expected to see in the Seven Stars that lunchtime, the missing runaway was not amongst them. He knew full well that it was quite inadequate, but he was right out of words, and as the boy shuffled meekly into the small room, the Reverend sank to his knees to speak to the petrified child. "The escaped runaway I presume?" asked Clarkson, first looking to the landlord for confirmation, which came with a nod and a glance behind, just to check that there was no one else in earshot. There wasn't, the bar was still almost empty save for the rescued shipmate who was now fast asleep with his back to the whitewashed wall, his empty tankard on the table and his food bowl scraped clean.

"The boy was hiding out in the yard last night" the innkeeper explained, anticipating the next question before it came. "I thought it was the damn cats getting into the bins again, so I went out with my pistols to see 'em off. Found this young fella, crouched amongst the waste. He must have been starving, he'd been eating the peelings and had knocked over the buckets which is what had caused all the racket. He's lucky I didn't shoot 'im."

"Has he said anything?" Clarkson asked, hoping for some clue or confirmation as to his identity.

"Not a thing" said Thompson. "Silent as the grave. I think 'is name is Jim, that's the name of the runaway that was in Farley's rag, he seems to answer to it anyway."

"Jim?," tried Clarkson. "Is that your name?"

The terrified boy didn't answer, he just looked up at their two white faces, clearly scared out of his wits and at a loss to know if either of these new white strangers were to be trusted. Judging by the others that he'd met in his short life, he had no reason to think that they would be, and so he continued to cower before them, his eyes lowered in deference and his hands tightly clenched into fists of fear. He had been locked down in a darkened cellar with a coal hole as his only source of light and air and though he may have been able to feel some sense of safety in his subterranean hiding place, any comfort that he'd been able to draw from such seclusion would have been short-lived.

Clarkson could only imagine what the boy had been through and the sights he had seen since his capture, and although it was a story that he hoped to hear someday from the boy's own lips, he suspected that any such communication between them might not occur any time soon. It was no wonder that a burly red-faced barman and a lanky red-haired clergyman, would not seem to offer up any relief in this cold and unforgiving land, but it was all that was available and so Clarkson did his best to convey his good intentions to him. After all, they really did have his best interests in mind.

"Have you given him something to eat and drink?" said Clarkson, hoping that the prospect of food might lift the boy's spirits enough to flush the fear from his timid and tearful face.

"Aye" the barman answered, "he wolfed down two portions of stew, I think he might have had another, but he'd already had the last of it. I was just about to put him up some pie and mash when you arrived. I'll just get it now, if you want to see if you can get anywhere with him."

Clarkson didn't even try, sensing that a clumsy attempt to force his friendship upon the boy would only make matters worse. Instead, he offered him a weak and sympathetic smile as he slumped down on his haunches against the bare wall opposite, his hands between his knees. He knew only too well that the child must have viewed all white men as a threat and when he looked into the boy's eyes, Clarkson found that he could not hold the child's stare. He found his thoughts drifting back to The Brothers, its sole purpose to make a healthy return on investment for its shareholders and he felt a heightened sense of shame, as if the actions of his own countrymen were his own. That the venture would see untold pain and misery inflicted on boys and girls like this one was certain, but the prospect felt personal, as the boy regarded him with a newfound interest.

He could not take his eyes off the giant of a man, who appeared tall to the average adult and so must have loomed over a mere child like a colossus. He just stared into his new captor's face, as if he was reading his intentions, considering whether or not he could trust him and scanning his features to discover what this latest master had in mind. Clarkson's thoughts, for good or evil, his lusts and desires, his anger, and his pain; all of his feelings seemed suddenly to have been laid bare, as if each thought and deed were written down on parchment and put up on display around the room.

It was Thompson that broke in to sever the growing tie between them, a plate of steaming hot food at the ready, which he handed to the boy who wasted no time in diving in to gobble it up. It was as if he had not been fed in days, and so he was intent on making up for his enforced fasting just in case supplies were running low or his turn of luck wasn't to last.

"Gentlemen!" the Chairman thundered, "can we make a start please. Gentlemen, we have a lot to get through this morning, the sooner we begin the sooner we can take our fill of Mrs Patterson's marvellous luncheon."

The assembled members grumbled in agreement, a sentiment that was quickly followed by an air of general good cheer, which he took as his cue to declare the general meeting of the Bristol Society of Slaving Ventures open.

"Firstly, some notices," he announced. "A couple of absentees send their apologies."

Lack of attendance at these important meetings was seen to give offence to The Trade and to their collective calling and so gave rise to a round of booing, which only abated once the Chairman raised his hand and motioned with a flutter of his fingers when he felt that enough was enough. He allowed it to go on for rather longer than he should have – and signalled to the clerk to have their feelings noted for the minutes – before continuing unchecked.

"Farr is in Liverpool on business, he is represented here by his nephew," the Chairman informed them, looking to the furthest end of the table where a nervous young man glanced around without once making eye contact with any of the generally jovial, yet severe looking faces. "Welcome young Farr" the Chairman nodded, and his salutation was met with a chorus of approval.

"Last month's minutes?" he asked, moving quickly through the standing points on the agenda. "Any comments or amendments? I assume that you've all read them?" It was clear from the way that he scanned the room, menacing everyone with an accusatory stare until his eyes fixed on one old rogue, who was nervously shuffling through his papers in search of his meticulously copied record. No one raised any objections or begged his leave to read them there and then, and so he declared the minutes approved and moved on to the official order of business for the day.

"Now then" he continued in the same gruff tone, "this recent voyage of The Molly Snow, I hear that it all went surprisingly well Anderson?"

The implied suggestion that this particular venture had not been expected to go well at all, caused quite a stir in the room, a couple of the older members elbowing each other in the ribs, as they shared a private joke at Anderson's expense. Their actions did not give rise to any objections by the chair or anyone else, other than the victim of their jibes, who was left feeling thoroughly uncomfortable at the ribbing to which he had been subjected.

The previous venture that had been presided over by John Anderson had been a bit of a disaster and quite a few members in the room had lost a hefty sum as a result. They had put it down to bad management, although the Agent had excused himself with the usual hard-luck stories.

"Yielded a tidy profit" he said proudly in spite of the banter, "which has now been distributed amongst the investors." As he said it, he looked around at some of the most notable investors who were present in the room, who each nodded their confirmation and made a few congratulatory grunts.

"Well done, young Anderson, well done" added the Chairman, though to call him 'young' was a bit of a stretch as he was forty years old, but he had sailed with his father and so Anderson took it to be a term of endearment. "Always good when a plan comes together. No problems to report? I hear that prices on the coast were high?"

"Yes indeed" Anderson agreed, seizing on the chance to expound on his knowledge for the benefit of those in the room. "As much as twenty pounds per head for an adult male" he conveyed to a ripple of surprised annoyance. "Our Captain drove a hard bargain though and managed to offload most of the goods that we had taken to trade," he went on, "though the demand for copper was less than usual, so it is reported that most of it had to be sold at a slight loss."

"And what about on the other side, any problems to report there?"

"No Sir, not of any note," he replied, "we fared well on the middle passage, only losing one tenth of the cargo, though the Captain did jettison a few as he was afeared that they had the flux, and he did not want it spreading amongst the rest."

"Wise man" the Chairman applauded. "Decisive Captain that one" he said, "he's saved many a venture in his time through timely interventions like that."

"Not afraid to call it when it needs calling," snorted another agreeable voice.

"I had him once in the sixties when he was first abroad," said another, "first class, even in his early twenties. A bit severe with the crew and the cargo some said, but I never had any complaints about his skippering skills, though his price is too severe for me these days."

"Five pounds, plus a hefty share in the profits, should be enough for any Captain" roared the Chairman, "even one that likes to take a barrel or two of rum on his own account for the return leg."

Another peel of laughter reverberated around the room, bouncing from knowing look to guilty frown - even the oil portraits of former Captains, that stared down over proceedings like caged hawks, seemed to twitch in displeasure.

"Well, if there's no more to say on that," he paused for a moment to look into twenty or more sets of mostly attentive eyes. "No? Well, can we please note in the minutes that The Society would like to congratulate Mr Anderson and Captain Howlett on a very successful enterprise, and we hope that he can repeat the trick on his latest voyage aboard The Brothers which has just left port this very morning."

"Hear, hear!" the co-owner of The Brothers hailed from the head of the table, his fellow Slavers banging the oak to time in noisy support.

"Talking of The Brothers, that brings us to the second item on the agenda" announced the Chairman, directing the committee to a second bound set of papers before them. "The muster roll, manifest and assorted other documents for the ship and its crew. Mr Rogers if you please Sir, anything to add or to share?"

James Rogers, a regal looking ship owner and former Agent from a long-established Bristol slaving family, sat back in his chair and flexed his fingers, as if readying himself for a long and boring account. "And keep it short James, if you wouldn't mind, we haven't got all day." It was the Chairman who had interceded, much to the relief of the assembled guests, who were all very well aware of this particular member's tendency to hold court whenever the occasion allowed. As it turned out, he didn't have much to say for once and as soon as that fact became apparent, he was cut off in mid-flow by the Chairman, referring those present to the documents for any further details. He did ask one more question though, and it led to quite a debate. "I hear that you had some troubles assembling a crew this time Mr Rogers?"

"It's become a problem for us all," another of the owners butted in, a consensus quickly building around the huge and heavily polished table, over which a multitude of papers were now scattered.

"We are seeing the same thing with The Pilgrim" another added, "we just can't get the bastards to sign their articles, and we sail in a week."

"Don't you always get them in the end?" the Chairman asked crustily, "from the drinking dens and whore houses on Marsh Street, I hear. No ship has yet been stuck in port for want of a crew has it, not in my time anyway?"

No one responded and instead looked away from the Chairman's gaze, careful not to catch his eye for long. He was a powerful man with a lot of influence over them and their business dealings and no one wanted to get on the wrong side of him, even for a moment. When he had an opinion, you agreed with it, if you knew what was good for you and when you had an opinion you kept it to yourself, especially if it was likely to be at odds with his own.

"No, I didn't think so" he went on, "so before we all start saying anything stupid like 'we should be raising their salaries' and eating into our profits still further – and I know that some of you have been suggesting it even if you don't have the balls to say it here – I am telling you this, we stick to our guns and keep their wages where they are. If just one of you raises your rates, then we all have to follow suit, so keep 'em where they are, or you'll have me to answer to."

If there was any discord bubbling beneath the surface, a rising crescendo of "hear, hear!" soon drowned it out, echoing around the hallowed hall to stifle any opposing views that may have been starting to form in the heads of the less experienced. "Minute it as a vote on the matter" the Chairman dictated, "carried unanimously. Subject closed."

And so, the conversation continued, subjects ranged from the worm infestations to the latest outbreak of scurvy on The Ruby, until the agenda was exhausted, and the Chairman asked the restless assembly if there was any other business. One hand went up. It belonged to the young Mr Farr and was followed by several objecting groans from the room; those whose stomachs had started to rumble, and from the alcoholics amongst them whose first drink of the day was already long overdue. Yet what he had to say was set to start a debate that would keep them busy for a further fifteen minutes, and for many months after the contents of the meeting had long since been inscribed in triplicate, and left to gather dust in the filing room for future generations to peruse.

"There's a stranger in the city, asking questions about The Trade," he piped up nervously. "I've been asked to raise it, as a matter of discussion, in case anyone else has seen him. He's been in the ale houses, talking to the crews about their treatment on board the ships and he's been seen around the docks, with that Quaker Gandy and a couple of the ship's Doctors."

"Which Doctors?" It wasn't a joke, but the irony wasn't lost on the gathered group and the Chairman was quick to pick up on his unintended pun. "Yes, witch Doctors, most appropriate. Because none of them are qualified in any way that would be recognised at the infirmary. I wouldn't let a single one of them near a member of my household, that's for sure. Not even the ugliest of my housekeeper's chamber maids."

"Falconbridge and Gardiner, I believe," another of the more informed owners replied as the obligatory laughter subsided, having heard the rumours at his club only the night before.

"And Arnold as well" added Rogers. "He was seen in The Stars with them the other night. Looked as thick as thieves they did, or so my man told me."

"Well to refer to any of those quacks as Doctors is stretching a point" the Chairman smarted, "none of them is much more than a surgeon's mate, I want none of us to employ any of them on any of our ventures from this point forward. Yes, I know before one of you pipes up that Gardiner is out on The Brothers already, but who knows, maybe he'll do us all a favour and fail to return."

For a moment a stunned silence descended on the room, as they considered the difficulties that all of them had encountered in finding surgeons for their voyages with even the most basic level of medical understanding. It seemed that some had heard rumours of this man and his recent dealings, whilst others remained uninformed and so simply looked perplexed at all the fuss. But there was one amongst them who knew more, and he was more than happy to share that knowledge with his peers.

"Aye" said James McTaggart, owner of The Pearl. "I've seen this man, hanging around the quayside. He was on board a couple of the vessels yesterday morning talking with your men." He was looking to the owners of The Prince and The Pilgrim, both of whom looked concerned, at the news, especially once he'd shared more of what he knew. "He was with that damn Quaker, Gandy. Asking after their treatment on the ships and the state of the slaves on the middle passage and whether we acquires 'em with force or not."

"Well, who is he? This stranger?" the Chairman demanded, "what does he look like?"

"Striking" McTaggart continued. "You can't mistake him. He's Irish looking, though by all accounts he's not an Irishman."

"Well, that's something he's got in his favour then" the Chairman scoffed, but no one else was laughing this time. This was no laughing matter. Strangers about town were rarely a welcome sight and were never to be taken lightly, especially those who had an immediate penchant for asking awkward questions of people that they didn't know.

"He's a clergyman of sorts, apparently" McTaggart continued. "He's over six feet tall, with a shock of red hair. Always seems to be dressed in black. He's been staying up on Park Street and he's been in the company of that meddling innkeeper Thompson, from The Seven Stars."

"He's been seen with the other Quakers too" another voice added. "About the docks and up at Clifton with that conveyancer Chandler – they seemed very friendly by all accounts."

"Bloody Quakers" the Chairman stormed. "They're a thorn in our backside, we should have got rid of them when we had the chance. What with that Methodist preacher Wesley and now this Anglican minister, we've got the whole bloody set" he cursed. "Don't they know, we are doing God's work here? It's us that has God on our side, not them. They need to remember that, before they carry on with their insults and condescending codswallop from their high and mighty pulpits. Who do they think they are?"

Ever since the transatlantic trade in African slaves had begun in the middle of the sixteenth century, the slave-trading families had held onto this self-perpetuating truth as if their standing in society depended on it. Their rationale was that the prevailing trade winds and currents that ferried their slave ships down to Africa, across the Atlantic along the middle passage, and back home again were somehow pre-ordained for their benefit. The triangular route was carried on the breath of God, they said, and that made The Trade and their resulting affluence, His providence.

"How do you know all this anyway?" the Chairman asked curiously, his thoughts of divine approval rapidly receding.

"I've had him watched since he started poking around my ship" the Scottish ship owner smiled, tapping the side of his nose for effect. "I don't like people interrogating my men, not unless I know what they're about."

"Or unless you've asked them to" a voice around the table quipped, at which all present shared in the well-timed joke, which McTaggart received in good humour for a change.

"Good man" the Chairman nodded in approval. "Good move. Well, keep it up and let me know immediately if he interferes in anything that is in any way harmful, to our business. If not, let's get our man at St. Mary's to have a word with him, vicar to vicar, so to speak. He's a reliable fellow, not the squeamish type like that Wesley toad, they can say a few 'Hail Marys' together and get this damn concern out of our hair. Now let's bring this meeting to a close and get off to the dining room for a spot of luncheon. I'm famished, I don't know about you all."

"One more thing Mr Chairman" It was McTaggart again.

"Yes, my fine fellow, what is it now that's so important as to get in the way of these ravenous gentlemen and an excellent piece of prime beef?"

"Have you seen this week's Journal?" he asked, waving a roughly folded newspaper in his general direction. "It would seem that our opponents are upping the stakes, take a look at this."

The cantankerous merchant grabbed the copy out of his comrade's hands and reluctantly perused the page, his eyes closing in on a larger-than-usual advertisement on the right-hand side, whose outline had been crudely encircled in smudged black ink.

SOCIETY

Instituted in 1787 for the purpose of effecting.

THE ABOLITION OF THE SLAVE TRADE

Encouraged by the success which has attended the publication of sundry tracts against Slavery, this society was formed in order to excite still more the Public attention to the Slave Trade and to collect such evidence or information as may tend to its Discouragement and finally to its Abolition. For these purposes (which have been already attended with and cannot be effected without considerable Expense) a subscription has been opened and a Committee appointed to manage the Funds. The principal Aim of this Society is to promote among the Members of both Houses of Parliament, a Disposition to inquire into this inhuman Traffic, and they have the satisfaction already to number, amongst the Friends to the Cause, several Men of distinguished Character and Abilities, who enter into the Business with a Zeal, which affords a reasonable Ground to hope for the Accomplishment of its Design. They have also the peculiar Pleasure of seeing Men of different religious Denominations unite with true Christian Harmony, in the cause of Humanity and Justice. Names of the Committee appointed for procuring Information and Evidence and for directing the Application

---

of such monies as are already, or may be hereafter collected for the purposes of this Institution:

CHAIRMAN
GRANVILLE SHARP, Esq. Leadenhall Street

TREASURER
Mr SAMUEL HOARE, JUN, Lombard Street

COMMITTEE
Mr Robert Barclay, Clapham, Surrey

Mr John Barton, Milk Street, Cheapside

Mr Thomas Clarkson, Wisbech, Cambridgeshire

Mr William Dillwyn, Walthamstow, Essex

Mr George Harrison, Wood Street, Cheapside

Mr Joseph Hooper, Walworth, Surrey

Mr John Lloyd, Tower-Hill, London

James Martin Esq. M.P. Downing St. Westminster

Mr James Phillips, George-Yard, Lombard Street

Mr Richard Phillips, Lincoln's-Inn

William Morton Pitt, Esq. Arlington Street

Mr Phillip Sansom, London Street

Mr John Vickris Taylor, St Helena's, Bishopsgate Street

Mr Josiah Wedgewood, Greek Street, Soho

Mr Joseph Woods, White-Hart Court, Gracechurch Street

The Society will thankfully receive any Communications on this Subject, addressed to the Chairman, at the office No.18 in the Old Jewry; or to the Treasurer in Lombard Street, London.

"Pfff" hissed the Chairman, screwing up the newspaper in his workmanlike hands and flinging it into the corner of the room, from where a finely carved redwood coat stand stood unmoved. "'Humanity and justice', my arse."

"Isn't it kind of them to list out their members and to tell us where they might be found" sneered McTaggart, as he hatched a plan, "it's as if they are inviting attention to themselves. Should we be 'encouraging' the good Reverend to leave Bristol, do you think?" the wily merchant then proposed, not wanting to act alone and without the backing of at least one other of their number. "I've got a gang of my finest enforcers standing by to intervene at our behest. I just has to give them the nod."

For a moment the Chairman considered the underlying threat in the suggestion, but although it was tempting, he wasn't yet convinced of the need for any strongarm tactics and did not want to bring unwelcome attention down upon their heads. They were, after all, dealing with a man of the cloth who, though clearly misguided in his mission, was most likely well intended. No, a quiet word or two would do to begin with, and only if he proved himself not to be open to their finely tuned inducements, should they decide to be a little more 'encouraging' in their efforts to return him from whence he came.

"Not yet" seemed like the right answer, for now. "But put a watch on The Stars, let's see if we can't find out what our religious friends are up to this time."

At that chairs scraped, and portly bellies bulged as servants scurried to clear the plates, and to avoid the wandering hands that pinched and groped at their passing skirts like piranhas in the Tropics might at the sound of wading feet. Pipes tapped and scraped as hats were restored to heads and long coats returned to hang from sagging shoulders, providing cover for breaking wind that poured forth from many a sweating arse. Finally, papers were stuffed unceremoniously into satchels as this unkempt herd of the newly and undeservedly rich, shuffled towards the heaving oak doors and the waiting feeding troughs.

CHAPTER SIX

"When the women and girls are taken on board a ship, naked, trembling, terrified, perhaps almost exhausted with cold, fatigue and hunger, they are often exposed to the wanton rudeness of white savages ... where resistance or refusal would be utterly in vain, even the solicitation of consent is seldom thought of."

John Newton, Rector of St. Mary Woolnoth – Thoughts Upon the African Slave Trade

John Wesley was a man on a mission and whilst he had always been very singular in his ambition to share the glad tidings of salvation from every pulpit in the land, since the turn of the decade his focus had shifted to the desperate plight of the African and the merciless horrors of The Trade.

He was not a Bristolian by birth and was not yet what he would one day become – her adopted son – but his mission had taken root in the Spring of 1739 at the brickyard in St. Phillips, Marsh Street and had continued until this present day. He was unrelenting in his life's work, to spread the word of the Gospel and to damn all those purveyors of injustice who failed to heed The Word, though in more recent times, he and others had spoken it aloud weekly along the streets of Bristol.

Born an Anglican in the Lincolnshire backwaters at the turn of the century, he had been educated at Oxford, where his Methodist ministry had taken hold, and had spent time in the colonies of North America and in Europe, before turning his attention to the receptive ear of Bristol and the West Country. The city had stood witness to many dissenting voices, since Tyndall's English translation of the Bible had paved the way for the official King James Version, and long before his arrival, Bristol had become well known for being a hotbed of religious tension.

As interest in his message continued to strike a chord amongst the populace, his church had grown in leaps and bounds and before that same year was out, the first New Room meeting place had been built and its doors were open to its first congregations who came from all over the expanding city just to hear him speak.

Persecution had been rife in the second half of the seventeenth century and although actual assaults had begun to dwindle as the next half century drew to its close, there were still pockets of unease that all too easily descended into violence, especially when the subjects of Wesley's preaching hit a little too close to home. He had often stood accused of inciting the resulting riots, as the prospect of eternal damnation did not sit well with the average resident, a city that had been built off the back of the traffic in human beings and which was continuing to prosper, as Wesley took to the streets once more on a May day in 1787.

Amongst the audience was a certain red-haired Reverend, who was eager to hear for himself the sermon of a man that he had long since admired, albeit at a distance. His height was proving to be an advantage as the crowd thickened around him, enabling him to see right above the gathered masses as the soberly dressed Methodist scaled the steps of the hastily assembled scaffold. A noticeable ripple of excitement drifted on the breeze, as people caught sight of the familiar man in the black robes and plain white collar, a palpable buzz that sizzled in the unexpected warmth of late spring, to hasten in a sudden hush as the man of the moment began to speak.

"Dearest Brethren," he started, "my favoured Bristolians, hear me now, for there is a pestilence upon you. You have heard my 'thoughts on slavery', some of you may even have read it, but I tell you now, a poisonous pall hangs over this fair city and it must be finished with. Better no trade, than trade procured by villainy. It is far better to have no wealth, than to gain wealth, at the expense of virtue. Better is honest poverty, than all the riches brought by the tears, and sweat, and blood of our fellow creatures." There was a cheer from some, booing and jeering from others, but most people remained silent, shuffling on their self-allotted spot, in full knowledge that this was just the beginning of a long and damning discourse.

The city held its breath.

"Give liberty to whom liberty is due, that is, to every child of man, to every partaker of human nature. Let none serve you but by his own act and deed, by his own voluntary action. Away with all whips, all chains, all compulsion. Be gentle towards all men; and see that you invariably do with everyone as you would have him do unto you."

Some in the crowd were nodding now, others had their hands in the air, palms upturned in supplication. Many others stood stock still, arms folded, regarding Wesley with suspicion and scorn, waiting for their moment to unleash their wrath upon the primary object of their anger. The majority were passive in the moment, listening intently as he shared his thoughts on the most controversial topic of their times, but not yet giving anything of themselves to the cause.

"And first to the Captains employed in this trade" he continued, scanning the crowd for likely candidates whose ugly profile best fitted the cap. "Most of you know, the country of Guinea: several parts of it at least, between the River Senegal and the Kingdom of Angola. Perhaps now, by your means, part of it is become a dreary uncultivated wilderness, the inhabitants being all murdered or carried away, so there are none left to till the ground. But you well know, how populous, how fruitful, how pleasant it was a few years ago."

The object of his accusative rhetoric was not lost on his audience, and almost all of them now glanced to their left and right, in full knowledge that many a guilty man was hidden in the full bustle of this crowd. The turning of heads became a ripple; the pointing of fingers gave rise to a wave; until a spring tide of eyes had someone else in their sights and every single someone returned the stare with a look of defiance.

"You know the people of that land were not stupid," the preacher scolded, "not wanting in sense, considering the few means of improvement they enjoyed. Neither did you find them savage, fierce, cruel, treacherous, or unkind to strangers. On the contrary, they were in most parts a sensible and ingenious people. They were kind and friendly, courteous, and obliging, and remarkably fair and just in their dealings. Such are the men you hire," he said as he scanned each of them for a measure of understanding, "their own countrymen, to tear them away from this lovely country; part by stealth, part by force, part made captive in those wars, which *you* raise or foment on purpose." A voice from somewhere towards the back of the undulating crowd called out in objection, casting doubt on the claim, but he was shouted down as others began to shove and barge, intent on starting a brawl that might stop the minister in his tracks. But the rumpus relented and so he continued, for the moment.

"You have seen them torn away, children from their parents, parents from their children: husbands from their wives, wives from their beloved husbands, brothers, and sisters from each other. You have dragged them, who have never done *you* any wrongs, in chains from their native shore. You have forced them into your ships like a herd of swine, them who had immortal souls as your own." More booing, more hissing, and one or two missiles were launched towards the podium, clattering against the wooden frame, and falling to the ground from where they would later be collected as evidence for the riot that was to follow. "Oh yes, you have shoved them together as close as ever they could lie, without any regard either to decency or convenience and when many of them have been poisoned by foul air, you have seen their remains delivered to the deep, till the sea should give up its dead. You have carried the survivors into the vilest slavery, never to end but with their life."

He paused there and let his accusing silence fall like a pall upon their heads, ignoring the continued rumble of dissent from the slaving community and their many sympathisers, amongst them one Horatio Mullins. A hard and pointed pillow for their collective conscience, one on which they would never find rest. Even the seagulls seemed to cease their squawking to observe the pause in the preacher's patter. Many in the crowd that day knew personally of such people, both Captains and crew; they were their brothers, their uncles, their grandparents, even their fathers. For some of them, it was themselves around whom the preacher's words were wrapped. No one came forward to berate him man-to-man, no one yet walked up to the front to hurl abuse or to trade insults face-to-face; there was no pillory or derision, there was only a sudden silence, and the preacher traded on its power.

"Are you a man?" he asked, knowing too that the women in the audience would not feel excepted by his use of the masculine pronoun that morning. "Then you should have a human heart. But have you indeed? What is your heart made of? Is there no principle of compassion there? Do you never feel another's pain? Have you no sympathy? No sense of human woe? No pity for the miserable? When you saw the flowing eyes, the heaving breasts, the bleeding sides, and tortured limbs of your fellow creatures, were you a stone, or a brute? Did you look upon them with the eyes of a tiger? When you squeezed the agonising creatures down inside the ship, or when you threw their poor mangled remains into the sea, had you no relenting? Did not one tear drop from your eye, one sigh escape from your breast? Do you feel no relenting now?"

He allowed the question to hang above their heads like a Frenchman in the shadow of the guillotine, as its victim steps towards his fate.

"Yes" a cry came from the depths of the crowd. "Yes" another from the back. "Aye," a voice from right next to Clarkson sounded out, as several men fell to their knees in apparent repentance and in certain guilt for crimes that they knew only too well were on their hearts. But many of the former slave crews, their Captains, ship's surgeons, and their mates, were all regarded with the cold and accusing eyes of their fellow Bristolians, as they stood proudly with arms folded and chins out, spoiling for a fight with anyone that was brave enough or sufficiently foolhardy to take them on. It wasn't yet a movement, but as Wesley cast his eyes across his audience many could not hold his gaze, and by that simple test alone, he knew that he was getting through to them. To some of them, at least. And 'some' was a start.

"If you do not," John Wesley preached, his right hand clenched into a fist that landed into the cupped palm of his left with a cushioned thump, as he pressed home his advantage. "If you do not, you must go on" he scoffed, "'til the measure of your iniquities is full. Then will the great God deal with you, as you have dealt with them, and require all their blood at your hands. And at that day it shall be more tolerable for Sodom and Gomorrah than for you."

A stark warning indeed, and though many were not of a Church-going persuasion, they knew only too well of the biblical towns to which he referred. He had struck fear into the rock-hard hearts of the staunchest of his enemies, though it would be folly to suggest that all were touched by his words that day, but for some that swayed and swooned before the pulpit, The Trade would never come calling again.

"But if your heart does relent," Wesley continued on a less damning tack, seeing with his own eyes that some amongst them had been touched by his words. "Though in a small degree, know it is a call from the God of love. And today, if you hear His voice, do not harden your heart. Today resolve, God being your helper, to escape for your life."

The crowd roared its approval. Hands were up all around, clapping and cheering and amongst them some men were weeping openly, their women consoling them or standing by their heads in their hands at the wonder of the message that they had just heard preached. Clarkson too was weeping, his tears in recognition of the importance of his own mission and the inspiration of the speaker, whose name was known across the land as a great orator and man of God. Of that there could be no doubt.

For several minutes, the crowd did not disperse and there was no way that Clarkson could make it through to the front, to shake hands with the man whose written word he had read many times. It was an opportunity that he dare not miss, and so as soon as he could see a way forward, he started to gently push through the barricade of bodies until he found himself at the front, or at least within a few yards of it, where a human wall was now erected. Some only wanted to touch the man, others wanted to get a closer look, but a few like Clarkson wanted to converse with him, even if only for a moment, to say to their friends and family that not only had they heard the great John Wesley speak on the sins of slavery that day, but they had actually spoken with him on this most important of subjects.

Thomas Clarkson was not seeking out the glory or the fame of coming face to face with a man who stood right at the forefront of the Abolitionist movement. Neither was he looking to justify his own views to a kindred spirit, that would no doubt give him some of the comfort and support that even he craved. He simply wanted to share his own plan with a fellow activist, to get a sense from Wesley of his own ideas and to draw on the Methodist man's dreadful experience, so that they may soon achieve their aims of bringing the whole sordid affair in front of the Parliamentary benches, before any more innocent lives were lost to its brutal regime.

"Mr Wesley, it really is an honour to finally make your acquaintance Sir."

The Methodist minister was forced to crane his neck a little to take in the full length of his unexpected admirer, but as he did so, a flash of recognition passed across his face and Clarkson was shocked to be recognised by his hero. "The Reverend Clarkson, I presume? Your depictions do you justice Sir, I could have recognised you anywhere. I had heard that you were in Bristol. Welcome Sir, to the most dissenting city in England."

He said it with a sardonic smile, and the two of them shared a moment of amusement that filled any theological divide that may have existed between them. Though Wesley never intended his Methodist movement to replace the Anglican church, only to supplement it, there were many in the established Church of England, including those who preached from the pulpits in the diocese of Bristol, who viewed Wesley's dissenting voice as a direct threat to the power of church and state.

"What brings you to this fair city Thomas? I hear that you've already ruffled a few feathers amongst the slaving community?"

"I hope that I have Sir" smiled Clarkson, "for that will remain my approach, until this foul plague is wiped from our nation's face."

"On that we are agreed, my friend" said the minister, "most vigorously, yes."

Their meeting had started better than Clarkson could have hoped and so he decided to grasp the nettle and push home his advantage. "I was wondering if we could meet for dinner one evening," he asked politely. "There is so much to do, that none of us can succeed alone. If we could find a way to join our forces together, also with the Quakers, then I am certain that we can bring the people's will to bear against this evil employment."

"We are cut from the same cloth Reverend" Wesley declared with a smile and a hearty pat on his collaborator's back, much to Clarkson's undisguised delight. "I have read your recent tract, the one that you are to shortly submit to the Parliamentary committee I believe?"

"Yes, Mr Sharp is in discussions with William Wilberforce this very week" Clarkson informed him, "I am hoping for news before the week is out."

The Methodist's face turned sour at the very mention of the Member for Parliament's name. "Do you really think he will back our campaign Thomas? His allegiances seem to turn with the tide from what I hear. I have grave misgivings that when the mood takes him or if another crisis looms abroad, that he will drop our great struggle like one of those hot potatoes in favour of another, less controversial cause."

"He does have a short attention span, that is certain" admitted Clarkson, "but he is a good fellow and committed to the cause. I have no doubts and neither does Granville Sharp, of whom he is a close friend, that he will raise our flag in Westminster very soon. I am here to gather evidence for our movement, to be presented to Parliament at the very earliest opportunity, but there is no time to lose, and I have much still to do before I can return to Cambridge."

"I don't doubt it Thomas, and yes, we must indeed dine together this week, we have many things to discuss. Where are your lodgings, so that I can get a message to you if I need to?"

Clarkson gave him the details of the inn on Park Street where he had taken rooms but added that he wasn't certain for how much longer he might find him there. "I am on the lookout for another place to lay my head," he admitted. "Too many prying eyes and eager ears, it seems that the slavers have their spies in all quarters of this city."

"They do indeed Reverend," he smiled knowingly. "My message will find you, do not doubt it. Listen, I will put the word about, I am sure that there are several good Methodist families, and many Quakers besides, who will be more than delighted to offer some home comforts to a God-fearing man such as yourself."

Clarkson thanked him vigorously and after bidding each other a good afternoon, he walked with his head held high above the still-restless crowds, towards his rooms and a well-earned rest. It had been an exhausting few days, both physically and emotionally and he was starting to feel the strain of every life lost, real, or imagined, and each one weighed heavily on his heart.

His short time in Bristol had gone far better than he could have hoped for, and his roughly laid plans had already borne enough fruit to fill a fair-sized basket. He needed time to write it all up and to get his plans in the proper order, but first and foremost he needed an afternoon nap.

-OOO-

On 22nd May 1787, whilst the Reverend Thomas Clarkson was walking the streets of Bristol for the first time, an unlikely group of nine Quakers and a couple of Anglicans had come together in a gloomy print shop in the back streets of the City of London. Chief amongst this unlikely gathering of Englishmen, Welshmen and one single but crucial American, one man stood tall as pivotal to their embryonic campaign to rid the world once and for all of the 'impolitic and cruel' trade in human lives: Granville Sharp.

He was a man of striking features, with a rather large and pointed nose and a prominent chin, that was impossible not to notice on first making his acquaintance. His high cheekbones completed a severe complexion which, if not accompanied by a welcoming smile, could be quite off-putting at the first-time of meeting. Though he was a gentleman, born and bred and so well used to putting his visitors at their ease, he was not averse to reducing his adversaries at the bar to a quivering wreck with one well timed quip and a fixed stare of regal proportions.

It was the eccentric Sharp who had first lit the flame for the torch that Clarkson had carried so heroically to Bristol in April of that year and he who had stood alone against the prejudice of a British legal establishment that still viewed the black man as the inferior property of a superior European race. It was he, that had put his legal brain to the test in the defence of the black lives that were lost in the Zong Massacre, where the only issue at stake for most, seemed to be whether or not an insurance company would have to stand liable for the losses. It was also he who had fought valiantly at Westminster Hall in the face of a white man's will to force a freed black slave, James Somerset, to return to an enslaved life in Virginia.

And these were not the only cases that he had championed in the latter years of the eighteenth century, so much so that he was held in high regard amongst the growing community of freed slaves who had come to call the streets of London their home. And so, it would have come as no surprise to those who knew him, when he'd joined forces with the Quakers and other like-minded ministers, to change the British public's perception of The Trade and all that it stood for.

Richard Phillips and his brother James were two of the Quaker businessmen who owned that small print shop just off Lombard Street and on that day, it was already being put to industrious use, rattling out copies of Clarkson's recently upgraded essay, the one that had won first prize in the Cambridge competition. It was, however, a shadow of its former self, having been the subject of numerous edits by Phillips and after ready input from the rest of The Society. It wasn't the first, and several tracts had already seen the light of day, with many more on the drawing boards and study tables of the more enlightened members of English society.

Yet those who were ready and willing to stand with this new movement, to do away with their sugar and tobacco and to oppose the might of the British establishment, were still few and far between - The Society had a very long way to go before they could ever hope to persuade a patriotic yet myopic public to accept their campaign as their own.

That the Quakers would be at the heart of it was never in any doubt; within their number they had the ear of an international network of influential businessmen, and more importantly, of their wives. Their dissenting voices had been drowned out ever since their inception, and whilst their existence was now tolerated by wider English society, no one that sat in the House of Commons or in the Lords were yet of a mind to take their views seriously. Let alone the views of Quaker women, who were amongst the most vocal in their meeting houses across the shires of England, but who knew only too well that their objecting voices would be ignored by their county's elected representatives, for whom even the basic right to cast their vote was still denied to them.

On the other hand, the Anglican church, or to use its more commonly known title, The Church of England, was all powerful and their influence extended well beyond the confines of their morose and archaic Norman churches, into the very heart of government. However, few of the army of clergymen, that presided over services in a thousand sleepy English villages, knew of the official Church of State's extensive investments in plantations across the West Indies under the guise of the little-known *Society for the Propagation of Christian Knowledge*; or to address it by a different name, the Foreign Mission Society of the Anglican Church. It was a church that, preferring to lean towards hypocrisy than to lean into humanity, was not for turning.

As it turned out, the three Anglicans who stood shoulder-to-shoulder with the Quakers, Methodists, and other dissenting factions of English religious society, were simply evangelicals by another name, and they mobilised the Quaker network that were already proven to be willing and able to rise to this particular challenge. Quakers knew from their own bitter experience what it was to be a persecuted community, having suffered greatly at the hands of the established church, and they now refused to sit idly by and watch as another branch of the human race suffered the similar sting of persecution at the hands of the same bigoted bullies.

The Society had dispatched Thomas Clarkson to Bristol to begin gathering the evidence that they needed for an all-out assault on the country's outright racist agenda. The belief that the British Empire and economy depended on the slave trade and would be bankrupt without it; the argument that the British Navy relied upon a steady stream of able recruits from amongst the slave ship crews; and the widely held illusion that the African slaves were being saved from a life of hardship and war on their own continent, were all falsehoods that The Society longed to expose with as much evidence to the contrary as it could gather. Only by exposing all of these figments for falsehoods, could they hope to break the stranglehold of resistance that had already squeezed the life from a continent during almost three hundred years of prejudice and lies.

Sharp was an avid pamphleteer and as each voice rose up against The Trade, he would seek them out, to capture their words and to have their case documented, with the printing machines at the ready, cranking into life to disseminate the evidence on an industrial scale. A propaganda machine it certainly was, but it was fed with facts from as far afield as Africa and America and all of the islands in between.

As time wore on there would be no shortage of witnesses willing to step up and share what they had seen on the African coast, on the slave ships themselves and at the plantations. Some needed to be coaxed into joining their ever-expanding pressure group, but with Clarkson's drive and determination and Sharp's eye for legal theatre, the two of them quickly became a force to be reckoned with, as the 1780s drew closer to its end, without a Parliamentary hearing in the offing.

"Am I not a man and a brother?"

None of them could remember who had first suggested it, but whoever it was, had been too modest to say so, a demonstration of reserve that would have been quite normal amongst their ranks. What each of them could recall was the day they made the decision to adopt the motto as their society's seal.

A black slave, kneeling in chains with his hands clasped and held high in a plea for mercy.

It would soon adorn thousands of hat pins, brooches and medallions and once Josiah Wedgewood, the great pottery magnate from the English potteries, had finished with designing it in relief, it was an image that would become instantly synonymous with their movement.

"Is it not a little too, submissive?" wondered the ruddy-faced Dillwyn, "like we are begging for mercy, pleading with the white master to take pity? I don't like it."

"It needs to be that way" said Sharp, "for any perceived threat will be used against us. It's a strong message, but if it appears to be too 'revolutionary' they will have us all in the Tower before we can say

'Abolitionist'." Sharp had given it his full and categorical support at one of their regular meetings at Old Jewry, in London's fabled square mile. "It encompasses all that we stand for in just eight simple words."

It would become their rallying cry.

One hundred and fifty miles away, Thomas Clarkson had just arrived back at his lodgings in Bristol. He kicked off his dusty black shoes, removed his white kerchief, stockings and garters and hung his black tailcoat, breeches, and waistcoat on the back of the door, leaving him in nothing but a frayed long sleeved grey shirt, that had seen better days.

He had intended to sleep the afternoon away, but as on most days, he found rest hard to come by and so instead, he had retired to the desk where he took out his writing utensils. He was a man who found it hard to shut out the darkness of the world and every horror that he encountered would trouble him throughout the day and long into the night. Exhaustion would eventually overcome him, but it was not unusual for him to still be awake well into the early hours, especially in the summertime when the light would only just be petering out, as the church clocks struck ten.

So, at two o'clock on a spring afternoon, convinced that any chance of sleep was beyond his reach, he had turned to his letters and his first bulletin since his arrival in Bristol. The object of his news would be Granville Sharp, who would no doubt be waiting with bated breath to hear of his progress.

My honourable friend and fellow protagonist,

I write to you now after one month of headstrong interference in the Bristol trade, the like of which I had never thought myself capable. I have gathered much evidence from amongst the maltreated crews of this port. Our Quaker friends and John Wesley are working tirelessly to keep the public conversant with the horrors of this dreadful business. Thus far I have encountered no real dangers to my person, though I have been aboard several slavers and have been in conversation with many of the Captains and crew in the most deprived parts of the city. More of that when we meet again.

You will recall our exchanges on the matter of the dinner party and who should be in attendance. I will return to London in a few weeks, once I have taken the road to Liverpool - I hope that Doctor Alexander Falconbridge will accompany me thence to keep watch as I fear the Mersey will be heavy laden with snows. He knows the city and The Trade and so I think that he will be the perfect travelling companion, though I do not know if he will submit to my request.

Wilberforce must be in attendance when we dine, and Newton too and any others that you know to be useful in our noble cause.

I leave all provisions in your able hands. God's speed to all who stand with us.

Your friend in haste.
Rev. Thomas Clarkson.

The note was business-like, he had no time for anything else, and after carefully folding the paper along its length, he sealed its edge with his wax candle, to deter anyone who might have a desire to pry into his private affairs, especially those that might be on the payroll of the slaving Slavers. He propped it up on his desk and made a mental note to ask the maidservant to take good care of it later, when she dropped by to replenish his candles and to turn down his blankets.

He leaned back between the pillars of the four-poster bed and plumped up his pillows, intending only to close his eyes for a moment and to think over his day, picking over his ideas for the next and fine tuning each carefully planned step.

But instead, and to his complete surprise, he went out like a candle in the wind.

CHAPTER SEVEN

"When I have charged a Black [man] with unfairness and dishonesty, he has answered, if able to clear himself with an air of disdain, 'What! Do you think I am a White Man?'"

John Newton, Rector of St. Mary Woolnoth – Thoughts Upon the African Slave Trade

Doctor Gardiner stood on the deck of The Brothers watching the sun slip behind the Welsh Mountains and his heart sank with it. The waters of the Severn estuary were calm, the wind was at their backs and the journey out of the river's lower reaches had been rapid and, since Mr Sheriff's untimely eviction, uneventful. The ship remained hemmed in by a familiar green and pleasant land, but the rolling hills of the Devonshire countryside had now started to fall away, as the vessel rounded the headland and, in full sail, pushed ever onwards, past the flat uninhabited island of Lundy and out into open water.

He knew only too well what horrors lay ahead.

This was not his first slaving trip, but he prayed that it would be his last. Were it not for his rising level of debt, which had now reached almost insurmountable proportions, he would not have been there at all. But the ready supply of ships' surgeons was falling in the face of rising awareness of what the job entailed, and so the wages on offer had become irresistible to all but the most principled of men. Not quite a king's ransom, but enough to pay off his significant arrears and so, in the end, the prospect had proved too hard to resist in return for just one more commission.

Much to his shame, he had succumbed and had accepted the owner's offer with little time to spare. Had he had more time to think about the implications for his own health and sanity, then he would almost certainly have come to his senses and declined it.

A couple of days notice was all he'd had, just enough time to fill his chest with the few things he knew that he would need and to sign his Articles of Agreement, before climbing aboard and locking himself away for the duration of the first leg. Other than a daily dinner in the Captain's quarters together with the uncouth First Mate, there were very few official duties until the cargo was loaded at the Guinea shore. Then he would be required to start earning his keep and so, other than writing in his journal and keeping a look out for any signs of insurrection or disease amongst the crew, for now his time was his own.

Despite Wesley's words of warning, which he had heard preached upon the streets of Bristol more than once these past few years, his heart was not yet hardened. He knew The Trade and all it's terrible truths first hand, but as the only trained surgeon for many a nautical mile, he told himself that his part in all of this was not entirely dark. There were moments in a long and dangerous voyage when his skills and knowledge could be put to good use, when his expertise could save a life or at least prevent a death, and so preserve the chance of life. Whether it be for the crew or for the cargo, his role was not always for evil, or so he told himself.

He was meticulous in his record keeping and his journals were amongst the most thorough ever set before the Bristol Society of Slaving Ventures. He recorded everything he saw, all that he heard on board his ship, every decision, every deed, and every death. His purpose was singular, and had the Slavers known of his true motivations, he would never have been allowed to set foot on another slaving vessel again. In fact, if anyone on board this ship was to find out his real intentions anywhere on their triangular route, he would almost certainly find himself fed to the fishes or worse still, manacled to the deck and flogged within an inch of his life – before being fed to the fishes.

Before leaving the port at Bristol, he had met with a most striking and unusual fellow. A large and intense clergyman, with a shock of red hair upon his head the like of which the Doctor had never seen, even amongst the Celtic folk of Ireland, Wales, or Cornwall. Having met at the quayside only a few days before, they found that they had a mutual acquaintance, the landlord of the little inn at the top of Thomas Street, and they had quickly hit upon their common cause. They had talked long into the night and the Reverend had revealed all, about the new Abolitionist movement and his involvement in it, imparting his reasons for being in the West Country and his need for evidence. Once Gardiner knew what was required of him, his way forward had become crystal clear, like the fog lifting across the coastline to allow a ship to navigate its way into port.

"Of course, I will testify," he had happily told Clarkson, "and I will gather more information for the cause this year, but first tell me what you need."

"Evidence" Clarkson had demanded. "Names, places, events. Detailed accounts of maltreatment of both Africans and the crew and witnesses, should anyone be willing to testify against any of those in authority, I need to know their names."

Clarkson was on his mind as the darkness descended, and as the Doctor carefully navigate the stairs and stepped into the stuffy solitude of his cabin, he could not rid the red-haired rebel from his thoughts. He had readily agreed to help this unlikely cleric, and though this would be his umpteenth voyage in eight miserable years, at first, he embraced it with a new lease of life and a newfound purpose, but the feeling wasn't to last. The decade had not been kind to him and his penchant for alcohol had quickly turned to obsession, consuming far more now than was good for him, often until late into the night. Strong ales, dark porter, Caribbean rum, scotch, or Irish whisky – was there anything else?

He had been just twenty years old at the start of the decade and an inexperienced surgeon's mate to Alexander Falconbridge on board The Pilgrim. By June 1787 he felt like a fifty-year-old, and not a particularly healthy one, yet he knew then that he faced a lifetime's addiction, and he was not disposed to change his ways, wherever it may be leading him. His fellow crew members were a ragtag collection of young and eager novices, many heading out on their first voyage in complete ignorance of what awaited them, but sold to them on the promise of untold riches and readily available women. Others amongst their ranks were seasoned scoundrels, running away from prosecution or persecution at home and without a trade by which they could scratch out a living on land. Whichever they were, Gardiner had no interest in getting to know them any better, in the sure and certain knowledge that any one of them might be inclined to slit his throat and throw him overboard at the slightest provocation.

Brawls amongst the crew were commonplace in the first phase, as old scores were settled, and boredom took its toll. Though the ship was heavily laden with gin, port, and whisky, it was all kept firmly under lock and key and set aside for bartering with the local Portuguese and Spanish Agents on the coast, where it was sure to fetch a high price. It was not intended for general consumption, though some watered-down rations were permitted, just to keep their spirits up. Invariably, this small allowance did more harm than good, as it simply made the crew sullen, irritable, and generally ill-tempered which, if they weren't kept busy with a whole range of menial tasks, would then give rise to squabbles and scrapes, some of which caused injuries and that was where his skills would be called upon.

So, they were generally kept busy, cleaning down the decks, working high in the rigging to ensure the ship's safe passage or continually tightening and adjusting the cargo nets below as the harnesses shifted and settled on the rolling tide. They had already been hard at work, the whole crew engaged in raising the halyard for the main sail, to set the point of sail at beam reach, much to the Captain's satisfaction as it made for a quick getaway. Their clamouring cries had completely drowned out what would have been a perfectly calming morning, one that the Doctor had hoped to spend on deck, standing witness as the last of the land sank down beneath the farthest horizon. Eventually their shouts and cries abated, as the mates relented in their ferocity and now that the Captain's commands had been obeyed to the letter, each man felt a sense of relief that their arduous journey was now properly underway.

As they eased out onto the open ocean, the rhythm of the vessel as it rose up and crashed back down on the fearsome waves was almost soothing to his soul. Even when, on every seventh wave, the ship rattled and shuddered as if its creaking frame would soon crack under the pressure, he remained at ease. The feeling often left new recruits green with sickness, which always led to an enforced cold shower at the hand of his crewmates. Bucket after bucket of freezing cold seawater would be hurled at him from all sides in a kill or cure remedy that had nothing whatsoever to do with the poor boy's wellbeing and everything to do with a spot of sport for his more seaworthy shipmates. At the end he would be blue with cold, as he was left dithering on the deck, but Gardiner had never seen it fail.

The seasickness was always cured. The end justified the means.

The Captain was often nowhere to be seen on this first leg, preferring instead to keep a low profile in his quarters, plotting the course ahead and his strategy at the coast. The day-to-day running of the ship was left to the First Mate and his team of sadistic officers, whose primary objective was to keep the rest of the crew in line and to avoid the skirmishes that all too often gave rise to unrest, through the regular application of discipline. Floggings and beatings were only dished out at this stage of a voyage in the most deserving of cases; there was a long way to go and plenty of time for feuds and wounds to fester and so, appeasement was often the name of the game. But should the need arise, then examples would always be set, and so it wasn't unusual for an insolent sailor to find himself held down by three or four of the officers, whilst the First Mate forced salt water down his gullet until he pleaded for mercy. The more imaginative forms of torture, like the thumbscrews and the other instruments were usually kept back, but seasoned sailors were well aware that they were only under lock and key until the need arose to bring a dog to heel.

Gardiner would dutifully record such things in his journals, should he be unfortunate enough to witness them, but such reports would hardly ever draw any attention on their return, as so much worse was sure to follow later on their triangular route.

As the ship lurched again, there was a hard knock upon his cabin door and the surgeon called out to give his caller leave to enter. It was Meadows, the First Mate, and he looked troubled, but then again, he always did. He was as unlikely an officer as he'd ever clapped eyes on; lanky and bedraggled, with greasy shoulder-length hair and a cratered face of spots, some of which looked ripe to burst whilst others had already formed into sorry looking scabs.

"Captain wants to see thee" he squawked. There was no need to reply. Captain's orders.

Gardiner stood and dutifully followed the second-in-command to the Captain's quarters, stooping through doorways as he lurched on the swell until, high up at the stern of the ship, he knocked in turn and was immediately met with a suspiciously cheery welcome.

"Ah, Doctor Gardiner, good to see you, are you well?"

"Quite well Captain Howlett Sir."

"That'll be all Meadows" ordered the colourfully dressed commander, his comically large black tricorn hat, which seemed to be a permanent fixture, shading his face from view as he ushered his cowering lieutenant from his room. "So" he continued once his door was firmly secured, "what trials and tribulations await us on this venture good Doctor? How might we fare at the coast, I hear that prices are high, and supply is low. The Traders will drive a hard bargain you can be sure of that Doctor, we will have to be on our mettle, if we want to make a tidy profit for the investors, and for ourselves besides."

Gardiner wasn't sure if he was being asked for his opinion, or if he was just being lectured and so he was wary not to ignite this Captain's infamous temper by saying anything that would put his back up. "I have heard the same Captain," he said nonchalantly, "I was told that the price is now above the usual for a healthy adult male, and I fear that our prizes down below will be stretched pretty thin if that is the going rate."

The Captain stroked his short and unkempt beard and regarded his ship's surgeon with dark and brooding eyes, weighing him up before deciding if he was to be the loyal sidekick that he'd hoped for. He had never sailed with this man before, but he had known many such medical men who, when push had come to shove, had not had the stomach for the venture after all. He was wondering which of these categories this rugged fellow fell into and hoped that he would be made of sterner stuff. Time would tell, but he wanted to get a sense of him before they dropped anchor in the Tropics.

Forewarned would be forearmed.

"You've sailed twice before on The Pilgrim I understand?" he asked, knowing that to be the case, but wanting to hear it in the man's own words. When Gardiner nodded, he pressed him further. "And what did you learn from those 'adventures" he probed, "any juicy tales to tell?"

"I try to keep a professional outlook" the ship's Doctor answered cryptically.

"Meaning?"

"Meaning that I don't fraternise Sir, with the crew or with the slaves. My job on board ship is to ensure that those under my care are as healthy as I can help them to be."

"Your job Sir on board 'my' ship" Captain Howlett roared, taking full advantage of this early opportunity to assert his full authority. "Is to do whatever the hell it is that I ask you to do. And as for 'fraternising', I hear that you are less choosy when it comes to red-headed Reverends?"

Gardiner was shocked to learn that he'd clearly been under observation in recent days, though when he did answer, he did manage to appear unruffled by it. "Yes, Sir", he said as obediently as he could manage in that moment. "Understood, Sir!"

"You have probably heard all about my 'methods' I presume?"

"Your reputation does go before you somewhat" the Doctor admitted, making the assumption that his Captain would take any fame as flattery. He wasn't wrong.

"Indeed," he laughed, "I have been told that I do have a certain 'quality', that is so often lacking in others who are called to serve in this noble business."

Gardiner had the strong sense that lines were being drawn and he needed to tread very carefully if he was going to stay on the right side of this character.

"We will talk some more Doctor Gardiner in the coming days" announced Howlett, seemingly willing to let bygones be bygones when it came to the company they kept when on dry land. "I want to deal you in on my plans for the Guinea shore, we will need our wits about us if we are going to achieve a quick turnaround. The middle passage must be in our sights within a month of our arrival, I will accept nothing less."

"I understand Sir," said Gardiner more respectfully than he would have liked, "will that be all?"

"Yes, my fine fellow," said the sly Captain, "until the morrow, you will be joining us for breakfast?"

"I will Sir, goodnight then." He knew that to decline would not be in his best interests.

Ten minutes later, as Gardiner lay with his legs up in his hammock, he began to seriously wonder what he had let himself in for, but he knew that there was no turning back now. What was done was done and he knew that he would need to have eyes in the back of his head if he was going to survive this trip and live to tell the tale before Clarkson's enquiry.

-○○○-

For three long weeks, Thomas Clarkson and his innkeeper friend scoured the drinking dens of Marsh Street in search of willing informants. They were not short of volunteers when it came to anguished tales of cruel Captains and monstrous First Mates, but many fewer were willing to testify when asked outright, and quickly clammed up as soon as the unlikely duo's true intentions were revealed. The stories they had to tell were remarkable in their consistency and almost every landlord on the strip seemed to be implicated in some way or other in pressing the crews of Bristol's fleet of thirty or more slave ships into service.

On more than one occasion they had been forced to stand witness as some poor youth in the throes of submission was forced to accept his fate in the face of the insurmountable odds.

"All you have to do is to sign my boy," some wily old sea dog would be heard to utter, "just here, that's it, your mark is all we need."

For most of them, a simple 'X' would have to do, scratched on the surface where their signatures should have been, illiterate to the words of bondage that for many would be their death sentence. Malaria, yellow fever, and dysentery were the three biggest killers for virgin crew members on their maiden voyage. But if they survived that, and the scurvy that would soon be rife especially when trade was scant and a month on the coast became three or even six, then it was not uncommon for them to die at the whim of some unscrupulous officer.

And whenever further persuasion was needed, the landlord would be on hand to chip in, to ensure that the Captain or his First Mate secured the deal, in return for a small fee of course.

"You've racked up two pounds, twelve shillings and sixpence on your board and drink this last month," Clarkson heard one landlady say to an inebriated victim, "so it's either service on this man's lush slave ship or its Newgate for thee, if you can't pay yer way." She had spoken to him like a scolding mother, and like a dutiful son, he would obey her every word.

The threat of Bristol's infamous gaol, with its stinking pits that somehow passed for cells, was usually enough to persuade any wavering would-be sailor to sign on the dotted line. Its threat was enough to drive even the most hardened criminal onto the first ship out of port, but if that failed, these roguish recruiters were not averse to slipping something stronger into the man's drink. They even heard of one that was slugged around the head with an improvised cosh, though such means were usually a last resort, employed only when the journey was almost upon them, or they had a need for a particular skill, be it a carpenter, cook, cooper, or blacksmith.

The Dublin Yacht, the Venice Frigate, the Golden Fleece, and the Foul Anchor, alone handed over more than two dozen sailors in the time that Clarkson and Thompson were trawling their depths, and there would have been many more besides. Unwitnessed dealings, underhand agreements, devious schemes; filling the hold of each and every slaver that ever departed from Bristol's waters.

But the seaman's' tales of woe were not the only information to be extracted from their drunken countrymen and many more stories centred around the slaves themselves, and their sickening treatment at the hands of these degenerates and their officers. For all the sympathy that each sailor's tale of entrapment had invoked in Clarkson, it was dwarfed into insignificance by revelations of torture, in which many of them had been active participants.

To Clarkson's shame as a clerical man, it often left him wanting to abandon them all to their collective fate, or to take charge of their punishment himself. And whenever he heard retellings of floggings and brandings, mutilations, and rape, it shocked him back to his real purpose for being there and pushed any thought of mercy for these dubious wretches far from his mind.

"I never did it myself," was the usual pre-amble, "but I saw some terrible things done by them that talked of the slaves as being savages. It was the other way around most times." If Clarkson could have had a farthing for each time he'd heard those words on the streets of Bristol, he'd have paid for his lodgings twice over with the proceeds. In addition to the beatings and the rapes, which were so commonplace as to hardly be worth a mention by the drunken seafarers, both the male and female slaves were often sodomised at the first sign of insurrection. Most slaves kept their heads down at all times, as to look straight back into an officer's eyes or worse still to hold his stare would be punished with the most humiliating weapon in their bestial armoury. Shackled face down to the deck, arms and legs outstretched, and often in front of a group of other slaves, the poor unfortunate would be subjected to a lengthy ordeal at the hands of the officers and crew, which would leave them bruised, bleeding and ashamed.

Another common abuse that was told of readily in the drinking dens of Bristol's harbourside, was often imposed by any one of the ships mates for 'talking back', even though the captive's words were rarely understood. In this scenario, the slave would be shackled to the deck face-up, have their nose pinched until the jaw dropped open and then to have a white miscreant defecate into their open mouths, their jaws being fastened shut with a ready string for maximum effect. Again, a performance that was often carried out in front of their countrymen, just to ensure that word wouldn't fail to get around below decks as to what would happen if any of them dared to challenge the authority of their scrawny overlords.

It was tyranny. It was the rule of fear. Terrorism in its purest form, inflicted by the powerful on those in enforced servitude. It was intended to keep them in their place, a barbaric system that had been finely tuned over two centuries of trial and error, and most of the time, it did its job. Slave revolts on the high seas was a rare occurrence, so much so that when one did take place, it was always a massacre.

Each time a tale was told, Clarkson would wait with trepidation, fearful of any new barbarism for which his defences were not yet prepared. Every time, a new macabre twist on the same torturous narrative would jar his senses, in disgust, pity and most of all rage. He found himself wishing that the worst of all punishments would befall those perpetrators and fantasised at length about being their hangman, or being able to hold their feet to the fire whilst turning the wheel of a gruesome rack on which their limbs would be slowly stretched and broken. The fodder of dreams, the stock of nightmares.

The weather had turned unseasonably cold in the weeks after The Brothers' departure, and Clarkson had been caught several times in the rainstorms that had lashed down on Bristol's streets, causing streams of muddy filth to flow down the middle of Marsh Street on its shortest route to the river. Though the pubs were tightly packed, moving between them and sometimes having to queue up in the rain just to get inside, had left both him and Thompson chilled to the bone. On his return to his rooms, he had been forced to light a fire in the grate in spite of the season, just to dry his sodden clothes and to raise his temperature high enough for him to be able to sleep.

Even in his exhaustion, sleep still failed to come easily to him, and his nights would be haunted by a thousand anonymous black faces. Each one walked with him, even in the cold light of day, but at night he saw them clearly and they stared accusingly back at him, imploring him to heed their prayers for deliverance. To send his mighty God to crush their persecutors before it was too late. Clarkson feared that even at God's speed, the answer to his prayers would be too slow in coming.

As the list of accusations against the slave traders grew ever longer, so did his conviction that he would see them in court to stand trial for their heinous crimes. He decided to consult a leading Bristol attorney, who also served as the Deputy Town Clerk, but much to his all-too-obvious disappointment, Mr Burges did not offer any encouragement, but rather did his best to persuade him not to bring any cases before the local magistrate.

"Should you decide on this course of action," Burges had said, "then you must take up the grievances with all who sail in The Trade, indeed I know of only one Captain who did not deserve to be hanged at Tyburn long ago." Clarkson had heard the tale before, but it remained a shocking admission, and Burges was adamant that any attempt to bring these men to justice was doomed to failure. "These seamen are so dependent on the sea for their upkeep that once all means are expended, they will simply take the next boat out once more – they do not have the luxury that landsmen do to maintain themselves on shore.

Are you prepared Mr Clarkson to meet all of your witness's expenses as they wait for months on end at the court's leisure for your show trial to begin?"

"I am sure that our society's benefactors have deep pockets," said Clarkson, his pride hurt at what appeared to be an amateurish oversight on his part.

"And what actions do you think the ships' owners will take?" he continued, "once they have knowledge of your plans? Do you think that they will stand meekly by and wait 'til the time of the trial, or will they spirit these men away on the next available venture, where some unfortunate end will no doubt befall them? When the trial comes around, you will find your precious witnesses dispersed and gone, and your expensive case in rags at your feet."

Thomas Clarkson was left feeling dejected, for he knew that in spite of the lawyer's obvious allegiance to the slaving families of Bristol, whose patronage paid his bills and bought his expensive clothes, his opinion on this matter was not wide of the mark. Burges was fully cognisant of the facts, and the facts were, that should Clarkson bring a case against any one of these scoundrels, he would come up against the full might of Bristol's wealthy merchants and the best defence that their huge reserves of blood money could buy.

But he was a stubborn clergyman, and on reflection, the infuriating exchange made him even more determined to build a cast iron case that only a corrupt magistrate could find against and if they did, then he would appeal to the highest court in the land to have that judgement quashed. The case would not be long in coming and when it did, it was for a capital offence which carried with it the ultimate penalty; if found guilty, the accused would go to the gallows to be hanged by his scraggy neck until he was dead.

As he continued to amass his evidence, he found that his determination grew stronger with every passing day. It was his duty to see to it that they paid the hangman his dues, or he would die trying.

-ooo-

It was Thompson who had first relayed to him the story of The Thomas, a slaving vessel under the command of Captain Vicars, currently in port in Bristol and facing lengthy repairs after a long and taxing journey. Three members of its crew were in a similarly poor state; one had been left blind as a result of a fever contracted in the Tropics; another was lame, his legs covered in painful ulcers which had left him bed-ridden; the third seemed to be suffering from an as yet undiagnosed nervous disorder, shaking uncontrollably as if some biblical demon had invaded his person and was busily feasting upon his soul.

Clarkson had managed to meet with all of them under the guidance of the ship's surgeon, Alexander Falconbridge, who had done his best to prescribe effective treatments, but had not been able to come up with a cure for any of their ailments.

All three told them the same story of William Lines, a crew member on board the same ill-fated voyage, that had been murdered by the First Mate, though none of them were willing to admit to having seen the act. He had been cruelly treated and had later died as a result of his injuries and without witnesses, any case against the officers would be dead in the water. Clarkson had thought the matter closed, the absence of willing testimonials leaving him without a case to answer, until quite out of the blue, he had received an unexpected visitor at his lodgings. It was the murdered man's own mother, and she had her heart set on revenge. She was able to provide him with the names of several other potential seamen whose testimony might yet bring those responsible to justice.

"They killed my only son in cold blood," she cried, "there are four more men who have already sworn it to me, but the magistrate is having none of it and the owners have washed their hands of the whole affair."

"How can they do that?" asked Clarkson, as she openly wept.

"They can do anything they wants," she sobbed. "That's what they says anyway. They offered me some pittance of a pension, but it weren't worth taking. I said I'd take my chances in court before I accepted that in return for my precious boy's life."

Clarkson spoke to each man in turn and found that the stories did not vary in their retelling, so he arranged for all parties to assemble at the Common Hall the following day, where he would confront the Bristol magistrate with their evidence. Word had obviously got around in the intervening hours as the hall was full to the rafters and, much to the Reverend's alarm, there were many slave traders and their Agents in attendance, with one or two sat upon the bench. He could feel real menace in the room and heard the abuse that was spewing from every side. As one more cheap shot hit a little too close to home for his liking, he could not resist responding to their slanderous outbursts, which he directed towards the bench.

"You Sir may know many things which I do not," he said, "but this I know, that if you do not do your duty, you are amenable to a higher court." It seemed to have the desired effect and as a guilty hush descended over the room, the hearing was spurred into life.

Each of the four witnesses were called in turn and after facing the same questions and providing the court with almost identical answers, the light of justice fell on Captain Vickers himself.

"What do you say to these accusations of bad usage Captain?" the magistrate asked him outright, but Vickers denied all knowledge, claiming wilful mischief on the part of a disgruntled crew. "And what of the death of the boy, what is your recollection of events? Was he killed unlawfully?"

The Captain again denied any involvement. "He died of the flux as I remember it" he claimed, "As many do their first time in Guinea, I remember very little about him, he was just a boy. A landsman. Not even an able seaman and so not one that I needed to give much notice to."

"Liar!" came the cry from the gallery and when Clarkson looked up to the balustrade above, he saw the victim's mother bearing down on them, brandishing a Bible about her head, which she waved like a weapon at the people below. "Tell him to swear his words upon the Good Book," she screeched, "he is false, he is a murderer."

The magistrate reminded her that he was already under oath, but he thought her reminder very timely and so, he asked Vicars again if he had had any hand in the boy's murder. "With your hand placed upon the Bible if you please!" The request may have only been for effect, but it had no effect at all on the Captain who was sticking firmly to his version of events.

"None my Lord," he pleaded, "it was dysentery that did for him, like I said."

The magistrate seemed dissatisfied with his answer and although he was unwilling to offer up any verdict, he instead astonished both Clarkson and the watching audience by taking the unusual step of deferring the case to the Lords of the Admiralty, at their forthcoming sessions in Greenwich. Until then he ordered that the Captain be held, pending their next sitting, but the wait would prove too long for the wheels of eighteenth century justice to bear.

"You blithering idiot!" a voice called from the audience. "Call yourself a magistrate!" It was the Agent from The Brothers, and he was not backward in coming forward. "How do you suppose that our good captains are meant to keep these men in line, if their authority is to be questioned like this whenever they are deemed to have made a slight error of judgement in the heat of battle? And by landlubbers like these", he spat, pointing at the boy's mother and Clarkson himself, with whom he locked eyes as he vented his fury. "They've never been on the beach, never mind to sea!" At that the remaining slaving contingent, of which they were many, roared their agreement, as several around him slapped Hal's back or reached out to shake him vigorously by the hand in a sudden show of camaraderie.

"Keep it down Mullins!" ordered the Magistrate, "one more outburst like that and I'll see you sent below!"

Clarkson did not engage him, knowing full well that he was not short on evidence, but now was not the moment to lock horns with the enemy. Although his compatriot Thompson soon found himself custodian of the most popular public house in Bristol, as disgruntled seaman from across the city descended on Thomas Street for counsel from the now infamous red-headed giant.

Crews of The Alexandria, The Fly and The Wasp told of savage beatings and unnecessary amputations, and even more witnesses from The Pilgrim and The Princess, The Little Pearl, and The Africa, shared personal accounts of physical abuse that had befallen them or their shipmates on previous voyages that went back decades. Clarkson was left in no doubt that he had disturbed a hornet's nest of trouble, but whilst he had Christian sympathy for the plight of these men, their misfortune was not the focus of his mission. Though their accounts were useful as anecdotal evidence for the cause, he refused to be detracted from his real purpose.

That said, he recorded each tale, the dates, and circumstances of each maltreatment against the names of their ships and the perpetrators, until there were literally thousands of claims spread across several leather-bound journals, which he stored safely in his travelling chest that was soon to be sent on its way to London and to Granville Sharp.

-oοo-

Extracts from the Journal of Doctor Gardiner, ship's surgeon on board The Brothers

5th August 1787

It's a full moon and the ship's timbers are bathed in its light. A vertical shimmer crested by a halo of silver as the sea spray showers our full compliment of sails. The deck is open, and I have walked its length a dozen times, a hundred yards or more from bow to stern and back. My quarters stand above the stern chasers, a couple of five-pound cannon that can be used to fire chain-shot should the need arise. I sleep below the Captain's cabin, which in turn sits under the poop deck, to which I have climbed to stand with the helmsman at his wheel. I look below at our white-

water wake, before turning to regard the grandeur of the ship once more, its masts at attention one behind the other like a line of guardsmen on parade. I count the wooden blocks that gather up the sheets beneath the crow's nest, but many are hidden from view, playing peek-a-boo behind the square tarpaulin sails. I duck beneath the boom, and stand next upon the quarter deck, then down to the half deck where wooden casks are brimming with water, each armed with a sawn-off rifle barrel. I have seen men fight like alley-cats over these metal tubes when water is scarce, especially in the middle passage when the Captain hangs them high up on the mizzenmast to preserve supplies. I step down to amidship and walk alongside the gunnel, where a stiff net stands ready in its oblong frame – once the first slaves are boarded it will be raised into place, to bar all but one route to shore. I step across the sturdy metal grids, through whose trapdoor four hundred lives will soon be forced before climbing the steps to the gun deck where a small hatch offers access to the stores. Here at the prow of the ship, the foremast rises up to join its sisters in the night sky, keeping lookout for the slumbering crew, though there's is a temporary abode. For once the enslaved are brought on board, their quarters will be set aside behind the barricado, a fortified screen that will halve the ship to form an unsafe haven for the women and children. I take my seat in the shadow of the foresail within the arc of the swing guns and stare up at the canopy of stars, a brief moment of tranquillity away from the cursing crew and the Captain's insanity. I meditate for an hour or more to the sway of the sea as the wind flaps at the triangular jib on the bowsprit, and the soaring masts stand like sentinels against a dark and starless sky. In my snug solitude I call upon the salty breeze to rain down on me like spittle, and I imagine myself to be free from this world and all of its evils, as the Captain navigates our course to hell.

CHAPTER EIGHT

"If we were to withdraw suddenly from this commerce, like Pontius Pilate, we should wash our hands indeed, but we should not be innocent as to the consequences".

The Reverend Thomas Clarkson, The History of The Abolition of the African Slave Trade

On first meeting with his Quaker friends in Bristol, Clarkson had impressed on all of them his need to get access to as many of the slave ships' muster rolls as possible. He had set his sights on the Custom Houses of London, Liverpool and Bristol and was curious to see whether or not these detailed records would corroborate the chilling conclusion that his field research had already inferred: that this wicked trade was a death trap for all but those who stood to profit from it.

He had almost given up hope when, just a couple of days before his intended departure, a young Quaker clerk revealed that he'd not only managed to get access to the information, but had also meticulously copied and supplied the records of every slave ship that had departed Bristol's docks since the middle of the century. It included an account for both the outbound journey via the coast of Africa and the return leg from the Americas, enabling the Reverend to trace the fortunes of each crew member from their point of embarkation to their final destination. Such fastidious record keeping would ultimately be the slave traders undoing, as it allowed Reverend Thomas Clarkson to compute the death toll of both sailors and slaves, as less personalised counts were also kept for those that were stowed away in the ships' holds on the second leg of the perilous journey.

Clarkson and Alexander Falconbridge, the athletic and resolute looking Doctor, and a veteran of four slaving ventures, sat at a table in a cool corner of The Seven Stars, and reviewed the comprehensive set of documents. Each sheet laid out the names of the ship and its master, its intended journey and the identities of each and every member of the crew, their usual place of abode and time on board the ship. It was used by the ship's Agent at the end of the voyage to account for the pay that was due to each man, on the all-important proviso that they had survived the journey. It also recorded those who had died enroute, those who were presumed to be deserters - having disappeared without trace in Africa or in the Americas - and those who had completed the voyage for whom any resulting hospitalisation might also then be payable by the insurer. It was all about maximising profits by minimising losses.

"This is remarkable" said Clarkson, as he explained the importance of the evidence to Falconbridge. "So much information, that can only help to incriminate those responsible."

"Though it doesn't tell us the cause of death" Falconbridge complained, "we must rely upon eyewitness testimony for that, mine amongst them."

"The death rate from leaving to returning is regularly more than one third on each ship," observed an astounded Clarkson, glancing at his notes and revelling in the mathematics, which had been his major at Cambridge. "At best, one in ten men are lost, at worst almost two thirds."

"And I'd wager that such a significant loss would have been due to one of two causes," the Doctor attested. "Either a rampant outbreak of disease, often flux, on the middle passage, or insurrection on board, usually a slave revolt, occasionally a mutiny by the crew themselves against their bad usage at the hands of the officers."

"So out of thirty or forty men who board each ship in Bristol, ten to twenty never make it back again" said the Reverend, shocked to the bone by the story that was unfolding before them. "Is anyone in authority even aware of this?" he asked. "The Admiralty, The Magistrates, The Government?"

"It's an extraordinary number," remarked Falconbridge, "I had no idea it was so high, even on the voyages that I was on, we never lost more than one third, though I saved a few along the way even if I do say so myself."

"And of the cause?" asked Clarkson, "you've said that disease was often rife, but what of all these statements we've collected? So much cruelty, so much wanton thuggery. What say you to the portion slain by the officers or by the Captain?"

The Doctor didn't answer, as he took a moment to recall his own journeys and the times that he had intervened to stop an officer in the midst of a flogging or a full-on fistfight. "It's hard to say," he said after due consideration. "But it's got to be two or three, three or four maybe, on every venture, that can either directly or indirectly be laid squarely at the feet of those in command."

"Indirectly?" asked Clarkson confused.

"I've seen examples," Falconbridge continued, "where the Captain has instigated a quarrel between two shipmates, promising one the other's share of the profits if some unfortunate incident were to befall that person. The Captain doesn't really care which one of them lightens the load, as he has no intention of paying either of them if he can get away with it, at least not in the King's currency."

"I have heard of this" Clarkson noted. "They pay them in some depreciated foreign coin and pocket the difference in the exchange?"

"They do indeed, the sly devils," the Doctor said with a crafty wink of an eye. "Those who have been to sea before are wise to the game, but for those that are new to it, they are taken in by the quantities of coin that they are handed at some foreign port and think that they are rich until they try to spend it of course. And their Articles make it quite plain, should anyone try to challenge it later, for they state that fully half of their dues will be paid at a port of the officers' choosing and in the currency of that country."

"It is a cruel trick indeed," Clarkson acknowledged, but he found himself all out of sympathy for any losses incurred. "Some might say it is all that they deserve, and I would be happy to be counted amongst that number." The results were very much in keeping with the pattern that he'd observed from the London musters, and he was almost content that they now had what they needed, but they were still missing the accounts from the biggest slaving port in England, and those were records that they could scant do without.

"We must make haste for Liverpool," he declared, "and I would very much like for you to accompany me there, your expense will be met by The Society of course."

"It would be an honour and privilege" Falconbridge said proudly, "when do you plan to go?"

"I must first head back to London," Clarkson informed his newly appointed sidekick. "I need to take the boy to Sharp, and I have asked him to arrange a dinner party with Wilberforce and a few other notable dignitaries. It's high time that we took this battle to Parliament."

"How is the boy?" the Doctor asked. "I examined him at Thompson's request the other day and in himself he seems to have come through his ordeal relatively unharmed, at least over recent months. There is no sign of anything untoward about his body, but he still wasn't speaking."

"Is he mute?" Clarkson wondered aloud. "There was no suggestion of that in the newspaper."

"No, I don't think so," was Falconbridge's medical opinion. "He just seems unwilling to speak, maybe out of fear, maybe he doesn't speak English. I'm not sure, but I can suggest no medical reason why he should not be able to converse with us, even in his own tongue."

At that moment Thompson appeared at the bar motioning to The Reverend that he wanted to speak with him in the back room. It was the same spot where Clarkson had last seen the boy, but this time the room was vacant and there was no sign that it had been recently occupied.

"Where's the boy?" Clarkson asked, a little alarmed that he was not there.

"He's safe" answered Thompson, "the fewer that knows where he is the better. There have been some types hanging about the alley these last few nights, I'm told by my regulars that they are slaver men, sent to spy on us. I think it's high time that you made off Mr Clarkson, with the boy as well, I'm hearing that they're none too happy at your snooping and they might be about to do something to stop you."

"Thank you Thompson," Clarkson said appreciatively. "I would have been lost without you these past few weeks. I am planning to return to London in a matter of days and will take the boy with me. I know of people who will care for him there, but again, best that few people know who or where he will be."

Thompson nodded in understanding. "And what about the Doctor?" he asked looking towards the bar. "Is he going too?"

"Not exactly," Clarkson said. "He's the advance party. I'm meeting him in Liverpool in a week or so, we have more work to do with those northern scoundrels. I am led to believe that their slaving industry is almost quadruple the size it is in your fair city."

"You need to take great care there Reverend" the innkeeper warned. "I have heard that they are expecting you. These men are a well-connected mob and I fear that they've been told of your plans to pay them a visit. Who have you told about it? We may have to be more careful in future."

"Only you, though we have been talking of it openly," Clarkson reflected. "It would not have taken much for it to be overheard in here, or at another public house."

"I have heard that they are less tolerant of strangers in the north," Thompson continued, "and so you can count on far less of a helping hand than you've had here."

"As I am led to believe Thompson," he replied, "that's why I have asked Alexander along, he is going to do some digging up there for me. He knows some of the characters, having been aboard their ships in foreign ports to help the sick and dying, and so no one should suspect him. He has only recently turned towards the light."

"I hope so Reverend," the innkeeper added. "It has been an honour to serve, I hope that we will meet again soon and that we will be able to celebrate a great victory when we do."

"I hope so too," Clarkson said gratefully. "You have played your part valiantly Sir. I will forever be in your debt."

He left with Falconbridge in tow. They parted at the bridge, agreeing to meet at The Kings Arms Hotel in Liverpool in ten days' time. Clarkson had already written to make reservations in the good Doctor's name, knowing that it would be less conspicuous than his own. He had also noticed a change on the wind around Bristol and as he walked back up Baldwin Street, several men with whom he had made a passing acquaintance in the last few weeks, crossed over to the other side as soon as their eyes met. A sea Captain that he had been in conversation with not two nights earlier, propping up the bar at the nearby Angel Inn, would have nothing to do with him and even John Aveline, the landlord of The Black Horse, had refused his custom when he'd stepped out of the midday sun in search of some refreshment.

A more sensitive soul may have been offended by these slights, but not Thomas Clarkson. He was delighted by it, for it meant that his presence in their small but influential city was starting to get under their skin, and that was proof positive that his tactics were working. His next appointment on his penultimate day in the West Country would have him strike at the very heart of their devilish ambition; he had arranged to meet with the very men whose capital had funded each and every foreign venture in recent years and which had paved the streets of Bristol with their ill-gotten gains.

He arrived at The Bristol Society of Slaving Ventures unaccompanied. It was his intention to face these men with no one but God at his side. As he strode up the elegant staircase and entered the prescribed chamber, he was surprised to find that he was the first in attendance. He made himself comfortable, drawing a glass of cold water from the crystal decanter in the corner of the room and sat down in one of the ornately carved high-backed dining chairs, from where he was able to take in the room in all its glorious detail. The ceiling was adorned in a brightly coloured fresco, a maelstrom of classical cherubs that stared down upon the assembly, and on each wall the steely eyes of several oil painted shipping magnates regarded him with more than an element of suspicion.

They were right to do so, but it was not just the portraits of previous chairmen and their benefactors that hung like guardians around the room. Several ships adorned each elegantly fashioned wall, most of them built to carry human cargoes, or converted from a former purpose to a much more profitable one. Sloops and snows surrounded him, their names etched for all eternity onto brass plates that were firmly tacked to each sturdy gold leaf frame. It put Clarkson in mind of the drawing rooms of some of the grander families in the East of England, where portraits of favoured pets or racehorses gilded the otherwise tasteful décor with their unabashed opulence. The Nevis Planter, The Molly Snow, The Britannia.

His eyes were still working their way around the room, when the heavy panelled door burst inward and the portly frame of a red-faced rogue followed on behind, like a well-dressed Christmas pudding on legs or an oversized human cannonball. Hard or soft centre, remained to be seen, but Clarkson suspected the former and so prepared himself for the worst.

The Reverend rose to his feet as was his training, "The Reverend Thomas Clarkson, at your service Sir," but was soon reminded that polite conversation would have no place in that elegant room on that day. Perhaps on any day. This was indeed a pig iron cannonball in human form, and he had his sights set on the lanky landsman that had just made himself a bit too comfortable in his backyard.

"Pray Sir, tell me, what it is that you want with my society and my city?" the latest Master of the Bristol Slavers demanded. It was an honorary appointment, the incumbent selected annually from amongst the rank and file of its mercantile members, and Harry Hobhouse had been a popular nomination. His family had played a prominent part in the rise to prominence of the port of Bristol, his Uncle Isaac owning 44 slaving vessels in the first half of the century, and although Harry himself was not directly involved in The Trade, he remained proud of his family's heritage and applied his legal training and family connections to maintain a diverse and growing share of its increasingly global interests.

"I think that you are well aware, as to my purpose here, Sir" Clarkson replied, refusing to be drawn or rattled by the combative introduction.

"I'll have you flogged back to London with your tail between your legs," the Master replied, "You'll wish you'd never heard of us by the time I'm finished with you. Poking your nose around in our business, firing up our sailors and threatening our good Captains with gaol time. Tis you who'll see the bars of Newgate, Reverend."

Clarkson was unmoved by such empty threats, but instead sat calmly waiting for the predictable tirade to die down. Once it looked like his adversary had run out of steam, the Reverend was only too pleased to give him his answer.

"I am here to investigate a most abhorrent trade Sir" Clarkson began. "A trade in human lives, but in so doing I have discovered a parallel scandal, that will bring dishonour on your company. The malpractice that engenders the untimely deaths of up to half your crews on every slaving venture, often at the hands of none other than your own officers."

"You are right my ginger friend! It is scandalous indeed!" the Master screeched. "It is a preposterous claim. How dare you Sir. Our Captains are fine upstanding members of this community. You talk of criminals and murderers; they are nothing of the sort. I will have your apology Sir, and so will they."

"You will get nothing of the sort" mocked Clarkson, staunchly certain of his facts. "Your Captains are rogues and scoundrels. I cannot yet say if they are murderers, but I have seen with my own eyes and heard with my own ears how they 'persuade' and entice fully half of their crews aboard, in the drinking pits of Marsh Street."

"I have heard that you have frequented the brothels and bars of our city, Reverend" snarled the Master. "Not a place where our Bishop would expect to find his clergymen on a Sunday morning." The inference was intentional, but if he thought that the implicit threat behind his words, would throw his uninvited guest off beam, or cause him to back down in a sudden realisation of an imminent risk to his own reputation, he was completely wrong.

"Your Bishop is a buffoon!" snapped Clarkson going on the attack, his fiery temper surfacing in a moment of unchecked rage. "Your Bishop is a sympathiser in The Trade, I am well aware that his investments are most welcomed by your business, but I will not flatter him by calling him a brother. I have spent my time in those places, purely to furnish me with the information that I need and now that I have all that I was looking for, I plan to return to London to plot the course of your undoing."

"You can try" the stout master laughed raucously, slamming his hand down on the table in time and leaning back in his chair like a tyrant surveying his kingdom. "Do you ever wonder Sir, what this nation would do without its tobacco, without its sugar, without its cocoa? A thousand coffee shops would be in mourning, not to mention the lords and ladies of the land whose tea mornings would be bereft without their beverages and their sweeteners. And what of the many trades that supply our lowly business with cloth and metal and guns and gin. The nation would be bankrupt Sir, your movement is a folly. Your evidence is corrupting. Go back to your pulpit and to your schoolbooks."

"I will Sir" said Clarkson, forgetting for a moment that he had no parish of his own. "I will preach the Abolitionist cause from my pulpit, and so will John Wesley and every other worthy pastor in this land until we have rid our country of your industry's stain. The people are for turning Sir, and when they do, your stinking trade will feel God's wrath."

"God?" thundered the master. "Don't speak to me of God. God is at 'our' backs not yours. God favours our every voyage, his trade winds and ocean currents hasten our journey around this vast globe of ours, don't you know that? If God was not on our side, then why would it be so? Answer me that eh, why would the winds blow in our favour all year around? Why would the ocean sweep us on our way if it were not the result of some divine providence?"

"Then you and I must worship a different God" Clarkson answered, unable to furnish him with a satisfactory explanation for this well-known earthly phenomenon, but certain that it lacked anything of the divine about it.

"So, now you are a blasphemer Clarkson" said the master haughtily. "For there is only one God, as well you know, and he is 'for' The Trade, not against it. You are standing in defiance of God's will and have your country-bumpkin arse set in the way of progress Sir."

"There is only one God, you are right there, Sir" blasted Clarkson, "and he is the God of love, as Mr Wesley preached only this week in your city, attended by thousands of *your* people. I see no love in your undertakings – the only God that you and your kind worship is the God of greed, and I will not rest until we have brought his Empire and all who profit from it to its knees."

"We will see who is first to be 'on his knees' Mr Clarkson," hissed the Master. "I will see you kneeling in the dirt, in chains with your 'brothers'. They are cattle and horses Clarkson. They are mules and asses. They are mere beasts of burden, and you are not even fit to be their field hand."

"They are human beings!" Clarkson raged. "They are made in the image of our Lord as we are and differ only by the colour of their skins. Your words are an outrage, but I expected nothing less from a man whose crumbling fortune is built on the backs of a million African lives."

"Be very careful Reverend" the master warned. "There are men far wealthier than I that stand to lose their livelihoods through your interference. And they have noticed you."

"I'm very glad to hear it" said Clarkson defiantly, "and I can assure you Sir that they will continue to take note of me, in fact I intend to be noticed by many more of their sort before my work here is done. I bid you good day" though Clarkson meant not a word of his final farewell, as he stood up to leave. "You and your kind have benefited from years of exploitation, and those days will soon be at an end. I ask you to consider a more wholesome and righteous trade with Africa. Turn away from these evils, before it is too late."

"Farewell Mr Clarkson," the Master smiled, "I hope never to see you in Bristol again, for your sake, and not mine."

-○○○-

The unlikely duo stepped up into the stagecoach at noon the following day, Thomas Clarkson barely fitting inside such was his stature, the small boy perched opposite him, his eyes wide in wonder. Clarkson had lent his horse to Falconbridge, who planned a more leisurely path up to the Northwest port, lodging with Quakers along the route at Stratford and in the Potteries, handing out The Society's literature and giving talks on his route. Their journey would take them two days, with stops at Bath and Windsor along the way, where passengers would disembark and alight. There were two others squeezed inside the cabin, and both had stared astonished at his appearance and that of his unusual companion; Clarkson could not decide which of them they considered to be the biggest sideshow on view, as the hosteler removed the short wooden steps, climbed up onto the sprung box and cracked his whip.

As they trundled on along the heavily forested road to Bath, the countryside opened out as they wound their way alongside the Avon and the boy watched entranced through the window at the rolling hills and English meadows beneath. Despite his ordeal, he did not seem to be at all traumatised, though he had not yet spoken, and Clarkson found himself wondering if he ever would.

On first arriving at The Seven Stars, the boy had been wearing a plated silver neck brace, a horrid practice that the sea Captains liked to employ as a way to announce their status to the world. Such brutal methods were secured by way of a tiny key, of which they had no copy, but the ever resourceful Thompson had paid a locksmith friend of his to tamper with the simple locking mechanism, and so had managed to remove it with relative ease.

He had handed it to Clarkson to squirrel away in his slowly accumulating box of evidence, along with various other items that he planned to use as props in sermons and speeches, and to engage the minds of fellow guests at dinner parties, like the one that he and Sharp had planned. Not as some unsavoury party gimmick, but to prove to the sceptics amongst them that the things he would tell them were true, and not a pack of lies as some of his opponents were already contending.

As was the practice, the boy's assumed name and that of his master were expertly stencilled onto its silver surface, but Clarkson didn't recognise the Captain's name and he hoped that it was now an irrelevance to them both. The boy would shortly be free – or as free as he could ever hope to be outside of his homeland - and once Granville Sharp had settled him amongst the black community in London, Clarkson prayed that he would never have to set his eyes upon another slave trader again. As they trundled along the pitted country lanes, he found himself wondering what the boy's real name was, his birth name, the name his mother had given him. The name that the slave trade had stolen from him.

"Addae." At first Clarkson wasn't sure who had spoken, but the other two paying passengers left him in no doubt, for they were staring straight at the boy. It was the boy that had spoken.

"That is my name." His words were spoken in perfect English, but heavily accented, the way that natives of some parts of England would distort the words of their own language. How did he know? How could he know what Clarkson was thinking at that very moment? It was a queer coincidence, but it would not be the first time that the boy would seem to know what his protector was thinking, at the very moment he was thinking it.

Clarkson smiled back, a big beaming smile that the boy could not help but meet with one of his own, and by comparison, the boy's smile won the day. It was infectious and even the strangers with whom they sat could not resist the urge to join in.

"I am Thomas" he informed him, and the boy repeated his name back, just to be sure. "Ad-day" said Clarkson, checking he had got the pronunciation right.

The boy nodded back.

It seemed enough for a beginning and the boy stayed silent for the rest of their day's journey. Other passengers came and went. The two that had joined at Bristol, stepped down at Bath, neither engaging the Reverend in conversation as they squeezed past him to descend the steps. They were replaced by a new couple, an elderly gentleman, and his young daughter, with whom Clarkson engaged in some pleasant conversation about the weather and the local sights, chief amongst them the beautiful and recently dubbed 'Royal' Crescent, that was the latest iconic addition to the growing architectural fame of Bath. Another swelled their number at the quaint hamlet and market town of Swindon, a young maidservant, on her way to take up a new position in service at a fine West London mansion and their compliment was soon complete when a smartly dressed lawyer squeezed himself into the space between Clarkson and the maid.

It had been an uncomfortable journey, especially for Clarkson, whose preference was always to travel by horseback wherever he went, leaving him free to enjoy the open air and to make unscheduled stops whenever it took his fancy. Being cooped up in a tightly cramped carriage, was never something that he enjoyed, and he would usually only give in to such an ordeal, when the weather was too unfavourable, meaning that the badly made roadways of England would be too treacherous for his steed to navigate, or too hazardous for his own health.

As they arrived in Windsor for their overnight stay, like some doting father, he ushered Addae inside the hostelry, where they would both pass a peaceful and uneventful evening in each other's quiet but unassuming company.

CHAPTER NINE

"England supplies her American colonies with slaves, amounting in number to about one hundred thousand every year. That is, so many are taken on board our ships; but at least ten thousand of them die in the voyage: about a fourth part more die at the different Islands, in what is called the Seasoning. So that at an average, in the passage and seasoning together, thirty thousand die: That is, properly are murdered. O earth, O Sea, cover not thou their blood."

John Wesley, *Thoughts on Slavery*

Extracts from the Journal of Doctor Gardiner, ship's surgeon on board The Brothers

2nd September 1787

After a brief landing at the Canary Islands to take on supplies, today we crossed the Tropic of Cancer, an event that never fails to be marked with a baptism or two. The poor unfortunates whose fate was already sealed before we put out of Bristol were the two landsmen, who until this morning had no notion of the terrors that the day would bring. Even when it was announced by the First Mate at the morning call that each was to be baptised by King Neptune for "crossing the line," they remained ignorant of their fate until, hooded and bound, they were told of what awaited them. First to the prow was a whimpering boy of no more than fourteen years, whose cries for mercy were met only with jeers and jibes, as he was lowered gingerly into the waves, the ship plunging him into the hungry waters and then raising him up like a babe in arms before a doting congregation. But it was only on emerging from the third dousing, coughing, and spluttering on the salty brine that his shipmates hauled him back aboard and removing his harness, hailed him as if reborn. Somehow he was soon smiling again, though the stench that was about him was evidence enough that he had fouled himself when in fear of his life, and he soon retreated beneath the decks. The second was a man of middling years who, having seen what had just befallen the first of King Neptune's victims was none too keen to go through the same torture, but despite his vigorous resistance, the crew proved too much for him. They would have their sport, and this rite of passage was not to be put off for another day. He was struggling against his bindings, hands held afore him and the sheets secured around his waist and up over his shoulders, before being bundled overboard and lowered to the waiting waters. For defying them and in view of his age, the mates insisted on a long-drawn-out ordeal and wave upon wave swallowed him whole until, begging for clemency he emerged almost drowned before being dumped like a catch of fish upon the wooden boards, his skin white with the scolding cold and his eyes red with the ocean's rage.

17th September 1787

After more uneventful moorings at the Cape de Verde Islands and then Cape Palmas, at a latitude of 4 degrees 4 minutes North and longitude of 7 degrees 26 minutes West, we have made good on our expected journey time and have arrived at the Guinea Coast ahead of our expected time. The crew have been busy readying the ship, a party sent ashore to gather the mangrove wood needed for its preparation. It took the whole crew a full day under the constant threat of the whip, but the timber barricado is now in place, topped off with sharpened wooden spikes and mounted with the small-bore cannon. It stands like a wicker screen, dividing the ship into two parts behind which the officers make their plans, a blunderbuss mounted at the fore in case of insurrection. Several trips ashore have sourced the reeds and bamboo needed to fashion the lattice, which offers the crew a makeshift shelter against the rains as their berth below must now be surrendered. The poor bosun is covered in sores from the swarms of midges which have seemingly taken a shine to him, the mosquitos have dined upon his flesh so badly that his back and legs are a running sore and no amount of treatment from my store can provide relief. Howsoever, the crew have thus been kept busy, and there is no sympathy afforded to them for their suffering, though their expedition to the shore was just the start of their misery. On their return they were muddied up to their necks and those that weren't, were burnt red by the sun, bringing back tales of monstrous snakes as thick as their legs, and lizards that spat poison from their mouths. The officers gave no quarter to their tales, but at least two have been badly bitten by something unknown, their broken skin swollen and bruised, and I fear that they may soon succumb to its poison. The Captain and his officers made haste for the African shore to enquire of the state of trade and thence to the local King with whom several other Captains will vie with us for their cargos, several French ships being anchored amongst the English under their tricolour flag. Some of their names are familiar, but I can see none other from Bristol. The Pilgrim cannot be far behind us, though I hear that their Captain has a preference for Sierra Leone, but two from Liverpool and one from London stand like us, idle in the mouth of the great river.

The coastline is green and lush, the tropical forest now receded from years of logging, but the islands that lie just offshore are redolent in colour and the foreign sounds of monkeys and other screeching creatures are unfamiliar enough for some. I am not alone in noticing the fins of sharks all about us; these fearsome creatures are so used to feasting on human flesh from years of trading that they now rely upon it and encircled the boat immediately on our arrival. The unwary landsmen are much alarmed though even the ordinary seamen have never seen the like and are much afeared. Today the sharks go hungry, but they will soon eat of their fill, I do not doubt.

18th September 1787

The local King Pepple and his entourage come aboard to receive beef and brandy and presents of chintz and silk from India. It is the custom, and once the King is satisfied, his agreement is sounded by one of his men, with the news trumpeted from an elephant's tooth announcing that we have permission to trade. I am informed by Captain Howlett that an acceptable duty for the purchase of slaves has been agreed, payable to the King for every head on our departure - the local traders will now be persuaded to make a sale of only healthy slaves, though our Captain has warned his officers to be vigilant. On the shore sit a handful of captives, but most were already rejected by the other ships and so the Captain says they made for a poor choice. He trades the watered-down brandy for two males, a gesture of goodwill he says, and they are numbered, shaved, and chained hand-to-foot to stop them from running, then put aboard and shackled to the deck behind the barricado, where they will now remain. These wretched souls will soon be numbered in the hundreds and those that bear but a single digit will be a rare commodity by the time we reach our final landing place, as the longer they lay in the belly of this ship, the less likely they are to survive. One of the crew has died quite horribly after falling foul of a black snake's bite, foaming at the mouth and delirious, the whites of his eyes reddened and his skin purple around the lesions. It has left the others unwilling to make more collections of the green wood for the fires that now burn under the copper cauldrons, without which we cannot hope to ward off the mosquitos and so more will be sent on their way tomorrow. It is the lesser of two evils, though all of our eyes are now irritated and sore from the smoke. There is no sea breeze to carry if off and its choking menace is thick about us, day, and night.

20th September 1787

The scantness of trade hereabouts has led Captain Howlett to send four of the crew 'boating', in the lower reaches of the Bonny river. It is well known amongst the crew that men may not return from such a venture, as skirmishes with the local traders, who do not hold with the intrusion of white men into their lands, can often be bloody encounters. The men drew lots amongst them and the four who got the shortest straws disembarked in the large canoe, which last saw service at Hotwells ferrying the Reverend and our ex-officer to shore, but now fixed at its prow with one of the swivel cannons for protection. The winds and rains have battered the barricado. Cavernous holes in the latticework canopy now let in a steady stream of rainwater and the officers have shown no mercy upon those who laboured on it, flogging them worse than beasts as they go about the repairs. Some have already been ashore to sell their clothes for liquor, so that they now stand almost naked at their work, but in this humidity, they see no need for linen and would rather drink away their living as we wait impatiently for The Traders to arrive, or for our expeditioners to return.

26th September 1787

The First Mate took much offence this morning at a young sailor's lack of attention, he falling asleep on watch last night. He had the other officers tie him to the main mast, stripped him of his shirt and then flogged him without mercy. The blood poured in rivulets before the mate relented, but even then, the punishment was not at an end, and he ordered the agonised boy to be strapped to the cannon for a further thirty lashes with the cat. I was obliged to inspect his wounds afterwards, but other than applying seaweed pickle, there was little to do to ease his suffering. We heard his wailing all day, from atop the bowsprit where he was hung out to dry in the tropical sun. On his being set down again, his skin was burned scarlet, and he was delirious, though the First Mate was pleased with his own work, which he says 'will stand as an example to the rest of the dogs'. Still no sign of the negroes, though the Captain has assured us he has heard good tidings of an upcoming fair that is soon to be held on the foreshore. Several parties are set to arrive, though the prices will be high, as our number has now been swelled by a small Whitehaven brig that has weighed anchor to our stern. The Captain has made clear that he wants to avoid The Quaw, who we know by their sharpened teeth and darker skin, for they often clash with the Eboe and have been known to be quarrelsome and, so he says, 'the cause of many a mutiny'. He has instructed that local Eboe – or Heeboes – Brasses, Appas, or Brechés are his 'commodity of choice' on this trip.

2nd October 1787

The boating crew returned one man light, slain as they fell upon a small band of negroes in a village some fifteen leagues to the interior. A hefty price to pay for *the two small boys that they have captured, neither of them more than ten years old, but the Captain seemed pleased with the outcome and as I examined them, both seemed healthy enough - free from any visible ailment anyway – though there was a fearsome look about their eyes. I am told that many are of the belief – when first captured - that they are about to be eaten and, having never seen a white man before, they do not know what kind of beast it is that has made them captive. It is a beast indeed, and I amongst them, for I play my part to the full in this most odious of industries. As is the usual order for kin, the two are not chained together, but are separated and fettered instead to one or other of the adult males, hand to foot to thwart any thought of escape. There is very little chance for them, but if they do slip their oversized shackles and find a way through the barricado and across the netting to jump into the waiting waters, then sharks the size of small carriages will be waiting. It is the perfect deterrent for all but the most despairing.*

<u>*4th October 1787*</u>

The scouting canoes arrived today, and they were full to bursting with captive Africans. It is like a feeding frenzy with the Captains, all of them eager to fill their boats and be away from these shores. I counted twenty-five or so of the large vessels, though more have since arrived, and each with thirty to forty slaves laid along their length. At most then, twelve hundred men, women, and children, to be split between the hulls of six or seven snows and brigs that are now afloat in the eight fathoms of water on this side of the sand bar. Some were already half full on arrival, and one may only need a dozen more to be exceeding of its true capacity. I have seen slavers so overloaded that their hulls sit low in the water, the rows of human flesh laid one on top of another below deck, with no care or modesty afforded to them. I prayed today that the salivating Captain Howlett was not put in such a mind, as he watched the rich flotilla coming closer to the river's mouth, as so many more would then surely die of suffocation and disease in the middle passage.

The fair was underway within an hour and each slaving party divided their catch by sex and age to best effect the process of inspection and barter. The Captain and his officers sifted the human herd, inspecting each file of black bodies for the most saleable assets. Young men and boys are always highly sought and so make up more than two thirds of the catch, but women and girls are also prominent – I saw several in the crowd that were with-child, after months of abuse since their kidnappings, and so they are often left unsold upon the beach until they are relieved of their heavy burden, which they are often forced to leave behind on the sand. The sea is no place for a babe-in-arms, and the death rate so high, that the Captains think it not worth the effort and so baulk at the prospect of an extra mouth to feed. Howlett takes his pick, ignoring the few Quaw that stand out from the rest, a proud and combative race who look upon their white captors with clear intent to injure and main at the first opportunity, and then he summons me to inspect the favoured few for disease or deformity. My rejection could result in their beheading by their captors if they are left unselected, and so I gave them all my consent, though they may not thank me for it later. A quick death might have been better than two months in the hold and a life in cruel servitude - but I could not see them so treated on my intelligence. I bore witness to many summary executions and watched in horror as the blood pooled around the toes of other desperate natives before being submerged in sand, leaving a dark patch on the strand that will be gone on the morning tide. This anguish and horror once seen, is now unseeable. The count numbered one hundred and fifty – one hundred and twenty enraged and terrified males, twenty shrieking women and ten traumatised children of all ages - chained and naked, they were forced aboard with sharpened sticks to the sound of cracking whips and bestial cries. Each of the adults were branded in turn by Smith, the third rate third mate - a red hot iron, its glowing and twisted end, curled into the initials of our cruel Captain, forever emblazoned on their bodies as a permanent reminder of this day. A long line of soft black tissue, forever scarred by methods honed at the inquisition and wielded by these willing demons. The Ottams, their bodies already greatly adorned with intricate and distinctive tattoos which mark out their status amongst a skilled and beautiful people, now have added another less decorative wound that they will bear to their graves. There were no exceptions made, but I will spare the details here, for it sickens me to recall and I cannot commit the memory to paper for the dreadful sense of it, lest the words rise up off the page in a sweet and stupefying stench to smother me in my sleep. The smell of roasting flesh hung like a pall upon the beach, as each victim kneeled to receive the branding iron upon their shoulders in a continuous train of terror — I have heard the screech of a multitude of sea birds when a single dog is set amongst them, but there was no dog and the birds had flown. As each ship filled its belly like a ravenous sea monster, I begged for such a natural sound to drown out their torment, but as I set my sights upon the agents of their agony and stood witness to their grinning devilry, I had to stop my ears and turn my back on it all. After the branding, and to the sound of much wailing and weeping, the slaves are led two by two in the aforementioned fashion to stoop through the open iron hatches, their fists closed around individual fetiches of shell, claw and feather which hang upon their chests from beautifully beaded necklaces. Some, which appear to be sharp and so could be used as a weapon, or as a tool to pick a lock, are torn from their necks by the crew and thrown overboard, much to their anguish, but they have little time to grieve as they are immediately forced below deck, where their fetters are fastened to the rusted iron rings that are affixed in lines. There they are left to fester cheek-by-jowl, until the Captain is ready to put to sea, from whence their screams and moans will be heard day and night, and no diversion can drown out their agonies. I can write of it no more.

12th October 1787

Though the ship is built to take but two hundred and fifty souls, the Captain wished to take full advantage of the good trading and so he ordered all studding and fair weather sails raised to journey along the coast towards Calabar, where we arrived at another fair. Today the same dreadful circus unfolds, where the officers bask in their cruelty and barbarism and the crew do their duty by the terms of their Articles, though some seem to revel in their newfound power. This time our Captain had free rein with no other slaver in sight, and so he supped until his thirst was quenched, driving down the price in exchange for our remaining goods, to fill his vessel to the brim, emptying our hold of its remaining linen, calico, muskets, gin, and brandy. He stretched out the gunpowder with fake layers set into several of the barrels, insisting that the measure was a full one, and similarly by adding our precious water to the supplies of Dutch gin and French brandy, he tricked his way to swell the boat to the bilge line. This time more females were taken, and naked they were left to roam behind the barricado, where they were easy prey for the crew - but not before the officers had made their own selections, escorting the most enticing below deck, where they will no doubt remain until their captors' lusts are satiated. If only that would be the end of it, but they will be swapped and shared until the voyage is complete, to make way for further unspeakable suffering at the hands of the planters. One fearsome girl, on realising her fate, managed to loose herself from her tormentor's intruding hands, by biting off a slice of flesh from his face, as he was busy molesting her, from whence she burst through a loose portion in the lattice fence and leapt from the side of the ship. She was seen no more, and is assumed to be shark food, but the foul man has had her price deducted from his wage and I have been forced to treat his wound with iodine. It should heal, though I am glad to say that he will be forever disfigured to remind him and others of his crime. You may ask why I have not succumbed to my desires in the same fashion – am I not a man too? Yes, I too made my choice, as to decline an officer's allowance would raise questions about my persuasions, though I feel sure that they would not have been concerned had I chosen to take a boy instead. A young girl sleeps on my floor beside me - I have not yet touched her and I hope I can resist the lustful urges that Satan sends my way. I have noticed that she doesn't sleep, so I have hidden all sharp objects, in case she has a mind to take one to my

throat or to her wrists, but I hope I can keep this small mercy and so, ease my own
sickly conscience. If I cannot - if it proves too much to ignore her nakedness and I fall
foul of Satan's urges - then I am damned and there can be no hope for me.

21st October 1787

The Captain is well pleased with our work, as the ship is fully stocked in
advance of expectations and so, we will take up the sails tomorrow. The barricado
has been dismantled and set upon the sea, where the waves will have utterly destroyed
it before the day is out, its branches left to crash upon the shore with the other flotsam
and jetsam that now litters the bay after years of trading. The slaves have each spent
time on deck today, manacled in twos in groups of twenty or thirty, along the chain
line, unable to stand upright as their shackles constrain them hand to foot, even with
the walls down and the sea in sight. Several have already died, most likely from
suffocation, their absence providing short relief for their close-shackled neighbours on
either side, who had been forced to lay all night chained to a corpse. I am made to
check each lifeless form for any signs of infection or disease - which if left unchecked
could spread amongst the living even before we have disembarked – and then their
carcasses are hurled overboard to the delight of the waiting sharks. The Captain is
most concerned to keep the slaves clean, and so has ordered that the decks below are
washed down with sea water once a day, a chore that the crew are most afraid of, and
several have been flogged for their refusal. The rains have been heavy today and all
have been forced to sit it out, without opportunity of shelter since the barricado is now
removed. The helmsman has been waiting for the high tide, to navigate the ship out of
the treacherous bay, avoiding the fate of many wrecks that lay upon the long and
deceptively shallow sand bar. The Captain is well aware of the dangers, and so is
keen to avoid any such catastrophe, which we are told would involve offloading the
whole ship - to free her weight from upon the bar, before the next high tide can set her
loose.

We are indeed fortunate that in spite of our excess weight, an unusually high tide has moved us across the sands, and I heard the cry go out as one of the slightest crew members was sent aloft to hand the main top gallant sail. We are now at sea, the ship in full sail and the crew in good spirits. The two dozen black children are now free to roam the decks unchained, and the women, though still in leg irons to handicap them should they attempt to jump, are also free in their captivity as they do their best to avoid the lustful clutches of the crew. The men remain in chains below deck and are only brought up in smaller groups of ten or twelve, though still in chains from hand to foot. I saw the boy again today, one of the first two aboard the ship – he was alone and free of chains to walk about the deck – but instead was sat hunched up on the half deck next to the chicken coop, observing the scene below and seemingly lost in thought, his dark eyes regarding the crew in sullen contemplation. I watched him for a while, until he noticed me and then I wished that I had remained a stranger, for his eyes laid claim to mine and reached inside to weigh my soul, and judged me guilty before God. We are making for the Portuguese island of Annabon, which is entirely populated by Africans, though it is a staging post for vessels like ours and not another place to trade, and so in less than ten days we will take on water and fruit before continuing Westward.

-○○○-

The impressive gathering of the great-and-the-good within The Society's inner circle of more amenable contacts, had been put in motion by Granville Sharp on receipt of Clarkson's recent letter, and they were both rather pleased at the response. Almost all of the invited guests had accepted and were in attendance, most of whom were keen to hear for themselves all about the Reverend's recent excursions in the

West Country. It was hosted by Bennet Langton, co-founder of *The Literary Club*, at his fashionable Cavendish Square home, and Thomas was not surprised to see Bennet's friend and confidant, James Boswell, at his side. Sharp saw Boswell as a potential activist to be put to work amongst London's genteel classes, if Boswell could just see his way to completing the biography of his late friend Doctor Samuel Johnson that is, which by all accounts had been his sole obsession for some time. As for Langton himself, he too would soon be briefed on his assignment by Sharp, to spread the word amongst the rank and file of his regiment and to other officers who frequented the same exclusive gentlemen's clubs in the capital. Though he looked every bit the aging thin-faced aristocrat, descended from a landed Lincolnshire family and with a seat in the House of Lords, he had spent his working life in the military, rising to the lofty rank of Major in the Lincolnshire militia. As such, he fitted the eighteenth-century definition of "influencer" very well indeed, a fact that was not lost on the core members and one that Sharp was determined to keep onside.

Other than the usual courtesies that befitted such an occasion, neither man would be the focus of Thomas Clarkson's attentions that evening, as both were already firm allies in their cause. Both he and Sharp had their sights set on other leading dignitaries of the day, who were busy admiring the recently installed Robert Adam fireplace, whilst waiting to be served with pre-dinner drinks. Right on cue the Langton's fashionably black manservant appeared, expertly balancing a silver platter upon his right hand, which served as a platform for six crystal goblets brimming with sparkling refreshment. Clarkson regarded the handsome servant with interest, wondering to himself what stories he could tell, and if he too considered himself to be enslaved or in service to his white masters.

It was a question that would have to wait, and despite the distraction, the Reverend only really had one man in his sights. William Wilberforce was already deep in conversation with another familiar figure, when the Reverend John Newton caught Clarkson's eye from the heart of this small gathering and beckoned him to join them. But before they could begin to talk in earnest, they were summoned to dinner and like a well-turned-out flock of sheep, they heeded the call without delay. Each were ushered into the adjacent dining room, whose oak panelled walls put Clarkson in mind of a galleon's war-room, as they milled around an elegant rosewood dining table, that was busily laid out in time-honoured fashion. Each place setting was strategically set, so as to leave no conversation to chance, and Clarkson could tell that Sharp must have had a hand in the seating-plan, with he himself seated at one end of the long table and Langton at its head.

"My Lords, Ladies and Gentlemen," it was Langford, and he was calling for their undivided attention. "Pray charge your glasses and join me, in a toast to His Gracious Majesty, the King."

They each stood to attention and joined together in the toast, raising their glasses skyward and only after affording the ladies time to settle themselves into their seats, did the men then make themselves comfortable for what would no doubt be a long affair. Though there were only ever three courses at these social gatherings, each one could last an hour or more and consisted of several separate dishes, many of them drawing inspiration from Britain's growing Empire and its ever-expanding trade network. For quite some time, business matters were put aside, and conversations were of friends and family, of the latest innovations and discoveries and the unfathomable behaviour of foreigners, especially the French, whose habits and dispositions were a constant source of amusement to the English. Anything controversial was to be avoided in these early exchanges; nothing remotely private, personal, or risqué would be mentioned and if there were a slip of the tongue, it was immediately charged down by the seemingly omnipresent host and his socially adept wife.

So, it wasn't until the ox soup had been consumed and the roast lamb with all its trimmings devoured - and just ahead of a divine chocolate orange dessert, generously decorated with peel and a sprinkling of cocoa - that anyone dared to turn the topic of conversation in the direction of the newest Deacon of Winchester Cathedral.

"So, is there anyone at this table that hasn't read the Reverend Clarkson's essay yet?" Langton asked, taking the lead as was his duty for the evening.

There were some around the table who admitted that they had not, which prompted Sharp to make copies immediately available, with a little too much haste for some people's tastes. "Why don't you give us a quick summary of your findings Thomas, bring everyone up to date, and whilst you are at it you can tell us what you've been doing these last few weeks in the West Country, other than partaking of their infamous apple cider."

All eyes were upon him, and he suddenly felt a little self-conscious, as he stared into their inquisitive faces. He could feel a rising flush about his own face and neck and although he quickly blamed it on the arrival of the port, that had already been passed around in readiness for the cheese course, his discomfort at suddenly becoming the centre of attention was obvious to all. He decided there and then to do away with his rehearsed monologue, the one that he always held in reserve for such occasions as this; he was already a little tipsy, which may have been the root cause of his snap decision to speak to them from the heart. He would not regret it.

"To begin with it was merely a competition, an exercise in Latin, and an opportunity to win a prize, which those of you that know me well, will know is usually motivation enough." A great start, it broke the tension that had been building in the room and he was off and running, his earlier nervousness forgotten, and his audience encapsulated. "But it quickly became so much more than that, because it is, 'so much' more than that."

"So, for those of you who are not well versed in the classics, the title of the essay was quite simple. '*Is it right that one man can own another?*', a very old and very pertinent question for our world today and for the scandal," he said, letting the word resonate, "that is The Trade." He took a drink from his refilled glass and contemplated each face in turn, finally settling on Newton, whose eyes were immediately downcast and his countenance noticeably sombre.

"I've been gathering evidence in Bristol" he continued, "and will also be very shortly heading to Liverpool, to continue in that effort. I have already spoken with several crews, and their tales of woe can be compared to that of the slaves themselves, because almost half of these young men never make it home again, dying of disease or most terribly by the wilful neglect of their own officers." An expression of disbelief seemed to pass from one dinner guest to the next as he looked upon their faces in turn and though they were too polite to say so, it was clear from their frowning expressions that they doubted his word, and so he continued with his evidence. "Everywhere I turned, I found some other dark secret, under every rock another tale of terror was hiding, and yet those men who perpetrate The Trade dare to continue to speak of its virtues and of its overwhelming economic benefits to our nation. Whilst thousands die upon their ships in squalor and disease."

"I have met with many ship's surgeons, who have turned their back on that most immoral of livings," Clarkson continued, "and are now willing to testify against the venture capitalists themselves, whose speculative investments are driving this dreadful business to ever higher stakes. Some of their stories, I cannot repeat around this table, as they have no place in civilised society, but if you can imagine the most heinous crimes against our fellow man, you will still not come close to the truth of it." The room was tense, each unsure of what was coming next and nervous that, whatever it was, it might not be to their liking.

"I will tell you what I have learned, the basis of The Trade and the many lives and livelihoods that it feeds on; I know not everything and every day I learn of another abomination, on the shores of Africa, on the ships that ferry the captives bound and shackled below decks and on the plantations in the New World; from whence our everyday 'essentials', our sugar and tobacco, our cocoa and cotton, are cultivated for our convenience. But remember the next time that you sweeten your tea or take a draw on your well stocked pipe, that you do so on the backs of a thousand dead Africans, who are far from the 'savage' that they are purported to be; a term which far better describes the officers and crew that prey on their souls."

His words were having the desired effect and one or two amongst his audience were looking visibly uncomfortable, willing him to finish his little recital, so they could retreat back to their drawing rooms and feign ignorance. Their embarrassment was only too obvious to the orator, and the denial that he saw stamped upon their privileged white faces, only served to drive him on, to share more of the brutal truth that underpinned their affluence.

"In this last year alone, almost eighty thousand Africans have been wrenched from their lands and shipped across the sea to the Caribbean islands or to the southern states. Of those that made it there alive, it's likely that twenty thousand are already dead and that a further ten thousand will soon be so, under the lash of vicious overseers or on their knees in exhaustion under the unforgiving sun of Barbados, St Kitts, Jamaica, and the other tropical islands that supply so many of the fruits that we have eaten our fill of this evening." The timely reminder led a few to dab their mouths with their napkins and to push the last of their plates away, as if to disassociate themselves from the painful truth.

"The death rate is so unrelenting amongst those innocent men, women, and children who toil on your behalf, that the populace has to be continually replenished with a new intake each season, just to keep the fields tilled and the crops harvested." The room was silent. Even the servants were quietly listening, seized by his words, and for some a festering anger was rising up inside them. But not for everyone.

"Are you for full emancipation then?" It was their host that posed the question that others were thinking, but who as yet were unwilling to put their name to their thoughts. "For if you are, then I would contest that the economy could not take it, the whole business would sink this country into recession, from which it would take years to recover."

"And wouldn't the other slaving nations, the French in particular, simply step in to fill the void that we had left behind?" said another of the guests, leading several around the table to nod in agreement or concern, whilst others looked troubled, embarrassed, or simply irritated.

"Full emancipation must be the ultimate prize."

It was Sharp who had spoken up, and everyone turned their heads towards him, as he put his case in the strongest possible terms. "But it may not be possible to achieve it in one step and we must impress upon our trading partners the full impolicy of their intentions. Firstly, we must put a stop to the supply of slaves, by banning The Trade in human lives across the Atlantic; this will force the plantation owners to treat their existing stocks more humanely, and so keep them alive and enable them to replenish their own supply, without resorting to this inhumane transatlantic trade."

"You mean to say that they should be encouraged to breed?" It was Lady Langton who had spoken, and the attention of the room now turned towards her, as she was forced to reconsider the implications of her words. "If that is not too vulgar a consideration for this dining table?"

"Not at all Madam," Clarkson said, "for it is a vulgar trade and if we cannot debate the full vulgarities of it, then we cannot hope to understand it, and so put a stop to it. But as we are now getting down to the 'brass tacks' of the matter, I am forced to share with you some of the evils of this stinking cesspit of wickedness, things that I want you to take with you, to tell your friends and family about, and to pray over when you take to your beds tonight. And please do not doubt the exactness of their retelling, for I have heard so many faithful testimonies to know that these tales are not the exception amongst those planters and sea Captains. These are the damning rule. They are the normal run of things, and I may still not know the half of it yet. Should anyone wish to leave us before I continue, then I will take no offence, for I know how it is to sleep on this knowledge once obtained, and it has been an uneasy bedfellow for me these last few months I can tell you."

No one moved, though several pairs of eyes were suitably downcast, settling on their now empty dessert bowls, where the stains of chocolate sauce were all too visible, not unlike the stains on their reputations, and for at least one of them on their soul. As if on some silent signal, the servants moved in to offer tea or coffee to moisten the palate of their diners; most of them took tea, unsweetened.

"At the Guinea Coast, it is true that some of the slaves are brought to the shoreline by their countrymen, already in bondage. Lines of all ages and of both sexes, shackled together with wooden beams about their shoulders which keep them from escaping from the clutches of their captors. They are bartered for along the beaches; Agents and Captains trade the goods that have been shipped from our English cities, a couple of fine muskets and some well woven cloth, maybe a few copper pots or a bar of lead, provides enough currency for one tall strong black African male. The ship's Doctor then examines them all in the closest detail, and once it is assured that they are free from all manner of disease, then and only then, are they deposited together with the others further along the beach, in a space allotted for each ship. If they are fortunate, they may sit under temporary shelters, out of the heat of the day, but as the cargo increases, for my friends that is how they are categorised in the ship's records, they cannot help but sit in the full sun, until their skin is burnt and blistered."

"I had no idea" gasped Lady Langton, but Clarkson wasn't yet finished, and she would have to endure many more shocking truths before her dinner party was done with for the night.

"Once the Captain is satisfied that he has amassed the required quantity, he orders his crew to force their purchases aboard the ship; naked and trembling, with men and women mixed together and children torn asunder from their mothers to form a separate line. They can sit for weeks on the sand, as the cargo is assembled, but sometimes when The Trade is slow or competition high, the Captain may decide to go off further down the coast in search of a different source - and if so then the poor slaves' agony is extended, as they must wait for the Captain to be satisfied with his load. Often, when The Trade is good, the Captain will greedily stack as many into the belly of the ship as it will allow, in full knowledge that many will die in the crossing. For he is motivated only by the maximisation of his profit and to supplement his meagre salary with a sickening share of the spoils."

"Each is then branded like a new-born calf," at which point Clarkson took a breath, to see to it that the full horror of this admission was understood by all. "Yes, you did hear me correctly Madam," he said, looking to Lady Langton whose hand was now at her mouth, which had fallen open. "A red-hot iron is pressed against their breast, shoulder or buttocks, the initials of the man who stole their life away, impressed forever on their skin. The similarity to cattle cannot be ignored, and many of the Slavers will ease their conscious by such beliefs, but I tell you as I have told them - these are human beings, they are not beasts of burden. They are no different to you nor I" he said continuing to keep a horrified Lady Langton firmly in his sights, "they are human creatures, God's own, created in his holy image, the only difference being the colour of their skin."

"Hear, hear!" It was Sharp, his hand banging upon the table. One or two of the others joined in, but neither of them was Wilberforce, who still chose to keep his own counsel. Newton was also strangely quiet, though Clarkson planned to call on him soon enough, to bring his first hand experience to the fore for the benefit of all.

"And then for the middle passage, as it is known," Clarkson continued. "The torrid journey across the great ocean, which only two hundred and fifty years ago was thought to have led to the edge of the world. If only we had stayed ignorant of its true end, our world would now be a far sweeter place, if Columbus had only been blown off course or run aground on the islands of the Azores. Foul weather can be a source of tragedy in this time, whilst it is not uncommon for the ship to be becalmed in The Doldrums before it reaches the Bahamas, with disastrous consequences for all on board. The longer the passage, the worse it is for the slaves, as the ship runs low on food, and water if the rains have failed to replenish supplies. If any of those who are close shackled below deck were diseased before their capture, then all will be in danger by the end, and this my friends, is where the real horror begins."

"As Reverend Newton well knows" Clarkson knew that on his cue, all eyes would then veer towards the former Captain and slave trader, turned evangelical preacher, and he found Newton's all too obvious discomfort to his own liking. The Rector's moment would soon be upon him, but it wasn't to be just yet, as Clarkson continued to call the tune.

"And what of the women?" Lady Langton asked, her hackles now up and ready to speak up for the cause, but her fight would not be with the Reverend Clarkson. He knew already that her support was guaranteed. "How is their modesty protected, are they kept separate to the men?"

"I regret to say Madam, any separation of the sexes is but brief, and as for their modesty, they are afforded none." He knew that should be answer enough, but he pressed on, spelling out the whole brutal truth to aid their digestion of the cold hard facts. This was not the time for niceties. "The officers take first pick, selecting the finest amongst them for their own personal usage, at least for the duration of the trip. Some are permitted to take one slave each at the end of the voyage, a prize that is usually limited to the Captain, the Chief or First Mate and to the ship's surgeon, but most choose not to do so and instead receive their sale price to augment their own personal profit."

"Did you ever take advantage of such a 'privilege' Reverend Newton?" the horrified Lady asked, fearful of the answer lest it might make her regret the company that she was keeping.

"To my everlasting shame Madam," Newton coughed, "I must confess, and have confessed, that I did as a youth partake in such notions as this. Though I have since ensured that any and all profits that came my way as a result of their sale has been paid over in full to the church and its adopted causes." The gathered group were shocked, and Clarkson let the silence do its work, to humiliate his clerical colleague just for a moment or two, but then his good nature got the better of him, and he allowed the Captain to make a rush at redemption.

"As the Good Book teaches us, Madam" Clarkson said, "we must all go down to the deep, before we can rise to the heights of glory, washed clean by Him who died for our sins. So long as we have truly repented, only then shall we be forgiven." The meaning was not lost on Newton, but Clarkson would spare him any further embarrassment, choosing instead to defer to a later and more private hearing.

"A whole month or more, spent chained close hand in the darkness of the ship, leaves all weak and terrified, the poisonous air and squalid conditions requires the decks to be hosed down daily with sea water, in the hope of warding off dysentery and death. It is a terrible state, worse than a farmer allows for his pigs, and yet on every vessel that takes its cargo from the coast of Africa, the scene is the same until they make landfall in the New World. Sometimes, the slaves are elated at the sight of the lush green islands, their yellow sands a reminder of home, and some amongst them may think they have arrived in paradise; and a paradise it is, but it is not theirs to share in. For them they have not arrived at a 'heaven on earth'; for them it will be worse than the fires of hell, and it's there that they will labour in the fields until they die an early death. I am told that seven years is all they can reasonably expect, for seven years of hard labour is all that the human body can endure in the heat of the Tropics and under the steady lash of the cruellest of men. Many don't come through the first season, so much so that the planters have a name for it; they call it 'seasoning' where each slave must endure their first cycle of planting and harvest and should they survive, then they might prevail for longer, but it is such that an early death may well be a blessing and not a curse. For the lives that they are forced to live on the very plantations where so many ignorant Englishmen have invested their wealth, are plainly not worth the living. All hope is gone and once this terrible truth is fully understood, many choose to destroy themselves, or to run. But those who try to run are tortured to death in the most horrific ways imaginable, as an example to others."

"Is there no one who will help them?" a tearful Lady Langton asked. "Is there no refuge?"

"The problem is, my Lady, that on an island, there is nowhere to run to" said Sharp, pointing out the obvious for any of them that might still be in denial. "On those islands, there are plantation owners and their families, their wicked and reviled overseers, and their slaves. And that is all."

"Is there no good that comes from this whole sorry tale?" It was James Boswell who had spoken up, his late friend Doctor Johnson had kept his own black manservant and the two of them had formed quite an attachment since his patron's untimely death. "To hear you talk, the whole thing is the work of Lucifer, is there no one in this savage business who is worthy of some credit?"

"There is none," Clarkson responded promptly, unwilling even to give the question time to settle in the room. "From the Slavers of Bristol to the Portuguese Agents of the African coast, to the sea Captains of Liverpool and Lancaster and their downtrodden crew members - they and the planters of the New World are profiteers to a man. They have no cares for the labourers in the fields, who are worked to death to bring them success. Their blood money is made off the backs of slavery and their wealth will stand for all time as their damnation."

"Something must be done!" It was Wilberforce, and at the unmistakable sound of his voice, which had conducted many a Parliamentary debate to a crescendo in the past, Granville Sharp's eye caught Clarkson's in a small moment of victory. A secret signal must have passed between them in that moment, for the two Abolitionists resisted the urge to fill the subsequent gap in the conversation and instead, stayed silent to let the only elected Member for Parliament in the room have his authoritative say on the matter. "These things are not news to me, I am sad to say" he continued, "for I have known of Mr Sharp's interventions and of Reverend Clarkson's sterling work for many months and have encouraged both in their noble efforts. For it is facts that we need, not emotions, if we are to table a bill before Parliament that will win over the sceptics and those whose money drives this evil commerce."

"Hear, hear!" Again, it was Granville Sharp's hand that rapped upon the table, but this time he was not alone and several amongst them joined him, much to Thomas Clarkson's delight.

"You must do all you can Mr Wilberforce to raise this abhorrent business amongst Parliament, immediately" Lady Langton implored him. "If all is as the Reverend has presented here tonight, and I do not doubt a word of your testimony Reverend Clarkson, then it must be brought to the attention of Westminster and to a swift and final denouement."

"I give you my word Lady Langton, as I have to Mr Pitt," Wilberforce committed, "that I will be raising this matter in the very next session. I will be working closely with these gentlemen and others from their admirable society, and with the Prime Minister's support, we will engineer a path to achieve our goal before the end of this eighteenth century, though I fear that it may be so entrenched in our commercial undertakings that the wheels may yet turn too slowly for our liking."

"Then we must turn them more quickly" said her husband. "For the wheels have been stuck in the mud of our own making for far too long."

"Indeed, they have Sir," said a victorious Granville Sharp, "indeed they have."

His words were met with nothing but a contented smile from Thomas Clarkson, who took solace in the knowledge that after months of weekly updates in hastily arranged one-to-one meetings with Mr Wilberforce, in the end, it had taken a woman's touch to tip the balance. Reams of paperwork, charts, statistics, tables, and tracts had passed between them; hours of debate and argument had ensued; nights spent poring over each and every word contained in circular letters; and early mornings pacing the pavements with Richard Phillips at Lincoln's Inn when all other God-fearing people were long since asleep. Yet when a Lady of the Realm showed her disgust for The Trade and all it stood for, the Right Honourable Member of Parliament for Hull did not hesitate to take up the cause as his own.

-oœ-

It had been a successful evening and as the visibly shaken guests began to take their leave, only The Society's founding members were left, alongside Wilberforce and Newton, who would also soon bid them goodnight. But not before the Reverend Thomas Clarkson had had his say. The urge to bring the man to heel had been burning a hole in his heart all evening.

"Reverend Newton," he said, "I look forward to reading your long-awaited *Thoughts on Slavery*, how is it progressing?"

"I am almost done with it," Newton informed him. "It is now undergoing its final edits and Richard Phillips will soon be printing five thousand copies for immediate circulation."

"That is splendid news" remarked Granville Sharp, "it will indeed be an important and long overdue testimony. But will five thousand be sufficient? The Quaker network alone has many thousands of members, and we will need several hundred for Parliamentary distribution after the summer recess. Shall I speak with Phillips to ask for the numbers to be reviewed?"

Newton nodded in agreement, and Wilberforce seconded it, agreeing that the more literature was in circulation the greater their chances of success in the upcoming campaign. Bennet Langton had now joined his only remaining guests and added his voice to the debate. "The Literary Club will be only too pleased to circulate your memoirs Reverend Newton. Your evidence will be crucial, as will your condemnation of those who have played a part in this cruel business."

"Better late than never, I suppose!" said Clarkson a little too sarcastically for some. "It has only taken you some twenty five years or more since you left The Trade to speak out against it, despite your 'finding God' so long ago, on your first voyage I believe, and yet you managed two more and would have made another had God not intervened and laid you low with a fever just two days before The Bee was to set sail. How far do your words impress upon the slaving community at large that they need to desist in their endeavours" asked Clarkson directly. "Are they left in no doubt that it is they who must seek new ways to trade with Africa, if we are to abolish the traffic in human lives?"

Newton was silent for a moment, unsure of how to respond and suspicious that a trap was being set for him, should he say the wrong thing. "They are my memoirs and mine alone," he started. "For it is for me that I speak, and I alone who has trodden this despicable path. After all that has been said already, I do not wish to interfere unnecessarily in the path of righteousness, that our nation at long last seems ready to follow. I see my testimony here given is to my shame and mine alone, for my untimely public confession, which however sincere, comes too late to prevent or repair the misery and mischief to which I have formerly been chief accessory."

It seemed a well-rehearsed speech and one that would avoid any accusations of hypocrisy from the midst of the leading slaving families, with whom he was still rather too well connected. He continued to talk of 'humiliating reflection' and of his 'headstrong passions and follies' that had seen him knee deep in the trappings of The Trade throughout his younger life.

"How many voyages did you personally oversee Reverend Newton?" Wilberforce asked, interested to learn more from this first hand witness and wanting to be sure that he had fully understood the depth of his sordid involvement in the trafficking of Africans.

"Three in all, from 1745 to 1754, though I was resident in Africa and living amongst the white Agents long before that, and so learned much of their business and how they first acquired the negroes for the slavers. I was due to sail again but indeed, I did fall ill and so resigned the Captaincy. In the thirty or so years since, my memory of those events has become less clear, although I remember enough to continue to vouch that it is indeed an evil undertaking. They were indeed ticklish times for me personally, ones that I do not look back upon with any pride or fondness, only with the utmost shame."

"I find it strange," countered Clarkson with an air of disbelief, "that your memory fails you in these matters, for I cannot forget a word of what I have read of this sordid subject over just a couple of years. I feel sure that had I played an active role in it, had I seen for myself the treatment that I have merely been told about, then those horrific recollections would be ingrained on my very soul and I would not so easily and conveniently forget."

The rebuke was intended, but Newton had no further words with which to defend himself, and so he continued, the hole around him getting deeper with every word. "The Trade was always indefensible, but inattention and interest prevented the evil from being perceived and as I say in so many words in my tract, the monies that still arise from it, are 'not lawful to put into the Treasury of this nation, because it is the price of blood.'"

"And yet still you are invested personally in the ships that trade upon the Guinea Coast Sir?" It was Clarkson again and there was no let-up in his fury. "You continue with your affiliations, and you still choose not to use your power and influence to talk them down from their high and mighty views. Your actions speak louder than your words Sir."

"I am humbled by your passions Reverend Clarkson," Newton said solemnly, "but I have now relinquished all shares in The Trade and have divested myself of all my interests. I know now that it is something I should have done long ago, but I am a poor sinner who knew no better, and I am truly sorry in the sight of God for my transgressions."

"You mean you have now seen which way the wind is blowing" snapped Clarkson, his hot-headedness for which he was becoming famous, once again coming to the fore, but like the professional politician he was Wilberforce stepped in to soothe the growing tension between his two co-conspirators.

"This pamphlet does your soul credit, Reverend Newton," interrupted a flustered Wilberforce. "I have read a draft and commend you for your honesty and candour, even if it is a little overdue, but right now is very judicious. Your testimony will be of great value to me before the Royal Inquiry and I would ask you all to use it to our advantage." His eyes were fixed on Clarkson as he said it and Granville Sharp's fixed stare also impressed upon the red-blooded Reverend that he should now abstain from his impromptu cross-examination of this misguided but important witness.

The last word on the matter though, would be Newton's.

"The facts as you have presented them are certain Reverend Clarkson, and as for the crew themselves, I can surely vouch that a great number of them do perish in the course of The Trade. I have known those who have lost half their people and some a larger proportion still, though I am far from saying that it is always thus. I believe that I shall state matters sufficiently low, if I suppose that at least one fifth of those who go from England to the Coast of Africa in ships which trade for slaves, never return from thence. I dare not depend too much upon my memory" he continued, glancing in turn to regard the rest of the quartet. "I judge it probable that the collective sum of seamen, who go from all our ports to Africa within the course of a year cannot be less than eight thousand. So, if upon an average of ships and seasons, a fifth part of these die, the annual loss cannot be much less than fifteen hundred persons. I believe those who have taken pains to make more exact enquiries, will deem my supposition to be very moderate indeed."

"So much for the argument that their number swells the ranks of our Navy in times of national crisis then" scoffed Wilberforce, as Sharp and Langton nodded in agreement.

"I know of none that made that transition in my time," said Newton.

"And I was told of none in the drinking dens of Bristol," confirmed Clarkson.

"Then I will conclude that it is a myth" said Wilberforce "and until someone can prove to me to the contrary, I will commit to slay that myth in the halls of Parliament in the very next session. I have come up with another notion gentlemen", he continued, "one that I believe might help to ease the ill treatment of the slaves on the middle passage".

"Pray continue", said Sharp encouragingly, though Clarkson couldn't help but think that whatever idea was about to be aired, it might not be to his liking.

"Would it be prudent", began Wilberforce, "to provide some level of government funded 'bounty', payable to a ship's company – its owners perhaps, but for maximum effect I would propose to the ship's officers. Particularly to the Captain, though we may also wish to extend the offering to the Chief Mate and Surgeon, to reward them for arriving at the West Indies with a full compliment of healthy slaves?"

Both Clarkson and Sharp must have looked dumbfounded at the suggestion for neither of them spoke, and the Reverend may have accidentally let his mouth fall open in horror at the very suggestion. In the end it was Newton who spoke up, and to their horror, it was with encouraging tones that he proceeded to heap complements on Wilberforce for the concept.

"A most ingenious suggestion if I may say so Sir", he said, fawning like a puppy at feeding time. "I can only see such an idea having great benefit, both for the slaves who will be treated more humanely as a result, and for the officers, who will have even more motivation to land a healthy cargo at the islands and so return to

England with a sufficient profit to keep the shareholders happy. After all, they do what they do for money, and so, as their prime motivator, such a bounty should appeal to their senses."

It seemed an opportune moment to call the evening to a close, before any other madcap 'solutions' were aired, and after thanking their hosts for a most agreeable evening, the two Abolitionists took their leave, receiving their coats and hats from the doorman and heading out into the grandeur of the square where their carriage was waiting for them.

CHAPTER TEN

"They frequently geld them or chop off half a foot: After they are whipped until they are raw all over, some put pepper and salt upon them: Some drop melted wax upon their skin. Others cut off their ears and constrain them to broil and eat them. For Rebellion, they fasten them down to the ground with crooked sticks on every limb, and then applying fire by degrees, to the feet and hands, they burn them gradually upward to the head."

John Wesley, Thoughts on Slavery

After three days on the dusty roads of middle England, Thomas Clarkson was once more in the company of Alexander Falconbridge at the Kings Arms Hotel in the heart of Liverpool's busy and bustling port. He had taken diversions to both Worcester and Chester on his journey north, primarily to meet with prominent members of the Quaker network who had expressed their support for his campaign and had been pleased to hear that they would be willing to distribute The Society's literature widely, within their mercantile and landed circles.

Mr Dale of the Kings Arms had also been most accommodating and in addition to their own bedchambers, he had procured a small area downstairs near to the public bar, where Clarkson and the Doctor would be able to read, and to meet with any visitors at their convenience. They were situated in the heart of the town, and but a short stroll down to the Old Dock, which acted as a gateway through to Salt House Dock and George's Dock. More docks were in the process of being built at the eastern fringe of the port, to meet the pressures of the recent economic boom, that was showing no sign of slowing down. The rapidly expanding canal network had given rise to an industrial feeding frenzy, and the pent-up demand from the mills and factories for raw materials - like cotton, sugar, cocoa, coffee, tobacco, and timber - was enticing an exponential increase in supply. The outward trade was even more impressive; coal, salt, glassware, pottery, hops, leather goods, textile goods and a whole kaleidoscope of other manufactures, were heading in the other direction and making full use of the expanding square footage of quayside space. So much so, that even the new docks would soon find their additional capacity outstripped.

To begin with, both men had been able to keep a low profile about the town, as Clarkson was a complete unknown and his companion was personally known only to a handful of locals. The rising national publicity for their cause had prompted some vehement reactions, but so far these had been limited to outraged letters in the local press or items raised and debated under 'any other business' at meetings of the regional Boards of Trade. As a result, their anonymity was not set to last, as a stream of visitors would soon be arriving at their temporary place of residence; some came just to gawp at the city's unwelcome guests, others to put their case for The Trade and some came looking for a full-on confrontation. The events that led up to their sudden notoriety took root in just a few days and the people of Liverpool were primed for a prize fight. Having heard of the goings-on in Bristol through their many commercial contacts, they were on the lookout and as soon as a strikingly tall man, dressed in black and with a mop of red hair, had started asking awkward questions around the port, any cover that they had hoped for was quickly blown. An ability to be inconspicuous was something that God had not seen fit to bestow on Thomas Clarkson, but he had learned to use his God-given ability to stand out in any crowd to his full advantage.

The muster rolls had been his first objective on his arrival, and just as in Bristol and London before them, he was surprised by the ease with which he was able to gain access, once his local Quaker friend,

William Rathbone, had made the necessary arrangements. The Custom House officials had simply provided him with entry to their reading rooms and he was able to browse through the rolls at his leisure, quickly noting that the volume of trade in this northern port was far greater than in the south, and that the number of slave ships registered to Liverpool had risen dramatically throughout the current century. But it was the death rates that he wanted to confirm, and before too long it became crystal clear that the pattern in Liverpool was no different than it had been elsewhere. Anything from one-third to two-thirds of the crew that had set out on voyages from the River Mersey, would not return to their home city, the records struck through and the words 'deceased' or 'deserted' imprinted across their entry, with zero money paid out on their behalf at the conclusion of the trip.

It was during these investigations that Clarkson's attention was drawn to a table of dock duties for the previous decade. He had almost missed it, but on closer inspection he found that it revealed the entire history of the port of Liverpool, and its exponential growth over one hundred and fifty years, from a small fishing village at the mouth of the river. What had struck him in the statistics though, did not concern the crews and their treatment, nor the number of slaving trips undertaken. It was the clear evidence that in spite of the fall in slavery that had resulted from the American wars during the years 1772 to 1779, the entire volume of goods entering through this Northwest seaport had continued to rise. In fact, trade had increased by 10% in the war years as the colonists fought for their liberty, and despite a fall in the number of slaving vessels from one hundred ships fitted out for Africa at the start of the period, to just eleven in the last year of the decade, Liverpool's economic success story had continued unchecked.

Clarkson was delighted to have come across such clear proof, that would help him to debunk the widely held view that, without slavery, the town's economy would be left on its knees. Satisfied with his first day's work, he headed out to walk the short fifteen-minute journey back to his lodgings, where he would share his findings with Falconbridge. However, he was stopped in his tracks by a most repugnant sight, one that he had never expected to see on the streets of an English city, but one that would prove pivotal in his campaign, and which would swell his growing box of evidence to bursting point.

There, as bold as brass displayed like everyday kitchen utensils in the window of a Liverpool shop, he came face to face with the whole range of instruments that formed the basis of the slave trader's arsenal; handcuffs, leg shackles and two iron appliances that were so unwieldy to the eye, that the Reverend found himself quite unable to comprehend their purpose. The shop was open and so he went inside, where he was determined to find out more and, if affordable and relevant, to make a purchase or two.

"Good day to you Sir" the shopkeeper called out as Clarkson stooped to enter. "The weather is unseasonably cold these last weeks, don't you think?"

"It is indeed," Clarkson agreed, "I had hoped the climes would be better in the north, but sadly not." For a few moments they exchanged further pleasantries and the Reverend imparted some, but by no means all, of his travel plans. He did not mention his true purpose for being drawn inside, nor his reasons for being in Liverpool on that July afternoon. He was there 'on business' was all he said by way of explanation, and he hoped that it would suffice.

"What can I help you with today?" the peculiar curator asked, as if his shop were a haberdashers, butchers or some other outlet filled with everyday mundane purchases for the home or kitchen.

"I was intrigued by your wares in the window display," Clarkson answered honestly enough, though he thought that his interest required some form of explanation, if only to banish any considerations that he had any clandestine use for them in his own home.

"I am doing some research, writing a paper for my university actually, on the plethora of ironmongery that keeps our industrial entrepreneurs busy in various parts of the country."

"Well, these are truly wonders of the engineering age," the shopkeeper enthused, fetching the two mysterious items from the window as he spoke. "Especially the instruments of correction, which I don't doubt would have been useful to the Spanish in the inquisition." It was a joke and as the older man chuckled at his own indelicate humour, Clarkson felt duty bound to at least crack an out of place smile in response. But it didn't sit well and so it was soon banished.

"If you don't mind me asking, what are they?"

"Not at all" the shopkeeper responded cheerfully, "the first is a thumbscrew, the second is a *speculum oris*." He demonstrated quickly how the thumbscrew might work, pointing out its use in interrogations, where the pressure could be slowly brought to bear upon a victim's thumbs until the blood vessels burst. "Most effective" he chuckled, with a little too much mirth for Clarkson's tastes. "I have never had the occasion to deploy them for my own personal use you understand, but I have no doubt that they would serve the purpose well if you were so disposed."

"And the other, contraption?" asked Clarkson, still none the wiser despite his competence in classical Latin.

"Used by physicians in the treatment of lockjaw" he announced, leaving Clarkson surprised that it was intended for use in the medical profession and not as an outright invention of some sick and twisted torturer. "Though most of my customers have a different purpose in mind. I sell quite a few of these to the Guinea traders in fact."

The Reverend felt his stomach turn at the thought of how it might be used in the slave trade, but now that his suspicions were confirmed he wanted to understand its purpose, before adding it to his collection of evidence to put before Parliament. He would want to be able to demonstrate it to them after all. "For what purpose are they employed?" he asked, truly dreading what the answer might be.

"Well," the merchant began, as if about to impart some delicious secret. "I am well informed by some local fellows in The Trade, that often times these slaves can be very 'sulky' when captured and are quite taken to refusing to eat their daily sustenance, with the intent of ending their existence. As a man of the cloth Sir, I am sure that you would agree that it is the Christian duty of our seafarers to rid them of such intentions and so, this little tool allows the officers to prise open their mouths, so that the food can be piled in - they must then only choose if they are to swallow or to choke."

"My goodness" Thomas Clarkson exclaimed in horror, though the shopkeeper may well have mistaken his reaction for admiration. "And are these, implements, all made locally, in English workshops?"

"They are indeed", said the shopkeeper proudly, "from England's finest toolmakers in the growing factories of Birmingham and what is becoming known as the Black Country, where many an ironmonger works hard at his forge to give form to such intricate designs as this. I am always in awe of their ingenuity, I have to say, and have yet to find a design that is beyond their capabilities."

"That is quite some apparatus, I would never have guessed it. I'll take it."

"Excellent choice Sir."

"And one of each of the handcuffs and the shackles, and the thumbscrew."

The retailer was taken aback. This would be a good afternoon's business and whilst he didn't completely buy the man's story, he had never had much interest in the uses to which the contraptions were put, once they had left his shop. So long as he was paid the asking price for his produce. He asked if he would like to set up an account, but Clarkson explained that he doubted he would ever be back to Liverpool and so he agreed to arrange for a banker's draft to be drawn up. The shopkeeper then agreed to set them aside, asking Clarkson to stop by again in a few days to pick them up.

The Reverend found himself wishing that he could have been there to see the look on the shopkeeper's face, when the cheque was drawn care of *The Society for Effecting the Abolition of the Slave Trade* and had no doubt that it was news that he would not be able to keep to himself. But for now, Clarkson intended to leave him ignorant of his customer's true intentions, and so he bid him good day and left the store, feeling more than a little queasy for the experience.

-◌◌◌-

On his return to the Kings Arms, he was surprised to find Alexander Falconbridge in the midst of a heated exchange with two dubious looking characters, whose very appearance marked them out as slave ship Captains. Each wore a colourfully embroidered tailcoat, waistcoats adorned with gold or silver plated buttons, silk kerchiefs, gold threaded breeches and white stockings made of the finest wool. Even their shoes were flamboyant in their design, each possessing an impractical silver buckle, with inscriptions that were too small to make out at his present distance, but he had no desire to get any closer for a better look.

"Ah, Thomas, good to see you back so soon" his colleague in arms admitted, a little more flushed than usual. "May I introduce former Captain Chaffers and present Captain Lace, most recently commander of The Edgar. Apparently, the good Captain was informed of your presence here by Mr Norris, and so he has called in the hope that he can 'set us right' on our intentions in this city."

"Ah yes, Mr Norris, I have been meaning to make myself known to him," Clarkson admitted frankly. "We have been in correspondence for some weeks now and he had offered to impart some of his former experience with me."

"You don't want to be talking with the likes of 'im" snarled Lace, "he's gone soft. Not set foot on a ship in years. It's us you need to be talking to – I tell you, without our honest business this city would be bust and this country too."

"And what of the Africans?" Clarkson bit back. "Are their lives not worth anything to you?"

"If it wasn't for us they'd be slaves anyway, where they'd be treated even worse" Lace replied. "They's brought to us in chains, and we takes 'em in chains, it's just we takes 'em somewhere that's better for their constitutions. They'd be dead within weeks at the Guinea Coast, those they don't sell gets their heads lopped off anyway, so we's doin' 'em a favour, ain't we?"

Chaffers looked uncomfortable but seemed to know better than to offer an opposing view on the matter, at least not within Captain Lace's earshot. "The Trade does have its problems, Reverend Clarkson," admitted Chaffers, sensing the need to cool things down a little. "We all know that, but then doesn't every industry? I hear of iron foundries and cotton mills not fifty miles from here, where men die daily in the heat and dust, where girls and children are crushed beneath the clattering looms every day of the year, all for the sake of a few yards of thread."

"Not to mention the pits." It was Lace again, jumping on the chance to deflect attention away from his precious profession. "In all directions from here – across the Pennines in Yorkshire, and Wales, right across the Midlands, there's thousands of deep mining pits dug with no account for safety, men being lost underground every day, or killed by fumes. Can't you 'do gooders' worry about their black faces, instead of ones thousands of miles away, that should be no concern of yours?"

The Reverend was riled now, and he had remembered where he'd heard the ship's name before, almost certain that the Captain was the very same man that had been associated with a voyage to Old Calabar in 1767. A fateful engagement that had led to over three hundred dead townspeople, and many others that were taken into slavery as a result, in what had come to be known as the 'Old Town Massacre'. He could not resist sharing the memory with their visitors.

"How long have you been the Captain of The Edgar?" he asked, feigning ignorance.

"Ever since she was first commissioned," the Captain stated proudly. "I'll be almost thirty years her skipper now, I reckon."

"So, you were the commander twenty years ago then" Clarkson said, preparing to fire another accusing volley in the Captain's direction. "When along with the Duke of York and the Indian Queen you tricked the people of the Old Town of Calabar into coming aboard your ships, only to execute their leaders and to send their sons and daughters into slavery in the New World?"

Chaffers was dumbfounded. This was new news even for him.

"How do you know about that?" stormed Lace, with an explosive mixture of embarrassment and fury. "I'll not have you put about such slanderous lies as that. I'll, I'll ..."

"From me," Falconbridge answered. "To my everlasting shame, I have been on several slave ships over the years, and in my four voyages as Doctor of The Tartar, The Alexandria, and The Emilia, I have heard this tale told several times. In fact, I have heard, Captain Lace, that you were a prime combatant in this little fracas?"

"Preposterous" Lace roared, "I'll have your apologies for this, or it will go very bad for the both of you. How dare you. You have no idea, no idea at all. You'd best be leaving town this very day or I will see that you rue the day you came to Liverpool."

"We seem to have struck a nerve there" said Clarkson with a wink to his partner, as the slaving men turned tail to leave, their cover well and truly blown.

"Good day to you gentlemen," said Falconbridge, showing them to the tavern door.

"Come on Captain Lace, I think it's time we left them to their, inquiries" Chaffers said ushering him out, as he took both of their tri-cornered hats from the stand in the corner, firing a determined final look at them across the room. "You don't know what you've done, the word will be out now, you'll get nothing but trouble here, I'd leave immediately if you know what's good for you."

Neither Clarkson nor Falconbridge were willing to oblige him with an answer, but neither had any intention of leaving, in spite of such thinly veiled threats. They had work to do, and they had only just got started.

-○○○-

Extracts from the Journal of Doctor Gardiner, ship's surgeon on board The Brothers

1st November 1787

The middle passage has us in its sway, having left our Portuguese island refuge behind us and we are now at sea again, the ship's daily routine is becoming tiresome even though we are only a few weeks out of Africa. So far the cargo seems healthy and there is no sign of the flux. Each morning at eight, or thereabouts, they are brought up on deck in groups of twenty to thirty and made to dance to the beat of a drum to shake the seizures from their legs after a night of cramped confinement. Then they are chained to the deck again, but in the open air to take advantage of the pleasant weather which so far has been in our favour, though there are some contrary winds which have kept the boatswain gainfully employed. Once the deck is filled with bodies they are hosed down by the crew with sea water, whilst the rota requires a team to go below to clear the gutters of excrement and blood, that has soiled the floors in the night. Several buckets arranged for that purpose are emptied of their slops, those that have not already been upended to add to the filth about their feet. Today Evans vomited after his shift, having found a small child drowned in one of the necessary tubs, and only under threat of flogging did he venture back down to finish his assigned duty. At noon, the slaves were fed their usual servings of pulped horse beans heated on the stove by the cook, but some refused their share — no one noticed this time, but several of the wooden spoons were left unused. The water, though rationed at a ½ pint each, did not go undrunk today. No slave has yet shown a sign of rebellion, though their eyes speak of their hatred and the crew has a heightened sense of it and watch them every second when they are not busy about the ship. The officers are wary of the ever-present threat and so are always tense, keeping a permanent watch from atop the quarter deck. The blunderbuss now mounted on the half deck, ready to blast a hole in any slave that gets loose of their shackles. I have seen the aftermath of the gun before - it is never clean, the man in direct line is always killed instantly - anyone thereabouts caught in the shrapnel from the splintered wood and flying metal will be lucky to survive its blast, leaving me to clear up the mess — in spite of our attentions, most always succumb to the inevitable and their bodies are committed to the deep. So far it has been quiet, and I pray that it remains so, for all our sakes. I saw the boy again, and he saw me too. He may have been watching me first. He seems frail now. His ribs stand out in his sides and his cheekbones are more pronounced than they were. His eyes bulge in their sockets, as he fixes his accusing stare upon me. If I were a tyrant like the others, I would have him punished for his insolence, but he is justified in his look. His thin frame made me consider my own appearance. I know that my waist is narrower now than when we left England. I have no mirror in my cramped cabin and so cannot tell if my face is also showing signs of fatigue, but I suspect I am a shadow of the man that I was. The rats are getting braver now, I have seen three today. I hate rats.

3rd November 1787

I fear that our luck has now run out as a most terrible storm came upon us yesterday, that has rolled the boat about and threatened to break her apart. The slaves have been most afeared as most have n'er been to sea in their lives and fear that evil spirits are now afflicting us, yesterday being the feast day of some Congolese deity. Many are sorely seasick, having been restrained below deck throughout. Their sickness has added to the stench and effluent that now pours about the floors like an internal tide, but the rocking of the ship has made it impossible for anyone to go below to clean up. All of the portholes are closed and bolted to keep out the waves that crash continuously against the timbers. The humidity makes the foul odours thick and nauseating, but on Captain Howlett's orders, I did try in a moment of calm to move amongst them, to ascertain the number of dead and dying. It proved an impossible task, my feet engulfed by salty brown effluent, I fell down twice and had to be removed lest I swallowed any of it. I couldn't make out anything of their foreign clamour, though there is not a need to translate the fear which they all feel and though I could not understand a word, I knew enough to know they were calling out for mercy. I was unable to grant them any, though I sorely wished that I could, but I know that aboard this ship there are few that would be so inclined. The crew have been all-hands upon the weather side of the vessel, working tirelessly to keep the ship facing into the waves as it is buffeted about, lest we are rolled by the squall, and the helmsman is battling every moment to keep The Brothers on its course. The storm trysail and jib are set into the teeth of the tempest and the main sail is reefed, as the exhausted crew do battle with the elements for the sake of their lives and ours.

5ᵗʰ November 1787

The storm has finally blown itself out and though the ship still rolls on every gust or gale - and I can hear each mighty wave crash upon the deck to the sound of much clamouring from below - its power has receded. I have lighted a candle as the darkness is all pervading and I sometimes think that I am landed in purgatory. If I am, then my judgement awaits, and I am not confident of a kindly fate. The girl sleeps silently now, I can hear her soft breathing, but it sounds double, and the sinister sound unnerves me. Like an echo. Or a shadow.

10th November 1787

After several days the winds have now fully abated, and the men are put to work repairing all manner of damage. The Captain was in a foul mood having been locked in his cabin these last few days, his slave has now been passed to the crew who set about abusing her in turn until she begged for mercy. I interceded under the premise of checking about her person for injury, but it was only a small respite, and I was unable to stand before the line of shipmates who continued to take their turn. By evening she was refusing to eat and was curled up on the deck, battered and bruised from her mauling at the hands of our own white savages – they refer to themselves as the 'white slaves', a self-demeaning term that is meant to highlight their plight to the officers, but I prefer my term. I knew that her melancholy would not go well for her if it came to an officers attention and when it did, it was that villain Meadows who ordered her set before the coals to lighten her mood. I protested this treatment most vehemently but was threatened with the same by the Second Mate, who made it clear that she was 'an attention seeking bitch' and 'deserved to be made an example of'. In that moment I prayed that ill-fortune would befall O'Shea before the venture's end. The coals from the ship's furnace were held before her face on a shovel and she was left to rue her refusal when her mouth was forced open to receive her punishment. I could not stand to hear her screams and went below to cower in my cabin where I regarded my supposed concubine with new eyes and vowed to keep her from their clutches, for as long as I was able. I haven't seen the boy since the storm. I pray that he is not harmed or sick. Or washed overboard in the typhoon.

13th November 1787

These last three days over thirty dead and dying slaves have been raised to the deck and thrown to the sharks, their diseased bodies a very real and present danger to the rest of us. The slaves have been shackled in the sunshine during daylight hours, but their imprisonment these last weeks has left many weak and infected with the flux and for some, their bodies are wasting by the day. We started out with many more, but now we are now running closer to two hundred and the profits are now at risk. The Captain grows more quarrelsome by the day and the crew are quick to make themselves scarce whenever he comes into sight, but they often react too late and I have witnessed several floggings for the slightest misdemeanour, which has left all of the crew wary and close to mutiny. The boy is nowhere to be seen. I fear that he is lost.

<u>19th November 1787</u>

There has been no let-up in the climate, so close are we to the equator that the humidity is nigh on unbearable, even for those of us who can walk upon the deck at nights to take in the air. I walked there this night, under the light of the stars. I thought I saw the boy, darting between the masts and stairs, but I was mistaken, and it was just the shadows dancing in the light of the lanthorn. During the daytime, with the wind at our backs and in the sails, the ship has been running dead down wind and has made steady progress towards our ultimate ambition – I look forward to that day, for at least then we will be released from our entombment and some relief can be given to the slaves for their ailments. But at night the Captain has forbade any such luxury for fear of rebellion under the cover of darkness when all slaves must be secured in their bays below and so their nocturnal tortures are unrelenting. There has been some relief from the feverish illness that has struck down so many, but I know that it can return without warning and so every morning when I go below, I do so in fear of a fresh quota of dead bodies that call upon me to declare their loss. Today, but three went to a watery grave, and I pray that we will soon be done with the middle passage, when this torment will be at an end, though another will then begin. The boy is most certainly gone, he is nowhere to be found. I have reported him missing, presumed washed overboard in the tempest.

<u>23rd November 1787</u>

The rains have returned though the swell has lessened, and the winds are less fierce and now blow in our favour, so our stocks of water have been replenished and everyone has drunk their fill. They would no doubt prefer a draught of the strong spruce beer that they brewed at the coast for this leg of the journey, but that has long since run out. Another tortured black female jumped to her death today, leaping from the side of the ship to slip unseen into the depths below, from whence she did not surface. The Captain was much aggrieved at her loss, not for any other thought than that by her actions he was thirty pounds poorer. He had the mate, who had been assigned a watch over the women today, severely flogged - he was dealt with by Meadows with whom he has had many quarrels of late. Meadows seemed to enjoy every moment. The white flesh of his victim's back, buttocks and thighs was torn asunder, deep gouges of flesh that no amount of ointment could heal, only time and much of it could hope to heal his afflictions. Another five dead slaves were today taken up and sent to their graves. It is a most distressing sight, not least because for every dead slave a second is brought to the surface in tow, only to be released from his dead compatriot on the deck and from thence returned shackled anew. I will not go up to the deck alone at night anymore, I have been most disturbed of late, and fancy that I can see a small figure standing behind the shrouds, a whispering voice that beckons me from behind the timbers.

It is only my imagination, or my guilt, I think.

<u>28th November 1787</u>

If the Captain's calculations are to be believed we will soon be in sight of the Leeward Isles and then to the beautiful St. Thomas, the first two 'friendly' islands in the archipelago where the British slavers may make landfall. It may not be our *final landing place but provides an opportunity to bring the cargo and the crew ashore, to feed and water them with fresh produce and so reinvigorate their looks, before taking them to market. The crew were disappointed that no such sightings were made before dark, as was I, but my fear is not the same as theirs. I could feel eyes burning into me as I tried to sleep in the pitch blackness of my quarters tonight, the girl no doubt awake and watching me, but then I heard her breathing and she sounded to be in the deepest of sleeps. Yet I knew that I was being watched until the very first light crept over the eastern horizon, and I heard the bosun holler, "land ho!"*

1st December 1787

After a brief landing at the Portuguese island of St Thomas, we put to sea again, but in full and frank knowledge that we would soon be laying anchor again, the officers had all-hands busy to prepare the cargo for an immediate sale. The slaves had been roused at the sight of land after so long at sea - they may have been so elated in belief that their ordeal was almost at an end – even if I could have spoken their languages, I would not have had the heart to tell them that the cruelty on board was to be nothing as compared to the short and squalid lives that lay ahead of them. The slaves were brought up in the usual groups, and secured in their chains to the deck, their eyes fixed on the small and seemingly deserted wooded islands that had sprung up all around. Great care was taken to shine their torsos, arms, and legs by generous application of palm oil and bees wax, whilst the weak and sickening amongst them were marked out to be retained 'til last or mixed amongst other pre-determined 'parcels' for sale as a job-lot. It was late afternoon before we had circumnavigated the Captain's island of choice and weighed anchor off the port. The light was fading, and the Captain had decided to put off any sale 'til morning, but he and his First Mate went ashore to spread the word amongst the taverns that a fresh and healthy cargo had just arrived from the Guinea Coast. The harvest season was not yet upon them and so our timing was optimal, and the Captain was well aware that he would now be able to drive a high price for the best of his catch. The girl has now left my cabin to retake her place in the line – she regarded me strangely as she left, as if confused as to my purpose, and she looked about her as if waiting for another to walk beside her to the deck. I wondered what would happen to her and felt ashamed that I had been part of her ruin – I felt no pride at my intervention, only remorse that it had been but a short-lived reprieve, and I was powerless to intervene in her favour. As I lay in my hammock last night, the lanterns that lighted up the quayside left their mark upon my timbers in a black and grey dance, and I thought that I could still hear her shallow breathing. I told myself that it was just the swing of the ship at anchor, the gentle waves lapping around its bow and did my best to ignore the sound that seemed to accompany every creak, as the boat listed and righted itself in the wash of a nearby frigate. I prayed for some small comfort, but there was none. I looked to thoughts of home, but this dreadful reality has put up its own unyielding barricado in my head and I cannot bring such memories to mind. Instead, my visions are all of this and other sailings and I find that I can no longer distinguish one from another. Long-dead features fill my mind's eye; a thousand dreadful mutilations that creep ever closer, until my cabin is crammed with their frigid flesh, and I cry out in the darkness, fearing for the moment when the lights are lit once more. For then I will be forced to face my fears alone, with nowhere to hide.

CHAPTER ELEVEN

"The time they work in the West Indies, is from daybreak to noon, and from two o'clock till dark, during which time they are attended by overseers, who, if they think them dilatory, or think anything not so well done as it should be, whip them most unmercifully, so that you may see their bodies long after wheeled and scarred usually from the shoulders to the waist."

John Wesley, Thoughts on Slavery

In the weeks following the revelations of that first day, the port city of Liverpool became a tinder box, ready to strike into flame at any moment. There was outrage amongst the mercantile classes that an uninvited outsider could have the sheer gall to stride into their city, intent on tearing at the very foundation of its economic miracle. Bristol's reaction had been amicable by comparison, but on the streets of Liverpool, the people's blood was high, and Clarkson and Falconbridge resolved to go nowhere without the other.

There was a steady stream of visitors at the Kings Arms, as news spread far and wide, but the mood had changed now and although the landlord was happy at his increased custom, he was forced to endure his town's bile for letting these 'ship wreckers' lay anchor under his roof. Slave-merchants and their Captains were the most regular amongst his new clientele and the most vociferous, but even those whose families had only a peripheral interest in The Trade were just as likely to put in an appearance, some of whom on hearing the other side of the story, were persuaded to take away abolitionist literature for distribution amongst their friends and associates. Such 'vile propaganda', as the slavers called it, would only serve to fan the flames of their anger, and it wasn't long before it all came to a head.

"To the success of The Trade" a Captain cried out, saluting their adversaries from the opposite side of the busy public bar, which despite its growing popularity as the local pub-of-choice, still allowed thrice the room for manoeuvre that was ever afforded to any slave on Liverpool's vast armada of Guinea-bound ships. Several others raised their glasses in solidarity and a group of six or seven stared the pair of Abolitionists down, almost willing them to raise theirs in reply, or to raise their voices in defiance. The Kings Arms had become a debating hall, with just one topic up for discussion, but it was never Falconbridge or Clarkson that would choose to lay the topic on the table.

"Where do you hail from 'red'" one salty old seadog called out one evening, knowing full well what the Reverend's name was, but choosing instead to single him out based on the colour of his hair. "I doubt that you've even seen the coast of Africa?"

"I have not" Clarkson replied, much to the former Captain's delight, "but I sup with a Doctor who has journeyed to the Guinea Coast many a time and who knows of every evil deed that has ever been done along that subjugated stretch of land."

It was true, Falconbridge's presence had been a blessing and without his quick and ready evidence, Clarkson may well have been sent packing from those lodgings a defeated man. For every challenge, the Doctor had an answer, for every lie, he had the proof of it, and he used it to great effect, whenever they were called upon to defend themselves and their actions. It was usual for these long and drawn-out conversations to descend into a tirade of insults and threats before the night was through, and each night the menace seemed to grow more alarming.

"You'll be leaving us soon Reverend won't you?" and on no reply being received, "if not you'll be sent back to your posh southern school in a long wooden box."

"Don't say you weren't warned" and then a pause for breath. "What we used to do to the Quakers in these parts will be done to you before long."

"It'll be your funeral next Padre."

"You'll leave if you know what's good for you."

"You'll have no need of a Doctor, by the time we've done with thee."

"Mind what yous doing around our city la', wouldn't want yous to have an accident."

Mr Dale was adamant that whilst he didn't want the two of them to leave, he had heard things and been told things that made him think that they should go, and not just from his establishment. "It's no good just finding new lodgings Reverend," he advised, "they'll track you down, they'll follow you home and if you're there alone, I dread to think what might happen."

The Reverend started to say that he wasn't going to be scared off by such hollow threats, but it was Falconbridge who interceded on his behalf. "It's not about whether or not you can defend yourself Thomas. It's that they will find a way to ambush us and if we are alone, then there will be no willing witnesses, not in this town. And don't forget, it wouldn't be the first time that witnesses have disappeared or that the guilty have left port on the very next ship and the very next tide."

Clarkson was disappointed to be forced into an early departure, but under duress he knew that he must resign himself to an early departure. "I already have more than I expected to get from this place" he reasoned, "so we should probably head back at the end of the week.

I will take my horse, as I want to stop in Manchester, so Alexander, you best go back to London on this Friday's stagecoach."

"Don't you think you should take a rest Thomas?" It was Falconbridge and his expression was the concerned look that his profession have made their own. "You have been on the go now for months, you've been all over the country and, if you don't mind me saying so, you look like it."

"Well thank you my friend" the Reverend smiled, choosing to see the complement behind the obvious concern. "Though it's good advice, and I will heed it, but after I have been to see the local Society in Manchester and not before I have attended to one more piece of business, that I swore I would get to the bottom of whilst in this city."

"Which business is that?"

"Do you remember being told of the death of Peter Green?" Clarkson asked, "by the crew of The Alfred, that very wet night on Marsh Street?"

"They were all very wet nights, if I recall the West Country well enough" smiled the Doctor, "but yes, I do remember talk of it, but not too much of the detail, I think I may have been quite far along the wrong side of the yard arm by that point."

"Well, it was after one in the morning" Clarkson grinned, unsurprised at his companion's lapse in memory. "We were told that he was on a Liverpool ship called The Emerald, I believe. He was beaten most brutally by the Captain, after an altercation with a black woman, which was not his doing by all accounts, but on Captain's orders, the mates had punished him with the cat o' nine tails for two and a half hours, until the whip was so frayed it was unusable. He had then been lowered in chains to spend the night in shackles on a small dinghy and left at the mercy of the elements, and when they pulled him up in the morning, he was dead. He was buried at Bonny Point without ceremony."

"Yes I do remember now," said Alexander. "I also remember being told that the hard knots of rope had struck his head with such force, that not only was his body pock marked by its impact, but his skull was also fractured with it. I was told on a separate occasion, that when Green was found in the light of day, they saw that his brains had seeped out upon the deck, much to the delight of the Captain's Jack Russell, whose bloodied snout was said to be a gruesome sight to behold."

"Yes, that's exactly what they said in Bristol" remarked Clarkson sadly. "It was all done by the light of the moon, with just a candle to mark the time. The Captain had come back intoxicated from shore leave with the rest of the officers in tow, and was angered by the money he had lost in some gaming den or other. What was the Captain's name again?"

"I don't know, it was never known amongst the Bristol crews," Falconbridge said, "but I'm sure we'd find out more if we asked around up here."

"My thoughts precisely" said Clarkson, still in combative mood. "If we can take two cases of cruelty before the courts, then the obvious defence, that the William Lines case is just a one-off, will be carry far less weight."

So, they were agreed that, in this their final week, they would each do all they could to unravel the murder mystery of The Emerald, starting with Clarkson's return to the Custom House at the Old Quay the very next day, and its goldmine of muster rolls. For once Thomas Clarkson slept like a baby. His plans were coming together nicely.

-oΟο-

Extracts from the Journal of Doctor Gardiner, ship's surgeon on board The Brothers

7ᵗʰ December 1787

No matter how long I live, I will never put the cattle markets of these islands from my mind. Today we sold at least half of our cargo and I fear that half of them again may yet be dead by winter. As always, the strongest and fittest were taken first, but the manner of their sale is the final atrocity that I will see of this unscrupulous trade. The Captain and officers went ashore early and had secured a place not far from the quayside where the 'scramble' would take place. Never was a system more aptly named – the first line of fifty or so slaves were led, now in singular chains, through the streets up to the marketplace, where a bustling crowd of menacing overseers and their rough plantation masters were gathered. The Captain had already set the price at £60 per head and he'd told me days ago, that he was of a mind not to budge from his valuation in that first batch. He told the gathered masses that he was not open to bartering and so, if they made a claim to expect to pay the asking price in full and that no credit would be given, even at the most profitable of rates. The line of terrified men were led to a side door, with the whips cracking around them to deter any from bolting and once inside, the bar was lifted, and the doors flung open to allow the slavering mob entry. They burst through like brutes, pushing, and shoving, barging, and yelling and with ropes at the ready, drew circles around the men that had caught their eye in the parade outside. Once they had their 'catch' encircled, the chains were loosened and re-fixed in these small groups, so that each purchaser had now laid claim to their own preferred troop – they were then permitted fifteen minutes to look them over, checking their teeth, their eyes, their mouths, and every other orifice for signs of illness or disease and then they were told they must decide, yea or nay, one by one. Any rejects were brought back to the centre for others to inspect and make a counter bid, as the whites of the poor men's eyes grew wider and wilder, in growing realisation of what was happening to them. The Captain knew only too well, that this was just this season's crop, a replacement for the one-third or more that had since died in 'seasoning' or been murdered at the hands of merciless overseers, into whose charge the new cohort were now being sold. Then the next fifty were made to stand 'at market' and the show was put on for a second time, the price set again, this time at £50 per head, and this time there were even more rejects, some of whom didn't look fit for sale at any price as they seemed unlikely to last the month under an oppressive sun and venomous whip-hand. Finally, the women were ushered out, their naked bodies glistening from the palm oil that the crew had attentively spread upon their ebony skin. I watched in horror as the owners and their overseers licked their lips, their faces betraying their true intentions and with just one thing on their minds, they regarded their 'soon to be' property as less than whores, and I cast down my eyes as I saw mine in the middle of the line. Our eyes met for a moment and although she hails from a foreign land, I knew the meaning behind them, and I bow my head in shame for my willing compliance in this wicked business. This time when the men were freed to make their choices, the inspections were even more invasive, their hands pawing at their naked bodies in salivating packs, like dogs about a carcass. Purchases were now made in a rush, their stained trousers straining about their manhood, and after making their commitments to meet the asking price of £30 per head, they were quick to drag their newly acquired property onto the backs of their carts, or behind the sides of buildings, to mark them as their own. I am ashamed to the core, and I will have no redemption for it, for I have played my part to the full. And later, I succumb to take the £20 in lieu that the Captain gifts to me and sign my mark upon his ledger, though I will not see the value until the venture is done with, and the Agent settles all credits and debts. But my work wasn't done there; the pitiful remnants of our cargo remained, and I am ordered back to the ship to attend to their appearances and to suggest a fair price for these dreadful wretches. Those that are still afflicted by the flux, I am ordered to 'bung up' using tightly wound strings of old rope rolled up into the size of high calibre musket balls, which I have to force into their anuses to fool potential buyers into believing them to be in 'good condition', only for long enough to make a sale. The low price is proof enough that they ail from something more than exhaustion, and some would-be purchasers are already wise to this trick, checking themselves for blockages before parting with their monies. In the case of our final twelve slaves their price was as low as £6 per head, amongst them some of the oldest and youngest examples, who are unlikely to survive for long in this intemperate climate. The second boy, now unchained from his lost kin, is amongst their number. I do not notice his sale price, for by then I am gone from that place in shame, an imposter for the man I thought I was.

14th December 1787

Unburdened now from all other duties, the crew are put to work on the ship, making her ready to sail again. The Captain and his officers are ashore and return each night intoxicated and irksome, so the crew make themselves scarce for fear of further abuse at their hands. Some ship's surgeons fall in with these bands of ruffians, but I will not sink to their level, a fact that Captain Howlett is well aware of. He already suspects me of being a spy upon his ship and he seeks to keep me separated from his men, lest I infect them with my 'mutinous character'. This night I was on deck as they returned and I did not make myself scarce, instead I watched them aboard and bid them 'good evening', to which most gave a polite reply. The Captain scowled at me and asked me 'what my game was?' threatening to maroon me there without provisions. I heeded his threats, but gave no ground, and he soon grew tired of our little fracas, which in his stupor I fully expect him to have forgotten by morning. I will have to watch my back in case he cares for one less pocket to fill on our return. It would not be the first time that the Captain of a slave vessel had thought to reduce his losses in such a dastardly manner. He seemed disturbed as he slipped below deck, and called out wildly as he entered his quarters, as if to ward off some sprite, though his words were slurred, and I couldn't make them out. I saw a small shadow dart across his path as his lantern swung in his hand, though it could've been cast by the lamp itself, but it didn't seem to move in time and he re-emerged a few moments later, a troubled look upon his disagreeable face, before turning angrily to slam the door to his cabin behind him.

25th December 1787

Christmas Day, but there are no festivities. The speed of our return now hangs on The Trade Winds. We will embark for home tomorrow and although three of the crew have now 'disappeared' according to Meadows, presumed deserted for which their pay will be made forfeit, a heavy-set man with piercing blue eyes has joined our number, in need of a way back home and so has boarded for 'the run' as it is known amongst the slavers. It soon became apparent that he is of a vocal disposition, and I quickly took a shine to him, as he began to recite some bawdy ballads, to remind us of better times. I could hear his singing from within my cabin as I blew out my candle and saw the whites of someone else's eyes just inches from my own. In my panic, I fell from my hammock with such a clatter, that I heard another man shout out in alarm. I could still hear the same quiet breathing about me, that I had been hearing most nights and which on other nights I had put down to my neighbour, whose snoring could often be heard around the deck. A few fumbling seconds later it stopped, the moment that my fingers settled on the fire-starter, which I struck hard to spark my extinguished flame back into life.

My room was empty save for me, and as I write this record down in the cold light of day, I am less fearful of what I think I saw, but I remain unnerved. Did I dream it? Perhaps, though I fear for the nights that are to come. I am certain; yes, I must be certain, for anything else would be absurd for a man of science, that it is my guilt that prods so harshly at my heart, worse than the pangs of unrequited love for it is the same organ that weighs so heavily within me.

For the first time in many days at sea, I prayed hard this night for someone other than myself – I took to my Bible for an answer and squinted at the scriptures until the light of the candle had almost burnt to the wick, yet I found no comfort in the prophets.

Not for me, not for them.

For none of us.

CHAPTER TWELVE

"One would have thought, considering the great enthusiasm of the nation on this important subject, that they, who could have given satisfactory information upon it, would have rejoiced to do it. But I found otherwise, and this frequently to my sorrow."

The Reverend Thomas Clarkson, The History of The Abolition of the African Slave Trade

The advertisement in the Liverpool newspaper *Gore's General Advertiser* was placed by Alexander Falconbridge, with the sole intention of flushing out witnesses from amongst the taverns and back streets of the port. He and Clarkson knew the Captain to have been the guilty party, they knew who his accomplices were, and they knew the cause and place of death, but they needed eyewitnesses. Ones who were willing to testify in the highest court in the land and to secure just one credible and willing crew member, they needed as many as possible to crawl from the ship's woodwork.

> HEINOUS MURDER AT BONNY RIVER, GUINEA COAST,
> AFRICA
> PETER GREEN CRUELLY AND UNLAWFULLY KILLED
> 19th September 1786
> ALL INFORMATION C/O REV. T.CLARKSON, KINGS ARMS
> HOTEL, LIVERPOOL

"Do you really want to do this?" Falconbridge had asked him nervously.

"We have to," Clarkson said, certain in the moment that the tactic was the right one. "It's the only way to bring these devils to justice."

"But with the ship in port, won't they just put to sea again."

"They might" Clarkson agreed, "but not if we can get our witnesses to come forward first."

Thomas Clarkson had been back amongst the muster rolls that morning, and so he now knew the names of every crew member on that fateful day, including whether or not they had returned to Liverpool alive. Though he had not been able to write everything down under the watchful eye of the clerk, he now knew the Captain's name. He had also been horrified to learn that sixteen of the crew had died in transit and he couldn't help but wonder whether some of them had also been killed for what they might have seen, or heard, that night. He needed more than hearsay and conjecture if he was to wield the sword of justice and bring the plight of slave ship crews to the attention of the nation, and in so doing, call out the evils of the slave trade in all its gruesome depravity.

"We need to get on board the ship today, before this is seen" Clarkson urged. "It's been in dock since early June, so it'll be due out again soon."

"That might be a dangerous undertaking Thomas" his friend warned him, "but I'm game if you are. As long as we go there armed."

"It's the only way and our only opportunity" said the Reverend, "who knows, there may be some sailors on board who are ready and willing to help us."

"Or to push you overboard after hitting you around the head" said Falconbridge, who always had a way of looking on the gloomier side of life and this occasion was to be no exception. "It's a risky proposition Thomas, but if you are sure, then let's do it. There's no time like the present."

Without further ado, the two of them made ready and set out on the short walk to the docks, an easy find by virtue of the many masts that kept a constantly changing vigil over the waterfront. When they arrived on the Goree Causeway, named after an island off the coast of Senegal where the Liverpool slavers first made inroads into the African trade, the quayside of George's Dock was packed three deep with slaving vessels. A line of new warehouses was under construction to their rear, and even more were breaking ground further along the piazza towards the riverside fort, another sure sign of the city's trading prowess. The fortifications, that had sprung up to defend the estuary in the civil war years, marked the city's edge and behind it, a smattering of windmills were strewn across the surrounding fields, their sails steadily circling on the breeze that blew in off the Irish Sea. As Clarkson's red hair flapped about in the wind, he stepped up to the first snow and its familiar two and a half masts, their booms stretched out like the arms of the guilty, just waiting to be searched for stolen booty.

As bold as brass, and much to the Doctor's surprise, Clarkson wasted no time in boarding the first vessel in line, as if it was his own vessel. It was possible, even from the quayside to make out two persons busying themselves aboard the ship for its impending departure, so busy that they somehow did not see the six-foot frame of the Reverend Thomas Clarkson as he strode up the ramp. Again, there was no doubting the ship's purpose, and he noted several barrels crammed full of irons and shackles that stood above the horizontal grills, each fixed in place like a lopsided portcullis waiting to be hauled into place above a castle drawbridge, and through which he was able to peer into the murky underworld below.

A light of recognition then sparked in the faces of the crewmen, as they caught sight of the red-haired Reverend, each a little unnerved to have a man of the cloth aboard their vessel, especially a man about whom they had been warned to have no dealings, on pain of a flogging.

"A slaving vessel?" Clarkson asked, getting straight to the point.

"Aye" the stocky one replied reluctantly, not looking up from his labours.

Their inquisitor nodded before probing further. "How many slaves did she carry on her last voyage?"

"I couldn't rightly say" the same man said, eyes averted, back turned.

"What about you?" asked Clarkson directing his attention towards the other unremarkable shipmate, "did you sail out to the Guinea Coast on her last summer?"

"What's it to you?" An Irish drawl, shifty, sullen. "But yes, I went aboard her last time out."

"I hear that some of the crew didn't return, is that right?"

That particular question really gave them the jitters and they looked at each other in a moment of panic, as neither knew quite what to say or do. There was something about a man in a dog collar that made a fellow want to confess, and it was certainly proving true on this occasion.

"I couldn't say, no more than usual, I would reckon," the taller one admitted after a momentary pause to gather his somewhat limited wits.

"So that would be at least one third of the crew then?" Clarkson went on, putting his research to the test. There was no reply either way. "And what about a steward called Green, and please don't say 'who'. I know for certain that he went out on this ship, and he was one of those that didn't come back."

"He's buried at Bonny point," the youth said, unable to stay silent, but his words were trailing off before he finished his sentence. "He died there."

"Yes so I believe," answered Clarkson. "What was the cause of death?"

"Not, not… not sure," he stammered, realising too late, under the fixed stare of his stout companion, that he was talking much more than he should have been. "Mostly was the flux that killed 'em, so I suspect it was that."

"Had he been ill-used by his Captain?"

It was a question that sent the shorter one scuttling for cover and his taller shipmate looking for the quickest route to shore. "No more than any of us," was the best he could manage. "It's never easy on these slavers mister, now we have to get on with our work, or there'll be hell to pay."

Their guard was up now, but the two investigators had already achieved their goal. Their strategy had been to panic their adversaries into acting rashly and into saying more than was good for them, but there was now a growing risk of violence, and although any assault would find favour with the Abolitionists in a court of law, it was a chance that neither of them wanted to take.

"Looks like that ship will be out of sight before the month is out," said Falconbridge as they made their way back to the inn.

"Indeed, it will," said Clarkson, "but they'll spread the word, you can count on it, and when the officers read of our intentions in tomorrow's press, the rats will start deserting that ship, long before it sails."

The very next morning, just before the midday chimes sounded in the hallway of the Kings Arms, in walked a contrite George Ormond, right on cue. At first sight he looked like a down on his luck street hawker; he was dreadfully scruffy, clearly malnourished and his matted nest of fair hair had not seen a comb in a very long time.

Mr Dale was about to eject him back out into the street with the other beggars, having misjudged his intentions, just as the vagrant spluttered out that he was there "about the murder."

"The murder?" asked Dale, "what murder, what are you talking about?"

"Sorry landlord" Clarkson interceded, "I did not find an opportune moment to brief you last evening. I was early to my bed for once, and then at breakfast I clean forgot." He filled Mr Dale in with an abridged version of events and led the bedraggled boy into the side room and out of harm's way. "Could you bring us some sweet tea please Mr Dale? I think we could all do with a cup. Now my fine fellow, what can we do for you?"

"My name is George Ormond, once of The Emerald and I saw the whole thing with my own eyes" he confessed in a garbled blast of local dialect.

Clarkson and Falconbridge looked at each other in a brief moment of triumph, before regaining their poise and formally introducing themselves to their soon-to-be witness. "Take your time now Mr Ormond, we have all day. Just recount the events in your own words and Doctor Falconbridge here will transcribe. There is no need to be afraid, you will have the full protection of our Society in London."

"Will I have to stand before a Liverpool magistrate?" the fidgeting boy asked, seemingly ready to turn tail and run if the answer was not to his liking.

"Not at all," Clarkson reassured him. "If you did indeed witness the whole thing and are prepared to say so in court, then I will personally guarantee your safe passage to London, where you will be taken good care of until the case comes before the bench."

"And what about afterwards? What happens to me then? They've already put it about town that any squealers will be 'buried at sea', so we know what that means."

"If you can help us to bring these officers to heel, then we will find you gainful employment in London," Falconbridge promised. "We have a wide network of God-fearing businessmen who are able to provide an honest job for those who are willing and able to testify. You'll be able to start again. A new name and a new life, away from all of this."

"You mean it?" the boy asked, unsure if he should be elated or terrified at the prospect.

"As God is my witness" the Reverend answered.

The boy gulped half of the hot tea and quickly scoffed down two of the freshly baked Eccles cakes, in case either of his interviewers had designs upon them, before summoning up sufficient courage to recount the events of September 1786 on board The Emerald, moored in seven or eight fathoms of water in the Bonny River. Once he started, he couldn't stop.

"Peter Green was steward on board our ship, he was decent enough, but was wary of the Captain as he'd already had a few run-ins with him. A black woman named Rodney belonged to the ship's owners and had been sent on board as an interpreter for the purchase of the slaves, you know, for when we got to the coast. About five in the evening, the Captain went on shore and with him out of the way, the woman asked Green for the keys to the pantry, which he rightly refused to give her - the Captain had already beaten him for giving them to her once before, when she'd downed a full flagon of wine in ten minutes. The woman hit him, and they had fought a bit, though Green backed off, knowing he'd likely get in trouble for it. Between eight and nine the Captain come back on board with the Captain of The Alfred. Rodney told him that Green had assaulted her, which we all knew was not true and said so, but he didn't want to hear it. The Captain then beat him severely - he ordered his hands to be made fast to some bolts on the starboard side under the half deck, and then flogged him, using the lashes of the cat upon his back and the double walled knot upon his head, only stopping to rest now and again and using each hand in turn, that he might strike him harder each time. The pain had got so severe that Green cried out and begged the Captain of The Alfred to intercede, but the scoundrel said that he would have served him in the same manner. He then called upon the Chief Mate, but this only made matters worse, as the Captain ordered the mate to flog him, which he did for some time. Green then called in his distress upon the second mate, but the second mate was immediately ordered to perform the same cruel offence and was made to persevere in it until the lashes were all worn into threads. But it did not stop there, and the Captain ordered another cat, with which he flogged him as before, beating him over the head with the double walled knot repeatedly, changing his hands and cursing his own left hand for not being able to strike so severe a blow as his right. The punishment as inflicted by all parties had now lasted two and a half hours, as one candle had been extinguished and another was a quarter gone, when I was ordered to cut down one of the arms and the boatswain the other. This being done, Green fell motionless on the deck. He tried to say something which I understood to be a plea for water, but the Captain refused it, saying that he was not yet done with him and ordered him to be confined with his arms across, his right hand to his left foot and his left hand to his right foot. For this purpose, the carpenter brought shackles and I was compelled to put them on him. The Captain then ordered some tackle to be made fast to his limbs and he was hoisted up, and afterwards let down into a boat. Michael Cunningham, the boatswain, was then sent to loosen the tackle and we were all ordered to leave him there for the night. In the middle watch, between one and two the next morning, I looked out of one of the portholes and called to him but received no answer. Between two and three, Paul Berry was sent down into the boat and he reported Green dead. He made his report to one of the officers and at about five in the morning, the body was brought up and laid near the half-deck door. The Captain on seeing the body when he rose, expressed no concern, but ordered it to be knocked out of irons and to be buried at the usual place of interment for seamen on Bonny Point."

As the boy finished recounting the horrors of that night, Clarkson blew out his cheeks in horror and called for more tea, his mouth dry and his heart heavy. He had no doubt as to the accuracy of Ormond's testimony, but he knew that if it was to stand up to the scrutiny of the Bench, it needed to be corroborated. Although Falconbridge had heard a similar account from the very mouth of the Captain of The Alfred, who had stood witness to the whole thing, securing substantiating proof from another willing witness would be a not insignificant achievement.

"That is indeed a terrible tale," the Reverend replied having recovered some of his composure, "but are there others who will give the same evidence? You mention some who were there; Cunningham and Berry for instance, do you know of their whereabouts and if they would be willing to step forward to help us bring this evil rogue to justice?"

"Cunningham and Berry are already out to sea," the crestfallen witness said sombrely. "And the boatswain has already been promised an officer's post aboard The Emerald when she sets sail in a few days. I have told him that they wants him out of the way and that he should watch his back at nights when he's alone at sea, because they know what he saw, and they might take the chance to quieten him for good."

"Did he take you seriously?" Clarkson asked, "I'd be in fear of my life if it were me."

"I don't think so," said the boy. "They have made him a promise of untold riches that he'd need to make three or more voyages to get his hands on, and he is so far in debt from drinking and gambling in the taverns of Dale Street. He thinks he can handle himself and so says it's a risk worth taking."

"Will he confirm your story?" asked the Doctor, "if we ask him outright?"

"Not if he knows who you are, no" Ormond answered. "Though he has been known to tell the tale in all its gory details when he wants to impress an audience. I've heard him tell it in The Hole in the Wall, which is his favourite haunt, but only when he's well-oiled and in cahoots with his cronies."

"Would he discuss it openly with you do you think?" the Reverend asked, the seed of an idea sprouting in his head, as he glanced across at Falconbridge to see if he was of the same mind. A smile from the Doctor suggested that he understood perfectly.

"Yes, we've talked of it a few times these last weeks."

"I know of a drinking house which would be perfect for such a plot as that," announced Falconbridge. "It has a small side room with a serving hatch cut out of the wall. A man who was sat beside the hatch in the smaller room, could easily hear the conversation on the other side without fear of detection."

"Could we set this up tonight?" asked Clarkson, "we will pay for a hearty meal and as many rounds as you can manage, to loosen his tongue. Will you seek him out, maybe offer to pay for his fayre, as a farewell gesture between old shipmates? Tell him you are going to London to seek out new fortunes, so as to talk it up a little, to entice him along?"

"Well, he was never one to turn down free ale" Ormond recalled, "but what of me, what if he tells the Captain that I've been asking after this murder? My name will go to the top of his hit list, and I don't want to fall foul of his temper."

"Tomorrow morning you will leave for London with Doctor Falconbridge" Clarkson proclaimed. "The Doctor is leaving in any case, so you can join him in the carriage, and we will see you safely lodged in London until the trial. No one but us will know your whereabouts and you can go by a different name until your evidence comes before the bench, even amongst our circles, to ensure your safety."

"But first, we must be completely certain of your credibility" and with that, Clarkson laid out his freshly laid plan for the evening, as the Doctor and their soon to be star witness hung on his every word. It would need to go like clockwork if it was to work at all. Nothing would be left to chance.

-○○○-

The tavern was tiny, being situated in the back streets of the port and hidden away behind a rickety row of other timber framed warehouse buildings. Thomas Clarkson had been sat hunched in his agreed spot for almost an hour already, arriving before the bar had got busy with the evening rush and seated just to the left of the hatch through which ales and spirits would be posted on busier days. He found himself wishing that Falconbridge had not shared what he knew about the room; that it was often used as a makeshift morgue in the winter, when the bloated bodies of storm victims, which had been washed up on the tide, were laid out for identification by their nearest and dearest. He couldn't decide if the fishy stench was real or just a figment of his overactive imagination, as he sat crouched amongst the barrels and crates that littered the flagstone floor. Whatever the source of the smell, he steeled himself to keep only one eye on the hatch. The other would be firmly fixed on the gloomy space to his rear, just in case a grey and wrinkled hand of a long dead sailor should fall upon his shoulder before the night was through.

On the other side, the Doctor positioned himself at the bar, so that he would be just out of sight but still within earshot and in case of trouble, he had come well prepared. Beneath his long coat, his trusted pistol was tucked away along with a long-bladed knife, whose ivory handle jutted out a few inches from the top of his leather boot. Neither item was exactly inconspicuous, but so armed he would be less easily overpowered and a glimpse of either could be enough to dissuade a potential assailant from making a move.

To the innkeepers of Liverpool, Falconbridge looked like just another punter, unremarkable in every aspect, but Clarkson was an altogether different proposition. His instantly recognisable form marked him out for celebrity wherever he went, and so he was best kept out of sight, lest their adversaries be alerted to his presence in this most inhospitable of public places. Time passed by slowly as they each waited patiently and alone, so much so that Doctor Falconbridge was on his third tankard of local ale, when the tavern doors finally burst inwards to the tuneless sound of some bawdy song.

It was clear to the Doctor that their financial contribution to the evening's activities was being well spent. He hoped that George Ormond was simply putting on a show, as he led his worse-for-wear pal to his appointed seat and tottered back to the bar for a fresh round. It seemed that they'd either already eaten or were intent on having a liquid dinner, for no food was ordered and as Falconbridge dipped his hat to avoid detection, Ormond staggered past, spilling the heads off their ale as he tripped and almost fell.

"Here you go mate" he heard him cry, slamming down the short-measured tankard on the small round table.

"You mean, 'here you go - second - mate'?" the former boatswain slurred, and the two of them fell about laughing, smashing their pewter vessels together, squealing like a pair of alley cats.

To the Doctor's relief, their words were still intelligible, but he wasn't sure for how much longer, and he prayed that they would soon get to the point. He and Clarkson had primed George with what to say, should he encounter any difficulties in getting his old shipmate to remember out loud, but in that moment he was severely doubting whether the boy would be able to recall any of their advice. He was sailing solo, and they could only hope that he would be sober enough to stay afloat.

Just when the two eavesdroppers had almost given the evening up, the boy recovered enough of his senses to turn the conversation back to the murder of Peter Green. Maybe it had been his plan all along, to get his target's tongue loosened to the full extent possible, and if it was, then it worked to perfection.

"Do you remember that steward, Green?" asked Ormond, teeing him up.

"How could I forget" the sailor sniffed, "still keeps me awake at night that does, I can tell you. Glad it was 'im and not me though, awful business."

"What was the Captain so angry about, do you know?" asked George. "I've seen him riled up before, plenty of times, but he was right off his head that night."

"Dunno" his former shipmate shrugged. "I heard that he didn't like Green much, there'd been some argument over monies owed or somethin', and the Captain had to pay him out. That's what I heard anyways."

"No reason to kill him though, was it?" said George, bringing to mind one of Reverend Clarkson's planted questions.

The newly appointed officer shrugged his shoulders again, but didn't speak up, much to their eavesdropper's annoyance. Almost, he thought, but to his credit the young man did not give up on his task and pressed on in the same vein.

"It was really gruesome though wasn't it?" Ormond prodded. "I didn't get to see the body up close but wasn't you one of the ones that took him to Bonny Point to be buried?"

"Yeh," his drinking partner mumbled, taking another swig of strong local porter from his jug. "Yeh, I was, and – I've never told no one this before so keep it to yourself – but before we laid him to rest, I put my finger in the holes in his skull, don't know why I did it, I just couldn't believe a doubled walled knot could leave wounds like that. They was like a musket ball had gone in and not come out the other side."

"Do you believe that Peter Green was actually 'murdered', like illegally killed I mean? Some say it was only accidental like." Another pointed question, the answer to which both Clarkson and Falconbridge waited on with bated breath. It wasn't long in coming and when it did, it was a bullseye.

"Well, I tell you for one thing" said the former bosun and newly appointed mate on a sharp intake of breath. "If Peter Green was not murdered by our Captain in cold blood, then no man ever was." It was the perfect reply, but the sugar-coating was still to come. "I've seen men hanged at Execution Dock for far less than that, I can tell you."

They had heard enough. Clarkson quickly upped and left without delay, relieved to be free of his claustrophobic cell, where the shadows were already getting longer as the night closed in. On his way through the bar, he tapped Falconbridge on the shoulder, caught the eye of George Ormond to signal that he had given them all that they needed, and slipped out into the worsening rain.

The very next day, Doctor Falconbridge departed for London, their witness safely delivered into his hands and stowed away at his side. As the two Abolitionists bid each other a hearty farewell, the Doctor implored his clerical friend to take good care of himself. "Don't take any risks now, I want to see you back in London in one piece before this week is out."

"I won't," Clarkson assured him. "I want to copy down the muster rolls for The Emerald first thing, and then I will be away to Manchester in the morning. My horse is well rested and so I intend to take the road back to Bristol, just to avail myself of all developments there, and I promise to be back in London for the next committee meeting." He waved cheerily as the stagecoach pulled away, watching the team of six silk coated black horses clatter along the cobbled street in what was still the swiftest available journey to the capital.

The Custom House was his first destination of the day, but as he strode down Paradise Street towards the Old Dock it became apparent that all was not well. It was the same reaction that he'd encountered upon the streets of Bristol, once his intentions had become known; no one would acknowledge him. One or two people actually crossed the street as soon as they saw him coming, and more than one openly spat at his feet in a disgusting display of ill will. Chief amongst these men were the dandily dressed Captains, who each regarded him with menacing looks as if, given the chance to do the crime, they would find the time and occasion to do him some serious harm.

This time the Registrar was called away on another important matter, leaving Clarkson to complete his investigations in peace and the muster rolls came up trumps once more, the register confirming the names of every potential witness that George Ormond had given them in his detailed account. He knew it to be highly unlikely that each man would be prepared to testify at the forthcoming trial, but the irrefutable evidence of their presence aboard that ship, was proof enough that the reports had their basis in hard truth. Not only was the Captain named amongst the protagonists, his was the first on the list, and it came complete with his signature, a formal sign-off on departure and return and his stamp of approval that the record was a full and complete one.

Together with the testimony of Falconbridge, who would explain what he had heard said in several ports, and their joint affidavit from the tavern, Clarkson was sure that their case against Green's murderer would hold water, if they could just get it in front of the magistrate in time.

It was blowing up a storm outside, the wind rising off the sea to clatter the plate metal street signs off their hinges. But as the rain was not yet pounding, and as he would soon be on the road again, he felt inclined to take one more look around before heading back to the Kings Arms to pack up his things. Most of his belongings had gone with Falconbridge on the stagecoach, including his chest of evidence and all of his writings, lest they be lost on the road. He had only his overnight items to cram into a satchel, which would then sit across his horse's haunches for the duration of his journey south, so as to make the load as light as possible for their long journey.

By the time he reached the edge of the quayside, it was blowing a gale and the boats secured there were buffeting up against the stone harbour wall like the blocks on a ship's rigging. The gulls were screeching warnings from above, their white wings turned into the wind and hanging like toy kites, as he walked along the centre of the pier, carefully avoiding the green slime that was spread across its length, in case he should slip on it and tumble headlong into the dock.

There were others milling around too, in spite of the weather. Some were working on the decks and others upon the quay, fetching and carrying, stumbling to and fro in the rising onslaught and turning their shoulders into the teeth of the storm. What the Reverend Clarkson had failed to notice was a shifty gang of eight to ten men, clearly intent on something more than sightseeing and as he turned back from the final ten-yard stretch of the stone pier, he came face to face with them.

Amongst their number, were several that he recognised, including last night's informant and the very man that he was about to have summoned before the court; the Captain of The Emerald himself. Their voices didn't carry on the wind, as each word was beaten back in its barrage, but as each base threat left their lips, their coarse countenance made their intentions as plain as day.

Clarkson glanced around for an escape route, but his path was blocked, and the Doctor's words of warning returned to him like an ill-timed omen. He had stupidly put himself in danger, and despite his lofty stature that had him towering above every snarling animal in the pack, he knew that he would not be able to take on all of them and hope to be victorious. They were closing in on him now, edging forward like wolves to a kill. The space to his rear had shrunk in the few seconds since he'd first seen them, and the edging stones of the promontory were now but a few inches behind him, marking an unguarded twenty-foot drop to the fierce waters below.

"You didn't really think you could take us on and live to tell the tale, did yer?" the Captain snarled. "Reverend Clarkson isn't it? You should've stayed in your pulpit Reverend, you've no business in the north, our business is our business."

"I will see you in court Captain," Clarkson shouted back, his defiance drowned out by the gull's cacophony as a blast of wind hurled his words back in his face. "You are a murderer Sir; I have submitted all the evidence that will see you hanged. If anything happens to me, your fate will be sealed."

"I am away to the Guinea Coast on the morning tide vicar man" he laughed, bidding his men to do the same, amongst them his newest officer. "Murray here tells me you're quite the chatterbox. Well, you'll soon be silenced for good, and as for your little chat with Georgie Boy Ormond - we have men down in the capital who owe us some favours, they'll smoke him out for us."

There was just a yard now between his back and the water and Clarkson knew that if he was going to do anything, the moment was upon him. And so, without warning, he launched himself into a run at full pelt from a standing start, straight into their midst like a French boule, smashing one man in the midriff who then took down another two like nine-pins, a third clumsily tripping over the newly formed pile and turning his ankle, as he stumbled to his feet in an attempt to give chase after their lanky prey.

Clarkson felt their rough hands grabbing at his clothes and withstood a hard blow to the side of his head, which served to send his carefully secured hat flying on the wind, never to be seen again.

"Get 'im" he heard the Captain spit, "he's gettin' away, strike 'im down." But with God's providence he had broken through their ranks, his long legs proving their worth as he raced across the harbour like a misshaped greyhound. He glanced around just once, to see that the Captain's foul temper had once again surfaced through the melee, as he pushed the former boatswain to the ground, kicking him mercilessly in his side and groin.

In that moment he feared for the young man's life, an impressionable boy who had sat just a few inches from his ear the night before, but even his Christian faith was not strong enough to make him want to fight the boy's corner. He had learned in the weeks spent in this underworld, that theirs was a dog-eat-dog existence and as he slowed to a trot, Clarkson found himself thinking that that particular seadog might be best served to turn down his latest commission, lest he found himself served up as a pickled appetiser on the Captain's table.

As he arrived back at The Kings Arms Hotel and his temporary sanctuary, the Reverend Thomas Clarkson finally admitted to himself that he'd had enough of Liverpool.

It was time to head south again.

CHAPTER THIRTEEN

"The stench of the hold now that the whole ship's cargo was confined together became absolutely pestilential. The closeness of the place and the heat and the crowding, which meant that each had scarcely room to turn, suffocated us ... the shrieks of the women and the groans of the dying rendered the whole a scene of horror almost inconceivable."

The Interesting Narrative of the Life of Olaudah Equiano, or Gustavus Vassa, The African

Had Reverend Clarkson stayed in residence for just one more day, he would have received a letter from his friend Granville Sharp, imploring him to make a speedy return to London. The trial of James Lavendar and his fellow officers aboard The Thomas in the case of the murder of William Lines had been called before the magistrates, without a single witness in attendance. As it turned out, he would not hear of it until his arrival in Bristol, three days later, and so Sharp's well-chosen words were destined to go unheeded.

My dearest Thomas,

I trust that you are well and that your trip to Liverpool has been an entirely successful one.

However, I must insist that you cut short your investigations and return forthwith, as your witnesses in the case of The Thomas have absconded. It seems that some may be back at sea on another vessel, bribed by the owners into positions of office aboard the latest venture and the others, having resisted the slaver's coin, have returned to the coal mines of South Wales, but we know not which, and the time is fast upon us. I have dispatched a local man to Neath and Swansea to see what can be done, but we are close to our time, and I fear that the court's patience is fast running out. I am led to believe that the accused has no defence whatsoever and that so long as our evidence can be presented, he has no hope of being acquitted, but without witnesses we have no hope of justice being served upon him.

I hope my letter finds you well.

God's speed.

With my greatest respects and esteem, Granville Sharp.

-ooo-

The mill towns and market towns that littered his eastbound journey were clogged with carts, laden with wool, which so obstructed his route that he decided to take a diversion along the towpath of the newly constructed Bridgewater canal. It's thirty-mile route proved to be most convenient, cutting through the south Lancashire countryside and striking right into the heart of Manchester's mill district. The air was full of wispy trails of white mist, the evidence of a cotton magnate's industrial strength which, unbeknownst to the local people was at that very moment settling in their lungs like desert sand.

As before, Clarkson had planned ahead, corresponding with the Quaker community and other leading manufacturers, whose businesses were the beating heart of the city's burgeoning economy. He arrived on the Friday evening, just as the mills were shutting down production for the day; a sea of men and women, boys, and girls, that poured forth from the base of the multi-storied monoliths. Dozens of brick-built chimneys stretched into the sky, to lord it over each regimented row of windows that sucked greedily on the last of the remaining light.

It was quite a sight, but as he trotted alongside, he found that his admiration for these bold industrialists became increasingly diminished, as he regarded the exhausted features of each man, woman, and child, their clothes little better than rags and their reddened faces weary from the week's excesses. Another form of slavery in all but name, and as each human specimen slouched away from the place where they spent the majority of their limited lifespan, the parallel was not lost on Clarkson. But they were not his fight, and so he pushed all thoughts of their hardship to the back of his mind and instead, set himself the task of tracking down his lodgings for the night.

He dismounted at the pleasant looking Waterside Inn and went inside, leaving his horse in the hands of a willing stable lad, and then settling himself beside the fire to take some sustenance, before making a hasty retreat to his rooms. He spent some time writing up his notes, carefully recording the events of that morning, and bringing to mind with sudden anxiety how he had only just escaped with his life from the clutches of a Liverpool mob. He was certain that they had been intent on driving him off the quayside, but had they succeeded, then they would have no doubt pleaded otherwise. It had been their intent to kill him, of that he was certain, and having now seen up close what such men as these were capable of, he was left in no doubt at all as to the true character of a slave ship's officer. He had stared into the eyes of a devilish fiend that day, and he was now more determined than ever to bring their kind to justice.

The very next morning at breakfast, he was greeted by Mr Thomas Walker, together with Mr Cooper and Mr Bayley, all local industrialists who had received his essay with heightened anticipation and had expressed a desire to be kept abreast of progress. That he had been able to do so in person had been very well received, but Clarkson was left astonished when they told him of the progress they had made amongst the mill workers of Manchester, who it seemed, had also been well informed of the Abolitionist cause and his part in it.

"The people hereabouts have already put-up petition t' Parliament, Reverend Clarkson," Mr Walker explained in his unusual mancunian accent. "I reckon there'll be ten thousand names afore long, there ain't a person round here who's names not on it."

"That's incredible" Clarkson answered in genuine amazement. "I had no idea that the movement was already so strong in the mill towns."

"Indeed, it is," added Mr Cooper, his face flushed with pride. "The people are deeply moved by the plight of the African, and your pamphlets have been in high demand. I have only recently sent for another two hundred copies and Mr Newton's is also much anticipated."

"Yes, I was with John Newton just recently," Clarkson said, but on this occasion chose to keep his own opinions to himself. "I have read his draft and I have to say it makes for sobering reading, I'm sure that it will persuade any waverers that are still undecided to join our cause."

"I hear that you've been into the lion's den yourself, Reverend?" asked Mr Bayley. "It's good to see that you survived unscathed."

"Only just, I can tell you" and he didn't hesitate to do so, recounting the events of the previous day and the evidence that he and Alexander Falconbridge had uncovered in their local port, through which most of the related raw materials and finished goods were shipped. The men were shocked and saddened by his account and vowed to retell of his experience far and wide in every corner of their county.

In a break in the conversation, his key correspondent spoke up again, making a request of the Reverend that Clarkson had not been expecting, and that had him doubting his own abilities to deliver on it. "Reverend, we have put it about that you were planning to visit our humble corner of England, and it seems that many people have expressed an interest in hearing you speak upon your subject, so much so, that the local vicar has kindly offered to give over his pulpit for tomorrow's sermon, should you be willing to address us on the matter."

It was a very long way of saying, 'we have already made arrangements', and so Clarkson did not feel that he was in any position to decline. "But I shall have to prepare, for I have no sermon planned," he said, glancing up at the grandfather clock in a moment of panic as he saw that the day was rushing by. "In fact, I haven't delivered a sermon in so long, that I fear I may be out of practice. I hope that I will not be a disappointment to you all."

The men all assured him that they thought such a possibility to be improbable, but sensing that he needed time, they declined the offer of hospitality and bid him a good rest of his day, giving him sufficient time to ready himself for the town's event of the summer.

-ooo-

The following morning the local church was packed to the rafters, with a congregation that must have been drawn from not just one parish, but several of the surrounding ones too. He found himself wondering whether all other churches had closed their doors that morning, such was the clamour to get inside and as he made his way through the arched doorway, he found that his passage to the pulpit was blocked by a sea of eager bodies. It was standing room only, even in the aisles and down each side of the seven-hundred-year-old building, and he doubted that its stained-glass windows had ever borne witness to such a multitude. Thomas Clarkson was quite overwhelmed and not a little nervous, as a human corridor parted through the melee and he was soon able to reach the front, where he shook hands with the local clergy and sat down in the front pew to gather his thoughts.

The first hymn was a new one, published just eight years before. Since when it had quickly become a favourite of preachers and churchgoers alike, who found in its twee verses and easy-to-remember tune, a timely reminder of their own failings and hope for redemption. These parishioners were no exception, as they stood to sing, and belted out the words of John Newton's classic.

Amazing Grace, how sweet the sound, that saved a wretch like me;
I once was lost, but now am found, was blind but now I see.
'Twas Grace that taught my heart to fear and Grace, my fears relieved;
How precious did that Grace appear, the hour I first believed.
Through many dangers, toils, and snares, we have already come;
T'was Grace that brought us safe thus far, and Grace will lead us home.
The Lord has promised good to me, His word my hope secures;
He will my shield and portion be, as long as life endures.
Yes, when this flesh and heart shall fail, and mortal life shall cease;
I shall possess, within the veil, a life of joy and peace.
The earth shall soon dissolve like snow, the sun forbear to shine;
But God who called me here below, will be forever mine.

Their rendition had almost moved the Reverend to tears, in spite of the double standards and hypocrisy that he knew lay only skin deep in Newton's words. As the audience settled back in their seats, the white-gowned vicar gave a nod in Clarkson's direction and without further ado, he hauled himself to his feet, propped himself up behind the lectern and began to speak of what would become his life's work. It was only then that he noticed, much to his initial shock and rising shame, that standing just to the left of the first few rows, a gathering of forty or fifty black faces regarded him with suspicion. Above their bare and folded arms, their eyes belied a lifetime of hurt and pain and, for a moment, he felt like an imposter - a fraud even - a faux champion, without authority to stand before them and to talk of his great struggle. After all, they and their kin had long since lived it and he had – as yet – made so little progress against The Trade that had blighted their lives and those of several generations before them.

Three thousand miles away, all down the west coast of Africa, from the Windward shores, along the Gold Coast and down through the states of Benin and Angola, people of the oldest earthly ethnicities and most ancient of human languages were being shackled, chained, and entombed in the bulging bellies of ships that had been fashioned just thirty or so miles to the west of where they were standing. As they bellowed out John Newton's 'little ditty', four thousand miles away in the idyllic islands of the West Indies, the enslaved were being sold like beasts. Their collective fate to be worked to death planting and slashing the sumptuous sugar cane, that danced above those cobalt blue seas and yellow sands on sun soaked paradise islands. All so that the foreign produce of those fields, and of the newly established American states to the north, could be sold on at profits that far exceeded their costs; to rattle the painted teacups of the English ladies in their drawing rooms or to cram the ornately carved pipes of the English gentlemen at their clubs.

"Brothers and sisters," he began self-consciously, as these fervent thoughts became the kindling for the fiery speech that he hoped to deliver. "My sermon today draws its inspiration from just one verse of scripture; chapter twenty-three, verse nine of Exodus: *'Also thou shalt not oppress a stranger: for ye know the heart of a stranger, seeing ye were once strangers in the land of Egypt'.*"

The sermon was long, and in the rising heat of an early summer Sunday, a healthy portion of those in attendance were left thinking longingly of other pursuits well before the end. The unseasonal storms of earlier in the week had passed and in their wake, a warm influx of air from the southern continent had taken the temperature to new heights. He was no John Wesley, and his public speeches and sermons lacked the inspirational punch of the self-styled Methodist. But what the Reverend Thomas Clarkson lacked in delivery, he more than made up for in guts and guile, and as his hastily prepared sermon closed in on its climax, he was determined to bring it to a telling conclusion. One that those listening would remember for weeks to come, maybe even for years, so that they could repeat it to friends and family and spread the Abolitionist message far beyond the confines of this close-quartered country church.

"Are there no strangers whom we oppress? I fear that the wretched African will say that he drinks the cup of sorrow, and that he drinks it at 'our' hands. Great numbers of these strangers, who are carried from Africa to our colonies, are fraudulently and forcibly taken from their native soil. Consider the person who is thus carried off by the ruffians who have been lurking to intercept him. Separated thereafter from everything that he esteems in life, without even the possibility of bidding his friends adieu, behold him overwhelmed in tears, wringing his hands in despair, while his family at home are waiting for him with anxiety and suspense, till length of absence confirms their loss and they are plunged into inconceivable misery and distress. If then we oppress this stranger and if by a knowledge of his heart we find he is a person of the same passions and feelings as ourselves, we are certainly breaking by means of the slave trade, that fundamental principle of Christianity, that we shall do unto another that which we wish to be done unto ourselves. I fear that in not doing so, those who are guilty of these crimes are cutting themselves off from all expectation of the Divine blessing. For how inconsistent our conduct is, if we come into the temple of God and fall prostrate before Him, and pray to Him to have mercy upon us. But how shall He have mercy upon us who have shown no mercy upon others? We pray to Him again that He will deliver us from evil, but how shall He deliver us from evil, who are daily invading the rights of the injured African by heaping misery on his head?"

Some members of the congregation were weeping now, others were standing stock still in solemn consideration, several stood awkwardly and self-consciously no doubt contemplating their own misdeeds, whilst more than a few others were openly angered by the speaker's choice of words. But Thomas Clarkson wasn't finished, and drawing inspiration from his Methodist mentor and co-agitator, he added one final blast of recrimination for them to take home to their communities.

"If then, we wish to avert the heavy national judgement, which is hanging over our heads – for we must believe that the crimes towards the innocent African lie recorded against our names in heaven – let us endeavour this very day to assert their cause. Let us withstand the torrent of evil, however inadvertently it may be fixed amongst the customs of our times; not by using our liberty as a cloak of maliciousness against those who have the misfortune to be concerned in it, but upon proper motives and in a proper spirit, as the servants of God. So that if the sun should be turned into darkness and the moon into blood, and the very heaven should fall upon our heads, we may fall in the general convulsion without dismay, conscious that we have done our duty in endeavouring to succour the distressed, and that the stain of the blood of Africa is not upon us."

In the aftermath, the sacred space fell deafeningly silent; it was just for a moment or two, but to Clarkson it felt like a lifetime. Not a word was spoken, not a pin was dropped. It was like the silence of a million African graves, until a single pair of hands began to beat in approval, then another and another, until the whole hall resonated with the sound of it, ringing around the ancient gothic arches and between the dusty cloisters in a cacophony of approval.

Clarkson glanced across to the gathered black community in hope of seeing some evidence of their endorsement too, but it was not forthcoming. Instead, they stood in silent scrutiny, the whites of their eyes offering a solemn backdrop to their contempt; tears did not flow in memory of the friends and family that had been lost at the hands of generation upon generation of white thugs, for whom these hollow words came too late to offer up any release. Instead, they stood stoic, proud, insolent even - unimpressed by the crocodile tears of their white oppressors - whose brothers, fathers, uncles, and cousins, they knew would never be held to account for the deaths of theirs. Killed for resisting capture, mutilated, and murdered for defending their own, lost to the depths of the ocean after succumbing to sickness on the high seas, or worked to death in the fields of foreign lands. No amount of self-conscious reflection could make up for two hundred years of untold misery, inflicted by a stubbornly racist nation on an unwary and unexpectant continent. No amount of retribution could compensate for the innocent millions who'd been sacrificed to the white man's earthly idol.

In that moment, Clarkson knew for certain that there would be no glory for him in his life's work – only a terrible and dreadful urgency, that grew ever more pressing with every passing day.

-○○○-

The very next morning he began his journey south, a journey that took him through the increasingly industrialised landscape of England. From the new mills of Lancashire, through the kiln-strewn potteries of Staffordshire and into the blackened landscape of the West Midlands, its iron and coal industry already taking a terrible toll on its once green pastures. Brickworks and glass factories had sprung up a few miles from the open pits, that had scarred the land for charcoal to fuel the fledgling industrial revolution, and as Clarkson rode along its sooted pathways, he couldn't help but wonder how the next generation would fare in this new industrialised world. As thousands marched off the land and into the cities to seek their fortunes, he feared that the price of progress would be the working man's to bear, and that the produce that poured forth from the city of a thousand trades would only go to feed the growing appetite of an increasingly imperialist nation.

He made a stop at Worcester, at the house of Timothy Bevington, a prominent local Quaker, with whom he talked until late into the night. Like several men before him, Clarkson furnished him with the latest copies of his essay, and then onto Gloucester the next morning to visit with his friend Dean Tucker. There too, he spread the word of their growing success, which was already well known across the local Quaker network and asked for further petitions to be raised across the county in support of the cause. He may have hammed it up a little, but he saw that as his role when journeying amongst the network, to help to fan the flames of the Abolitionist movement and to bolster its support wherever he could. After all, 'success has many fathers, but failure is an orphan', and Thomas Clarkson did not intend to fail.

On his arrival at the same Bristol lodging house on Park Street, weary and somewhat saddle-sore from the ride, he was not surprised to find a pile of messages waiting for his attention. Most were from disgruntled seamen who had hoped to bend his ear about their mistreatment at the hands of various officers, which he would be only too happy to receive in the course of time. However, chief amongst the stack was a note from Harry Gandy, his local Quaker correspondent, requesting an urgent meeting on his return.

The very next morning, after sending a runner to inform his friend of his arrival back in Bristol, Thomas was met at his breakfast table by a much-agitated Gandy, who was quite unable to suppress his anguish.

"Thomas" he said, grasping his hand in the warmest of greetings, but the man's flustered appearance gave proof to his anguish. "It is so good to see you. I have grave news, of the utmost importance. I take it that you did not receive Granville Sharp's letter?"

The look on Clarkson's face was answer enough, but he confirmed that he had not, and as a much-troubled Gandy began a confused retelling of events, Clarkson held up his hand to call a halt to his ramblings. "Take your time now Harry, please. You're not making any sense, please take some coffee and let me understand what the matter is. You say that the witnesses have disappeared, what witnesses, disappeared where?"

Gandy took a deep breath, took his seat at the table and after sweetening his coffee with a scrape or two of sugar from the small loaf before him, he started again from the beginning. "The magistrates in London have called the murder of William Lines before the bench, but there are no witnesses to be found and without them, James Lavendar is a free man."

Clarkson was horrified, but though he could not understand how the case had come to court so soon, he chose to leave that question for later and instead focused his attention on the most pertinent point. "What's happened to them?"

"Two were bribed by the ship's owners to return to sea," Gandy explained. "Both instated as officers aboard another ship and offered extortionate amounts to make themselves scarce. They also tried the same trick with the others, but though resolute in their refusal, they had no way to sustain themselves further in Bristol without work on board the ships, and so they have been forced to return home, to the coal mines of South Wales."

"Can we track them down?" asked Clarkson, desperately aware that all of his hard work in bringing this case to court, might be about to fall at the final hurdle.

"We have sent a messenger to seek them out, but have heard nothing since," Gandy advised him. "He left on horseback a week ago with an instruction to go from pit to pit between Neath and Swansea, but I can only guess that he has not yet found them."

"How much time do we have left?" asked Clarkson.

"Not much," said Gandy, "the bench sits again on Friday, so just a few days I suspect, to bring them back here and then to get them shipped up to London."

"It's going to be very tight, but we can still make it if we can find them quickly," Clarkson reasoned, and after finding a few coins to cover the cost of their half-eaten breakfast, he called on Gandy to accompany him to the livery stables where his horse was being made ready for a gentle day about town, but those plans were about to change. As they walked he provided further instructions, intent on following in the messenger's tracks and hoping that he would either meet them on the road back from Wales, or that he himself would succeed where their courier had failed.

"What is the fastest route to take?" he asked Gandy as they rounded the corner to the stables.

"Down towards the Avon mouth where the rivers meet, then to take the ferry across the Severn at the Passage House," he explained, "but you'll need to be quick, it looks like a storm is coming and the ferry rarely crosses when the winds are this strong. The waves will be too high."

"He will today!" determined Clarkson, as he mounted his hastily readied and unwilling horse, pulled on the reins to turn him outwards and kicked hard.

"God's speed Thomas," Gandy shouted after him, but Clarkson was already headed into the rising storm.

-ooo-

His horse was white with sweat when the Passage House came into sight. He could see that the ferry boat was at its mooring on this side of the Severn and his heart leaped at the prospect that he might yet make it across the estuary before dark. The full fury of the storm was still some way off, although a bank of darkness had drawn a line across the sky to the west, that did not bode well for the journey ahead. There were other paying passengers who were milling around at the water's edge, which filled him with hope for a quick departure, but as he dismounted to make his enquiries for the next scheduled crossing, the initial response was not to his liking.

"Nay Sir," hollered a weathered woman in a pleated grey shawl. "No boat'll be going out tonight, storms a coming."

"But I have to get across tonight," pleaded Clarkson, "a man's life depends upon it." It wasn't entirely true, but it was a fact that the scales of justice, that would soon determine a man's life or death, were hanging in the balance. "I must get to Wales before sundown, it's imperative that I get across tonight."

"There's no boatman that'll take 'ee," the old woman warned. "It's a fool's errand. One big wave'll tip her about and see thee drowned."

"The storm is not yet upon us" Clarkson said pointing towards a line of darkened sky that was now a little too close for comfort. "We have time yet I'm sure. The other side is still in sight."

"Three guineas" a faceless voice called out, "three guineas and I'll take it out, not a penny less."

"Are you a fool?" coughed the old woman, as a well-timed thunderclap split the sky to fire a warning to the unwary, but Clarkson was in no mood to be deterred.

"Done" he said, his hand searching for his money belt and his purse, adeptly retrieving the three gold coins, much to the astonishment of the boatman who had not really expected his outlandish price to be met. "Here, three guineas, now can we be about our business, I beg you."

"This way," the wherryman motioned, with a crooked smile that was matched only by the worried frown that had appeared in triplicate on his forehead. As he led the Reverend away, a girl led his steed to its stables for the night, and Clarkson put his best foot forward, landing it on the unsteady gangplank that led to the small but sturdy wherry.

"I've been at sea in much worse a storm than this 'un," the old man said, in an attempt to reassure the both of them. "It might blow us back a way, but we'll make it ashore afore dark."

"I do hope so" the Reverend stammered, noticing only then that none of the other waiting passengers had joined them for the short sailing. "Is no one else coming?"

"There's none that have the nerve, but thee" the boatman sneered, "it seems all this talk of a storm has spooked 'em, but there's nay need. I've never lost her yet."

As the boat pushed off it was almost immediately caught by the strong current which carried it out into the slipstream of the river, but the winds were furious and battered the sail so fiercely, that even the boatman's nerve seemed frayed by its strength. The prow of the vessel veered against the wind, though the twin oars did their darndest to turn her as they struck the water again and again, and the rudder to the rear strained against the tide's fearsome force. There were three crewmen, one positioned at the end of each oar; each one had been invisible to Clarkson as he boarded, but he was soon acutely aware of the two hunched shapes that heaved in time and cursed with every stroke, as they inched a course across the channel. The rain was pounding hard, beating them into submission, as a sheet of lightning illuminated the Welsh mountains beyond; it was as if Merlin himself were casting out demons from the depths of each rugged peak and in that moment Thomas Clarkson recognised the full folly of his misguided mission.

In an instant they were wet through, as an almighty wave slammed against the side of the boat, tilting her high in the dark and threatening to capsize them, before crashing back down in a thunderous slap that seemed poised to wrench each timber rib from its spine. Clarkson clung on to the frame for dear life, as he silently mouthed the Lord's Prayer with his eyes tightly shut.

When he opened them again, his prayer had been answered.

"There, ahead, is that a light or the evening star?" Clarkson pointed frantically into the almost solid blackness, a veil through which one small light seemed to beckon them and the oarsmen battled against the elements to turn the bulk towards it. It was the flickering light of a candle and as they closed in on the opposite shore, it shimmered and danced, as if sheltered from the wind as it lighted some soul to bed. If it had been an outside flame, it would have been long since extinguished, but it wasn't, and Clarkson was determined not to let it out of his sight until his feet were firmly set on land once more.

As the boat edged its way into the shallows and out of the swirling waters of the main channel, all those aboard were visibly relieved to have made it to the other side, and each congratulated the other with a hearty slap. "That was a close 'un" the ferryman sighed, as one of the oarsmen eagerly leapt onto the gangplank to secure the rope around a waiting mooring hook, lest the tide should take a turn against them to drag them into peril once more.

"Thank God." It was Clarkson who had spoken, and as he gratefully stepped off onto dry land and strode up towards the Passage House on the western shore, he knew that he would have to wait there a while to let the storm pass and to give his saturated clothes sufficient time to dry out.

"Is there another way across the river?" asked Clarkson, "further upstream maybe?"

"Not for many miles Sir" the boatman answered, "not 'til Gloucester or thereabouts, a good half day's ride at least. Anyone from Swansea will come to this crossing, to wait out the storm. If they're coming back tonight, they'll be coming this way" and at that they bid each other farewell and a restful evening.

Once inside it was obvious that the old man was right, as several people were sat steaming at the side of the stove, where his clothes would soon be left to dry, and with the promise of a loaned horse that would be made ready for an early start, he begged his leave for the night. He was in no mood to make idle talk and so a small room was made available to him at a few pennies rent, and after undressing and pulling on a rough robe, he passed his sodden shirt and breeches to the maid, before laying down exhausted.

At just after five in the morning, the dawn chorus coaxed him from his slumber, and after peering out into the early light of day, he rose eager to resume his quest. He pulled on his garments, now dried, and ironed and left at his door, and with just a slice of bread and dripping for sustenance, he took the reins of a fifteen-hand mare and pressed on towards The Valleys. He made inquiries of the incoming despatch rider, just to see if he had passed anyone on his route and having been informed that no one else had come via the Passage House since his own late arrival, he kicked on in haste, knowing full well that time was not on his side.

After an hour or more's riding, just as the darkened scars of another industrial landscape had started to reveal themselves in the far distance, his heart jumped at the sight of three men approaching on horseback, galloping along the unmade highway. The spray from each heavy hoof was illuminated in the noon sunlight, and Clarkson wasted no time as he sped towards them as fast as his unfamiliar horse would carry him. They wasted no time on pleasantries and after just a brief greeting Clarkson turned and headed back the way he had come, but this time he had company. His witnesses sat astride the despatch rider, who had been sent out to find them, but Clarkson led the way, intent on keeping up the pace all the way back to the Passage House on the Welsh side of the river's mouth.

They made it back to Bristol the next day after being forced to wait out the storm, though the Reverend was now wracked with the aches and pains of a heavy cold. Gandy refused to let him leave for London without rest, but there was no time, and Clarkson knew that their cause was almost lost. In his place, the mother of the murdered seaman offered to accompany the two key witnesses to the Greenwich courtroom and so, the three of them were packed off in the fastest available stagecoach at The Society's expense, which they hoped and prayed would yet make it there in time. They knew that it would be a close-run thing, but after all the obstacles that had been put in their way, it seemed that even an outside chance was better than none at all.

The Reverend Clarkson took to his bed, his body shivering uncontrollably and a fever raging about him, which would lay him low for several days. He was made very comfortable in the household of Harry Gandy, with one of the maids keeping an almost permanent vigil just in case his chill should worsen. Taking no chances, the Quaker had paid for his family's Doctor to visit him twice, and the apothecary had ordered that Clarkson stay confined to his bed for a week, by which time he was finally well enough to sit up to take some chicken broth.

At the end of that convalescence, a letter arrived for him care of his lodgings, and as he read it aloud to the listening audience of Quaker kin, his strained words confirmed their worst fears.

My dearest Reverend,

I was most alarmed to hear from Mrs Lines of your sudden illness and I hope that this letter now finds you in better health, after your momentous efforts for our cause.

I do have some disappointing news to convey, however. The witnesses made it to the court by the stated time, but the magistrates had called the case early, on the previous day in fact, I suspect at the behest of the Slavers who will no doubt have heard of your success in tracking down our witnesses and sent their own riders ahead of you. In the absence of any person appearing against him, James Lavendar Esq. was 'discharged by proclamation' and so, whilst he had no defence to provide and would have surely hung for his evil doing, he instead walks free this very day.

As I understand it, the knave has already been put to sea to stave off any appeal against his untimely 'judgement'. I do not expect that we shall see him again on these shores.

I know that this must come as a huge blow for you Thomas, but you must not blame yourself for the outcome. Our cause has been much advanced by this hearing, and all who have read of its truths will know of the officer's guilt and of the terrible treatment that was handed out at his and others' hands on board The Thomas.

Addae is well and safe in my household. He wants to tell you that he dreamed of you and looks forward very much to seeing you again but wants me to tell you to stay away from the water. I don't know what he means, but he thinks that you will understand.

Get well my friend and come back to London, as soon as you are able, for we have much to discuss.

Your humble servant and friend,

Granville Sharp Esq.

CHAPTER FOURTEEN

"In general, a few roots, not of the nicest kind, usually yams or potatoes, are their food, and two rags, that neither screen them from the heat of the day, nor the cold of the night their covering. Their sleep is very short, their labour continual, and frequently above their strength; so that death sets many of them at liberty, before they have lived out half their days."

John Wesley, Thoughts on Slavery

Extracts from the Journal of Doctor Gardiner, ship's surgeon on board The Brothers

7th January 1788

It's been two weeks now since we set sail from the islands, loaded up with one thousand hogshead of sugar loaves for the coffee houses and dining tables of England. We are scheduled for a final stop at Jamestown, Virginia, to take our fill of tobacco and cotton, at the Captain's behest. He wants to maximise his profits on this leg having lost out on the slaves and since the cessation of hostilities in the War for Independence, he thinks he will fare well there. I dread this portion, for it is long and arduous – it can be weeks before we catch The Trade Winds and all too often ships fall foul of the weather, to be slung about by storms making the crew sick and tempers quick to fray. Boredom is the biggest danger, and too often I have seen men fight for no good reason, even killing each other over a mouldy slice of bread or a meagre slug of rum. The lime and lemon juice has been the reserve of officers 'til now and though we are stocked up for the return, the crew know of its medicinal value and at the first sign of scurvy amongst them, they will be at my throat for a taste. I don't trust Captain Howlett, nor do any, not even the mates; they know his conniving ways and don't dare turn their back on him, lest he tosses them overboard to save a penny of wages. He is a scoundrel, and I shall never again sail under his command, if 'command' it be, for I haven't seen much of that from him these past few months. He has kept himself a concubine for the short journey up the coast where she will finally be sold, but she has not been seen about the ship since the islands, so I do not know the extent of any ill treatment that he may have caused. Other than that, the ship has plenty of water and is in good repair and so, with a fair wind and good fortune, I pray that we will see the coast of Ireland before the winter is out. The rats have been quiet, I almost miss their scurrying, for without them there is only silence.

11th January 1788

The crew have become very restless after two more of their number have seemingly taken their leave in Virginia, with talk of a curse upon the ship, that has led them to try their luck in the new lands. They have reportedly taken their wage in Virginian dollars and were none too pleased at the rate of exchange, though both struggled to know the extent of the swindle, such was their confusion at the state-branded dollar bills. I could have told them that they had been paid only three-fifths of their dues but a greater number of notes in their hands seemed to please them well at first. Until they tried to make good on it and found that half was now worthless since the widespread devaluation following the war. The Captain would have none of it and claimed to have no knowledge of the cause of their complaints, but his dastardly behaviour has set the rest on edge, as they fear similar treatment. I think they have cause, but who am I to intervene? I am no counting house clerk. I only have a say in their physical wellbeing and as far as that is concerned, they are no less 'healthy' than they were at this stage of their last outing. I am more rested now, after taking up lodgings above the inn. The noise from the bar beneath could wake the dead, but I am glad of it, and have slept the sleep of the virtuous, though I know only too well that I am not.

15th January 1788

I was called to attend upon the Captain today in his quarters, for what is a nasty festering wound on his John Thomas. I had trouble to keep my face straight after asking him outright where he had been 'sticking it' to produce such a sore. He said it was a mosquito bite, but I have never seen a flying creature with incisors as big *as that before, though I took him at his word and prescribed him with some ointment. I asked after the girl. He told me she had fetched a goodly price in the Jamestown market, though I didn't believe him and intend to check the ship's accounts when they are submitted. I suspect foul play. Not that it will amount to anything more than a financial loss as, if she has indeed perished at his hand, then it will simply be marked down as another loss at sea, but I shall do my very best to hold him to account, or at least to ensure that the truth of it is added to his scandalous reputation.*

20th January 1788

The men are growing agitated now. They want to be away from here, but still the Captain delays and as long as he does, they will spend their credit in the taverns and the brothels, and our reserves become ever more depleted. If he has any motive for his madness, then it has not been shared with his officers, who are all as confounded and as keen to leave these shores as we are, but he has been reluctant to set foot on board except to seek my medical advice for his mouldy manhood.

21st January 1788

We finally set sail today. A gentle breeze chased us out of the harbour, and we were soon across the horizon, out of sight of land and of our former colonists. What the next three months holds for us, I cannot say, but I pray for kind winds and gentle waves. And for protection against whatever else may yet befall us.

Sir Samson Wright was a Bow Street magistrate and Head of the Police for the metropolis of London, home of the famous Bow Street Runners. It was to that recent Knight of the Empire, that *The Society for Effecting the Abolition of the Slave Trade*, turned for help in the case of the murder of Peter Green, determined that at least one notorious slave trader would be brought to justice before the year was out.

On his arrival back on the busy streets of London, Clarkson had immediately sought out Granville Sharp, for they had much to tell since their last meeting. Foremost in the Reverend's mind was the welfare of Addae and he was delighted to find him in rude health, dressed smartly in a page boy's uniform and capably serving in the household of his own good friend and mentor.

"He has been on my mind these past few months," admitted Clarkson, as he asked after the boy. "I had hoped to find him in good spirits after his ordeal in Bristol."

"He has been most amicably so," Sharp informed him, "but it would seem that you have been weighing heavily on his mind too, for whenever I have seen him, he has asked most passionately, if I have heard from you and was often desperate to tell me that you are 'in danger'."

The boy was brought up from the servants' quarters below stairs and on seeing the six-foot frame of Thomas Clarkson, he ran across the drawing room and threw himself at the clergyman, his short arms barely meeting at his back. Again, he didn't speak, but he seemed terribly relieved to see his former travelling companion in one piece and as he gazed up at him, a worried look still hung across his willing yet wary features.

"Well thank you for the wonderful welcome" laughed Clarkson, "to what do I owe the pleasure?"

"I dreamt of you," the boy said, "you were by the water, there were many ships there."

"Yes," said Clarkson mystified. "I have been to Liverpool, there *are* many ships there."

"There were many men, they wanted to hurt you," the boy went on. "They wanted to kill you."

"That's right," nodded Clarkson, confounded by the boy's words, before being prompted to recount to Granville Sharp, the story of his dice with death at the hands of the slave trader and his angry mob. "But how do you know about that?" he asked, "I haven't even told Alexander yet, in fact I've only told the Manchester Quakers, so unless word has reached here from them?," he asked, looking straight at Sharp who was shaking his head and at a loss to explain the mystery.

"Thank you Addae," Sharp interceded, "go down with Mrs Avebury now, Reverend Clarkson will see you again at dinner, when you can share with him more of what you have been doing since you joined us here. I'm sure that he would be interested to hear all about how well you've been doing with your reading and writing."

Dutifully, the boy tailed the housekeeper out through the ornate double doors, that stretched high above his tiny frame. "How can he know about that?" asked Clarkson again, perplexed. "No one knows about that, not even Falconbridge."

"I cannot say," answered Sharp, "but he said he dreamed it, as I mentioned to you in my letter, which I assume must have arrived in Liverpool too late?"

"I received no letter," Clarkson answered, "it wasn't until I arrived in Bristol that I learned of the court case, but then I was too ill to be of much use to anyone."

"You did all you could" said Sharp, "but you do need to take it easy my good fellow, you have been overdoing it these last months, you need to take a rest, a proper rest back up in the Fenlands." Clarkson's expression made clear that he was not about to listen, so Sharp tried a different line of argument in the hope of rendering his friend more amenable. "The Society feels that it's time you provided them with an updated version of your essay, one that will include all of your new evidence and all of the testimonies. There must be upwards of ten thousand now, it's time we catalogued them and made their contents known to the world."

"Closer to twenty thousand actually," Clarkson said with a wink, "and yes, I do agree, there is so much more to say now that I've seen it all with my own eyes, but isn't there more to do here?"

"I need you to be well" ordered Sharp, "and to write up all your evidence. Don't worry about things here, The Society are fully manned, and the Phillips brothers are busy finishing up with Newton's essay. Thanks to you, they will soon have Doctor Falconbridge's *Thoughts on Slavery* too, I hear that it's coming along very well indeed."

"I bow to your greater experience Mr Sharp" said Clarkson somewhat theatrically, "but first I must be done with the case of The Emerald. What's your advice there, have you spoken with George Ormond yet?"

"I have indeed" Sharp smiled, "and I have some additional news for you on that score too." he added, teasing his clerical friend for a moment, before enlightening him further. "We now have a second witness, a Patrick Murray."

"The boatswain?"

"No less!" answered Sharp, "the bosun."

"But wasn't he promised a commission?"

"He was, but he was so badly treated by the Captain in some scuffle or other, that he turned his back on the offer and instead, he found his way to me, thanks of course to Mr Dale at the Kings Arms Hotel."

Clarkson grinned at the irony of it. "The scuffle that he speaks of, is the very same altercation that had me wishing that I had learned to swim in my youth. But if his story also incriminates the Captain and backs up Mr Ormond's account, then I think we can overlook his involvement in that little incident – I am sure that he was coerced to stand against me in any case."

And so, Granville Sharp had made contact with the head of police who had now drawn up detailed depositions from both witnesses, confirming that each had corroborated the other, even in the finest of the details. Under his experienced cross-examination, the magistrate had failed to find a single discrepancy between their accounts.

"He has already applied to the magistrates at Liverpool" Sharp said, continuing to bring Clarkson up to date. "And has ordered the apprehension of all of the principal officers of The Emerald, before she sets sail again for the Guinea Coast."

"Let's hope then that the letter reaches them in time," said Clarkson.

"And if it does," Sharp concurred, "that the law-abiding magistrates of Liverpool remember that they swore an oath to uphold the law of The Crown."

"And what of the House?" asked Clarkson, "are the Members of Parliament for or against us?"

"It remains too close to call," sighed Sharp, but his tone was unconvincing, and Clarkson was suddenly overcome with anguish. His look was not lost on his friend. "But there is always hope Thomas, the House is divided but the vote can yet stand or fall on the smallest of margins, and I will summon all of our considerable influence to press home our advantage whenever and wherever I can."

"I fear it will be a long road Granville."

"Do not despair my friend" said Sharp doing his best to lift his mood, which suddenly seemed uncharacteristically morose. "Your only concern now is the report, I will harness our forces here and work with our friends to apply pressure where it's needed most. You on the other hand will head back to your parish and to your study."

CHAPTER FIFTEEN

"A toleration of slavery is, in effect, a toleration of inhumanity."

Granville Sharp Esq.

The letter made it in time, but the Liverpool magistrates failed to keep to their side of the bargain. Even as Clarkson and Sharp conversed on the matter a few weeks later in Sharp's smartly decorated study, The Emerald had already set sail with its renegade Captain at the helm, his newly appointed first and second mate and the rest of the ship's officers alongside him.

News of their escape would not reach the Abolitionists for another week, leaving them with the headache of what to do with their two retained witnesses until the ship's return. To hold them in London for a year or more at the expense of The Society - or as their own personal charges - hardly seemed feasible, but there was no way now to bring a case against the Captain until his return, and only then if he dared to ever make landfall in England again.

"It's a moral outrage" stormed Sharp, "an absolute bloody disgrace. How are we supposed to win this battle if even the judiciary are working against us?"

"It gets worse than that" said Clarkson, his temperament unimproved by recent events. "In advance of these developments, I had instructed my family's attorneys to bring a private prosecution at common law against the ship's owners, for dereliction of duty, and instructed them to pursue it as rigorously and speedily as was reasonable in the circumstances."

"Good thinking" answered Sharp, "so, why am I so fearful of what you are about to tell me?"

"Because their attorneys have also been swift in their reply," he explained, "and at the very mention of Sir Samson Wright's name they have capitulated completely. Offering a substantial out of court settlement to each of our two opportunists, for any injury that they themselves have sustained as a result of these events. In return for..." the Reverend started to say, but he was about to have his sentence finished for him.

"In return for their complete and utter silence," cried Sharp, having seen such things a hundred times before and he slammed his hands against the back of one of his expensively upholstered chairs in frustration. "Have they signed? The two of them? Ormond 'and' Murray?"

"Signed the release, received the monies and disappeared off the face of the earth, I should fancy" said Clarkson, still fuming at the sheer nerve of it.

"Well, that's that then" huffed Sharp, "back to the drawing board. And just in case that wasn't bad enough," he went on unfolding a letter in front of them both, "this morning I received this writ from a firm of Bristol solicitors representing a certain Mr Freke, demanding the return of his client's personal property, that was reputedly 'stolen' by your good self, and which is now being 'unlawfully restrained' by my good self."

"The boy?' asked Clarkson, knowing full well the 'property' to which he was referring.

"Addae," confirmed Sharp, "but they won't be getting their hands on him, that's something that I will stake my reputation on. I'll be representing him in court, personally. It won't be the first time will it, and this time I've got some personal skin in the game."

"Not that you ever needed that" said Clarkson. "Surely, they cannot win can they? The Somerset case was a test case wasn't it? Wouldn't that ruling need to be overturned for them to have any chance of winning?"

"It would," agreed Sharp, "but I would never say never, these people have money to burn, and where there's money on the table, even the most impartial of magistrates can be turned."

-OOO-

A few days later and Clarkson and Sharp were once more to be found on Lombard Street in the musty gloom of the George Yard print shop where, under the guise of a hastily arranged committee meeting, the Reverend was welcomed back like a returning hero. In its cramped upstairs room, eleven good men and true stood and applauded as their founding member and committee secretary took his seat, entreating them all to desist from their overwhelming show of admiration.

"Please, gentlemen!" he said, more than a little embarrassed by the unexpected overture. "I have done nothing more than any of you would have done in the circumstances. Now, please, let's get down to business," but his co-committee members were not done yet with their praise.

"Oh yes" chuckled William Dillwyn, "like boarding a sea-bound slaving vessel to rescue a wrongly indentured man from a year or more at sea. As if 'I', would have done that! Have you seen my waistline lately?"

"Or chasing halfway across South Wales in a hurricane," said Samuel Hoare, "in pursuit of chief witnesses turned coal miners, only to catch his death of cold from exposure to the worst storm the county has witnessed in living memory. I'd have been tucked up in bed if it was me."

Even Granville Sharp's usually severe features were forced to crack under the pressure, as the group shared in a rare moment of good humour, something that was rarely appropriate in their chosen line of work. "But our good Reverend is most correct in his reticence to celebrate our achievements gentlemen, for nothing has changed these past few months, other than another ten thousand Africans have been stolen from their homes and transported to a life of slavery in the colonies. Or to an early death."

It was a sobering call, and as the unwilling Chairman declared their meeting open, directing them to the day's agenda and order of debate, he made no apologies for absence and immediately asked each man present to confirm their approval of the previous meeting's minutes. The pressure group's membership included five of the six original members of the Quaker sub-committee, their numbers swelled now by four other Friends and three Anglicans, who were all united in their cause to bring about the abolition of the slave trade as soon as possible. Additional members from amongst the political and industrial landscape of the day, rarely attended in person, especially now that William Pitt had succeeded as Prime Minister and Josiah Wedgewood's fabled and fashionable ceramics business was inundated with orders daily.

"I'd like to start by thanking you all for your continued diligence and commitment gentlemen," said Sharp in a genuine flush of appreciation for all of their efforts. "I have been astonished to learn that in this year alone, Richard and James have printed and distributed 51,342 pamphlets in support of our cause and 26,536 copies of official papers, all of which have gone out across our ever-growing network of Friends and other associates for distribution in towns and cities across the land."

"Across the world actually!" corrected Richard Phillips. "We've now begun correspondence with both Philadelphia and Delaware after the cessation in hostilities there, and have been in close contact with our compatriots in France for quite some time." There was a general chorus of approval, as a ripple of table-tapping spread around the room, the Phillips brothers each acknowledging the committee's endorsement of their efforts, with a dismissing wave of their hands.

"As a result of our sterling work to raise the awareness of this despicable industry," said Joseph Woods, "we have seen an outpouring of support in local newspapers and letters to very many Members of Parliament, which has in turn seen the establishment of similar committees to our own, all over the country, each committed to vocally opposing The Trade in their own constituencies. And our coffers are filled by their kind donations, so much so that we now have sufficient funds to double the production of the pamphlets and to meet the expenses of our most important witnesses."

"That's wonderful news" said Clarkson, using it as a springboard to launch into his favourite metaphor. "I see them all as tributaries, each feeding the flow of one mighty river of Abolitionist fervour, pouring forth to swell into a torrent of objection that will ultimately sweep this evil from the face of the earth. The waters are on the rise gentlemen, but we must bring the rains."

"There is still much to do" said John Lloyd of Birmingham. "I understand that the industrialists of the Midlands are generally supportive of our movement, but that there are some, like the gunsmiths of Bath Street, who fear that the end of the slave trade will usher in a depression and a slump in orders, especially now that the American wars are over."

"There will always be those who put profit before principle," said Joseph Hooper, "but it is our burden to imbue in them such revulsion for The Trade that they will seek out alternate ways to make their profits."

"Hear, hear!" The grumblings of approval resonated around the room, as the Chairman moved onto the second item for discussion.

"Now you will all no doubt recall the cases of the Africans; Jonathan Strong, Thomas Lewis and James Somerset," Sharp began, "which I have defended in court these past ten years or more?" Whilst there was a general murmur of confirmation, Sharp took silence from some as an invitation to provide them with a brief recap. What he failed to mention was, that in the case of Strong, he himself had personally defended the former slave at a time when he had not a shred of formal legal training to his name, and at great personal risk to himself.

"The case of Strong, first beaten and abandoned by his owner David Lisle on a London street, then taken in by my brother and hospitalised at his expense for four months. Strong recovered sufficiently to hold down gainful employment for about two years, until having been spotted about the city by his former owner, was kidnapped and sold by the said man to a West Indies plantation owner by the name of James Kerr. The case was heard by the Lord Mayor of London, who admirably threw out the claims of his new owner and set Strong free."

"Isn't Lisle the scoundrel who challenged you to a duel?" asked Clarkson.

"The very same, for 'gentlemanly satisfaction', which I of course ignored." scoffed Sharp, recalling his own personal and professional satisfaction at the favourable outcome. "Shortly afterwards I wrote my tract *On the injustice and dangerous tendency of tolerating slavery*', which reminds me, the Archbishop of Canterbury still owes me his considered opinion."

Slavery had indeed been 'tolerated' in England up until that point, although prior to 1729, a ruling by Chief Justice Holt in the reign of William of Orange, had unequivocally ruled that a slave was a free man on setting foot in England. Holt had famously said that '*one may be a villeyn in England, but not a slave*', though this had been scurrilously overturned three decades later and it was this reversal that Sharp had successfully annulled in his defence of Strong.

"Then, there was the case of Thomas Lewis just four years later in 1771, I think it was. Again kidnapped off the streets of London by his former owner and with the aid of two London watermen, dragged to their boat which was moored on the Thames and from thence, held in chains on a ship bound for Jamaica, until I was summoned to intervene. Despite the well-publicised leanings of the Lord Justice Mansfield to find in favour of his master, a Mr Stapylton, the grand jury again ruled for Lewis and set him free."

"Though he did not rule that slavery itself was unlawful in England, did he?" remarked Woods.

"No indeed" confirmed Sharp, "Mansfield was very careful on that point and ultimately refused to pass judgement on it, as he himself was, and remains, an owner of slaves, and has investments in several plantations in the West Indies. His summing up was something to behold, for it did nothing to clarify the situation, as he sought to avoid having to bring a ruling that was against his own interests. I don't know what the consequence may be," said Sharp, his legal training allowing him to recall Mansfield's words to the letter and even to muster a passing likeness in his impersonation. "If the masters were to lose their property by accidentally bringing their slaves to England. I hope it will never be finally discussed; for I would have all masters think them free, and all Negroes think they were not, because then they would both behave better."

"So not exactly an impartial judge then? Is no one amongst the landed classes of this country untainted by this vile trade?" asked James Phillips, knowing full well the answer to his rhetorical question.

"Very few," answered Clarkson, "it is indeed a monstrous foe."

"And finally, the case of James Somerset in the same year," continued Sharp, "again kidnapped in London by his owner Charles Steward. He had brought him to England from his estates in Virginia, but I contended that having set foot on English soil, he was therefore a free man, as we are not subject here to the laws of the state of Virginia. Either all the laws of Virginia must apply in England, or none, there could be no middle ground. Unless there was to be a new definition of 'property' created in England, that could be said to encompass the person of an African, who is, after all, a man. Such a designation would be contrary to so many laws of our land, as to be indefensible. Again, it was Mansfield who presided, and though he was most adamant that Steward should back down from his claims, he knew that he must rule in Somerset's favour, but still did not want to set a precedent that would - by default - declare all slaves in our land, free of bondage."

"Is that a fact of law that is still in any doubt?" asked George Harrison, his voice sounding in the room for the first time that evening.

"It is a matter of 'fluctuating opinions'" said Sharp, "though Mansfield did conclude that 'no foreigner can in England claim a right over a man: such a claim is not known to the laws of England'. He didn't go so far as to say, that any slave being landed upon England's shore was automatically free, though his judgement has been interpreted as such. Mr Davy, summing up, did it for him, when he said that 'as soon as any slave sets his foot on English ground, he becomes free.'"

"Well, that sounds pretty conclusive to me" said Harrison, "so why does any doubt remain?"

"Let us not be fooled," continued Sharp, "to think that we English can talk from some moral high ground when it comes to the state of slavery in this beloved country of ours, as if it is just some foreign problem, for our own countrymen are also guilty of this unseemly prejudice. And there are still prominent gentlemen who are pressing Parliament to make new laws on the question of what constitutes 'property', in respect to the African. A few years ago, I saw this advertisement placed in a newspaper here in our own city."

> To be sold, a black girl, the property of J.B. – eleven years old, who is extremely handy, works at her needle tolerably and speaks English perfectly well; is of an excellent temper and willing disposition.
> *Inquire of Mr Owen Esq. at the Angel Inn, behind St. Clement's Church in The Strand.*

The excerpt was passed between them, each taking a few seconds to digest it before passing it on to the next man, until finally it was Clarkson that broke the ensuing silence. "In which tardy publication was this posted?" he asked, horrified at the content, and wanting to make a mental note of those who had thought it fit to be placed in the public domain.

"The Public Advertiser," said Sharp, "and not for the first time either. I have other examples in my files, but this is not my point, for now we have another case in the offing." He glanced back at Clarkson to take up the tale, which he did with relish.

He explained how he had first encountered Addae in Thompson's Bristol Inn and the circumstances of his arrival at the home of Granville Sharp in London. "It seems that we were being watched at The Seven Stars, not surprisingly and that our movement across the town to join the stagecoach must not have gone unnoticed that morning. Either that or they just put two and two together and made a lucky guess, but my presumption is that we were seen. We were, after all, hardly the most inconspicuous of travelling companions."

"And so, I will again bring this before the courts and I hope that Lord Mansfield will be appointed to preside" declared Sharp, "as we have come to an agreement on this matter and so he should be ready and willing to fight our corner."

The Committee continued their discussions until long into the night, such was their constitution, never starting their deliberations until the end of a working day. Clarkson updated them all on his findings into the treatment of the slave ships' crews and the evidence that he had amassed from thousands upon thousands of interviews with embittered sailors. "Few amongst them had shown any regret in the retelling for their wrongdoings abroad", he informed them, "though some were still haunted by what they had seen and for those who had found the weight of what they themselves had done too hard to bear, there was always the Church to offer some solace. After all, it had worked out well enough for John Newton."

Sharp then informed them of his efforts in Parliament, and the growing backing from amongst the men of the commons for a Royal Commission to investigate The Trade, whilst Clarkson told them of his success with several Doctors, Falconbridge, and Arnold amongst them, to offer evidence before such an investigation.

"As you heard, Falconbridge has also agreed to produce his own memoirs," added Clarkson, "and is in the process of writing up his tract, which he will submit for our publication and circulation. He wants no recompense for his efforts, telling me that he is 'done with The Trade'. He is happy to do whatever we need to bring about its demise."

"And what of Newton's memoirs?" asked Sharp, directing his question at the Phillips brothers, whose presses were already busy with its production.

"Almost ready for circulation," Richard told them, "a few days more and the first edition should be ready to ship."

"And what of your next works Thomas?" asked Sharp, putting his friend on the spot to commit to a publication date. "It's crucial that we have it in plenty of time for the next Parliamentary sessions. You know what some of them are like, they need weeks to read a recipe. Something as detailed as your essay could keep them occupied for months."

"I will be working in Cambridge over the winter, to lay out the impolicy of the slave trade in all its grisly detail," he explained, "but though I have seen the ports of Liverpool and Bristol and the beating heart of our industrialists in Manchester and Birmingham, I fear that I need to travel still further, south to the ports of Plymouth and Exeter.

I'll start at Gravesend in Kent and work my way down to Cornwall, then back to Bristol on my return. I seek the Committee's leave to expense such a journey in the spring."

There was no vote as such, the Quakers' ways outlawing such practices. Instead, they debated the proposal further until a consensus was reached and, with no objections tabled, approval was given for another journey into the jaws of The Trade. "But not unaccompanied, you must take Falconbridge with you" Sharp insisted, "and you must be fully rested over the winter."

"I must agree with our learned friend" added Hoare, which precipitated the general agreement of the rest of the gathered group. "You are much too exhausted to commence another gruelling trip Thomas. You must rest and write, and not by the light of a candle either, you need to recuperate and to restore yourself. You are quite worn out my friend."

"I thank you for your concern," said Clarkson, genuinely touched by their warm interest in his welfare. "And I will take heed of it."

"Good, that's settled then" said Sharp, casting a look of brotherly concern towards Clarkson in the hope that he would finally take some direction on the matter. "And if there's no other business, then I strongly suggest that, without further ado, we should all be away to our rest for the night."

CHAPTER SIXTEEN

"That man will take away all the people of Africa, if he can catch them, and if you ask him, 'Why do you take away all these people?', he will say 'O they are not like white people, why should I not take them?' That is the reason I cannot forgive the man who takes away the character of the people of my country."

Prince John Henry Naimbanna of Sierra Leonne

<u>*Extracts from the Journal of Doctor Gardiner, ship's surgeon on board The Brothers*</u>

<u>*29th January 1788*</u>

> *We have not yet found The Trade Winds and the Captain is growing agitated, striking out at the slightest provocation. The weather has been fair, which offers up a small blessing, but the ship seems strangely empty, even though the hull is packed with cotton and tobacco from the American states and with sugar and rum from the islands. I am overcome with a sense of melancholia. I have kept my own company, much to the Captain's vexation and he demands me to attend at dinner. I am in no mood for his poor nature and fear that if I sup with him, then my sense might not survive it. The crew are more contented now that they can again hang their hammocks below deck, but though it has been cleared, and despite its thorough cleansing at Jamestown, a stubborn stink remains. I lay awake all last night. The thought of it would not leave me. The ship's load continuously shifted below me and the rolling barrels and sliding strongboxes prised my eyes apart whenever I heard them slip their restraints on the heaving tide. Though I have grown accustomed to the noises of the night, each chafe of wooden skin on skin still scratches at my senses and tempts me to go below. The chatter has abated inside my wooden cell, but I have still felt a presence in the darkness, crouching in the corners or cowering beneath my hammock like an imp. My guilt makes me ponder the girl's fate, and I have prayed that by some miracle, she has chanced upon some kindly planter, or used her charms to eke out a bearable existence. But I know that it is fancy, and that if she is not yet dead, then*

she soon will be - in a month, in a year, or in three at most. If the eyewitness testimony of our new shipmate is to be believed, she may have already ended her own life before the ravages of time and toil can take their toll. I am tormented by his stories, which gnaw away at me like the ship's rats that only come out at night, lest they be hurled overboard by their tails. I know that I deserve the same fate for my compliance in this, the most dreadful of crimes, but here I am, and I have no doubt, will be again. The rats are back.

<u>4th February 1788</u>

    I have succumbed to the urging and have been below deck this morning. I heard noises emanating from beneath the waterline and I had to satisfy myself that it was not the boy; I can tell no one and have told no one. I slipped from my rooms and entered via the half deck hatch next to the gun deck, which is left unlocked now that we have left the islands in case of threats from pirateers. The port holes were all closed up to keep out the sea water, which would otherwise spoil the cotton and tobacco leaf – its scent is strong down there - and so the draw of daylight is limited to a few isolated shafts that pour in through the grating. The pungent smell of body odour is still rife, its stench absorbed into the boards, which are slippery underfoot. I crawl about on my haunches like some forest animal and squeeze my way between the unresponsive cargo. I wriggle on until I think I am positioned in the space beneath my cabin, contorting myself into position as I bend between the platforms where three or four bodies were so recently packed. Like those that went before me, I lay on my back, the bare boards pressing against my spine, and feel each roll and smack of the hull upon the ocean. The sound of it, just a few inches below the keel, drowns out all others, until I grow accustomed to its rhythm, and become attuned to the silence that waits between each wave. I wonder if this is how it was for them or if in their terror and torment such senses are scoured away. In the rationed light, I imagine their faces ingrained in the wooden hull– woodgrain eyes etched into every knot, like engravings on a print-shop block, immortalised in ink though their blood runs red. Once I think of it, I imagine that I can see them everywhere, peering at me in pairs from the perimeter. I fancy that I can hear them now too - those former occupants of this temporary tomb – who passed this way like cattle at market, living meat for the masses who care not for their suffering. Then I heard it. A heaving, snuffling, sobbing sound. Small. Pitiful. Human. I sat bolt upright in fright and hit my head hard against the upper platform, so hard that I saw stars and had to rub my crown vigorously to ease the pain. In fear of an infected wound, I took my leave and shuffled out of there. I was relieved to see no blood upon my hands. Nothing that was visible anyway, but I knew that there was already blood enough for one lifetime. My heads still hurts, and an egg-shaped bump has risen below my hairline. I did not venture below again and spent an uneventful night listening to the silence, as the ship shifted on the swell.

5th February 1788

The Trade Winds have arrived, and we are at last away. The Captain is in much better humour, after finding that a couple of landsmen have left us lightening his load and his wage bill when we get back to England. I am not. I haven't slept well, the overpowering stench of tobacco leaf permeates my quarters, and I am at a loss to understand from where it rises. I tell myself that it must be coming through the boards below, but that cannot explain why the aroma is so much stronger about me than it was in the cramped confines of the lower deck, and I can only think that the lingering reek of death and disease has overpowered it. It seems out of place. I wonder if it is my mind playing tricks on me, stoking my senses with more than my imagination can bear.

6th February 1788

The Captain's good mood did not last. More men are missing, without satisfactory explanation and the ship has been searched from fore to aft. They have been recorded as 'gone overboard' as there can be no other explanation – it is suicide, or murder, for there has been no bad weather that would account for their loss in a sudden freak wind or wave. None of them had seemed intent to destroy themselves and all seemed in fair spirits, and there has been no maltreatment by the officers of late, no more than the usual threats and harsh words. An all-hands call this morning assembled everyone on the half deck, but of a crew of nigh on twenty-five men when we departed at Jamestown, including the officers and our anonymous passenger, only twenty can now be accounted for, which is hardly enough to man the rigging should we fall foul of the weather again. It is a mystery, and the Captain wants answers.

8th February 1788

I have dispensed with my own rule and fraternised with the remaining crew and officers these last three days, the general consensus being that the Captain wants to reduce his expense and so has 'jettisoned' the men one-by-one since leaving port, though no one really believes it, least of all the officers who would need to be in on such a dastardly scheme. The Captain is old and fat, these men are young, he would not have had the strength to overpower them against their will. The thug Meadows thought he saw a light out on the quarter deck a few days after we put out from Jamestown, but on investigation, the upper deck was empty, and he found nothing amiss the next morning. The Captain has ordered a night watch in pairs from dusk until dawn, and I must take my part, doubling up with Evans as my partner every second week. Last night was the first and I'm glad to say that it passed without incident. A morning and evening rollcall has also been initiated, just before and after each watch and at last count we were still twenty. Everyone is now on their guard. I did not tell what I had heard. Maybe I should have, though I have heard nothing since. I am saying my prayers at night again now, a habit that I had long thought lost to me. I am sure that someone is listening to my mutterings, and I hope that it is God. I think that the rats are listening.

The impolicy of the slave trade.

Or to give it another less succinct title, how would Britain's economy have fared without it? How would the port cities and manufacturing towns of the kingdom have prospered? How would the wealth of the landed classes be impacted by its loss? Would the Empire continue its rapid expansion, were Britain to hand over the reins of The Trade to a rival nation like France or Holland, countries with whom England had only recently made a very tenuous peace. Moreover, what would the effect of cessation be on the plantation owners and their island economies, some of which remained under British rule and so provided a vital contribution to the financial state of the Great British nation.

Such questions had taxed more gifted minds that that of Thomas Clarkson and yet such considerations had already put paid to the Quakers' long-standing humanitarian argument for the abolition of what was, for those who had no personal stake in it, an abhorrent undertaking. An economist's dream, but a mathematician's nightmare, and one that Thomas Clarkson was forced to accept as his primary occupation throughout the long and hard winter of 1787 to 1788. He lost count of the number of times he had refilled his inkwell or of the number of quills that he had split, and the pile of parchment on which he wrote up his mammoth report, had littered his study floor long before the last snows had started to thaw.

The book was addressed to William Wilberforce Esq. 'one of the Members of Parliament for the county of York', and in true eighteenth-century deference, was signed off by Thomas Clarkson as 'I have the honour to be, Sir, your sincere and obedient servant'. He spelled out in clear and unambiguous language, that his purpose from the outset had been only to prove that, having already shown the injustice and inhumane basis for The Trade, 'the African slave trade has not that sound policy for its basis, which people have but too generally imagined'. In it he laid out the results of his research in four sections; the produce of Africa, which could be traded should a proper basis for economic trade be established, the cruelties of the officers towards the slaves and the crew, the loss of the seamen with seven or eight thousand men willing to testify to it and finally, a list of plantations and their owners that had proved to be successful 'without' the need for a slave labour force.

Clarkson took great care to emphasise the legitimate opportunities that Africa could offer up to the merchants of Great Britain if the nation could just see beyond its myopic obsession with the shipment of human cargoes to the New World. An honest trade in exotic woods like mahogany, camwood, barwood and the newly discovered tulip wood could, he argued, provide the country's army of skilled cabinet makers and luthiers a clear advantage over their European competitors in the manufacture of fine furniture and musical instruments. Superior pigments drawn from the bark of African trees and from the far superior strains of indigo, would be produced more cheaply than from current sources and result in much more vivid and long-lasting dyes, to the obvious advantage of the cotton and linen manufacturers of Yorkshire and Lancashire. Agricultural produce such as black and cayenne peppers, a variety of gums and a whole new world of spice, were readily available for commercial advantage. Not to mention exceptional strains of rice, cotton, and tobacco, that far outstripped anything that was available in the islands of the West Indies and on the mainland of America which, since American Independence, had seen unstainable price increases to the detriment of Britain's manufacturing base.

And Clarkson's point?

That all of this was within the grasp of the merchants of Great Britain, without the need for a trade in human lives, but rather as the result of investment in African cultivation and free enterprise amongst their peoples. In so doing, Britain could break the present monopolies of the French and the Dutch, whose own duties on slave-produced raw materials had pushed up the price of our own manufacturers and depressed their profits. Whilst he was not espousing the merits of 'fair trade', nor for the 'free trade' that Adam Smith had written of just a decade before, he was certainly in favour of a fairer arrangement for Africa.

"It's as if they are blinded to the possibilities," said Clarkson on his return to London, deep in conversation with Granville Sharp, as they prepared for their confrontation with the Board of Trade. "These merchants are so drunk on the profits of their present cargoes, that they simply cannot see that at a much-reduced risk, their businesses would stand to make so much more, and their eternal souls might yet be saved."

The Fenlands had endured another hard winter. The snowdrifts were still piled high along the dykes, enclosing the edges of the land in frozen channels, lying solid under winter's white blanket. Each ancient irrigation ditch was filled to overflowing, the land within gripped in Jack Frost's steely embrace, as Thomas Clarkson finally put down his pen and longed once more for the open road.

In the intervening months, he and his stoic Society had kept up their unrelenting pressure on the government of the day, with each of them agitating through letters published in local newspapers and submissions to every Member of Parliament in the land. Right across their network, a series of chain letters had been distributed by the Quakers, encouraging its members and their business contacts to make their horrified voices heard, 'topping and tailing' the letters to add their own personal stamp of authority, before bombarding the local population with their latest campaign literature. It was a pressure group like no other, one that did not discriminate based on station or gender. The lords and ladies of the land were to be fully engaged in the conversation and they were, dinner parties and coffee mornings being a prime target for the movement, along with the newly emergent factories of the mercantile and manufacturing classes. The wives of prominent Quakers also had a significant say on matters, taking full advantage of their equal footing in the confines of their meeting houses, to raise an unprecedented hue and cry about the town in a full rejection of The Trade and all of its evil trappings.

Chief amongst the marketing material was 'The Print', which would soon be disseminated far and wide across the nation, onto the very benches of the House of Commons and its more entitled equivalent, the House of Lords – where many would stare at it in disbelief and so, at first, reject it out of hand as 'pure propaganda' at the hands of the Abolitionists. In the preceding Parliament, a Captain Parrey had been dispatched to Liverpool to assess the slave ships at the quayside. It was an attempt to test out their capacity for human storage and so, to be able to prove or disprove the claims of Clarkson and his fellow agitators, that these ships were regularly stocked to brutal levels.

What they did not reckon on, was that once the true dimensions and capacity of these low-slung ships had been properly assessed, that the printing press would be put to work to produce the most powerful portrayal of human suffering that the world had ever seen.

The Brookes was the first ship that Parrey came across on that fateful day. It was the first ship that he climbed aboard and the first that he measured, taking his time to trace every line and to assign a number in feet and inches to its bulkheads and its beams. It was also the first ship named on his report and so the first one that would be discussed in Parliament that following spring, when Clarkson returned with its first edition, safely stored away in his satchel, lest the light might lessen its power, like some sacred book or ancient scripture from the banks of the Jordan river.

The engraving was taken at a scale of one-eighth of an inch to a foot and it marked every room and space on board The Brookes, in sections cut across its bows. Parrey had also investigated other ships in dock that day, The Kitty and The Venus amongst them, and was satisfied that the measurements that he had taken on board The Brookes, represented as close to the average for all nine ships as was possible to get. It was therefore a representative model, a good illustration of the dimensions of the average English slave ship in use across the triangular route in the late eighteenth century.

But this was not an exercise in engineering. It was not a 'make it at home' instruction kit for the budding sailing enthusiast. It was an insight into the savage depths that a man will sink in order to maximise his profit and satiate his greed.

A white man.

An Englishman.

A so-called 'civilised' man in those days. That those very same men were still capable of a level of depravity unknown since the days of Rome, with its gladiatorial battles and sacrificial games, was hard for Clarkson and his co-workers to fathom.

The stated capacity of this, an average slave ship, was four hundred and seventy human beings, a feat that would require precise packing below deck to use up all available space. It also required the insertion of additional platforms to split the space below deck into two, so using both the half and quarter decks to pack in the women and children. And yet, as The Print showed only too clearly, these cowardly Captains were somehow able to stow six hundred and seven people into the same spaces, giving each man, woman, and child a meagre width of just one foot in which to lie and a length that varied from six-foot one inch for a man or five foot ten inches for a woman.

Children had to make do with spaces of five feet or less.

The size of a coffin. As apt a measure as any.

Parrey had computed a twenty three percent surplus on an already staggeringly overloaded hull, with the double-decker arrangement affording each person a headroom of just two and a half feet. Meaning that any inclination that they may have had to sit up in their berths, during their long and torturous journey, would have been nigh on impossible. And beneath them a harsh rough timber floor. No bedding, no straw, nothing on which to lie other than the splintering joinery of a ship's skeleton. Conditions that would prevail for an absolute minimum of two months along the middle passage, which could sometimes last for two or three more if the weather was against them. It's likely that for many of these unfortunate souls, their enforced confinement would have begun months earlier, if they'd had the misfortune to be amongst the first to be captured on the African continent.

"I have it!" cried Clarkson, as he arrived back at the print room on Lombard Street. "This is what we have been waiting for gentlemen" he declared, bursting into the gloom from the cold of the courtyard and flinging his hat and tailcoat onto the floor in his haste. The Phillips brothers looked up from their printing presses at the same moment, their fingers blackened from their efforts to reposition the type-press into its frames, in readiness to hammer another revolutionary pamphlet into existence.

"What is it Thomas?" asked James, his interest aroused.

"How intriguing" smiled Richard at his fervent tone, delighted to hear his co-conspirator in full flow.

"It's a plan of a slave ship" said Clarkson, a little embarrassed that his explanation didn't sound quite as exciting as the build-up that he'd given it. He withdrew the drawing from the satchel and laid it out before the three of them, letting the picture speak for itself, and this time it did not fail to live up to the billing.

"Are those all bodies?" asked Richard, fearful that he already knew the answer to his question.

"Surely not" said James, incredulous. "Is each one of those really a human body?"

"Every single one" Clarkson sighed. "And they are forced to lie like that for many weeks. Only the women and children are allowed to roam around the decks, as they aren't seen to pose a threat of insurrection. The men lay in chains the whole time. If the weather is agreeable they might be allowed to come up on deck for eight hours in every twenty-four, though they must remain chained to the decks at all times, but when the weather is rough as it often is, then they are forced to stay below, with the portholes up. For weeks on end."

"It makes me want to be sick" said James. "I can't look at it a moment longer" and he turned his back on it, returning to his place at the printing tables, and the acidic tang of ink that permeated from the comfort of his own corner of a pre-industrial world.

"If we can print this out by the thousands and get it distributed throughout the country ahead of the Parliamentary Enquiry" suggested an animated Clarkson, "it could just be the rallying call that we need. It could turn the tide of public opinion, just in time for the debate."

"How quickly can we get it out James?" asked Richard, placing the diagram before his reluctant elder brother once more.

"It's quite complex," said James rubbing his chin, as he examined the engraving in more detail. "The typesetting is not easy, and the illustration itself is going to be challenging, as there's just so much detail. We also have to get the Falconbridge tract out next week."

"Sorry" said Clarkson, "I had completely forgotten about that, of course, Alexander's work must take precedence."

"Well, that one's almost ready," said James, "we've already printed out half of it, so once the rest is done, all four thousand copies of each page that is, then it's just the binding and the distribution, so we should be done with it in a matter of days."

"Let me go and talk with Sharp and he can show it to Wilberforce" said Clarkson. "Let them decide the priority, but I've a feeling that each of them will want to see a copy of both papers on every seat in each House, as soon as Parliament is back in session."

No one disagreed and as the two men got back to work, Clarkson departed in the direction of Old Jewry, to catch up with his friend Granville Sharp, before the working day was out.

-o0o-

"You say the local Society in Plymouth produced this?" asked Sharp, amazed by the latent power that now sat in his trembling hands.

"Yes," said Clarkson, "they based it on the measurements taken by Parrey and so took the initiative to get it drawn up. They've already distributed some copies locally and its caused quite a hullabaloo, but we have their permission to take it nationwide using the printing capacity at our disposal."

"What else did you discover on your tour of the southern counties?" said Sharp, arranging the document in a prominent position on his desk and not taking his eyes off it for a moment. "Any other scrapes with the local slaving community? Any more duels with old seadogs?"

"I've only one incident to tell you about," said Clarkson, a little defensively, unsure if he was being made fun of. "But I will leave that for another time. I managed to cover almost sixteen hundred miles and toured the naval towns of Gravesend and Portsmouth and the ports of Exeter and Falmouth, before returning through Bristol and the Medway towns."

"Quite the trip," said Sharp, "I was pleased to see that you completed the essay on the impolicy of The Trade, before you embarked on your little tour. I've read it a couple of times and I have to say, it's very good. I'm sure that it will hit the mark for the select committee, though I'm still concerned that the slave traders hold the whip hand. Tensions are rising with the French, *The Rights of Man* has caused quite a lot of noise - there's a revolution in the air they say and they're in no mood to join forces with us and if they do, we could stand accused of encouraging revolutionary forces in our own back yard. We need to tread very carefully Thomas," warned Sharp, "our very reputations are at stake."

"The lives of one hundred thousand Africans are what's at stake!" Clarkson snapped back "And that's just in this year alone. Bristol has moved four hundred thousand on its own since their first involvement in The Trade and Liverpool is now exceeding Bristol's annual totals by ten to one. It's out of control, but it has to stop before we empty Africa of all of its people. I'm told that the West Coast is already a waste land thanks in the main to this 'Great' land of ours!"

Sharp nodded gravely, knowing that his comrade at arms was well informed, but still concerned not to lose his place at the political table by overstepping his position before they were ready with all the evidence. "Wilberforce is very ill," he announced without warning, an unexpected piece of devastating news that was unknown to Clarkson until that moment. "He's taken to his bed for a few days now and is under his Doctor's strict orders to stay there. He is unlikely to be able to take his seat in Parliament for the next session and so is not available to speak at the Select Committee."

It was just about the worst news possible, as without their spokesman on the Parliamentary benches they would be voiceless at a most critical moment, just when the momentum for change was building. It was a disaster in the making and if they were to ward it off, then time was of the essence.

"You will need to talk to Pitt" instructed Sharp in a moment of inspiration. "It has to be you, he's a detail man and if it's his voice that Parliament will hear on this matter in Wilberforce's absence, then he needs to be properly briefed, by you."

"I hear that he is quite the orator."

"Yes, that's true," said Sharp, "but he doesn't suffer fools, and if he smells any kind of horseplay, he will drop us like a hot potato. He supports our cause, some say that he was the one that persuaded Wilberforce to take it on, but he faces pressures from all sides and answers only to the King. He has all of the Empire on his shoulders, and he knows that just because something is justified, it doesn't mean that it's going to get the support of the required number of members. He will want to know all of the details Thomas, and now that you have visited all corners of the kingdom, you're our man. It has to be you."

"I hope so," said Clarkson, a familiar self-doubt rising as nerves began to get the better of him. It was one thing to move amongst the mercantile classes and to rub shoulders with the gentry, but to walk the halls of the ruling classes was another matter entirely.

"I know so" said Sharp firmly, "and I will be impressing on him tomorrow, in person, that he must make time to see you before the week is out. So be prepared to be summoned at a moment's notice and have all of your facts to hand. And take your 'box of tricks' with you," he ordered, "he'll like that, he's a very tactile type, so let him handle them all for himself."

-oOo-

Thomas Clarkson's audience with William Pitt, the Younger, came far sooner than either of them thought it would. The very next day in fact, and Clarkson hurried to the PM's plush rooms on The Mall, weighed down with an assortment of books, papers and his trusted chest of 'African Productions', which had to be carried into the audience by two smartly dressed footmen. There was a lot to cover, and he was unsure of how to proceed, or the order in which to relay the fountain of knowledge that he had acquired. As it turned out, he let the Prime Minister lead the way.

Despite his popularist title, William Pitt did not look all that young, though in that year of 1788 he was still the right side of thirty. His short years in politics had already aged him long before his time and he was well known in parliamentary circles for his ability to get by on just a few hours' sleep a night. He was very welcoming though and more than keen to see and hear from slavery's 'moral-steam-engine', as Clarkson would soon be known. He had come armed to the teeth with all manner of evidence from the very eye of the storm and neither man could wait to get started.

"So, I hear that you've been busy this last year" said Pitt, "I have been kept fully abreast of your activities by Wilberforce and Sharp and they are most complimentary of your role in all of this. It is a noble cause Sir, one that brings you the utmost credit."

"Why thank you Prime Minister," said Clarkson, a little taken aback at the unexpected praise. "I will not rest until this evil trade is at an end. I am not prepared to sit back on my laurels, until its scourge is wiped from the face of the earth. And when it is, all of the glory will belong to God and not to me, for I am merely His instrument in this undertaking."

"That's quite a soliloquy for one man," said Pitt, a little overwhelmed by the response. "I fear that it may take time to achieve your goal, even a whole lifetime, are you ready for such a commitment?"

"I am Sir" said Clarkson stoically, "even if it takes charge of my whole life, I will stay the course. Or I will die trying. Every step that I have taken these past two years, every stone I have turned, has revealed yet more of its vile injustice in all of its shameful truth and, I fear that even now, there is yet more that lies undiscovered."

"Good man," said Pitt encouraged, but it was time to get down to business. "So, let's see what you've brought along."

Clarkson withdrew some examples of the muster rolls from his satchel and his own volumes of names and mortality rates, that he had gleaned from the annals of the Custom House records across England. "As I think you know Sir, the death rate amongst our sailors on these voyages is beyond belief, these are the records that I have used to prove it is so. There is no denying them."

Pitt was astonished at these revelations and although he had heard the rumours, and the counter-rumours from amongst the slaving community, seeing the muster rolls for himself, in all of their stark honesty, was almost too much for him to take in. He rifled through them for a full half an hour, looking at the sheets in minute detail and prompting Clarkson to explain some of the references and terms employed. Finally, he sat back in his fine leather chair and regarded Clarkson with steely eyes. "You mean to tell me, that it is quite 'usual' for a ship to lose up to half of its crew to disease or worse still, at the hands of the officers, in a single circular voyage?"

"It is Sir," Clarkson confirmed gravely, "it was one of the most shocking truths that I uncovered amongst the drinking dens of Bristol, that most crew members are terrified to put to sea, for they know that their chances of coming back alive are barely one in two, but they are often given no choice in the matter. Many take the first opportunity that comes their way to desert, even if it means surviving alone in the Tropics, so the death rate that I have been able to report, is most likely Sir, understated in the extreme."

"This is most valuable research" Pitt applauded, "most damning, as it strikes at one of the slaving communities long held assertions, that without these men, our navy would lose a steady stream of willing recruits. That would seem to be a load of poppycock based on these reports Clarkson. I have no doubts of that now, none whatsoever. I have had my own suspicions for many years on this matter, having discussed it myself with the Lords of the Admiralty, but now I have the facts. The facts are what we need. And what of the slaves?" said Pitt, striking at the heart of the matter. "What of their treatment? Are things quite as bad as I've been led to believe by Sharp and Wilberforce?"

Clarkson placed his one and only copy of The Print on the table before the Prime Minister and left him to absorb its contents for a minute or two, before adding to the narrative. "I have run out of words Sir, to describe their treatment at the hands of our countrymen. Their behaviour towards these poor Africans makes me ashamed to be an Englishman, but I believe that this engraving provides a sufficiently damning picture of how they are dealt with, at least upon the middle passage of the triangular route."

Pitt said nothing but endeavoured to read the explanations that were printed in small typeface at the bottom of the drawing. He was breathing heavily, his forehead drawn up into a frown and his fingers rapping on the polished surface of his red-brown rosewood desk.

"The Brookes is one of the ships that Parrey used to compile his data," explained Clarkson. "He will be presenting this to the select committee of the Board of Trade in their upcoming sitting, and he is very confident that it is a representative likeness, as he has been on board eight other of Liverpool's slave ships. According to his calculations and from what he has been told, over six hundred Africans - men, women, and children - were packed into spaces designed for no more than the four hundred and seventy that you see here displayed."

"How?" Pitt demanded, but Clarkson was at first reluctant to provide the answer. Both men were ashamed by what they saw before them, knowing that the mistreatment was still continuing at that very moment, under the banner and authority of the Union flag.

"By laying them on top of one another," said Clarkson eventually, plucking an answer from the air. "By letting the women and children roam free on the upper deck when the weather permits. So many die by this cruel treatment Sir, that between one and two-thirds don't make it to the plantations at all. They perish on board our ships in the utmost filth and squalor."

"The major cause?" asked Pitt, "other than their general mistreatment."

"The flux Sir, or dysentery to use its proper name" Clarkson presumed. "Smallpox sometimes, or yellow fever, though that usually takes a greater toll on the crew, especially in their first year in the Tropics. Suffocation also Prime Minister, when the portholes are closed and the bodies are laid double, it's often the case that many are found dead in the morning from asphyxiation."

"Sickening" muttered Pitt, a rising sense of anger gripping him "and I hear that you've managed to secure the testimony of several ship's Doctors for the committee?"

"Yes Sir," said Clarkson, "three have come forward, most notably Alexander Falconbridge whose written account is in production as we speak, and James Arnold who has recently sailed from Liverpool aboard The Ruby. I also know of another Doctor, Gardiner is his name, who is presently at sea as ship's surgeon aboard The Brothers and who is keeping a detailed journal for our use on his return."

"It is a most thorough and deserving piece of work Clarkson" said Pitt resoundedly. "You are to be commended and even though I know you won't accept it, I want to personally thank you for all of your diligence in this most important matter of our times. Quite possibly of all time."

"One other thing," said Clarkson, ignoring the unsolicited praise. "I have some African goods here, which I believe will show that we would be far better served if we were to trade with our African cousins, for goods and not slaves." He opened up the chest and began to withdraw examples of exotic wood and local manufacturers of leather and textile. Pitt was astonished, picking each of them up and turning them about in his hands, a look not unlike wonder on his face. His contemplation may have run for a full quarter hour, before he placed the objects back into the box, rose to his feet and navigated the circumference of his large table, to take Clarkson firmly by the hand in one final show of support.

"Thank you for shedding so much light on this grave injustice – you have given me so much food for thought on this great question."

"It is my honour and my duty, Prime Minister."

"Then you have acted most honourably and far exceeded all reasonable expectation in your duty, Sir" said Pitt. "I am in your debt. So is our nation, though I fear that not every corner of our land will prove to be as indebted to you as they should be."

CHAPTER SEVENTEEN

"How can you carry on the slave trade moderately? How can a country be pillaged and destroyed in moderation? We cannot moderate injustice."

Charles James Fox, Britain's first Foreign Secretary

It was Thursday 6th March 1788, a date that would go down in history, at least amongst the growing number of dissenting Methodists across the length and breadth of England and around the world.

On Reverend Thomas Clarkson's return from the wildest reaches of the West Country, he had planned to take a path through the low-lying Mendip hills to Bristol, a most appropriate place to end his tour of England's slave trading ports, for he was back where he had started. His reason for being in town on that inconsequential Thursday in March, had nothing whatsoever to do with the Bristol Society of Slaving Ventures; nor was he in the least bit interested in stopping by the quayside to check out the several slave ships, that were each in the process of being fitted out for yet another raid on the southern continent. His sole intention on that pleasant spring afternoon was to make a stop at the New Rooms on Horsefair, where John Wesley's much anticipated sermon on the slave trade was due to be delivered; a speech that would form the basis for the preacher's upcoming tract on slavery, and yet another print from the presses at George Yard.

He had arrived a day early and had been alerted to a much-anticipated performance of William Shakespeare's 'Othello – the Moor of Venice'. It was taking place at the Theatre Royal on King Street, just a stone's throw from the public houses that he had come to know so well on his first visit to Bristol. The lead role was being played by an up-and-coming actor who went by the stage name of James Middleton, an Irishman – James Magan - who by all accounts had once trained as a surgeon and as rumour had it, had spent his younger years as a surgeon's mate on board a Liverpool slave ship. It had seemed like too good an opportunity for Clarkson to pass up and so, shortly after his arrival, he found himself ducking beneath the ticket office doorframe.

"You're in luck, my lover," the attendant smiled, using a term of address that is solely to be found amongst the people of Bristol and the West Country. "I've a few tickets left in the pit, none for the boxes or for the dress circle no more, nor for the Gallery."

"How much for the pit?" asked Clarkson, struggling to extract his tightly drawn purse.

"That'll be two shillings and six pence Sir," she said, running him off a ticket and handing him an order of service before he could change his mind. "It's very popular, that Mr Middleton, he's so 'ansome, I think I might take 'im home later, if I can get me hands on 'im. He's gert lush, he is."

What she meant by that, Clarkson had no idea, but he had no time to ponder on it. The performance was due to start at six o'clock precisely, and so with little time to spare, he grabbed himself a rather dubious looking pie from one of the street vendors outside, before striding through the central arch of the flat-fronted and newly fashioned edifice and making his way inside.

Standing on the uneven flagstone floor of the pit, he was surprised to find it so claustrophobic, hemmed in by the rising hum of expectation. The wooden benches on which he was soon to be sat were crammed tightly together, surrounded on all three sides by a two-storey timber balustrade of enclosed circle and gallery seats, with two more pairs of elaborately framed boxes sitting one on top of another astride a tiny stage. The ceiling was ornately decorated in gold and green, and as he strained his neck to admire the stuccoed plasterwork of the most intricate design, he became suddenly aware of just how conspicuous he must have appeared to onlookers seated in the surrounding stalls.

He slunk quickly down, though he remained head and shoulders above everyone else, and without his hat, his ginger shock of hair must have shone like a beacon in an otherwise bland and boring sea of brown and grey. There was no way he could make himself any smaller and so he slouched down in sudden paranoia, certain that the eyes of Bristol's finest families were firmly fixed upon him. He was desperate for the curtain call to signal a dimming of the lights, but time seemed to be standing still, and so he did his best to keep his head down, trying not to catch the eye of anyone who might know him and so alert the outside world to his presence.

Finally, the candles were extinguished, the near darkness silencing the boisterous chatter from the audience like roosting birds at dusk, Rodrigo and Iago burst upon the stage. All eyes became transfixed upon an artistic backdrop of an imagined street in Venice, complete with canals and brightly painted gondoliers.

But it was too late. He had already been noticed.

-OOO-

During the interval, he couldn't help but eavesdrop on a few passing conversations, as he pushed his way through the crowd in search of some refreshment. It seemed that the young Mr Middleton, who's 'blacked-up' version of Shakespeare's anti-hero had so far gone down a storm, was of questionable character, having already built up quite a reputation for late night antics and bawdy parties during the show's recent run at the theatre's sister establishment in Bath. He was certainly every bit the slave ship officer, if his growing reputation was anything to go by, and Clarkson was very much looking forward to making his acquaintance backstage at the end of the night. He planned to ask how he'd managed to swap the wooden decks of a slave ship for the wooden boards of the stage, whilst at the same time, hoping to hear more tales of trauma to add to his ever growing collection. He rightly suspected that this, the unlikeliest of impresarios, would be so 'puffed up' with his own importance that he would be only too willing to speak of his experiences on the high seas as to do so would add greatly to his own mystique, a rare quality amongst the acting fraternity.

Just as he was about to heed the final call to make his way back to his seat, he was rudely intercepted by a flustered bell boy, who thrust several small calling cards into his hand, before retreating into the wings as if his tailcoat was on fire. In the dimly lit auditorium, none were easy to read, but as Clarkson peered more closely, he was soon able to make sense of the messenger's urgent errand.

'Get out of Bristol', read the first, scrawled across the back of Mr Pretor Pinney's business card; 'Leave tonight, you don't belong here', the next one read, a message from Mr J. Tobin; 'See you in Court," read the next, the name of Freke emblazoned on the other side in bold black stylised lettering. There were others besides, but he wasn't inclined to read them; he got their drift, and as the lights were already fading, he was ushered back to his place, or as near as he could get to it, for the second half of the night's Tragedy.

Clarkson didn't enjoy the final act very much at all. The acting was not to his liking, far too dramatic and extravagant, as the part of Othello was hammed up to full effect by a flushed Mr Middleton. He roared and ranted his way through his lines, bellowing over the more mellow tones of his fellow thespians, and beating on a desperate Desdemona with more force than seemed entirely necessary. Clarkson's attention had been drawn away from the stage and towards the exclusivity of the box to his left, where a brooding Tobin and a rather aloof looking Penny, sat in demure silence alongside their immaculately turned out wives. Each of the men was sporting a closely manicured white wig, that was pulled tightly into curls at the side and furnished with the same ponytails that had long since gone out of fashion in London.

As for the ladies, their fashionable wigs were much more substantial with no expense spared in their decoration; gaily coloured feathers about the tops, each tied up in an abundance of expensive French ribbon. Neither look impressed Clarkson, who like his Methodist brethren, took a dim view of such self-important shows of decadence; for the wealthy mercantile families of Bristol, it offered a fitting display of excess that they had no doubt at all was well in keeping with their newly established status. They were the 'new money' about town and so they were determined to show it off at every available opportunity and this 'opening night' show was to be no exception.

Every now and again, he caught one of the men regarding him, their eyes burning down on him in the pit, as if they were the Lords on high and he, the poor sinner cast down with the Devil. He watched them as they shared a joke or two at his expense, the object of their derision made all too clear by a synchronised turn of their heads. On one occasion they even engaged their wives in the joke, Tobin pointing out Clarkson's prominent frame amongst the crowd below whilst doing an impolite impression of an ape or monkey, their haughty laughter audible from his lowly vantage point. He did not wait to see how the play ended; he had seen it before in London, and though he was rather looking forward to watching this particular Othello's tormented demise, he could not bear to stand witness to his overzealous death throes. He picked his moment to excuse himself, during a scene change, and made his way through the packed auditorium to the streets outside, where he inhaled deeply and mopped his brow in relief.

The second that he reached King Street; he knew that something was wrong.

Since his dice with death in Liverpool, he had developed something of a sixth sense for danger, and though the cobbled street looked empty enough, it was eerily sparse for a pleasantly warm spring evening. In that instant, he decided against waiting around for the play to end on the off chance of an unlikely interview with a second-rate actor and determined to make it back to his lodgings before the rest of the bawdy audience spilled out onto the streets.

It was then that he caught sight of a ragged posse of men, loitering on the corner of the street and blocking the walkway through to Queen Square. He looked right in the direction of Prince Street, but another gang of paid ruffians were similarly positioned on the opposite side. In their hands he caught a glimpse of a hefty cosh or two, and the deadly flash of a silver blade, and the sight struck fear into his now racing heart.

As before in Liverpool, he knew that the element of surprise might give him a crucial advantage and so without hesitating for a moment longer, he darted ahead, aiming straight for a narrow alleyway between two buildings, just as the two sets of men took flight towards each other in a vain attempt to catch their target where they met. He reached the gap two strides ahead of his pursuers, but he could hear their cries and their heavy footsteps echoed against the walls on either side, as he burst out into the next street and into the waiting arms of his self-appointed local bodyguard.

And Thompson had brought with him a gang of his own.

As a crowd of twenty or more heavily armed lynch mobsters faced off against each other, it was Thompson who spoke up to prematurely disperse the opposing crew into the night air.

"Leave 'im be" he ordered, "you 'ave no business with this man."

One of them took a step forward, brandishing a blade of seven or eight inches. Another offered back-up, snarling like a caged animal as he raised his own cutlass in defiance of Thompson's words.

"Don't be a fool McNulty" said Thompson. "I knows most of you, if there's any trouble 'ere this night, you'll be up afore the magistrate in the morning. Whatever they've paid 'ee, it's not worth a hanging." The threat was enough to convince the ringleaders to call off their pre-planned attack, and as they turned their backs to return to their normal nocturnal pursuits in the nearby pubs and brothels, Clarkson breathed a huge sigh of relief as he turned to thank his friend and ally, without whom his life may already have been at an end.

"How did you know I was here?" he asked, wiping the sweat from his brow with a shaking hand.

"Word travels quick in this town," said Thompson. "One of the landlords sent a runner sayin' that a mob was bein' raised in the Marsh Street dens to set about a red-headed Abolitionist, who'd been clocked in the theatre. Well, it could only have been thee."

Clarkson declined an invitation to return to the Seven Stars with Thompson, preferring instead the safety of his room where he would spend what was left of the evening, but both men agreed to meet up the next day at The Africa House, where the clergyman would update his local informant on the progress made by The Society since their last engagement. In the end, they were destined to spend most of the following afternoon in conversation, and it would be time well spent. Thompson was keen to hear that real progress in the capital's corridors of power was being made against The Trade and in return, the publican was able to share more intelligence about recent and upcoming voyages, all of them embossed with further narratives of crime and skulduggery upon the streets of his adopted hometown.

There was no doubt that Clarkson was now a marked man amongst the slaving community and though another dice with death had come and gone, he knew that his luck was wearing thin. Though he thanked God for his divine deliverance from yet another close call, Thompson left him in no doubt that he had to be more careful, and that warning was still ringing in his ears as he approached the cobbled courtyard of the New Rooms - the chapel and Bristol residence of John Wesley. It was already bustling with people, a full two hours before the scheduled time, but rather than putting himself in harm's way once more by scouring the streets for a quiet coffee shop to while away an hour or two, Clarkson instead made his way inside. Wesley's fame as a fine orator had spread far and wide and people were known to come from miles around to hear him speak, and not only those, like Clarkson, who were in need of something spiritual to soothe their unsettled souls.

His topic for the evening had been widely publicised, and the expectant audience would be dominated by native Bristolians, who had more than a passing interest in the slave trade itself. Whenever he had broached the subject locally in past rallies, Wesley had often been roundly heckled, especially when a flotilla of slaving vessels had been confined to port due to bad weather or lack of hands. There were several ships in dock today and so he fully expected to be the subject of ridicule bordering on outright hostility, and Clarkson could already sense the rising angst in the courtyard outside, where a bustling audience were getting high on the atmosphere.

The Captains, Agents and owners would sometimes offer bonuses to those amongst their crews, who were most vocal in barracking the preacher whenever his words became too critical, or to hurl insults whenever his sermon came too close to the truth. They would gather in a pack, at a depth of thirty to fifty men, some of them straight from the taverns of Marsh Street, half-cut and spoiling for a fight; shoulder to shoulder with the shipping clerks from the customs house, fearful for their jobs, or with the bankers from the counting houses, concerned for their investments. Once in position they would barge and shove, their foul language offensive to the ears of the regular churchgoers and upsetting the sensibilities of the city's gentlemen and their genteel wives.

Clarkson strode in through the wooden doors to the front of the grey chapel, then dipped his head under the door to his left, before stepping into the modest but impressive meeting room. He was first struck by the quartet of tall stone pillars that marked off the imaginary corners of a hexagonal sky light, through which a deluge of daylight streamed. A balcony ran down both sides of the space, where a few people were already seated, intent on grabbing the best view of the pulpit, which stood at the front and was raised up from the floor by means of a few modest steps. A balustraded staircase skipped its way down into the seat from which John Wesley would soon deliver his sermon, a large vellum Bible at the ready, laid open upon the lectern, a great vantage point from which to look down upon the standing scrum beneath.

The church organ was sat almost on the pulpit's shoulder, perched into the corner of the upper floor, from where its melodious sound would soon smother the room in harmonious song. From there, the music would roll down upon the crowd's heads in an acoustic delight, and when the large latticed window to the rear illuminated the preacher's form in a saintly silhouette, the significance of it would not be lost on his predominantly Christian congregation.

Clarkson took his seat on one of the long and simple oak benches, that sat to the left-hand side of what would soon be the focal point. He sat at the back, knowing that whoever chose to sit in the seat in front of him would be unlikely to obstruct his view of John Wesley, but also being well aware that should he have chosen to sit closer to the front, his mop of hair would no doubt have been an irritation to whosoever was sat behind him. In any case, he wasn't there to look at John Wesley, he knew full well what he looked like. He was there to listen, so much so that in all likelihood he expected to have his eyes closed in silent contemplation as soon as the great man stood to speak, to let the word of God do its work.

As if in preparation for the moment's arrival, he leant back against the oak panelled wall and rested his head up against it, listening to the steady beat of the large grandmother clock that was secured to the gantry above his head, giving the time at ten minutes past four. When he opened them again, the black iron arrows had moved in what seemed like an instant, to five and twenty minutes past five and in those missing minutes the room had been filled to bursting.

On the bench right in front of him, a family of four were balanced like a brood of chickens, father and mother perched like bookends at either end. Their two young daughters sat snug in between, dressed in their best Sunday clothes with their hair tied up in pale blue ribbons and their matching bonnets in their laps. The anticipation was palpable, a steady hum of chattering voices that vibrated around the room, a hundred indistinct conversations rolling into one continuous peal of excitement. From the door, people were somehow still finding their way inside, despite the crowd that had by now almost blocked the entrance and though Thomas Clarkson could not see it, the courtyard to the rear was also brimming within its brick-built walls. Outside, a disappointed crowd shuffled around that walled garden, but whilst they were able to admire the roses and other climbing plants, they were almost certainly about to miss out on one of the last and most important sermons that John Wesley would ever deliver in his adopted city.

Five minutes to go and a respectful hush had descended upon the heads of the assembled masses. A handful of black faces stood out amongst the crowd; servants of Bristol's merchant class that had preyed on their homelands for one hundred years or more, or maybe the children of stolen status symbols, kidnapped and kept captive as an officers' prerogative.

There was as yet no sign of Wesley, but the room grew quiet then, knowing that the moment was almost upon them. Those in their seats sat silently, their view secured, whilst those in the pit held fast to their spot, their feet firmly planted, their clammy hands sat on the shoulders of loved ones or grasped within another's, a wife's or husband's, mother's or father's, sister's, or brother's.

It was time and John Wesley wasted none, being as frugal with seconds as he was with words. He strode into the room, ascended the stairs, and claimed his customary place in his pulpit, all in a matter of seconds. There was no applause to greet his arrival, nor would he have wanted to have heard any. The glory was God's and he His humble servant. His aging hands reached forward to grasp the worn leather binding of the Bible on either side, as he raised his head and challenged the room with his eyes, surveying the gaze of every pair that stared back at him, to feed on his aura.

"Brothers and sisters," he began in the usual fashion.

"The scandal of Christianity, of England, of humanity. That most excregable of all villainies. Slavery." He paused for a moment to ensure that he had the full attention of every man, woman, and child in the room. Every Methodist and every Anglican, every pauper and every gentleman, every Captain, and every crew member. He wanted them all in his grasp, seated or struggling in the palm of his hand.

The silence that greeted him told him that they were his to do with what he would.

"Now, it is argued that there is an absolute 'necessity' for it – if it is not 'quite right', yet it must be so, it is 'necessary' that we should procure slaves. Well, I answer. You stumble at the threshold. I deny that villainy is ever necessary, it is impossible that it should ever be necessary, for any reasonable creature to violate all the laws of justice, mercy, and truth. No circumstances can make it necessary, for any man to burst asunder all the ties of humanity – the absurdity of the supposition is so glaring, that one would wonder that anyone could help see it. But to be more particular I ask, what is 'necessary' and to what end?"

They were listening now, the Captains and the plantation owners amongst them. There was no doubt to whom this speech was being directed and they were caught in its sights, the crossbow's bolt locked in on their rapidly beating hearts.

"Well, it is answered, that the whole method used by the purchasers of the Africans is necessary to the furnishing of our colonies yearly with a hundred thousand slaves. Well, I grant you, this is necessary to that end, but how is that end, 'necessary'?" He paused for a moment to let his message resonate, before continuing. "How would you prove it necessary, that one hundred, nay even one, of those slaves should be procured?"

Silence. Wesley looked straight into the dark eyes of a known slaver, standing just a little way back amongst the throng, almost daring him to offer up an answer, but the man could not hold the preacher's stare for long.

Guilty.

"'Why, it is necessary to my gaining a hundred thousand pounds' says the slave trader," teased Wesley, his eyes still fixed on the same shamed man. "Perhaps so, but how pray is this, 'necessary'? It is very possible that he might be both a better and a happier man if he had not a quarter of it, indeed I deny that his gaining one thousand pounds of it is 'necessary', either to his present, or to his eternal happiness."

"It is then argued that the furnishing of slaves is 'necessary' for the trade, wealth, and glory of our nation. Well, here are several mistakes," scoffed the preacher. "For wealth is not necessary to the glory of any nation, but wisdom, virtue, justice, mercy, generosity, public spirit, love of our country – these are all necessary for the real glory of our nation."

"But abundance of wealth, is not."

"Better not to trade at all than have trade produced by villainy," a statement that precipitated several pockets of inflamed grumbling amongst the audience. "It is better to have no wealth at all, than to gain wealth at the expense of virtue, better is honest poverty than all the riches brought by the tears and sweat and blood of our fellow creatures."

The audience was stirred into life at that statement, the Methodists and Quakers amongst them expressing their wholehearted agreement with it, whilst the other merchants and their shipmates, regarded each other with mixed expressions that ranged from discomfort to dishonour and a festering sore of outright anger.

"May I speak plainly to you?" asked Wesley, not expecting any of them to give him an answer and he didn't wait for one. "I must. Love constrains me, love to you, as well as to those you are concerned with. Is there a God? Well, you know there is. Is he a just God? Then there must be a time of retribution, a time wherein the just God rewards everyone, according to his works."

"Well then what reward will he render to you? Well think betimes, before you drop into eternity. Think now, as the scripture says, he shall be judged without mercy that shows no mercy. Are you a man? Well then you should have a human heart, but have you indeed? What is your heart made of? Is there no principle of compassion there, do you not feel another's pain? Have you no sympathy, no sense of human woe, no pity for the miserable?"

It was at that moment that Wesley first became aware of a low rumbling sound, a vibration that echoed around the hall, rising through the feet of the congregation, which occasioned some to shout out loud in shock and awe. The first benches that moved were up in the gallery, a hard scraping across the wooden boards of the balcony, as if some beast was moving amongst them, pushing their way out of the crowd in a rush to get away. Those seated there stood up in alarm, then another bench moved on the opposite side of the room to the same effect, but this time someone screamed, and Wesley looked up, thinking that his enemies in the town were finally about to make good on their threats to disrupt his preaching with a violent show of strength.

In the pit, a man stumbled and fell, as if pushed by some unseen force, landing roughly on his knees, caught in the arms of another. A woman fell backwards as if her hair had been pulled, her head jerking back to strike another on the chin, which caused pandemonium to break out in the hall. The panic spread as if a fire had burst up beneath their feet, but there was nowhere to run. The floor was like a sea of skittles, as a wave of bodies fell over each other in a sudden rush towards the doors, like a stampede of spooked livestock, as Wesley called out for calm.

Thomas Clarkson watched from the side lines with his mouth ajar, as the inexplicable scene unfolded before him. On his side of the room, several of the benches had also moved, as if pushed by unseen hands, forcing their occupants to their feet and then, in defiance of the known laws of nature, two were upended with such force that one was smashed against the outer wall, its frame splintering on impact into sharpened shards. The other danced a pirouette around the stone pillar, ending upside down on the opposite side, and colliding with two modestly dressed women, striking them so hard on their ankles that both crumpled onto their backsides, crying out in shock and not a little pain. A semi-darkness descended, as if a shroud had been laid across the whole building. The daylight was shut out for a moment in a grey-black shadow of something that was not of this world, and then in an instant the light barged its way back in through the skylight, and whatever it was over almost as quickly as it had begun. As the panic began to subside, Wesley's composed and soothing voice could be heard above their heads, pleading with them for order and calm. It took a few moments for his words to be heeded, by which time some people had already forced their way out of the chapel and into the courtyard, never to return, whilst others were busy righting the benches or helping the injured to find solace amongst the seated.

The Methodist minister had no explanation for it then, but the event would be recorded in the annals of Methodist folklore for years to come, and in Wesley's own journal as a 'vehement noise' when 'the terror and confusion were inexpressible, the people rushed upon each other with the utmost violence, the benches were broken in pieces and nine-tenths of the congregation appeared to be struck with the same panic'.

But that was for later, for now Wesley had a sermon to finish and he wasn't about to be put off its portentous truth by the quarrels of the Devil and his minions.

"And this equally concerns," he started slowly, "every merchant that is engaged in this trade in slaves, for it is you, that induces the African villain to sell his countrymen, or rather to steal, rob and murder, men women and children, without number, for it is you that enable the English villain and pay him for so doing." Most people remained nervous, as if in expectation of another attack, whilst those who had been intent on disrupting events that day were no longer of the same mind, but they were at least listening again and soon enough, they picked up the thread.

"It is your money that empowers him to go on, so whatever anyone does in this matter, it is all 'your' act and deed. Is your conscience quite reconciled to this? Does it never reproach you? Has gold entirely blinded your eyes and stupefied your heart, can you see, can you feel, no harm therein? Is it 'doing as you would be done to'? Make the case your own." He was speaking directly to the slave ship Captains and crew now and judging by the continued look of horror that was etched across some of their faces, the hardened hearts of one or two of them had clearly been softened by his words.

"Have no more part in this detestable business" Wesley pleaded, imploring them to turn to the light. "Instantly leave it!" he ordered. "Be you a man, not a wolf, a devourer of the human species; be merciful, that you might obtain mercy."

But he wasn't done there.

"And this equally concerns every gentleman that has an estate on our American plantations, nay all slaveholders. Now it is your money that pays the merchant, and through him the Captain and the African villain, you therefore, are guilty. And principally guilty of all these frauds, robberies, and murders – you are the spring, that sets all the rest in motion. They would not stir a step without you. Therefore, the blood of all these wretches, who perished before their time, whether in their country or elsewhere, lies upon your head. The blood of thy brother, that criest against thee from the earth, from the ship and from the waters. Whatever it costs, put a stop to its crime before it is too late."

As the sermon drew to its close, a few of those that remained, made a point of shaking John Wesley by the hand as they edged out of the room. No one confronted him. There was no anger and no immediate retribution for his words from those whose interests had been brought into question. Even the merchants just slipped quietly away, stunned by what they had heard and seen in the New Rooms that evening. Only the Reverend Thomas Clarkson dared to raise the question that was on everyone else's lips, but he waited until there were only a few onlookers left who might overhear their unqualified assessment.

"A most revealing evening" said Clarkson a little shakily, taking his fellow clergyman by the hand. As he did so, he thought that he could feel the faintest tremor in Wesley's fingertips, as if even he had been unnerved by the evening's unearthly events.

"I'm glad it was to your liking Thomas," he answered, knowing that he would soon have to pass judgement on the other less explicable occurrence. Clarkson wasted no time in getting to the point, refusing to let the Methodist minister off without giving him an opinion on the matter.

"What was that?" he asked not really expecting to receive any kind of satisfactory explanation. "Was it some kind of earth tremor? I have experienced such a thing once before, in the Potteries, but never one so savage and so prolonged as that."

"It was no earthquake!" answered Wesley, with a level of certainty that his ministerial friend had not expected. When his answer came, it struck Clarkson like a lightning bolt to the heart. "That was Satan," said Wesley with all the conviction that he could muster. "That was Satan himself, holding on to his kingdom."

Soon after Thomas Clarkson's return to London, the Privy Council met for the first time to discuss the question that was on every Englishman's lips; the abolition of the slave trade. The crumbling walls of Westminster Palace provided a grandiose, but inadequate venue for the debate, its antechambers being so small and cramped that the effect was to render every participant quite irritable by the end of a day's debating.

The sessions were not over in a few days; they ran on for months, in the face of an increasingly agitated public, who were demanding an answer to the one hundred and three petitions, that had found their way onto the crusty seats of the House of Commons in the first few months of open campaigning by The Society. During the course of that first month, Clarkson and Sharp had both feared the worst when, on the morning of the 22nd March 1788, the following statement had been published in the morning newspaper:

"After due examination, it would appear that a major part of the complaints made against this trade are ill founded ... some regulations, however, are expected to take place, which may serve in a certain degree to appease the cause of humanity."

The conclusion was premature, put about by the pro slavery body and their supporters in the press, who having decided that the case put by Clarkson, Sharp and Wilberforce must have been exaggerated for political gain, were quick to leap to the defence of the slavers. The Liverpool contingent had played a most prominent part in proceedings, and they were first to present their case, dominating the podium for the first few weeks in an attempt to debunk the plethora of damning material that had by then come from every corner of the British Isles.

Mr Norris strenuously denied that any kidnapping ever took place on the shores of Africa, claiming that their only sources came from 'just' wars between nations or from the outcomes of criminal trials.

They also claimed, without blinking even once, that The Trade on which their livelihoods depended was 'full of Christian virtue', relieving the African of the threat of imminent execution or sacrifice at the hands of their own countrymen. Their contentions caused quite a stir in the chamber, but the merchants were adamant; African slavers would execute any or all slaves that they did not sell, and the palaces of the African princes were bedecked with the sun-soaked skulls of a thousand slain Africans, all of them otherwise destined for salvation at the hands of their white rescuers.

The fantasy didn't stop there. Evidence was presented by the anti-Abolitionists, as they had become known, that the King of Dahomey would sacrifice thousands of his own people each year. They claimed that an annual poll-tax would be called, and a pamphlet was presented, in counter to those from the 'Quaker press', that The Trade was in fact a most humane one, as it had saved the lives of millions who would otherwise have fallen foul of local injustices and barbaric sacrifices to pagan idols.

To give it its full title, '*Scriptural research on the licitness of the slave trade: shewing its conformity with the principles of natural and revealed religion, revealed in the sacred writings of the word of God 1788*', written by Raymund Harris, a former Jesuit priest turned slaving-house clerk from Liverpool.

"Do I take it from this that the accounts I have read from Falconbridge and Newton are pure folly?" asked a dismayed Bishop of London, his eyes burning a hole in Thomas Clarkson's forehead. "If these are but idle tales, put about to shame and debase those on whom we are dependant for our commercial success, then I'll have them both in the dock before the session is out."

It was Penney Snr, the shipping magnate and former Captain of his own slaving ship that leapt to his feet, sensing an opportunity to hammer another nail into the coffin of the Abolitionist camp. "The Trade in African slaves has long since provided these poor fellows with accession to a greater happiness in the Caribbean islands, than any they could ever have hoped for in captivity at home." The chamber seemed full to the brink with similarly minded people, who together made an appreciative noise, not unlike the deep and guttural growl of a mountain bear.

Clarkson was furious that so many supposedly intelligent people were being carried away on the back of these outright lies and was more than outraged that he would have to defend his Society's calling as a Christian movement, in their endeavours to have The Trade abolished. That educated people were even capable of spreading such distorted propaganda seemed abhorrent to him, but having now heard it first hand and in the highest office in the land, Clarkson knew that they were in it for the long haul.

Finally, there was a change in the wind, and a respectable Member of Parliament, Mr Devaynes, himself an Africa trader, conceded that there were no human sacrifices that he had ever witnessed and no poll tax where lives were held forfeit. His only admission was that the old, lame, and wounded slaves, that had been captured by black traders in readiness for sale to the white slavers, would sometimes be summarily executed, but that this was not the case for fit and healthy 'specimens' who would always be held over until the next available market.

The Abolitionists had not expected to have to thank a member of the enemy's camp for supporting their own cause, but by casting doubt upon the evidence provided by the Liverpool men, he had inadvertently boosted the Abolitionist's position and their morale, though his choice of words came from an entirely different dictionary than the one that they used.

Finally, when Doctor Alexander Falconbridge was called upon to give his evidence and to account for the contents of his own recently published pamphlet, his truths were not to be so easily denied and when John Newton, former slave ship Captain and, by his own admission, a 'wretch', gave similar testimony to the barbarism of his former paymasters, the balance was redressed. African goods were presented, and Clarkson shared the various contents from his collection that proved beyond doubt, that the continent was fruitful and luxuriant and could prove to be a highly profitable trading partner, were the route not so polluted by the ills of The Trade.

At the end of several weeks, the council retired to make their preliminary report to the House and although Granville Sharp impressed on them the need for abolition in its entirety, the Prime Minister was as yet unconvinced. He assured Sharp and Clarkson that his heart was with them and that he remained fully committed to their cause, but it was not his heart that they were worried about; it was his head that was seemingly about to steer the country on a different course.

"This subject is one of great political importance," Pitt stressed as he waited to enter the House. "One that will require us to proceed with a modest temper and much prudence." It was all he had to say, and he quickly swept away, his robes flowing in his wake, billowing about his expensively soled feet that tapped out his departure, echoing across the flagstones of the hall like a diminishing cry for help that would soon go unheeded. It was not a reassuring message after months of back-breaking toil, and as they watched the younger man climb the steps into the medieval chamber, neither was confident that they were about to win a resounding victory for the oppressed African.

"I fear that the voices of commerce may prove to be too strong this time my friend," said Clarkson, his hand resting on the older man's shoulder. Sharp said nothing but watched after the Prime Minister like an agitated child, fearful of what the next few hours might bring and what their one and only champion in Parliament might have to tell them on his return.

-ooo-

In the Chapel of St Stephen, all four rows of benches were completely full, the elected Members of Parliament turning out in their numbers for a Commons debate on a subject which was 'top of mind' throughout their constituencies. Each of them had been bombarded with letters from the landed gentry, and although their wives were not yet blessed with the power of the vote, they too had made their views known in the strongest terms. Most of the letters received were from those who had been moved to action, having read the accounts of the now infamous Doctors and their former Captains, but the port cities and some of the manufacturing towns had also witnessed an almost unprecedented backlash at the prospect of complete abolition, that they foretold would undermine the very commerce on which their livelihoods depended.

The current incarnation of the chapel in which the House of Commons held its sessions, had been extensively restored by Sir Christopher Wren almost one hundred years before, in a time when slavery was still the sole enterprise of the London based Africa Company, which then commanded a complete monopoly in the trading of African slaves. Following Wren's renovations, the Chapel was now very much enclosed, its vaulted roof hidden within thick wooden panelling, that also obscured the formerly whitewashed walls from view with a much-improved wooden façade.

As Prime Minister, William Pitt was granted the Speaker's permission to address the house, a first amongst equals, he wasted no time in getting straight to the point. "I intend to move a resolution," he said, his voice resounding around the enhanced acoustics of the chamber, "which is of more importance than any which has ever been agitated here in this house." But prior to launching into his well-prepared address, he apologised for the absence, due to illness, of Mr Wilberforce, who would otherwise have taken to the floor, and he took the time to wish him God's speed in his recovery.

It seemed like a diversionary tactic. It looked like an excuse.

"The subject at hand is no less than the slave trade," he announced rather sheepishly, and lacking the forthright sense of justice that the full House before him warranted. "The great number of petitions which have now been presented to us from all corners of the land, has impressed on us the urgency in which this issue is regarded by our constituents and one that it is our duty to address with the maturest deliberation."

There was a general murmuring of agreement, neither side in the debate could take offence at his opening remarks and all agreed that, in view of the level of public interest, it was a given that their attention in this matter was long overdue. The subject had been ignored for long enough, like some unfortunate relative with an undiagnosed deformity, locked away in some anonymous tower in a remote highland glen for successive generations.

"It has been generally held, that the African slave trade ought to be abolished, although there are those who have commercial interests in The Trade who are of the strong opinion that it is only in need of regulation. But all parties are, in my humble opinion agreed, that it cannot remain as it is at present, requiring of a cool, patient, and diligent examination of the subject in all its circumstances, relations and consequences." A self-conscious Pitt droned on, a monotone retelling of the work that had been undertaken at his behest and though it was delivered with the full backing of the aforementioned William Wilberforce, it was clear to the gathered audience that it wasn't his to give. He spoke only in general terms of the investigations currently underway in the Privy Council, that would shortly result in a detailed report to be submitted for their review, but he did so without his customary gusto, as if he lacked the stomach for the fight that would surely follow.

Something was amiss and then, much to the disappointment of his two listening lieutenants, all was revealed, and it was a bombshell that neither eavesdropper had seen coming. After reading aloud the names of the one hundred and three towns and cities where petitions to outlaw The Trade had been raised, sometimes from amongst the general public, in other cases from certain religious groups or manufacturing sectors, without warning the Prime Minister moved for an unexpected delay in proceedings.

"That this House, will early in the next session of Parliament, proceed to take into consideration the circumstances of the slave trade complained of in the said petitions, and what may be fit to be done thereupon."

In the semi-darkness of the gallery that ran alongside the main hall, Granville Sharp beat his hand against the wooden panelled wall in exasperation. The thump would no doubt have been heard on the other side, and he did not doubt that his Prime Minister would have held a very strong suspicion as to its source. But neither Sharp nor Clarkson much cared and were only thankful that they were not present in the room in that moment, for the object of their anger would have been obvious and their cause undone.

William Pitt took his seat, taking care not to sit squarely on the fence that he had just so ably demonstrated to his right honourable colleagues. He was succeeded by Mr George Fox, a staunch opponent of slavery and of the Prime Minister who, after talking at length of his experience and knowledge of The Trade, made his position perfectly clear. "The slave trade ought not to be regulated, but destroyed" he proclaimed, before shredding the notion of any delay. "I am sorry that the question should even need to be considered further," he stormed, "particularly where so much human suffering is concerned, that it should be put off to another session, when it is plainly obvious that no further advantage can be gained by it."

Others took their turn at the plate, the Chancellor of the Exchequer refusing point blank to offer any opinion on the subject in advance of a full and frank debate and lending his full support to the PM's motion to delay. More vociferous support for the slaving community came in the shape of Mr Edmund Burke, formerly the MP for Wendover and Malton, but now representing the safe seat of Bristol. His defence of the merchants and planters was mainly one of concern for their reputations as "just and honourable men," yet for The Trade itself he somewhat surprisingly proved himself to be an opponent. "It ought to be abolished," he admitted in his strong Irish drawl, "on principles of humanity and justice, however, if opposition of interests should render its total abolition impossible, then it ought to be immediately regulated, without further delay."

It came as no surprise that the fiercest opposition came from the Member for Liverpool, Mr Gascoyne who was visibly furious at Burke's apparent stand-down and could hardly contain his indignation at the suggestion that his constituents were somehow implicated in a sordid and savage trade. "These men are of entirely respectable character, and they have been so shamefully smeared," he roared, giving his full support to a delay that would give more time to the Privy Council to come to the right and proper conclusions. "But as to the total abolition of the slave trade," he continued, "why, such a draconian measure is both unnecessary and impracticable, though some modification and regulation as to the transportation of the slaves would have my full support."

It was the cue that Pitt had been waiting for, but he was determined to leave it to others to make the case for him, choosing instead to continue the political theatre by looking to his fellow Tory and zealous Abolitionist, Sir William Dolben, to bring the first debate to a worthy conclusion. He avoided entirely the question of any delay, which he saw as a foregone conclusion, re-focusing the debate on the infamous middle passage, and raising the spectre of what he called the "immediate state of tenfold misery, which those poor Africans undergo in their transportation."

He believed that it was this portion that was in need of the most immediate censure, and he was determined that if he was unable to stop it in its entirety then he must at least achieve a modicum of restraint by outlawing the most outrageous practices that had long since become the accepted way of things.

"Hear, hear," the echo of a dozen or more voices sounded around the chamber in a clear show of support. Others added their voices to the growing clamour for action; Mr Smith, Mr Grigsby, Mr Whitbread, and Mr Pelham all advocated immediate action to regulate or to completely abolish the 'odious business'. Yet in spite of the numerous petitions and the overwhelming voice in the House, the final decision remained a postponement, pending the conclusion of the Privy Council and the completion of its examinations.

"If the Chancellor had moved for an immediate abolition it would have carried this night," said Clarkson, who cut a dejected figure as he and Sharp left the Commons side by side.

"Even if he had done so, the motion would not have been carried in the Lords," countered Sharp, "they would have folded in the face of the lobbyists, the planters and the slavers, who would have pleaded for more time to make all necessary adjustments to their practices, lest their business be weakened, and their profits reduced."

"And so, it carries forward to July," bemoaned Clarkson, "in which time another ten, twenty, thirty thousand innocent African lives are torn from their mother countries, a third of whom will be dead by the end of the year, two-thirds by the end of the next one. And all the time, we talk, and debate and move motions and hold bloody meetings." Clarkson was exasperated and it showed. He was no politician.

"The wheels of government move slowly," sighed Sharp, "but at least they are moving, and that is in no small part down to your efforts and those of The Society."

It felt like scant consolation to the Reverend Thomas Clarkson, but as the two of them headed off in the direction of Granville Sharp's club for a night cap and a fine cigar, a small flotilla of predominantly British, and a smattering of French, and Portuguese slave ships were tracking down the west coast of Africa, each with the sole intention of enticing, capturing, branding, and enslaving another cargo of human souls, to carry them across the vast ocean to their doom.

CHAPTER EIGHTEEN

"You can choose to look the other way, but you can never say again that you didn't know."

William Wilberforce, Member of Parliament for Hull

Extracts from the Journal of Doctor Gardiner, ship's surgeon on board The Brothers

18th February 1788

The weather is now against us, and the seas are high, confining the officers in their quarters and the men below deck. Our number has fallen again, another two able seamen reported as missing, presumed gone overboard. The Captain tells us that we are making good progress, but hope is a rare commodity on board this ship and although the night watch has now been abandoned due to the elements, a roll call is now a thrice daily occurrence. So far our numbers have not diminished further, and the stocks of lime and lemon juice are holding up, there has even been a move to share a sip or two with the remaining crew members, a rare selfless gesture that did not go unnoticed, though I doubt that it was at Captain Howlett's behest. I passed a restless night, but there was no sign of anything untoward, except for the rats.

20th February 1788

We are down another man and his loss proved to be the last straw for the Captain. At this morning's all-hands call, his absence first came to light. A young seaman called Wintersgil, a shallow-faced soul who has not said much or been of any nuisance throughout the voyage. As quiet as a mouse he's been, well now he's quiet as the grave, and the generally held view is that his has been a watery one. The Captain ordered the whole ship searched from top to bottom, to leave no stone unturned or chest unopened. But the poor chap was nowhere to be found and we have reluctantly concluded that he too is gone overboard. The remaining men have now become beset by jitters, afeared that they will be next – they even have a name for it, they call it a 'wil o' the wisp' sometimes a 'jack o' lantern', a light that appears at night on deck and

- 328 -

which, if followed, will light a man to his end. I have heard of such things before, but know not what they are, be they spirits or demons, or just tricks of the light. The mind can play some fearsome tricks on a man who has been at sea for too long, out of sight of land and the comforts of home. As I sat there shivering in my hammock, I thought of a home fire, a roaring flame, and a fine glass of scotch. I must keep that thought close by, these next weeks, when the wind is howling, and the crashing waves are beating like a drummer boy about my head.

23rd February 1788

23rd February 1788

Another man down. Jackson this time, ship's carpenter, and a skill that we can scarce do without if the ship is damaged in this weather. Again, a thorough search was conducted, again no sight or sound of him was to be found. The Captain has reinstated the night watch and I am on first tonight, the first on the rota, with Meadows this time, and there are no worse to spend the night with. He has a stink about him, and he tells some tall tales, but he is free with his rum, and he is as scared as the next man that he may soon be called to account for his life's works. I am writing this now at dawn, the night watch being just finished, and I must write it down before I sleep on it and forget any part of it. Meadows is gone. The Captain is incensed, he would have had me flogged had I not pulled my pistol on him and threatened to fire it at any man that dared to raise a hand against me. I have locked my cabin door and dragged my chest behind it to wedge it shut in case the Captain keeps a skeleton key. I didn't see what was happening, at least not until it was too late to intervene. Meadows had talked of demons and ghouls all night long, until he finally fell asleep next to me, and he was soon snoring like a stuck pig in spite of the cold. He had his woollen blanket pulled up beneath his spotty chin and so, I let him sleep, knowing that if he was caught he would be flogged within an inch of his life, but thinking that as it was too cold for me to sleep, I would wake him the instant that I heard any movement from below. As it was, I too must have drifted off, because when I was next conscious, Meadows was no longer beside me, but I thought that I could see the light from his lanthorn bobbing about on the quarter deck and so called out to him, unsure of what he was doing up there. He didn't answer me and so, I hauled myself up, stamping my feet on the wooden deck to rid my legs of their stubborn sluggishness and then proceeded to mount the stairs towards his light. The light made only a faint impression against the blackness; it was like an orb, a ball of whiteness that wasn't quite a sphere and which seemed to shift its shape as it dodged behind each straining sheet and beam. It stopped to hover like a hornet at the very tip of the foredeck, and I had the awful sense that in itself, it was regarding my approach, for the light was not after all the glow of a candle enclosed in a metal casket, and I could see no shadow of a man to carry such a piece. It was simply a ball of light, but it wasn't solid, for it seemed to have a beating heart as if it was alive, as if it was watching and waiting for me to make my move. I didn't and instead raised the alarm, pulling hard on the rope to ring the heavy brass bell that would summon the rest of the crew and the Captain to my aid. But as the first man placed his heavy boot upon the deck, I watched as the light fell like a stone beyond the prow of the ship. I rushed forward and gazed down after it, but there was no sign, as if it had never been there at all, and in that moment I resolved to keep its secrets for I feared for my safety should I be responsible for spreading such a tale. Instead, I said that Meadows had made off to relieve himself about the boat and had not returned and that having given him a full twenty-minute grace, I had made my own search to no effect, before deciding to call all-hands to help in my endeavours.

25th February 1788

I have remained out of harm's way for the last two days and have ignored the Captain's ready requests for me to come upon the deck, for fear that he has designs upon my life. He assures me that he has not and has rapped upon my door to tell me so, but he is a dog and I do not trust him. I am running low on food and water so *will soon have to take my chances with the rest of them, but I have no doubt that more are now missing, having heard the all-hands call on two separate occasions. Something is amiss aboard this ship, and I no longer believe that it has an earthly cause. I am now a ragged version of my former self, a scraggy beard about my face and my clothes are hanging off my back, a belt tightened about my waist to keep my breeches from falling around my ankles. I am anxious of what will now befall us, and sit in trepidation within my timbered cell, starting at every real and imagined noise, which no longer sounds like rats, but I tell myself that it must be they for what else could it be?*

26ᵗʰ February 1788

Smith and Evans are lost, one on each of the last two nights, and so the ship is now bereft of officers, other than me and the Captain, who has tried and failed to appoint new mates from amongst the remaining able seamen. Along with our paying passenger, plus the Captain and myself, we are now short of hands to steer the ship being just 13 in number, and so I have re-joined their ranks and have been assigned my share of duties by a much-maligned Captain, who seems now more inclined to be considerate, for he knows that his life might now depend upon it. On my return to deck, I was perplexed to see the sails and timbers coated in a brown earthy substance which has not been washed away on the surf. I am told that it is the sands of the Sahara, caught on a wind called the Hermitan, which blows until March, and which can even keep the skies dark in the daytime. It feels like a bad omen, not least that it is now clear that our course is lost, and we are much further south and west than I had imagined.

-◦◦◦-

In the end, The Society would not have to wait until the following year for the matter of slavery to be raised again before the benches of Parliament. The debate had raised the hackles of the slave traders and they had done themselves no favours when they celebrated their stay of execution with euphoria, and not in humble acceptance that something still had to change.

As their puppet politicians in the West Country and on Merseyside gratefully accepted the plaudits at their supposed victory, their opponents in the Parliamentary ranks were far more numerous and their consciences had been pricked. Not least amongst them, Sir William Dolben who stood firm, refusing to accept the decision to delay. Haunted by the continued suffering on the middle passage, a few thousand miles to the south, he was determined to act. On 21st May 1788, he aired his grievances in the House of Commons, catching the anti-Abolitionist movement off guard and turning up the heat on those Parliamentary protagonists whom he knew were of a similar mind.

"I will but take up a little of your time gentlemen," he began, after rising to his feet to address the assembled mass of Whigs and Tories. "I wish to put a motion before you that will bring but some relief to the suffering of those unhappy persons, the natives of Africa, from the hardships to which they are usually exposed in their passage from the coast of Africa to the colonies." He knew full well that such a modification would be insufficient to address all the evils of The Trade, but he also knew that full abolition was still some years away and that he, most likely, would not live to see that glorious day. He needed to be able to say that he had done something, anything, to address the wicked and unjustifiable trade in human lives, which had taken root in his own lifetime and against which, he would go to his grave as the most staunch critic.

"The Bill which I am considering," he went on, "must strictly limit, on pain of significant financial penalty to be imposed on the owners, the number of persons that may be legally carried on board a slave ship according to her tonnage. This in order to prevent overcrowding, whilst ensuring that there is sufficient food and other provisions on board to make their transition as comfortable as possible, until this house can once again bring the matter of The Trade's abolition to a satisfactory conclusion."

They had all seen The Print and knew exactly the issues to which the Baronet was referring, having not only studied The Brookes diagram in detail, but also having read the musings of Falconbridge's much touted pamphlet from cover to cover. Even so, Dolben was determined to labour the point, just to ensure that no one was left in any doubt as to its providence.

"I know gentlemen that we have all seen and read the excellent account of Doctor Alexander Falconbridge, but just in case its finer details have slipped from your memories, Mr Speaker, I beg leave to read but a small section from his accounts of the middle passage, just to remind us of the horrors that are presently entrenched in that devilish voyage." The Speaker did not object and as there were also no objections from the floor, even from the less than honourable gentlemen for Bristol and Liverpool, who were shifting uncomfortably on the green baize covered bench where they were sat like a couple of thieves.

"Some wet and blowing weather, having occasioned the port holes to be shut and the grating to be covered, fluxes and fevers amongst the slaves ensued. While they were in this situation, and my profession requiring it, I frequently went down among them, till at length their apartments became so extremely hot, as to be only sufferable for a very short time. But the excessive heat was not the only thing that rendered their

situation intolerable. The deck, that is, the floor of their room, was so covered with the blood and mucus which had proceeded from them in consequence of the flux, that it resembled a slaughterhouse. It is not in the power of the human imagination to picture to itself a situation more dreadful or more disgusting. Numbers of the slaves had fainted, they were carried upon deck, where several of them died, and the rest were with difficulty restored. It had nearly proved fatal to me also."

"I could read so much more from within these pages, if additional evidence is needed," said the Baronet, "but I would hope that in the Parliament of a civilised and Christian country, such additions are indeed superfluous. I move to introduce such a Bill as soon as is practical."

Mr Samuel Whitbread, a prominent brewer and MP for Bedford stood to second the motion, which gained the immediate and vocal support of several others. Even the Chancellor of the Exchequer conceded that he could support the motion, whilst the MP for Liverpool, Mr Gascoyne, could see which way the wind was blowing and so, gave the motion a qualified thumbs-up and the Bill was accepted, at least in the Commons.

However, in spite of Sir William's best endeavours, its passage would not be a smooth one and although his initiative had its second reading just a few weeks later on the 2nd of June 1788, the Liverpool contingent continued to raise objections, seeking to water down any regulation that would in any way impinge on the profitability of future ventures. The very same witnesses as before were dispatched back to London, intent on disproving the need for regulation, for which they were forced to lie through their teeth. Lieutenant Matthews, an ex-navy man turned slave trader, tarnished his own flailing reputation, when he was called upon to bring evidence before the committee.

"The present mode of transport is sufficiently convenient for the objects of it," he lied, "and well adapted to preserve their comfort and their health. The slaves have sufficient room, air, and provisions on board every ship that sets sail from the coast and once aboard, are known to frequently make merry, with dancing and singing. So few of them have any occasion to be sick, that the mortality levels aboard are trifling. In short Sir, their voyage from Africa to the West Indies is amongst the happiest periods of a slave's life."

In itself, these ill-chosen words should have been enough to persuade any waverers in the room of the unscrupulous nature of the pro-slavery movement, whose only interest in being there that day was the preservation of their own livelihoods, but the deceit didn't stop there and several more made their own assertions against the Bill, with unsavoury claims that bordered on insanity.

"The African is so unhappy in his own country," began Mr Norris, the same man who had 'befriended' Thomas Clarkson in Liverpool, "that he finds the middle passage under the care of our merchants, little less than an Elysian retreat and I urge the committee to commence investigations into the source of these unfounded allegations." The very idea that the captured slaves were treated to some form of idyllic heaven-on-earth, when first captured and taken below decks to be shackled in rows barely two feet apart, was nothing short of ludicrous and yet the view is recorded there in the black and white of Parliamentary record for posterity. As a consequence of his ill-founded words, the Agent was subjected to a fierce barrage of questioning, and some of the most severe cross-examination ever seen before in a Privy Council meeting, at the end of which the case for the opposition of the proposed Bill was in tatters and the credibility of the

Liverpool-based lobbyists was shot. Further evidence was put to them that even the treatment of their own crews was barbaric, and when the indisputable evidence of the muster rolls was placed before them, their game was up.

Mr Dalzell, a slave ship Captain out of Liverpool who had skippered several slaving vessels including The Hannah and The Europa, bore the brunt of the Abolitionist's ire, when Thomas Clarkson himself had the opportunity to set the questions for the committee. Clarkson knew from his research in Liverpool, that this particular Captain had himself lost fifteen out of forty seamen on his last voyage, and it followed that the journey must have occasioned the deaths of many Africans. When Clarkson stood to make his presence known, the Captain blushed with embarrassment as he shifted uncomfortably in his seat, recognising the Reverend by his reputation and by his description, and fully cognisant of the fact that his 'testimony' was about to be exposed as a 'tissue of lies'.

"How many crew did you depart with on your last voyage aboard The Europa?" his inquisitor asked, fully aware of the answer, but wanting to hear it from the Captain's own lips.

"Forty Sir," he said sheepishly, knowing that that was the easiest of a litany of questions that would shortly follow.

"And how many died on the journey?"

"Fifteen Sir."

"So," said the clerk of the court, working from the information in front of him, information that had been supplied by Clarkson who was sat a few feet behind him in the public gallery. "You managed to lose over one-third of your crew in a single voyage, only last year, is that correct?"

"Yes Sir," he answered meekly.

"How many of your slaves were lost also?"

"One hundred and twenty," he muttered.

"One hundred and twenty" repeated the clerk for the avoidance of any doubt, "and was that all, or was that just those who had perished by disease?"

"Another twelve Sir," the Captain faltered, "another twelve were lost by accident, drowned that is, mainly at the coast."

"You mean they jumped into the ocean to avoid capture or in a futile bid to escape," the clerk asked him for clarification, and also to make him squirm some more under this very public examination.

"Yes Sir," said Mr Dalzell. "That's right Sir."

"And any more than this?" asked the clerk, pressing home his advantage. "Outside of the middle passage itself and before you saw them last in their sale?"

"Yes Sir," he admitted like a scolded child. "Another twenty to thirty died upon the sands of the Gold Coast, I couldn't say exactly how many."

"So," the clerk said, turning to the room to sum up. "This Captain, this champion of the merchants, this advocate for the health and happiness of the slaves in the middle passage, lost nearly one hundred and sixty of these unhappy persons committed to his supposedly superior care, on a single voyage."

It was enough and the counsel concluded its business on the 17th June 1788. Mr Henry Beaufoy, MP for Great Yarmouth, who was raised as a Quaker, brought his significant influence to bear on the outcome as he condemned the proceedings as a sham, and the behaviour of the anti-Abolitionists as abhorrent to the sensibilities of a civilised nation.

"Thus, I have considered the various objections which have been stated to the Bill, and am ashamed to reflect that it could be necessary to speak so long in defence of such a cause: for what, after all, is asked by the proposed regulations? That the Africans, whom you allow to be robbed of all things but life, may not unnecessarily and wantonly be deprived of life also. To the honour, to the wisdom, to the feelings of the House I now make my appeal, perfectly confident that you will not tolerate, as senators, a traffic which as men you shudder to contemplate and that you will not take upon yourselves the responsibility for this waste of existence. To the memory of former Parliaments, the horrors of this traffic will be a permanent reproach; yet former Parliaments have not known, as you on the clearest evidence now know, the dreadful nature of this trade. Should you reject this Bill, no exertions of yours to rescue from oppression the suffering inhabitants of Empire; no records of the prosperous state to which, after long and unsuccessful war, you have restored your native land; no proofs, however splendid, that under your guidance, Great Britain has recovered her rank, and is again the arbitress of nations, will save *your* names from the stigma of everlasting dishonour."

The motion was carried by fifty-six votes to five and despite further futile objections by the Liverpool lobby, the first move to regulate The Trade in human lives, made it to the House of Lords the very next day, but it took another month until its royal assent was granted, after which the ruling was finally able to pass into law.

A fight that had begun for the Reverend Thomas Clarkson three years earlier with the completion of a Latin essay, and which had taken him across the length and breadth of England in pursuit of the evidence to back up his claims, had ended in the corridors of power that housed Great Britain's political and aristocratic elite.

And all that had been achieved, despite the overwhelming popular will of the people, the support of many of its religious dissenting voices and the backing of several of the most influential and powerful men in the land, was a regulation that imposed upon the slavers the need to treat their cargo in a manner that would not result in an horrific and untimely death. Their capture and sale had not come up for debate and would not in any meaningful way for another three years, as Britain began to become entangled in a nasty scrap with France, when the Parliamentary agenda would have no room for topics such as human suffering at the hands of their own subjects.

One hundred thousand slaves a year were boarding England's ships on the west coast of Africa in the last decade of the eighteenth century, to navigate the middle passage to the islands of the West Indies and onto the former colonies of the motherland. And yet here in England, the swelling source of their destruction went unchecked, as a new river of affluence carried the few on a winding route through a scarred and fractured landscape. As the end of the eighteenth century loomed large, manufacturing production in England was at an all-time high, and an ever-exhausted workforce began to burst at the seams of cities like Birmingham and Manchester. An unrelenting crush of migrant workers, who had left the land of their fathers to seek their fortunes in the unregulated factories, mills, and foundries of what was fast becoming an industrial wasteland, poured forth like lambs to the slaughter so that rich industrialists could grow fat on their sacrifice.

Many were illiterate, reliant on their masters for their bed and board and on their preachers for a glimpse of a rapidly changing world, which they knew little of and understood even less. For them, Africa was as far away as the moon and just as incomprehensible, but like the displaced African, survival was the best that they could hope for and for most, when their turn came to die, it would be a blessing.

CHAPTER NINETEEN

"In the African trade, as in all others, there are individuals bad as well as good, and it is but justice to discriminate and not condemn the whole, for the delinquencies of a few."

Captain Hugh Crow – Memoirs comprising a narrative of his life, 1830.

<u>Extracts from the Journal of Doctor Gardiner, ship's surgeon on board *The Brothers*</u>

<u>6th March 1788</u>

There are no longer enough men to man the ship and we are far from our intended course, another 4 slipped away in the night, taking the smaller canoe as the quietest means of escape from this accursed ship. The Captain is uncertain how far we are from our plotted route, but we are some degrees further south than intended though a dense fog has now descended upon us which does not help us in our peril. The remaining crew now huddle together on the deck at night, refusing to go below in the dark and instead sleep beneath the tarpaulin in the boat which last saw service on the Bonny river. There are just nine of us now and there are hardly enough for the more strenuous jobs, so the sails are at risk when the wind changes, as we cannot be quick enough to reef or put about, even with the Captain's minimal help. The passenger has shared some strange ideas that he has about the slaves, having travelled all over the West Indies islands, believing that there is some ancient religion of sorts, which he thinks might be behind our disturbances. He wants to talk to me about it, but I am not of a mind to listen. I am not one for folk tales and will hear of no other power on earth but one.

<u>10th March 1788</u>

I have ordered the Captain to be confined to his quarters. Last night he came on deck brandishing his cutlass and armed with his pistols but was quite intoxicated and was overpowered by the rest of us, our gallant passenger striking the final blow with an empty gin bottle, which shattered on impact. Had he not done so then

Howlett may have done someone serious harm, and though both shots with his guns missed their intended targets, a stray musket ball has torn through the jib sheet, rendering the flapping sail loose of its mooring. The crew has emptied his quarters of all weaponry and all alcohol which they have divided up – much to his fury as we heard him cursing this morning at the discovery – but he has been left with sufficient water and provisions and his cabin door is now bolted and chained from the outside. He has no means of escape unless he wishes to drop from his window into the ocean, which if he does, will be his own undoing. This is not a mutiny and is for the safety of the remaining men, of whom I count myself one, for the Captain is quite insane. Even now he rants and raves about his room, kicking out at the door and walls in a furious temper, but we have two men standing guard at his only exit point with orders to ring the all-hands bell at the first sign of danger. So long as he stays behind the barricade, our fate is in our own hands.

16th March 1788

A mighty tempest has pitched us upon the ocean again for two days and two nights and is only now becalmed, a most frightful experience which, with our much-reduced crew, was almost too fierce to withstand. The half-mast is down and shattered, what is left of its sail is a tattered rag and the rudder is smashed against its housing, only half of its length now functional, severely affecting the bosun's ability to steer us home. And without a carpenter it is impossible to fix, even if we could reach it. We are now completely at the mercy of the sea and have concluded that two more men were lost overboard in the storm. There are now but seven crew members, including our passenger, me, and the Captain. Is there another that moves amongst us? If so, I have not seen him nor heard his breath these past few nights, but I think that something may be watching. I can sense his presence, and I am now certain that whatever it is, it is not of good intent. Even the rats seem to be wary.

24th March 1788

I am writing after a shocking incident discovered just this morning. It has not been my habit to write in my journal at this time, preferring the cover of darkness by the light of a candle, but my stocks are running low, and this morning's savagery has left me doubting my own resolve, though I have not the courage to try my luck in the remaining boat as some of the men have mooted. The hen coop was broken open upon the deck, and the chickens so wantonly mutilated, that we would think a rabid dog must be on the loose. The flesh is not fit for consumption for it is torn asunder and the feet and entrails were deposited together like an offering to Neptune, though the rats have feasted on it. If it was intended to terrify then it has worked and any steadfastness that we had left amongst us all is now at an end. The Captain is as yet uninformed of the event, as he has been quiet this last day and night and we are determined not to disturb his mind still further, if indeed he has at last found some peace. Not that he deserves any, but at least in his solitude he can do no harm to anyone else, though any suspicion that we held that it was he who was somehow behind all this, has now been put to rest, for the bolts upon his cabin door remained secured throughout.

25th March 1788

The events of last evening have left me certain as to the cause of all our troubles. It is a dark and wicked spirit that walks amongst us and last night we saw its form, for the first and I hope for the last time. Reader, if ever you hear this account you will surely cast doubt upon my words, if indeed this book is ever to be found or read but be not troubled by it, for I cannot deny it more. If it is but a boy, then it is one whose intent is driven by some preternatural power that is beyond any laws of heaven or hell that I have learned in all my academia. The six of us had gathered on the deck, as has become our habit and now that the rain has ceased to drive us below, we set about settling in for the night beneath a makeshift tent made up of the tarpaulin from the boat and the remains of the half-mast. We had eaten a hearty meal of heated beans and the scrags of meat that we were able to salvage from the chicken carcasses, washed down with the now plentiful water and our allocation of rum, when the troubling light once again appeared and beckoned for one of us to track its path about the deck. But we held firm, enticing it closer, for a full hour we just watched it as it passed along the half and quarter decks and right up to the prow of the ship, before it slid back to settle about the deck, not twelve feet ahead of our small circle. I regarded it closely, trying hard to look beyond its luminescence, trying to see inside its boundaries, for it was a circular mist, the size of a man's heart and it seemed to beat as if it had life caught within its glow. It was bright enough to illuminate the boards over which it hovered, a few feet up, about the height of a small boy and as I thought it, I saw him. I could not say if I thought it first or saw it first, but there was an outline of legs and hands, which became visible just for a moment, and then was gone. I wasn't the only one, the bosun started to point at it just as I traced its edge and he gasped out loud "it's a boy" just as the others started to look, but then its image dissipated into the dark. But that was not the horror of which I speak, it was just the harbinger, and what happened next scattered us like scared rabbits from the scent of a fox. A dark impenetrable swell began to form about the boards, a rising proliferation of nothingness, a spreading span that blocked out the light from behind it and it came for us like an outpouring of dark blood. It grew out of the spot where the boy had been, and though human in shape it seemed deformed, its arms extended like the chain of an anchor, adorned with two large and unwieldly hands, with fattened fingers bloated like a floating corpse. Staring down towards its head, as an artilleryman might do when caught in the enemy's sights, an oval shape stared back, without eyes or mouth, as if it was wearing a tightly fitted mask to shroud its face. Every man ran for his life, in all directions about the ship, including I who bolted below deck and into the safety of my quarters, where I cowered in the corner until the first rays of daylight came to my rescue and I plucked up the nerve to scribble down this entry. I saw others about me too, and felt them at my heels, but I know not where they went, only that like me, they did not want to face that thing alone, the name of which we all knew, for it was obvious to us. For it was of them all. And it wanted vengeance.

-◦◦◦-

"How can that scoundrel find in Freke's favour? It is absurd!" ranted Granville Sharp on his return from court. "Every magistrate in the land knows that he will lose it on appeal, there is no foundation to this immoral verdict, the only possible explanation is that he was under the influence of those Liverpool devils."

"You do plan to appeal then, I take it?" said Clarkson, equally disgusted by the outcome.

"I have already lodged it with the court," announced Sharp, "and that boy is going nowhere until the date is come, and we have had our share of justice from a more impartial judge."

The judge had clearly let his own personal investments sway his decision and had cited previous cases to show that although Addae was not, in fact, a slave under the English legal framework, the definition of 'property' continued to be challenged, and an unsympathetic court had ruled that he still 'belonged' to the slave trader Freke, only because he had been kidnapped off the streets of Bristol and so had been abducted unlawfully. The slavers had been cock-a-hoop at the verdict and saw the outcome of the appeal as a mere formality, and so were pushing for a quick about-face to the same courtroom and the return of Freke's property before the month was out, but Sharp was not to be so easily outwitted. He had already petitioned the Prime Minister to step in and to forcefully assign Lord Mansfield for the appeal hearing, a request that he would certainly grant, as none of them wanted such a high-profile case to find in favour of the pro-slavery movement, just as they were preparing for a second Bill to go before the house.

"But I am not prepared to wait and run the risk that Addae will be shipped back to Bristol, to that ogre" declared Sharp.

"What do you have in mind?" asked Clarkson intrigued.

"He needs to be settled amongst the black community in London, before the re-trial begins," he schemed, "so that, should we lose, which we won't, he will be nowhere to be found."

"Won't that leave you exposed?"

"It may," conceded Sharp, "but I'll be damned if he's going back to that guttersnipe. We cannot save as many as we should, but I have been able to save some these last few years, and if I do lose this case, then no amount of reputational or financial loss is going to stop me from saving the boy."

"But won't they just track him down?" asked Clarkson, fearing the worst.

"They may do, and that is why I have another plan, just in case I cannot get the verdict over-turned," said Sharp. "Should I lose, which I won't, but should it come to it, then we will ensure that a ship is readied to take him and others to Sierra Leone, immediately that the case is concluded."

"Sierra Leone?" asked Clarkson, "is that wise Granville? The expedition is but a few months old, I fear that it is not yet stable there, and would be worried for the boy's safety if he went there alone."

"Would you rather see him back in Bristol?" challenged Sharp. "I have no doubt that this Freke character will treat him sorely. I would expect that he will himself ship him back to his plantations on the very next slave ship, where he will toil in the fields until he expires, if he doesn't die on the journey that is. These are spiteful men Thomas, and I will not let Addae fall into their hands for a second time."

Sierra Leone was a state on the west coast of Africa, where a settlement had been established in the previous year, as a supposed safe haven for former slaves. Freetown was its rather clichéd name, and though its passage would not be an easy one, in 1788 hopes were still high that the four hundred strong black community in London and in the northern States of the new American land - most notably Nova Scotia - might find freedom back in the continent of their birth. The Sierra Leone Company had been established in 1787 and Thomas Clarkson's younger brother John, a British Naval Lieutenant, had agreed to become its first governor.

Sitting between two rivers on the Grain Coast, the region had been a hotbed of slaving activity since the days of the Portuguese, but the Abolitionists had managed to secure a deal with the Temne, an African tribe whose people lived in the region, to purchase an area roughly the size of a small British town. Sharp had written an essay on the matter, or what he called a "short sketch," laying out the system of government and other *temporary arrangements until better shall be proposed*', which included provisions for its establishment and ongoing political, economic, and agricultural governance.

It was a system based on 'Frankpledge', or tithing structure, which specified the basis for labour and currency, public service, and public health. Sharp had proposed a method of 'free labour' based on an eight-hour day, which ran from 6am to 4pm with time for breaks and an afternoon siesta, or 'festoo' as it was locally known. The prescribed day also allowed for five hours of 'leisure' time each day for citizens to cultivate their own land, with just six hours of labour on a

Saturday, whilst Sunday was set aside for God. Under the constitution sketched out by Sharp, any fugitive slaves were to be given full state protection and the opportunity to purchase land through their labour, with any and all being designated a 'free man' on setting foot in Freetown.

In many ways it would be a commune, with all lots of land subdivided equally from the outset and no man being able to accrue more than one 'town lot' and one 'out lot', being obliged to sell any that were obtained through marriage or other means within three years. Provisions included land for a 'general asylum', a poorhouse for any families that were in need of state support, a hospital for the sick and injured and a penitentiary, plus glebe land for the clergy and other arrangements for town clerks, schoolmasters and even allowing for a small militia in case of insurrection or an attack.

The public revenue was a particularly novel concept, levying taxes in the form of days of public labour to cultivate crops or maintain buildings, which could be substituted only if the taxpayer had the money to pay a free man to work on his account, ten minutes labour being specified to be worth the princely sum of one farthing, equating to one shilling a day. Sharp had even proposed a 'tax on pride and indolence' where those people of means, who declined to submit themselves to public works, must pay a fine equivalent to triple the value of a day's labour in lieu of their public debt, a record of which would be maintained for all citizens. Other fines would also be levied to swell the public purse, including penalties for drunkenness and immodesty and for fornication and adultery, as well as for breaches of the Sabbath.

Even in the early summer of 1788, Sharp knew that things were already going wrong with this social experiment. There had been issues, both within the newly formed society and between the settlers and the local tribespeople, who it seemed had not fully understood the basis of their agreement. However well-intentioned they were, naïve thoughts that an idyllic solution to the question of disenfranchised slaves could simply be carved out of the African land mass, by virtue of a simple legal agreement, remained a genuine proposal. Clarkson's brother, who was intimately involved in the scheme from the outset, had only recently sent him a worrying, but not yet hopeless, update.

"I have heard many melancholy accounts of the unfortunate colony of Sierra Leone. But I have however discovered that most of the evils have arisen from the allowance of rum distributed on board the ships; and the landing just in the rainy season on an uncleared woody country when they were so infatuated by the rum that there was no prevailing on them to clear the underwood as I had recommended. They have purchased 20 square miles of the finest and most beautiful country that was ever seen. The hills are no steeper than Shooters Hill and fine streams of fresh water run down the hill on each side of the new township and in the front is a noble bay where the river is about 3 leagues wide, the woods and gorges are beautiful beyond description and the soil very fine. So that a little good management and a prohibition on rum and spirits will produce a thriving settlement."

Sharp reminded Clarkson of his findings, as they discussed Addae's future and both agreed that should the appeal be lost, then his transportation back to Africa would be the only possible course of action open to them, whatever its inherent risks.

"It would be far better for the boy, than to let him fall back into the grasp of the slave traders," agreed Clarkson, but he was yet to be convinced that the tentative foundation of Freetown would survive another winter. Such experiments had been tried before, in the colonies of America when towns had faltered and disappeared, despite the best intentions of its founders and he feared having to abandon the boy to his fate, in a futile bid to succeed where others had so spectacularly failed.

"He needs a chaperone," said Sharp cryptically. "If we do send him there, he needs a travelling companion from amongst our number, someone that we can trust. Someone that has a shared interest in the cause and who will have his best interests at heart."

Unfortunately, there was no one that immediately came to mind.

CHAPTER TWENTY

"All the information I could procure confirms me in the belief that to kidnapping, and to crimes (and many of these fabricated as a pretext) the slave trade owes its chief support."

Alexander Falconbridge, Account of the Slave Trade on the Coast of Africa, 1788

As it turned out they need not have worried about the legal case.

Lord Mansfield was imposed upon the court as the presiding judge after the intervention of Pitt, and Freke's case was thrown out of court, his seething outburst at the conclusion of the re-trial almost seeing him held up in the holding cells beneath on a contempt charge. The judge was unrelenting in his condemnation afterwards, reproving in the strongest possible terms the callous actions of the Bristol shipping magnate in bringing the case in the first place and lecturing him that he was fortunate not to be on a kidnapping charge himself, leaving any other slaver in no doubt that any man, woman, or child that sets foot onto English soil is 'immediately' made free of any laws of bondage that may once have applied to them in foreign lands.

The introduction of regulation for slavery on board British ships had not marked a turning point for the Abolitionists and there was no let-up in the intensity of demands placed upon them in their endeavours. Instead, the opposition grew more fierce at the ports, especially in Liverpool, where a steady stream of witnesses were dispatched to stand before the London-based council and submit their evidence in defence of The Trade. In general, the thread of their accusations against the Abolitionists remained the same; that they had fabricated the evidence against the slavers, exaggerating the suffering in the middle passage and embellishing the peril of their situation in

Africa, which the slavers maintained was a place of constant peril for the slaves.

In consequence, Thomas Clarkson continued to spend his waking hours in pursuit of his own new witnesses, many of whom wrote to him with news of unimaginable horrors that they had been forced to endure off the coast of Africa or upon the islands and their plantations. Yet so few were ever willing to testify, pleading instead that they remain as an 'anonymous source', lest their livelihoods be affected, or their family name besmirched. It was not uncommon for him to travel two or three hundred miles in a single week after receiving an evidentiary letter that brought hope for their cause, and yet after a long journey on horseback or by stagecoach, he would find the witness unwilling to appear in court or on some occasions, would not appear at all, making the whole journey a futile one. He had accumulated a mass of correspondence, most of which was supportive in its content, though some was abusive and occasionally even contained physical threats to his person, should he choose to persist in his chosen crusade.

He could handle the threats, and simply handed them over to Granville Sharp who followed them up with a legal letter, noting their stated intentions and inviting them to discuss the matter before the local magistrate at a time of their choosing, which usually did the trick. What he struggled to come to terms with were the stories themselves, the suffering that they had witnessed and the horrible cruelties that had been inflicted upon them or, more often than not, on a black slave. He often read them long into the night, after the trials of the day had been negotiated, when by the light of a candle he would pore over their pages until he could no longer keep his eyes open. Yet when he lay down to sleep, he would imagine their broken bodies in all their terrible details and weep. He would then be roused from sleep by the dawn chorus and even when he had found some solace in their song and so slipped back into sleep's embrace, his dreams would always be full of the same dreadful imaginings, leaving him listless and fraught at breakfast.

It could not go on, and although his friends and fellow Abolitionists urged him to take some time off, to visit the coast or to take to his cottage in the country, there was to be no let up. Until this frightful curse was lifted he would have no rest and so he soldiered on. As 1788 became 1789, a now fully recovered William Wilberforce finally stepped forward to take centre stage in the House of Commons, armed with a vast catalogue of evidence, much of which was a direct result of Clarkson's legwork and his alone.

Despite their misgivings about appearing in public, a dozen or more willing witnesses had agreed to stand before the committee, but on the return of Doctor James Arnold from his latest voyage aboard The Ruby, complete with a compendium of evidence in his meticulously maintained journal, the council would not permit him another and so Clarkson was forced to choose. On the one hand he had the eyewitness accounts of family visitors to West Indies' plantations, unscrupulous crew members bemoaning their own foul treatment and various merchants with a wide array of insights into their slave-trading partners' evil undertakings. On the other, he had a relatively respectable ship's Doctor, just returned from the triangular route, and armed with first hand observations from the deck of a modern slaving vessel. In the end, the weight of the one outweighed the bulk of the dozen, and so, somewhat reluctantly, he stood down his carefully collected witnesses in favour of a single trusted ship's surgeon.

But the tide was turning, and it was turning against the Abolitionist cause.

The lobby on behalf of the planters, merchants, and investors in The Trade, had gained much ground, an impetus that was spurred on by generous donations collected from the slaving ports of western England, whose own self-interest in its continuation seemed somehow to captivate the minds of many leading politicians who had, up until then, committed their support to Wilberforce. That they should be so inclined was to their eternal shame, as it robbed The Society of several of its most prominent witnesses who, sensing a change in the wind, were no longer willing to stand before the committee in condemnation of their families and friends.

It was against this backdrop that William Wilberforce first took to the floor of the chamber, to add his voice to the call to arms against the evils of this commerce, asking the House to form itself into a committee, where all Members of Parliament would take their seats to hear the petitions of the people and to consider the report of the Privy Council.

"When I consider the magnitude of the subject, a subject in which the interests, not of this country, nor of Europe alone, but of the whole world, are involved," he declared. "And when I think, at the same time, on my weakness as the advocate who has undertaken this great cause, when these reflections press upon my mind, it is impossible for me not to feel both terrified and concerned at my own inadequacy to such a task. But when I reflect on the encouragement which I have had, through the whole course of a long and laborious examination of this question, and how much candour I have experienced, and how conviction has increased within my own mind. When I reflect that however averse any gentleman may now be, yet we shall all be of one opinion in the end. When I turn myself to these thoughts, I take courage and determine to forget all my other fears, and I march forward with a firmer step in the full assurance that my cause will bear me out, and that I shall be able to justify upon the clearest principles, every resolution in my hand. The avowed end of which must be the total abolition of the slave trade."

His words caused quite a fuss in the chamber, for many representatives in the room remained far from convinced that the whole trade required abolition, and still clung to the hope that their constituents would be free to continue in The Trade, albeit on a more regulated basis. Wilberforce paused for a moment and waited for the clamour to subside, undiminished in his intent to drive home his incontestable line of argument.

"I wish exceedingly, in the outset, to guard both myself and the House from entering into the subject with any sort of passion. It is not their passions I shall appeal to. I ask only for their cool and impartial reason; and I wish not to take them by surprise, but to deliberate, point by point, upon every part of this question. I mean not to accuse anyone, but to take the shame upon myself, in common, indeed, with the whole Parliament of Great Britain, for having suffered this horrid trade to be carried on under their authority for so long."

It was quite an admission, and a shared guilt that not everyone in the room was willing to accept, but Wilberforce was not in the mood to relent. His position on the matter was clear and his resolution fixed. "We are all guilty" he asserted. "We ought all to plead guilty, and not to throw the blame on others; and I therefore deplore every kind of reflection against the various descriptions of people who are more immediately involved in this wretched business."

He worked through the aspects with which they were now so familiar, even if his Right Honourable audience varied in their degree of support. He talked of the 'transit of the slaves in the West Indies', calling on the evidence already submitted and lambasting the counterarguments of the slave traders and their allies as 'wilful misrepresentations'.

"This I confess, in my own opinion, is the most wretched part of the whole subject. So much misery condensed in so little room, is more than the human imagination had ever before conceived." He stopped short of calling out the perpetrators, at the behest of Pitt, who warned him against making enemies of these men, those villainous creatures that Wilberforce assured the PM he would never want to count amongst his friends.

"I will not accuse the Liverpool merchants: I will allow them, nay, I will believe them to be men of humanity; and I will therefore believe, if it were not for the enormous magnitude and extent of the evil which distracts their attention from individual cases, and makes them think generally, and therefore less feelingly on the subject, they would never have persisted in The Trade."

Clarkson turned his head to the ear of the listening Sharp. "I fear that is wishful thinking" he whispered, to which his brother-in-arms nodded in solemn agreement.

"I believe therefore," continued Wilberforce, "that if the wretchedness of any one of the many hundred Slaves stowed in each ship could be brought before their view, and remain within the sight of the African merchant, that there is no one among them whose heart would bear it. Let anyone imagine to himself six or seven hundreds of these wretches chained two and two, surrounded with every object that is nauseous and disgusting, diseased, and struggling under every kind of wretchedness. How can we bear to think of such a scene as this? One would think it had been determined to heap upon them all the varieties of bodily pain, for the purpose of blunting the feelings of the mind; and yet, in this very point the situation of the slaves has been described by Mr Norris, one of the Liverpool delegates, in a manner which, I am sure will convince the House how interest can draw a film across the eyes, so thick, that total blindness could do no more; and how it is our duty therefore to trust not to the reasonings of interested men, or to their way of colouring a transaction."

The Member of Parliament for Liverpool, Mr Gasgoyne, pursed his lips at the very mention of his friend and sympathiser, in obvious indignation at the very suggestion that the evidence he had given to the Privy Council was anything other than the truth. But Wilberforce had anticipated this reaction and paid it no mind, staring the man down with a steely determination that bordered on contempt. He then put his plan into action to use their ill-thought-out claims against them.

"'Their apartments', says Mr Norris, 'are fitted up as much for their advantage as circumstances will admit. The right ankle of one, indeed is connected with the left ankle of another by a small iron fetter, and if they are turbulent, by another on their wrists. They have several meals a day; some of their own country provisions, with the best sauces of African cookery; and by way of variety, another meal of pulse according to European taste. After breakfast they have water to wash themselves, while their apartments are perfumed with frankincense and lime-juice. Before dinner, they are amused after the manner of their country. The song and dance *are promoted'*, and, as if the whole was really a scene of pleasure and sport. *'The men play and sing, while the women and girls make fanciful ornaments with beads, which they are plentifully supplied with'."*

The utterly ludicrous basis for this 'evidence' was not lost on the chamber, and Wilberforce was determined that it should be understood by all that listened, that their version of the truth was so far from it that it bore no resemblance whatsoever, to any single event yet recorded in the whole of the African trade.

"Such is the stain in which the Liverpool delegates, and particularly Mr Norris, gave 'evidence' before the Privy Council. What will the House think when, by the concurring testimony of other witnesses, the true history is laid open. The slaves who are sometimes described as 'rejoicing at their captivity', are so wrung with misery at leaving their country, that it is the constant practice to set sail at night, lest they should be aware of their departure. The pulses which Mr Norris talks of are horse beans; and the scantiness, both of water and provision, was suggested by the very legislature of Jamaica in the report of their committee, to be a subject that called for the interference of Parliament."

"Mr Norris talks of frankincense and lime juice; when surgeons tell you the slaves are stowed so close, that there is no room to tread among them: and when you have it in evidence from Sir George Yonge, that even in a ship which was short two hundred of her full compliment, the stench was intolerable. The song and the dance, says Mr Norris, are promoted; it had been more fair, perhaps, if he had explained that word 'promoted'. The truth is, that for the sake of exercise, these miserable wretches, loaded with chains, oppressed with disease and wretchedness, are forced to dance by the terror of the lash, and sometimes by the actual use of it. Indeed, one of the other evidences says, 'I was employed to dance the men, while another person danced the women.'"

"Such, then is the meaning of the word 'promoted'. It may be observed too, with respect to food, that an instrument is sometimes carried out, in order to force them to eat which is the same sort of proof how much they enjoy themselves in that instance also. As to their singing, what shall we say when we are told that their songs are songs of lamentation upon their departure which, while they sing, are always in tears, insomuch that one Captain threatened one of the women with a flogging, because the mournfulness of her song was too painful for his feelings. In order, however, not to trust too much to any sort of description, I will call the attention of the House to one set of evidence which is absolutely infallible."

"Death, at least, is a sure ground of evidence, and the proportion of deaths will not only confirm, but if possible will even aggravate our suspicion of their misery in the transit. It will be found, upon an average of all the ships of which evidence has been given at the Privy Council, that exclusive of those who perish before they sail, not less than twelve and a half percent perish in the passage. Besides these, the Jamaica report tells you, that not less than four and a half percent die on shore before the day of sale, which is only a week or two from the time of landing. One third more die in the 'seasoning', and this in a country exactly like their own, where they are healthy and happy as some of the evidence would pretend. The diseases, however, which they contract on board, the astringent washes which are to hide their wounds, and the mischievous tricks used to make them up for sale, are, as the Jamaica report says, the principal cause of this mortality. Upon the whole, however, here is a mortality of about fifty per cent and this among those poor unfortunate souls who are not bought unless they are sound in wind and limb. How then can the House refuse its belief to the multiplied testimonies before the Privy Council, of the savage treatment meted out in the middle passage?"

All about the room was now draped in silence. No one spoke, no one interrupted. Even the Bristol and Liverpool men were suitably subdued as they looked down, lest they catch the eye of a friend or colleague and be forced in their appearance to admit their collusion in these ventures and to a less than liberal commitment to the truth.

"Nay, indeed, what need is there of any evidence? The number of deaths speaks for itself and makes all such enquiry superfluous. As soon as ever I had arrived thus far in my investigation of the slave trade, I confess to you Sir, so enormous so dreadful, so irremediable did its wickedness appear that my own mind was completely made up for the abolition. A trade founded in iniquity, and carried on as this was, must be abolished, let the policy be what it might, let the consequences be what they would, I from this time determined that I would never rest till I had effected its abolition."

The following day, *The Morning Star* newspaper in London included this report, which was read widely throughout the capital and, throughout the country's network of local newspapers as the week wore on:

Mr WILBERFORCE then called the attention of the House to what he was about to propose. He said that he rose with a confession of what operated in his mind relative to the abolition of the Slave Trade. When I consider, says he, how long this has been suggested by many, and of what importance it is to a race of men, possessing qualities equally commendable with our own—how many millions are at present involved in the decision of the question—it is impossible for me to object in being instrumental to the business. He then remarked that he was convinced, whatever should be the decision, that in bringing forward the discussion, he performed nothing more than his duty; and he was so fully persuaded of the rectitude of his conduct, that no consideration whatever would make him swerve from his honour so far, as to dissuade him from marching boldly forward on the occasion. It was no party question, and he flattered himself that the voice of reason and truth would be heard. He was resolved to be regulated by temper and coolness and challenged a fair discussion. —It was not a proposition grounded upon particular motives of policy but founded in principles of philanthropy. It was no idle expedient or speculation of the moment but derived from the most mature deliberation. He came not to accuse the Merchants, but to appeal to their feelings and humanity. He confessed, that in the weak state of health in which he now appeared, and precarious as it might seem to many, he would stand against every personal idea, and bear the burden destined for a person who stood in his situation. The subject had already undergone many discussions, and he apprehended that previous to a final decision, it would undergo many more. What must make every man of feeling shudder was, that, after examining the annals of Africa, numbers had been carried every year from their native country, in order to satiate the avarice of a certain description of men whose whole thoughts were bent upon tyranny and oppression.

His speech had lasted three and a half hours and after a momentary pause, the proponents of the slave trade wasted no time at all in bringing their grievances before the House once more, convinced that his impassioned speech would sway the waverers in the room into backing the call for complete abolition. Lord Perhyn and Mr Gasgoyne of Liverpool both bemoaned the lack of compensation for the loss of their voters' property and belittling the evidence submitted against the slavers as 'misrepresentations', placing 'no reliance whatever' upon it.

Others joined them in their condemnation, but not before the Prime Minister had added his considerable weight to the pro-abolition argument. "I would like to thank my right honourable friend for having at length, introduced this great and important subject to the House," said Mr Pitt, his eyes scanning the room for any disputing voices. "I am sure that no argument, compatible with any idea of justice can be assigned for the continuation of the slave trade. At the same time, I am willing to listen with candour and attention to everything that can be urged on the other side of the question, though I am sure that the principles from which my opinion is deduced will be unalterable."

His intervention opened the floodgates, and although several leading politicians stood to confirm their full support, Mr Burke, Mr Fox and Sir William Yonge amongst them, a mounting voice of dissent rose up from the packed benches, and each one baulked at the prospect of complete abolition.

Aldermen Newnham, Sawbridge and Watson, representing the City of London raised objections and called for greater regulation to the commercial advantage of their merchants. Mr Dempster repeated the call for reparations for those who were set to lose out financially from the sudden and unexpected decision, begging leave for more time to consider the full effects and though others, to their credit, interceded to denounce these demands, their torrent of objections ensured that a decision was again put off until 21st May, when calls for further evidence would take centre stage once more.

In the end, the debate dragged on to such an extent that all momentum was lost and with it went any hope of an early resolution to the question of the slave trade and England's leading role in it.

Extracts from the Journal of Doctor Gardiner, ship's surgeon on board The Brothers

6th April 1788

There are now but four of us left – the bosun, the passenger, me, and the Captain. As for the rest, it would seem that they have all destroyed themselves, lost overboard at their own hand or at another's prompting, I know not which. The ship has been drifting now for weeks, and there are not the hands left to right it, even if we could read the charts and alter our course. We are at the mercy of the waves, the Captain has the sextant and almanac necessary for navigation, but he is still our prisoner. He may even have one of the new chronometers, but such an expense as that may have been too much for the Slavers, though if he has it we may be able to re-plot our course again. Tomorrow we will loosen the locks upon his cabin, for it is time to bring him to heel, for all our sakes.

8th April 1788

As we opened up his rooms, it was the stench that first assaulted our senses. The thick noxious fumes of death poured out upon us, and long before we could bring ourselves to take a look inside, I knew him to be dead. Yet still we were not prepared for such a sight – his green rotting flesh visible around his bruised neck and face, as the makeshift noose that had throttled him was cast upon the highest beam. His blackened tongue protruded, and his eyes were like cannon shot, black and bulging from his skull. His hands were strangely tied about his back in a mystifying manner, for there was no one else to so ensnare him, and the lock had not been tampered with since his incarceration. His heels hung less than an inch from the boards, and I felt sure that the faintest of stretches could have secured his toes upon them and so released the pressure from his neck and yet, he was hung there like a carcass on a butchers hook. *The passenger fled at the sight and was last heard vomiting over the gunnel, the remnants of his breakfast evacuated upon the waves. The bosun and I stood regarding the dead form for quite some time, before embarking on our civil duty, and with his knife we sliced at the knot of scarves to let his body slump to the floor in an undignified heap. The odour from about his person was most vile, evidence that he had soiled himself before the end, like so many executed souls before him, as the noose bites and the bowels loosen. We wasted no time in dragging him starboard and taking each an end of him, we lifted him up and, like so many before him, we swung him over without another word. The bosun wondered afterwards if we should have said a prayer on his behalf, but I would not have sullied the word of God with that man's memory, nor asked for his forgiveness if he had never thought to ask for it himself. He was now where he deserved to be and where he would no longer be of any harm, though his body may come to some use as the sharks continue to circle us in expectation of more meat.*

10th April 1788

The days pass slowly, though we still have good supplies of food and all necessary items for our survival. The bosun has done his best to make what he can of the quadrant, and we have all pored over the charts, looking to the night sky for guidance. The consensus is that we are drifting southeast, but without a functioning rudder and missing the mizzenmast, we have little means to go against the will of the wind and the current. We have spoken openly of the boy and of what we were witness to. We have all seen him and have thought we have heard his knock, though all agree that solitude can play tricks on a man, especially when cast adrift upon the ebb and flow of this mighty ocean. And what we have all seen is beyond human endurance, the inhumanity of humanity, the wickedness, the greed, it haunts us all. The young bosun is called Whitfield. He is on his first voyage and is adamant that it will be his last, says he has seen enough of the world now to last him a lifetime. The passenger has not given up his name, he seems intent to keep it, but he has tales of his own to tell and though he did not stand witness to our own atrocities, he has seen enough amongst the colonists and on the islands. I won't repeat them here, but one day hope to be able to recount them for the Commission and will work upon the passenger to join me in our confession to the inquiry. Who knows, it may help to rid ourselves of this curse and of our trepidations as we lay down our heads to sleep. The bosun now occupies the Captain's quarters for the scoundrel has no more use for it, and the passenger has taken the officers' quarters where they once plotted and conspired. I for my sins have stayed in my own cabin – I see no reason to try to run from what is hounding us. There is nowhere to run. It has marked its territory and its scent seeps into the craftsmen's caulk that keeps the brine at bay.

12th April 1788

The Brothers was built in 1771 and so has been at sea some seventeen years, or so the bosun says. We discussed the matter today as we scavenged broken biscuits from the bottom of the barrel. I assume that the ship could have completed one voyage for each year of its service, but then discount by three to allow for repairs and bad seasons, then we arrived at fifteen voyages to the coast. It's a snow, so was built for The Trade, the boat has no other purpose but to ferry a human cargo across to the colonies, and we found ourselves considering the number of lives it has stolen away and those that have died within its hulk. We arrived at an average of five hundred slaves loaded per landing, giving seven thousand five hundred lives shipped, and knowing that between one fifth and one third will have perished in the middle passage, our verdict was beyond all reckoning. Between fifteen hundred and two thousand five hundred dead upon its decks and tossed overboard before it had sighted the sandy shores of the Caribbean islands. All that blood, all that agony, their sweat, and tears, consumed by the ship, seeping into its ribs, sinking down to be absorbed into its keel. No amount of salt water could scrub away those stains, from fore to aft, from starboard to stern, its stinking frame is now saturated with the sorrow of two thousand African souls. That is a sin that can never be reconciled, it can never be mopped from its decks and scoured from its beams, it's very masts are admissions of its guilt, its hands held aloft in a confession to the stars. "It was me. I am guilty." And so, I am, and so is the bosun and all of those who have gone before us to meet their fate on board this boat, for there is no honour amongst thieves and we stand judged for our wickedness. It is a monstrous sin, and we are the most guilty of it for we have yet to pay the price. Though before long, we will. We will.

14ᵗʰ April 1788

Last night, I awoke with a start. It was still dark, but there was a full moon, and its light was cast about the creaking cabin, arcing through the port hole to illuminate my quarters. I breathed out hard and watched my breath rise like cold smoke, white on black. And then I saw it, crouched in the corner. It was more dense than the darkness in which it was submerged. I lay crooked like a hinge, my head elevated in the hammock as it swung me gently from side to side with the swell, as if trying to soothe me back to sleep as the mass moved in time, its smooth lines lost in a seamless soup. I lost track of time. I imagined it was just a shadow, but cast by what for there was nothing there? I fancied that I saw it move, breathe, vibrate, change its form; but then, it looked just the same, and I dared not look away, in case it leapt forward to feed and swallow me up. I puffed out my chest and waited for an attack that did not come, and it was only then that I realised that something had changed. It was dawn and as I glanced up to draw some comfort from the first light, I looked back to see only joinery, and a line of crudely hammered nails poking out of each stretch of English elm. About the floor, crumbs of caulking lay in piles, as if the carefully embedded fibres had somehow worked themselves loose from between the timbers, where they had been so expertly wedged at the ship's last refit. It occurred to me that the nocturnal scratching that I had heard so often within these walls could now have its cause, but whilst I could easily explain the force that had pushed those strands of flax into the gaps between each horizontal plank, I was hard pushed to understand what might have coaxed them out again.

15th April 1788

At first light, I went below again. I had begun to concern myself with the caulking as on closer inspection I saw how much of it had been forced out from between the planks in my own cabin and I got to worrying whether some force of nature about the ship was doing the same below the water line. If it was, I felt certain that we would soon sink and so resolved to see to its repair. I put my idea to the passenger who inspected my cabin's timbers and was of the same mind and so he agreed to accompany me thence, lighting a fresh candle in the storm lantern as we raised the iron grate that had once kept the slaves captive below and stepped down into the void. The hold was full of traded goods, raw materials for the cotton mills of Lancashire, the tobacco factories of Bristol and even for the Quaker's chocolate factories of Birmingham, from whence we stepped down another level, deep into the bowels of the ship where less perishable goods were stored. The vessel's sway sent us stumbling into the blackened walls of this timbered tomb more than once as we wandered in the path of the flickering flame, looking for signs of damage to the caulking, but we could see none. More than once I caught sight of a rat or two, large and unafraid down in their lair, though they dodged from our intruding light, preferring to lurk in the darkest corners.

We stayed close then, as we inched along the length of the boat until we came upon an unexpected sight.

A small open trapdoor that led down to the very lowest point of the ship below which, save for a few inches of timber, pitched a vast and watery grave. The torch did little to penetrate the dead pool of water that lapped beneath our feet, but we could see enough of the noxious bilge to perceive its ebb and flow. It moved like a tidal *lake and as I knelt down to peer beneath the boards, I didn't reckon on the overpowering stench that soon assaulted my senses. The ship lurched and the putrid well surged within its frame as it turned somersault to bring a jumble of swollen bodies to the surface like flotsam and jetsam on a secluded beach. Their skin was flaccid and grey, their unseeing eyes dull in the lamplight and their mouths ajar in death's last scream. Foremost amongst this final muster roll, the ravaged face of a tortured mate rose up like a bloated buoy, the skin of his cheek flapping in a savage wound that neither time nor tide would now heal.*

I don't know what I said then, I don't know what I did or if I was first to make it back upon the deck, I cannot recall, but I will never go below again on this or any other ship. I will never ever put to sea again, so help me God.

If I might just live long enough to tell my tale.

CHAPTER TWENTY ONE

"By purchasing so great a number [600] the slaves were so crowded that they were obliged to lie one upon another. This caused such a mortality among them that without meeting with unusually bad weather or having a longer voyage than common, nearly one half of them died before the ship arrived in the West Indies."

Alexander Falconbridge, Account of the Slave Trade on the Coast of Africa, 1788

The presentation of evidence before the whole of Parliament dragged on, a whole year being lost in sub-committees and council meetings, and with it went all hope of a reprieve. It would prove fatal to the cause and although Thomas Clarkson spent most of that period across the channel in France, drumming up support amongst the French Abolitionists, rumour and counter-rumour was killing their movement and raising the hopes amongst the slave traders that their commerce would never be called to account for its crimes.

Suggestions were put about in Parliamentary circles that even William Wilberforce had softened his stance on his call for total and complete abolition, and though he denied it vehemently in Parliament and before the Select Committee, the rumours persisted. No doubt it was the slaving community that continued to fan the flames, their propaganda infiltrating the homes, offices, and clubs of former staunch allies of the cause, to such an extent that some advocates had started to turn, believing that the Abolitionist stories had been exaggerated or at worse fabricated. The proofs supplied by former members of The Trade, particularly the crews, were also brought into question, their lowly status in society being held up as evidence of their unsuitability to be relied upon under oath, a challenge that Granville Sharp thought to be particularly odious.

"It is the worst of all hypocrisy" he roared, when first presented with the claims in discussion with Clarkson on his compatriot's return from the continent. "To accuse a man because of his station or living of being less honest than a merchant or plantation owner is scandalous."

"But what are we to do?" asked Clarkson in desperation. "Over twenty thousand of our 'evidences' are drawn from such men, the crews of slavers who have witnessed up close the horrors of The Trade. If they are not to be believed then our case is lost."

"I have heard that even the numbers are being questioned now," admitted Sharp. "Some are saying that it is 'quite impossible' for one man to have collected the testimonies of so many witnesses in so short a time, or to have travelled so far and alone, on horseback."

"But we both know it to be true" scowled Clarkson, personally affronted by the accusation.

"We do," agreed Sharp, "but if our evidence is not to be held up as the truth in this matter, then no matter how many witnesses we bring forward, their sheer number will go against our cause and not for us."

For a moment, a brooding silence fell about them, as each of them contemplated the growing possibility that they could be defeated. After all they had been through in bringing this matter to the attention of the people, and then before the benches of Westminster, neither was prepared to give it up without a fight.

"One of the biggest arguments put forward so far by the slavers," said Sharp in a moment of clarity, "is that they are somehow 'saving' African lives by taking them to the West Indies. That without them, these poor souls would die at the coast, through sacrifice or some other abuse. What if we could prove that they are not just taken prisoner as the spoils of war, but are being kidnapped from surrounding villages by force, in raiding parties either instigated by the slave ship Captains, or by the English crew to meet that need and that need alone?"

"I have heard that raiding parties are sent out to find victims, whenever several ships are in port," Clarkson confirmed, but I've not yet heard of a white man accompanying the party. There are stories of several large canoes heading upriver and bringing back hundreds of men, women, and children, but no witness has yet come forward. It's still only hearsay."

"So, what if we could find such a witness, one that is of unassailable character. A Royal Navy man perhaps? One of the King's own. And bring them to testify?"

"It's possible," said Clarkson, "but it would be like looking for a needle in a haystack."

"I think we have to try," said Sharp, "our evidence is exhausted, and we are losing ground. They've become immune to the horrors of the middle passage and the effects of the seasoning, and no matter what manner of degradations and cruelties we bring before them, it's as if they have heard it all before and so are rendered numb to its authenticity."

"Then I will try," Clarkson conceded, "there are still ports I have yet to visit and if I can find amongst their number, servicemen who have been along the slaving routes we may yet uncover such a witness. But it is one thing to find a Navy man, who was once aboard a slave ship, it's quite another to get him to testify."

"Do whatever you can Thomas," urged Sharp. "Pay him whatever 'expenses' need to be paid to bring him to London. House him in the finest hotel and furnish him with the best food and wine, but find him and bring him hither."

Thomas Clarkson wasted no time at all, leaving London the very next day.

In just a few weeks he had travelled over one thousand miles visiting the naval ports at Deptford, Woolwich, Chatham and Sheerness, interviewing hundreds of men on board one hundred and sixty vessels, but it was at Portsmouth that he received the information that he was looking for. A sailor who had indeed accompanied a slaving party up the River Calabar, on one of two African voyages, but though he had been in Portsmouth, he was there no longer, and the only clue that Clarkson could find as to his likely whereabouts was that he was a Devonian, and some had thought that he had returned home for a few weeks rest and recuperation, before taking on another journey out of the southern port of Plymouth.

He pursued this tenuous lead with haste, riding through the night to reach his destination. Once at the port, he spoke at length to the harbour master of his mission and his cause, but without a name to go by, he found that his search was becoming increasingly futile. But as luck would have it, as he boarded the very last ship in port that day, a frigate by the name of Melampus, and relayed the story to an officer on deck, he was finally rewarded for his diligence and fortitude.

"You'll be wanting to talk to Isaac Parker," the officer said in a broad West Country accent, "he's told that tale many a time, he be down at the quayside preparing the ship to leave on the next tide. Be careful though, he also reckons he sailed with Captain Cook a few years back!"

On finally coming face to face with a bemused Parker, Clarkson had an overwhelming urge to hug the bearded seaman, but unsure of the reaction that such warmth would invoke, he resisted the temptation, settling instead on a firm, but friendly handshake.

"I have travelled far and wide to find you Mr Parker," he explained to the puzzled mariner. "It is indeed a pleasure to meet you. You would be doing your country the greatest service if you would be willing to talk with me a while and if you are indeed the witness that I am seeking, if you were then ready to accompany me to Parliament."

Clarkson continued to explain the purpose behind his unlikely errand and the corroboration he was seeking. At first, Parker seemed unwilling to either confirm or deny the story and as the Reverend had begun to give up hope that they would ever find a willing witness to this most horrific of practices, the man spoke up to furnish him with his own account of the kidnapping packs who prowled the Guinea Coast.

"It be right that this goes on," he said, "it is common amongst the local tribes to find the cargoes in this way. If there's been no wars to offer up any ready prisoners and no disputes amongst the local chiefs, then ten or twelve of these canoes are sent upstream to find some."

"And how many are come by in this manner?" asked Clarkson excitedly, knowing that he was on the verge of uncovering some new and powerful evidence.

"Hundreds every time there are ships at anchor. Maybe thousands a month, tens of thousands every year in all I'd say," Parker said, "every time they'd send upriver. These canoes are not like small dinghys, they'd be large, big enough to fit dozens and dozens of bodies in their bellies and with a small cannon affixed to the front, in case of trouble. They has 'em lie down you see, tied up and squealing like pigs in the base of the boat one on of top of another."

"And how long do they stay like that?"

"Two or three days, I'd say," shrugged Parker. "They ambushes 'em in the dark outside their villages and brings 'em to the river by force, then packs 'em in nice and tight and gets away under cover of darkness. Sometimes they only takes the women and children, when the menfolk are out hunting, so they gets away sharpish like, before the men come back."

"So, there is no coercion, no involvement of local warlords?" asked Clarkson, knowing that he wasn't asking his question clearly enough. "They are not already prisoners? They are free men and women, taken from their villages in the dead of night for the sole purpose of being sold as slaves to the white slave ships?"

"That's exactly what they are" said Parker, "I've seen thousands on the beaches within a few days of the canoes being sent out, and the slavers prefer these to the ones taken in wars. They be fresh you see. They has no wounds about their bodies and are not exhausted by a long journey, just a bit shook up as is natural, and melancholy of course. Nobody likes to be kidnapped after all."

Clarkson couldn't help but think that Isaac Parker didn't really know the half of it, but having cleared the situation with the ship's Captain, he agreed on a generous sum for his transfer to London and for his board and lodgings on the way, sending him thence with Granville Sharp's business card and clear instructions for how and where to find his rooms.

In addition to Parker, he harvested another five additional first hand witnesses himself on a subsequent journey that took him North again, another dozen witnesses were persuaded to take the stand. But so many more declined his invitation and though they were willing and able to share their experiences in a 'private setting', the majority remained obstinately opposed to the prospect of any public appearance.

However, amongst the massed ranks of the opposition, the anti-Abolitionist movement were also getting themselves organised, and their wealth amassed over two hundred years of exploitation and persecution was being put to a new and even more ominous use.

-○○○-

The fortunes of John Pinney and James Tobin were secured long before they joined together in a prosperous Bristol based business in the middle of the 1780s. Both were born into the sugar trade, with family estates on the island of Nevis, and though both would return in 1784 to a mercantile career in England, leaving their plantations in the capable hands of locally appointed managers, neither had any notion of the domestic storm into which they were sailing.

In their appearance, the two men could not have been more different. Pinney was not blessed with a face for paintings, his high forehead and pursed lips giving him a stern and unwelcoming visage, which was not complemented by a pair of dark and brooding eyes that seemed to always be looking down in judgment on his subject. Tobin on the other hand, was possessed of almost girlish features, his red lips and complexion sat beneath prominent eyebrows to give him the comely look of a 'dandy', a look that he would use to good effect on the social circuits of Bristol and London, in the years before - and after - his well-arranged marriage.

Tobin's family owned the Stoney Grove estate together with one hundred and seventy-five slaves, whilst the Pinney line held the nearby Mountravers plantation, where nine hundred slaves would live and die beneath the misted hills of the Nevis island in the one hundred years of his family's tenure. Pinney had inherited the business from his guardian in 1764, changing his name as part of the conditions of inheritance, and aged just twenty-four had travelled back to the island, intent on clearing his debts by transforming an enterprise that was on the wane.

Nevis was once the disembarkation point of choice for slave ships arriving in the Leeward Islands, and though its pre-eminence was in decline by the latter years of the eighteenth century, its two thousand square miles of mainly rugged terrain, had been largely set aside for the cultivation and processing of sugar. Though small by comparison to the larger islands of Barbados and Jamaica and dominated by three volcanic mountain peaks of which Nevis is by far the most spectacular - rising almost one thousand meters above the azure seas in which it sits - the island economy was dependant on the African trade for its labour force by the time that William and Anne took to the throne of England.

Sugar cane had prospered in its well-drained soils, and the Mountravers estate took full advantage, sitting as it did on the lower reaches of the Nevis mountain and so able to benefit from the regular rainfall that fell on its gentle slopes. Sugar was a highly perishable commodity and the time spent in moving it from the fields to the boiler house and then onto the waiting snows, was an exercise in back breaking precision. Having the sea so close by gave a distinct advantage, where barrels of rum and sugar could be loaded onto ships at minimal cost in sterling and in time. Like all successful planters, the Pinney production line was a finely tuned operation, and although the sugar cane itself was nurtured over an eighteen-month cycle of holing, planting, manuring, weeding, and harvesting, once the leaves had been chopped away and the stalks cut loose, many large bundles of canes would have to be carted with the utmost urgency for processing. It was strength sapping work.

A highly labour-intensive process called for a diligent workforce of attentive and physical labourers, but a crew that laboured under the threat of an overseer's lash proved to be even more effective. Working in teams of four, they were tasked to twice feed the plants into the crushers, forcing the stems between the rollers to extract as much of the precious sugar as possible. Then, under the pressure of the wind powered millstones, a constant slurry of cane juice would flow into the boiling house, where a raging fire kept three or four copper kettles at boiling point, fomented by the sweat of the slaves who kept it stoked with the dried sugar leaves and their brittle husks. Another slave sweltered at the opening to each copper station, ladling out the steaming syrup into the next, his brow and body steaming with sweat and at an ever-constant risk of scalding, until the strike point was reached when the copper and the sugar syrup would be ready for curing. Here, the liquid would be ladled into the familiar conical pots where it would solidify, or into large wooden barrels, the uncrystallized molasses draining out from the bottom, to be fermented into rum or used as feed for both slaves and animals about the farm.

All of this, beneath the unforgiving glare of the Caribbean sun, a form of forced labour which had proven to be too strenuous for the weaker constitutions of indentured servants from Europe, whose lives had been made forfeit in the early years of the plantation one hundred and fifty years before Pinney had set foot on the island. The whole gruelling undertaking had been no overnight success, it had been trial and error of the most unforgiving kind, and only now was its process finally close to being perfected.

Pinney had immediately set about bolstering his labour force as soon as he arrived in the Caribbean, wasting no time at all in travelling to the nearby St Kitts on 11th January 1765 to acquire nine new males, all aged between ten and twenty years old. It wouldn't be the last 'scramble' that he would attend and far from being put off by the demeaning circus, he had rather enjoyed the whole spectacle and the opportunity to pit his wits against his fellow owners and co-dependants on The Trade. He also liked to be seen to be spending his hard earned fortune. It made him feel superior and it was a feeling that he had grown accustomed to. He acquired another one hundred or so slaves on his marriage in 1772, coming from his wife's estate, and throughout his time on the island was actively engaged in the sale and purchase of human labourers, who would toil their lives away on his intensively cultivated lands.

Pinney did not rest on his laurels, and after an initial period of good harvests, he continued to invest in buildings and equipment, rebuilding mill houses and replenishing his stocks of mules and other beasts of burden, shipping them in from England throughout the 1760s and into the 1770s, but it was not all plain sailing. Far from it. A series of bad harvests, accompanied by several devastating hurricanes, outbreaks of smallpox and other diseases and even attacks from French and American forces on the island and on his property at sea, had left his business on the brink of bankruptcy on more than one occasion. When he finally returned to England in the mid 1780s, along with his wife and many children, he did so a far wiser, and far more wily investor.

Tobin on the other hand was born in London and though he spent his formative years on Nevis from 1758 to 1766, he returned a decade later to manage the Stoney Grove estate once again, which had by then fallen on hard times. He was soon back in Bristol though and by 1784, together with Pinney, he would quickly become a vocal member of the Bristol West India Association in their stand-off against the Abolitionists. When the Reverend James Ramsay issued his damning *Essay on the Treatment and Conversion of African Slaves in the British Sugar Colonies*, published in the same year that Tobin arrived back in Bristol, it was Tobin that responded in kind, issuing his own 'little unpolished tract' to put the nosey clergyman in his place. According to Tobin, Ramsay was guilty of making 'uninformed', 'prejudiced' and 'misrepresented' claims, using 'gross misrepresentations', 'virulent invectives' – whatever that means – and 'absurd prejudices' in the process. His claims were 'fallacies', his 'injurious and ill-founded aspersions' a conspiracy, and his much-quoted work full of 'palpable and numerous contradictions'. And all this, at a time before Thomas Clarkson and his band of brothers had even begun to bring the truth of the colonies before the eyes of a disbelieving public.

"In short," said Tobin, as he read his now infamous works out loud before the attentive ears of the Bristol Society of Slaving Ventures, "when a preacher of primitive meekness, ostensibly desirous of spreading the invaluable blessings of liberty and Christianity, takes the most illiberal and unchristian-like manner of doing it, the true motives of his zeal, and the immaculate purity of his intentions may become justly liable to suspicion." And having got that off his chest, his next grievance, aired with a rising sense of injustice, seemed to strike a little closer to home.

"If after three or four generations of their ancestors have sacrificed their health and finished their lives in the toils, vexations and disappointments, necessarily attendant on the forming of new settlements, amidst the uncultivated wilds of an unhealthy climate, and under the scorching influence of a vertical sun, a very few of their descendants are happily enabled to return to their mother country in easy, or even affluent circumstances, is this the reception they merit?"

He seemed to be suggesting, both verbally and in writing, that 'the end justified the means' and having given examples of rehabilitated planters who had returned to a more civilised existence in the clergy or The Commons, he challenged Ramsay, a former clergyman on the Island of St. Kitts, outright. "If equity and truth obliges the author to answer these questions in the affirmative, with what appearance of decency or propriety, does he presume to paint the West Indian planters as a band of inhuman and unprincipled tyrants while abroad, and a set of useless unthinking, dissipated spendthrifts when at home?"

That line of argument really struck a chord with his largely Bristol-based audience, and a loud cheer rose from amongst them, that grew steadily in volume, rising to a crescendo of applause and forcing Tobin to take a momentary break, to gather his thoughts and to whet his whistle for another go at it. From then on, every challenge to Ramsay's words, every apparent falsehood exposed and every unaccepted insult, was met with the same resounding noise.

The English were not 'first' to enslave the African, it was the Portuguese and the Moors before them. Our slaves are not treated worse than on the French islands, the French being much more severe and cruel masters; the fraternisations between overseers and female slaves were nowhere near as prevalent as on the French islands, where even the planters had a string of black mistresses. The food was better, the clothing was better, the breaks were better and even, according to Tobin, the housing stock on the English plantations compared to the other slaving nations were too. But there was more to follow, as he turned his attention next to comparisons with the general people of the British Isles themselves, as he took a firm swipe at its wealthy landowners and the 'scandalous' treatment of their own labouring classes.

"On the whole, even the meanest of their dwellings are undoubtedly better than the turf-built hovels of the Scottish highlanders," he professed to another supportive cry, "or the demi-caverns of the Irish bogtrotters; and those of the better sort may more than vie, for neatness with the habitations even of the English labouring villages." He quoted the admissions of Ramsay to the existence of "doors, window-shutters, nails and hinges" as evidence against the accusations aimed at his compatriots, and fervidly defended their collective honour in the treatment of pregnant black women, who Ramsay asserted would sometimes be forced to give birth in the fields where they toiled.

"Supposing, however, that pregnant and lying-in women, on ill-conducted estates, are treated but little better than Mr Ramsay asserts," having already claimed to cries of 'shame' from around the table, that he had never seen a heavily pregnant slave still working in the fields. "Still their situation under those circumstances, will more than bear comparison with the lot of the lower orders of females in Great Britain, whom we frequently see taken in labour in the harvest field or at the washing tub – and who after three- or four-days recess are obliged to return to the same unremitted drudgery without the least assistance as to the care of their offspring."

His concluding defence of his West Indian clansmen drew comparisons with the English peasantry, in an attempt to claim that the treatment of slaves upon the plantations was no worse than, and likely better than, the torments endured by the supposedly 'unenslaved' workers of England. "The English peasants of both sexes may, without exaggeration, be considered as born to severe and hereditary labour," he said in an honest assessment of the lot of the labouring poor. "They struggle through the years of their childhood and the diseases, half naked and half starved, equally exposed to the heats of summer and the frosts of winter and in a state of untutored ignorance. They are no sooner able to handle a fork, or a rake, or to follow in the steps of a horse along a furrow, than their regular career of toil begins."

He painted a stark picture of the English agricultural labourer, asserting that "all the hardships of the English peasant are softened by the idea of liberty and yet that great part of liberty they are reckoned to possess is truly nominal and ideal, for they are absolutely bound either to work, or starve under the absolute dominion of some tyrannical overseer or unfeeling church warden, who in every country parish exercises an unmerciful sway over the poorer inhabitants."

It was a much shortened version of his tract, but as he happily distributed copies of its one hundred and sixty eight pages at the end of his address, he was content to have thoroughly dismantled his opponent's essay as a work of fiction, and laid a damning accusation at the feet of the English aristocracy that those in glass houses were in no position to throw stones.

As the gathered planters and ship owners each took their leave of the other's company at the end of the evening, Tobin lost count of the number of congratulatory remarks that came his way, noting with pride that several referred to his discourse as the "highlight of the evening," and promising to ensure that their newly furnished copy would be well-thumbed by all members of their extensive households, at least by those amongst them who could read.

Its impact was no 'flash in the pan' and by 1789, as the threat of abolition began to hit a little too close to home, its well-fashioned defence would once again be brought to bear before a willing readership in the House of Commons and amongst the Lords. The rising threat had given Pinney much to deliberate over and he had already given serious consideration to the disposal of his interests in the West Indies, as the two ruthless friends and business partners led the charge of Bristol's merchants in the fight against the radicals. Together with members of the other leading Bristol families, whose business interests extended to the African Trade, they forged ahead and organised themselves, holding their meetings at the historic Merchants Hall in Bristol, from whence they sought to mobilise the interests of the nation's ever expanding commercial Empire.

The Claxton, Protheroe and Baille slaving houses were all represented prominently in their meetings, as were the Bristol Alderman, Daubeney, and Harris, who had initially declared for Clarkson's cause, only to change their minds under the due influence of these paid-up members of the Bristol Society of Slaving Ventures. Between them they would raise three petitions from Bristol alone, and present each to Parliament in the capable hands of Henry Cruger, their

American MP, whose family also held extensive 'business interests' in Jamaica.

On April 9ᵗʰ, 1789, at the London Tavern in Bristol, they and others met to agree on a response to the outrages of the Abolitionist propaganda machine, that had gone from being a once a week irritant from the pulpit on a Sunday, to a continual and outright attack on their mercantile interests that was threatening to make inroads into their hard-earned fortunes at home and abroad.

At a General Meeting of the WEST-INDIA PLANTERS and MERCHANTS and other Persons interested in the SUGAR-COLONIES pursuant to Advertisement.

RESOLVED UNANIMOUSLY.

That it is the opinion of this Meeting, that the approaching investigation (in a committee of the House of Commons) of the Petitions against the Slave trade demands the most serious attention of everyone interested in the commerce of Great Britain but most particularly of such as are connected with the British West Indies.

That the cultivation of the SUGAR COLONIES cannot be sustained even to its present extent but must immediately decline without the importation of negro labourers from Africa.

That in consequence of a diminished cultivation in the British Sugar Islands, the Navigation, Manufacturers, Trade and Revenue of Great Britain, must suffer a proportional diminution.

That it be earnestly recommended to the different departments of his Majesty's Subjects, who may be affected in their respective interests or employments by the diminished cultivation and eventual decline of the British Sugar Islands, to make such representations to Parliament as they may think necessary in order to defeat the Injurious Tendency of the proposed Abolition of The Trade to Africa for Labourers.

RESOLVED.

That it be recommended to the Manufacturers, Traders, and others to appoint delegates to attend the Select Committee.

That such reflections be communicated to all the great Trading Towns throughout Great Britain.

It was a call to arms.

And to Great Britain's everlasting shame, their call would be heeded.

CHAPTER TWENTY TWO

"On whatever branch of the system I turned my eyes, I found it equally barbarous. The Trade was, in short, one mass of iniquity from the beginning to the end."

Thomas Clarkson, The History of the Abolition of the African Slave Trade

Eighteen long months had passed and as Mr Wilberforce begged Parliament to give him more time to call up yet more witnesses, the odds were becoming stacked against them.

On 4th February 1791, Wilberforce impressed upon Parliament that of the eighty-one days spent to date on the subject of the slave trade, fifty-seven of those had been spent listening to the complaints and curses of the pro-slavery movement and that this imbalance must be redressed to allow the Abolitionists time to bring their own latest evidence to bear on the case. Another committee was appointed, and its deliberations lasted from the 7th February to the 5th April, but events outside of The Society's command were spinning out of control and as the day of the final Parliamentary debate drew closer, it was other matters that were now front of mind for the government.

A revolutionary fever was in the air, and the landed classes, most prominently amongst them the House of Lords and the Monarchy, were running scared. Even those elected members of the House of Commons, whose properties and estates were not insubstantial, were feeling the pressure from across the channel, so when news reached them of slave revolts on the islands of Martinique and St. Domingo, their nerves were shredded and any compulsion that they may have held to support the Abolitionist cause began to unravel.

Finally, an insurrection on the British island of Dominica, led to calls for a military deployment from those whose financial interests were affected, and they were in no doubt that continued delays in Parliament over the question of the slave trade had led to this sudden unrest. They had been the architects of their own downfall. The pro-slavery movement had played for time and their delaying tactics had won the day, or at least had brought about a significant delay of execution and for many, that was all they were reasonably expecting. After all, many were aging gentlemen who could expect to see another twenty years at the helm, when their interests would pass into the hands of the next generation. Survival was the name of their game, and if they could eke out a couple more decades of deregulated free trade, then that would do for them.

On Monday 18th April 1791, William Wilberforce again rose to his feet before his increasingly less honourable Parliamentary peers to bring the matter of the slave trade to a close. The debate would last two days and finish at three thirty in the early hours of a shameful Wednesday in English history. This time there was no inspirational speech. Enough words had been spent on behalf of this most villainous of subjects to last for ten sessions of Parliament.

"I hope that the present debate," he said, outlining his most solemn expectation, "will, instead of exciting asperity and confirming prejudice, would tend to produce a general conviction of the truth in what in fact was incontrovertible; that the abolition of the slave trade was indispensably required of them, not only by morality and religion, but by sound policy."

He brought forward the evidence provided by Isaac Parker, that "armed parties were regularly sent out in the evening, who scoured the country, and brought in their prey." He accused The Trade of being a corruption to the morals of all those who were involved in it and said that "for the honour of the mercantile character of the country, such a traffic ought immediately to be suppressed." Of the middle passage, he chose this time to "spare the feelings" of the House by not diving further into its depths of depravity for the umpteenth time but did not hold back on the impolicy of the plantation owners themselves, who continued to claim a need for fresh supplies of slaves to "replenish their stocks". He denied the claims of the pro-slavery lobby that colonial laws had been passed in order to protect the interests of the slaves who were there interned, where the agents of savage beatings and brutish murders were never brought to justice.

He quoted a Mr Ross, whose strongly held belief was that "a master had a right to punish his slave in whatever manner he might think proper without fear of indictment" and that no man could be held to account for the destruction of his own 'property'. He finished with a call to the people of Great Britain of whom he was "confident would abolish the slave trade when, as would soon happen, its injustice and cruelty had been fairly laid before them."

"Already we have gained one victory," he concluded. "We have obtained for these poor creatures the recognition of their human nature, which for a while had been most shamefully denied them. This is the first fruits of our efforts. Let us persevere and our triumph will be complete. Never, never will we desist, until we have wiped away this scandal from the Christian name. Until we have released ourselves from the load of guilt under which we present labour, and until we have extinguished every trace of this bloody traffic, which our posterity, looking back to the history of these enlightened times, will scarcely believe had been suffered to exist so long, a disgrace and dishonour to our country."

To say that Wilberforce then had to withstand a barrage of opposition to his proposed Bill, would imply that he was under attack, but as politician after politician again stood up to have their say, it was soon clear to all on the Abolitionist bench that there had been a change in mood since the last debate. And it had not moved in their favour.

After Colonel Tarleton claimed that "it was the duty of the House to protect the planters," Mr Grosvenor aired the widely held view that "kidnapping and other barbarous practices were the natural consequences of the laws of Africa," coming to the outrageous conclusion that whilst "the slave trade was not an amiable trade, neither was that of a butcher, but yet it was a very necessary one." Mr Burton on the other hand, no doubt thinking himself a man of reason, wanted to "go gradually into the abolition of The Trade", giving the planters time to "replenish their stocks". Lord John Russell called the motion "visionary and elusive" and "a feeble attempt without the power to serve the cause of humanity." Mr Stanley continued to expound the myth that the tales of misery in the West Indies were "gross falsehoods," drawing his evidence from the Bible itself, that it was "the intention of Providence, that from the very beginning, one set of men should be slaves to another.

"The truth," he lied, "was as old as it was universal."

The final statement turned the tide for a while at least. Mr William Smith took exception to Mr Stanley's "misapplied passages" from scripture and Mr Matthew Montagu added his condemnation to that of Mr Wilberforce, pledging his unwavering support to the cause. But it was Mr Smith who then held court, bringing several examples of brutality before their collective consciousness, less the 'evidence' of the pro-slavery lobby should pass for the truth amongst them. The thought that he left them with should have been enough to melt even the most hardened of hearts, which he hoped would then pave the way for the final vote and the ultimate abolition of The Trade in 1791.

"I would now mention another instance," he began, "though I must warn you that it is of the most heinous sort imaginable. A child on board a slave ship, of about ten months old, took sulk and would not eat. The Captain flogged it with the cat, swearing that he would make it eat or kill it. From this and other ill treatment the child's leg swelled. He then ordered some water to be made hot to abate the swelling, but even his tender mercies were cruel; for the cook, on putting his hand into the water, said it was too hot. Upon this the Captain swore at him and ordered the feet to be put in. This was done. The nails and skin came off. Oiled cloths were then put around them. The child was at length tied to a heavy log. Two or three days later the Captain caught it up again and repeated that he would make it eat or kill it. He immediately flogged it again, and in a quarter of an hour it died. But after the child was dead, whom should the barbarian select to throw it overboard, but the wretched mother. In vain she started from the office. He beat her 'til he made her take up the child and carry it to the side of the vessel. She then dropped it into the sea, turning her head the other way that she might not see it."

A brooding silence descended upon the gathering of elected Parliamentarians. Such barbarity. Such evil. Such horror. A brutality that even the most wicked of Satan's hoards would have been hard pushed to emulate, and yet here it was, presented to the British ruling class, to its elite, as an act carried out on the High Seas in the name of progress.

In the name of a supposedly 'Great' Britain.

This account alone, should have been enough to warrant an end to it, once and for all, but Mr Courtenay rose and once again raised the spectre of France before the room, claiming that should we cease in our participation in The Trade, that England's arch enemy would simply take it up and strengthen their position as Europe's foremost power. And so, it began again, starting with an address by the Prime Minister, Mr Pitt, who in an attempt at an early summing up claimed with some degree of exaggeration, that "almost everyone appeared to wish that the further importation of slaves might cease, if it could be made out that the population of the West Indies could be maintained without it." Mr Alderman Watson defended the benefits of The Trade and Mr Fox shouted him down, restating his feelings on the matter from his last address. Mr Ryder and Mr Stanley gave their support for total abolition, Mr Smith, and Mr Sumner countenanced caution, preferring a more gradual cessation, whilst Major Scott called any attempt to curtail or regulate The Trade "a dangerous experiment".

It could have continued for hours, but once again they were burning the midnight oil and it was well past three o'clock in the morning when the speaker called the House to order, and the chamber was divided to cast their votes. In a civilised and Christian nation, whose people had spoken out against the inhumanity of the slave trade in their hundreds of thousands, where a catalogue of independent evidence had been amassed to demonstrate beyond any reasonable doubt that this trade in human misery was repugnant to the core, one hundred and sixty-three of its politicians voted against the motion.

Only eighty-eight had the courage and compassion to vote in favour of its abolition, overpowered by a collective sense of guilt and shame that it had been allowed to continue in their name for so long. They had been out voted, two to one.

-ooo-

The following morning, two hundred miles away in the City of Bristol, the bells of St. Mary Redcliffe church were rung in celebration on hearing the news that Wilberforce's Bill had been so resoundedly defeated. Effigies of the red-haired Reverend and his lapdog politician were carried throughout the narrow streets on the shoulders of a sizeable and jubilant crowd, before being tossed atop of bonfires and burned in triumph long into the night. The Trade had been saved, industrial ruin was averted and the mercantile classes upon which Bristol's very fabric depended would continue to prosper, for several years to come. Their victory had been so overwhelming, the margin of defeat so devastating, that many doubted the ability of the Abolitionists to respond and so the prospect for imminent change was at worst uncertain and at best unlikely.

"Not in my lifetime" a grizzly old sea Captain was heard to holler, as the festivities spilled out of the pubs onto Marsh Street and Baldwin Street, where the slaving community sang and danced until the light of dawn was upon them.

-ooo-

In the subsequent weeks, an almost fatal malaise struck the Reverend Thomas Clarkson like a cannonball. It was as if the exertions of the previous four years had afflicted him all at once, knocking him off his feet and sending him packing back to the countryside of Cambridgeshire, a shattered and broken man. Though The Society had called an immediate meeting after the defeat to proclaim it as a mere setback in their plans for full emancipation, the Reverend knew in his heart of hearts that their cause had been deeply wounded by the loss, and was inconsolable in the thought that many thousands of African lives would now be lost as a direct consequence of the sheer cowardice of the British Parliament.

He was shaken out of his stupor when a curious letter arrived at his home in Wisbech, which left him so intrigued that he was soon forced from his confinement and back onto the road.

My Dearest Thomas,

I know that you will have taken our defeat hardest of all, but I hope that my words have provided you with some small comfort these last months.

The vote against our cause shames our Parliament, not us, and I repeat that it is merely a setback on a much longer road. We have achieved many things together these past five years and I know that when the time is right, our Parliamentary friends will come to listen to their consciences and their constituents to abolish this evil trade.

I write to tell you of a recent encounter, one that requires you to attend on me in London, if you are quite well enough to take on the journey, though I implore you to come by stagecoach and not on horseback, I fear that such a strain would take its toll on your already weakened constitution.

I received a strange and striking visitor just yesterday, an unusual man that would not give me his name, but who told me of his recent return voyage on board The Brothers. He came back on 'the run' from Jamestown, with an extraordinary tale of Doctor Gardiner and the return crossing, which ended up back on the Guinea Coast where our good Doctor met his end. There is more, but I would wish to tell you of it in person and the stranger has agreed to return on Monday next to meet with us and to share with us the good Doctor's own journal which he claims to have in safe custody.

If you are too weak or not of a mind to make the trip then I will of course understand and will furnish you of all the details by letter, but if you are able and willing to visit then I will be delighted to accommodate you here at my London residence.

Yours in hope,

Granville Sharp Esq.

It was not the kind of news that could be ignored, and so Clarkson hastily scribbled his reply, accepting the invitation and immediately began preparations for the journey, sending his servant to enquire as to the most convenient carriage from Cambridge. Arrangements were quickly put in place and within a few days, a weary Thomas Clarkson's heart was set on a return to London to commence a new phase in the fight to secure a long overdue victory that would last for another fifteen years.

CHAPTER TWENTY THREE

"We will never desist from appealing to the consciences of our countrymen till the commercial intercourse with Africa shall cease to be polluted with the blood of its inhabitants."

Granville Sharp, Chairman of The Society for Effecting the Abolition of the Slave Trade

"I'd like to introduce you," started Granville Sharp, as the three men sat together in his study, a tea service laid out on the table before them, in preparation for a servant's touch. "To our informant."

"Pleased to make your acquaintance," said Clarkson somewhat bewildered, as he regarded the man with interest. "Though you have a familiar look Sir, have we met before, in Bristol perhaps, or Liverpool?"

"Indeed, we have," he said, "and I could hardly forget thee either, or the rumpus that followed our last meeting aboard The Pilgrim. We paid the price for our sociable swig of rum I can tell you, when the Slavers found out we'd been talking, it cost us all a flogging!"

"I'm sorry to learn of that" said Clarkson, placing the man in his mind's eye aboard the boat that had waited at quayside in Bristol, alongside The Prince and The Pearl. "I knew I'd seen those silver-grey eyes somewhere before, though I have to say you have aged since we last met. I don't believe that I had your name last time and I must say that whenever I have had the pleasure to make a new association in the confines of a gentleman's home, it has been my habit to insist on knowing who it is that I am addressing."

"Nor will you on this occasion either," he remarked, his countenance entirely unruffled, though his appearance was now of a much older man, for his hair had begun to turn white grey and his ashen skin had weathered far more than was warranted by the passage of time. "For I fear for my life should my name be known back in

England Sir. I was left for dead in the islands by a villainous Captain and now I have a perfect opportunity to escape from this evil occupation I intend to grasp it with both hands. My name, you shall not have, but my testimony is yours."

It was indeed quite irregular, but Sharp had allowed this break with etiquette, only because of the friend that they all had in common, and they didn't have to wait much longer before the memory of Doctor Gardiner came into focus as they put the awkward pleasantries to one side.

"I apologise for the mystery," explained their anonymous visitor, "but my sole reason for being here is to fulfil the good Doctor's intentions and to pass this into your safe hands, for use in bringing about the final abolition of this heinous trade." Reaching for his satchel he withdrew a bound binder and within it was pure gold, not of the kind that pirates fight to the death over, but of the literary kind. "I gave Doctor Gardiner my word that if anything were to happen to him, then I would do my best to get this to you. He had a fine reputation and though I never sailed with him in an official capacity, it was good to sail with him on The Brothers. Though it has taken me some time to pluck up the courage to return to England from Africa, and having found out your whereabouts easily enough – you are both very famous in this vast city it would seem – then I came to make good on that promise."

"Have you read it?" asked Sharp, taking care not to sound too accusing.

"No, for I cannot read," the man admitted with a wry smile, "but he told me much of what it contains and as I too lived much of it at his side, I am hopeful, nay I am certain, that it will lend much to your argument, even if some aspects are a little, strange."

"Then please proceed with your tale," said Clarkson turning the pages of the roughly bound book with care, "as I am most interested to know of our good Doctor's demise. It's been some years since we've had any news of him and I pray that he did not suffer in his final days, though I have misgivings that any such hope as that, may be false."

The expressions on the faces of both Sharp and their visitor, strongly suggested that his sentiments were not far from the mark. At that moment, the tea arrived, served by a robust looking Addae, who smiled broadly as he caught sight of Clarkson, laying the tea pot on the polished wooden surface, an ornate and inlaid ivory place mat laid carefully beneath its hot base.

"Addae" Clarkson beamed back, "you are looking so well, I hope that life in London in Mr Sharp's service is to your liking."

"It is Sir," answered the boy in a voice that still held a strong sense of his native tongue. "But I will soon be travelling with Mr Falconbridge and his family to the new colony, I hope again to be able to find my family, though I fear that my brothers are dead."

It was an avalanche of information and as Addae backed out of the room, in the full habit and attire of a London servant, Clarkson looked at Sharp for an explanation, but before one could be given it was their unknown visitor that spoke up, and he was clearly quite startled.

"Who was that boy?" he asked, a look not unlike shock upon his face.

"A young man that has been in my service these last three years," explained Sharp, "ever since he had the wherewithal to escape from the clutches of a beastly Bristol merchant and to hitch a lift east with this fine gentlemen."

"Why do you ask?" said Clarkson, "you look quite shaken by it if you don't mind me saying so Sir. I'd like to understand more and quickly, as I have growing concerns for your character."

"All will become clear," said the plainly dressed man, whom neither Abolitionist thought had enough credentials about him to be considered a gentleman. "I joined The Brothers at Jamestown and paid Captain Howlett a handsome purse for 'the run' back to England. I had made my way up the coast after being marooned at the islands you see."

"Wait a moment", challenged Clarkson, as he worked out the timeline in his head. "As I recall, your vessel put out to sea long after The Brothers left Bristol, so how is it that you were able to complete the return journey on Howlett's ship when you sailed out on The Pilgrim?"

"The Pilgrim had met with favourable trading on first making it ashore on the Windward Coast, and so – as I later learned - had started on the shorter 'middle passage' several weeks earlier than The Brothers, which sailed down to Guinea and so faced a longer second leg. But the prospect of rich pickings from a fully loaded and healthy cargo had set the Captain thinking, and so, though her profits were well ahead of all reasonable expectations, he got greedy and decided to 'lighten his load'. He paid off several of the crew in worthless local coin and abandoned them to their fate, and I was numbered amongst those unfortunates."

"Your testimony would have been most welcome a few months ago," exclaimed Clarkson. "We should talk in detail of your findings, in case there is anything that we may be able to put to good use in the coming years. Though it's unlikely that Parliament would accept your testimony without your name."

"Alas, I would not be prepared to give such a testimonial," said the man, "for the reasons that I have already given. Once I am done here with my tale, then I will be again to sea, I fancy that the northern states are a good bet for a man such as I – Boston seems to me to be a fine up and coming city, one where I may well lay my hat."

"Pray, continue" ordered Sharp, more than a little annoyed at the man's apparent lack of backbone.

"I met with Doctor Gardiner almost immediately and we became instantly on friendly terms," he said, "though the good Doctor did keep himself to himself for much of the voyage, staying within his cabin until things became too strange and too concerning. It was a few weeks into the crossing before anyone noticed our diminishing numbers, but it took an all hands call by the Captain to first identify that there was a problem aboard."

"The crew were not all present?" asked a bemused Clarkson, at which the stranger nodded in confirmation. "Well, what in heaven's name had happened to them?" asked Clarkson suspecting foul play on the part of the Captain and crew who, he knew only too well, were not adverse to lightening the load on the return trip and so saving themselves a bob or two on wages once it came to the final reckoning.

"At first we had the same suspicions," said the man, guessing the Reverend's line of thought, "but it was not the Captain or his officers who were guilty on this occasion for they too were amongst the missing and within a few weeks more, only the bosun and the Captain remained, along with myself and the good Doctor. Our fine ship had been battered in a storm and the half-mast was lost, the rudder barely functional from the mighty waves that had torn its upper beams asunder, and we were drifting far off our chartered course. The Captain had already been confined to quarters, for he had gone quite mad and was a danger to all about. The three of us overpowered him and removed all weapons from his person and from his cabin, then kept him prisoner lest he escape to wreak havoc."

"I can see why you wish to remain anonymous Sir" said Sharp, "for the High Court of the Admiralty would almost certainly see that as mutiny, a crime for which you would be hanged at Wapping."

"Of that small matter, I am well aware, and is why I have stayed away for so long" said the man with a worried look, "and so now I hope that you can afford me some trust in my intentions here, for why would I return to these islands and run such a risk, if it was not for a noble cause?"

It was indeed a strong argument and his audience of two glanced at each other as if in confirmation that they were of the same mind. "Go on," said Sharp, "your good intentions are duly noted."

"The Captain died not long afterwards," said the stranger, "we believe at his own hand, though how he managed to tie his hands and secure the noose is a mystery, but no one else could have arranged such a feat as he was a strong and heavy villain and, even had he been drugged, it would have taken the strength of two men to hoist him so."

"I have a memory Sir", interrupted Clarkson, "of that time on the wharf in Bristol, when you recounted to me your previous experiences of Captain Howlett and how you would 'never sail under his command again'. Now that I mention it, I am certain that you said he was a 'scoundrel' and I had the distinct impression that there was some bad blood between you. If that is so, then why did he let you back aboard his ship and why did you put your differences aside and come aboard for 'the run'?"

"You are right Sir", admitted the man. "He was indeed a villainous rogue, ask anyone that has ever sailed under him, and they will all tell you the same, whilst those that haven't will know of him and will, if they can, avoid ever putting to sea on one of his ships. But money talks, and I paid a handsome fee to make the run back with him, with a promise made of half on departure and the same again on arrival in any English port, which is my good fortune that I no longer need to concern myself with."

"Quite a motive?" said Sharp, suspicious as always from his years spent at the bar. "A motive for murder, perhaps? And I wouldn't be so sure that you are debt-free in this regard, but let us leave that matter to one side for a moment for there are more pressing things that we need to discuss."

"So, there were but three of you now?" Clarkson interrupted, letting the question hang there for a while longer and intent on getting to the heart of the man's tale. "Did all three make it to shore alive?"

"Yes" said the stranger, more uncomfortable now that Sharp had intervened. "Though only I survived. We drifted for months, fortunate only that the supplies that were intended for the sustenance of thirty men now only needed to be divided amongst three and so, we did not want for food or water. The bosun had some rudimentary knowledge of the charts and the sextant, but without the Captain and the other officers we could not set a course and without a crew we could not steer the ship. By the stars and the sun, we could get a measure of our general route and knew that we were headed in a south easterly course, but as the air became more humid we knew that we were closer to the Tropics than to the European continent."

"Are you saying that the boat drifted all the way back to Africa?" asked an incredulous Clarkson. "How is that even possible, even I know of the prevailing trade winds that would have set even an unmanned craft on a course for Ireland or even allowing for some roguish current, to Spain."

"That is what we thought too," answered the man, "but the landscape that we saw was unmistakably African and as we drifted closer into shore, our presence was noted by the other ships, and we were hailed and told to prepare to be boarded."

"It was then that I found Doctor Gardiner, dead." He paused for a moment, out of respect if nothing else. "I know not exactly when he died, but I rapped upon his cabin door in my joy at the news that we were about to be saved, and on there being no reply and finding the door locked, I fashioned a battering ram from a piece of broken mast and with the help of the bosun, smashed my way inside. He was slumped in the corner of the cabin, his eyes wide open and his mouth ajar, and the look upon his face is not one that I will easily forget."

"What would have occasioned such an end?" asked Sharp, "I would suspect a heart attack with no other evidence to the contrary, but what would have caused such a seizure?"

"That is the part of the story that I have not yet shared with you," said the stranger, "and one that I have not yet reconciled with my own heart, for it is too strange to be believed, even for me."

"Continue," said Clarkson, intent on hearing the man out and desperate for him to reveal all.

The man heaved in a fresh gulp of air, before continuing with his tale, as if it's very retelling was taking its toll upon his otherwise resolute constitution. "We had all seen the lights," he explained somewhat cryptically. "Once when we were all crouched together on the deck, and when we did, we all agreed that we had seen it before."

"The lights?" asked Clarkson, sure that nothing spiritual would be at the root of this evil.

"An orb of light," said the stranger. "No bigger than a small cannonball, that pulsed with life and hovered about the ship. Some of the men referred to it as a 'wil o' the wisp' others as 'Saint Elmo's fire'; we watched it lead at least one seaman below, and we assume that the rest were all similarly led, like the pied piper and the rats in the old legend."

"An extraordinary account Sir," mocked Clarkson. "Thank you for sharing it, but I think that I may speak for both of us when I say that it is 'balderdash'. But to complete the tale, and a 'tall tale' is seems to be, you have accounted for the Doctor and the Captain," said Clarkson, "what about the bosun? I thought he survived this, this curse?"

"For a time, he did," said the man ignoring the rebuke, "but he did not reach the shore. He was safe aboard our rescuers boat when he leapt from the side of it, the crew said that he saw the circling sharks and without a word, jumped into their midst, as if he was intent on destroying himself. He was quite delirious when he left the ship and was destined for the local gaol, the only place of internment at the coast where a madman can be safely held until a Doctor can be summoned. But like the others, he didn't make it."

"So, is that the end of it then?" prompted Clarkson, convinced that it was all a tissue of lies. "I'm not quite sure what to say, I have to tell you!"

"Not quite," he said, "there is more, and still more now that I have set eyes upon your servant, for I fear that there is a sombre twist in all of this, for which I do not have an answer."

"Addae?" asked Sharp indignantly, "what in heaven's name does he have to do with this whole sorry mess?"

"A most peculiar sight met my eyes as I regarded the deck, just as I placed my feet on the ladder to the waiting boat and turned about to make my way down. The light was there again. But I had never before seen it in daylight, and so I was taken off guard, though I couldn't take my eyes off it. It seemed to grow as it glowed, pulsing like a beating heart and around it I saw the faintest outline of a boy, his body clearly standing upon the deck and his face, most clearly, staring back at me, before the vision faded and the light moved off, over the stern of the ship and out of sight towards the land."

"What nonsense" spluttered Sharp, "we are talking spirits now are we? Demons, witches, and familiars next I don't doubt, it's like something from the days of King James. I cannot believe such a tale."

"Believe what you will," said the stranger, "but I have no reason to deceive you, yet I have travelled this far to tell you this tale and of the good Doctor's fate, putting my own security at risk as you have already observed. You can read it for yourself for I feel sure that all but the Doctor's own end will be contained herein."

"Was Doctor Gardiner laid to rest?" asked Clarkson, "in a Christian manner?"

"He is buried at Bonny Point," said the man, "and he was given a fitting tribute from those who were there. He was a good man, but a troubled one, haunted by his past involvement in The Trade and desperate to make reparations for it."

"And what of the boy?" asked Clarkson, "you said that Addae had something to do with this?"

"I cannot say," said the stranger, "but when I saw him just now, when I regarded his face up close as he served us with the tea, I had seen his face before. The very same features, the same dark eyes and beaming smile, the same as stared back at me as I descended from the side of the ship into the waiting canoe. The very same."

Clarkson looked across at Sharp and shook his head in denial. "This makes no sense; how can we be expected to believe this?" he said angrily.

"I cannot explain it" said the stranger, "though I do have a theory which I discussed with Doctor Gardiner the night before his death.

"Go on," said Sharp, "we must hear of all of it, if we are to know what to make of all this."

"There was a boy aboard the ship, so Doctor Gardiner said," explained the stranger. "He told me of it, but I did not see him myself, at least not in the flesh, as he did not make it to the islands. He disappeared on the night of 2nd November, when the ship was beset by a monstrous storm and he went missing, presumed washed overboard. I explained to Doctor Gardiner that this date, by some macabre coincidence, is the feast day of Baron Samedi, one of the deities worshipped by the slaves on the island formerly known as Hispaniola."

"The island of Haiti?" said Clarkson, checking his facts.

"Yes, Hayti as it is known locally and also formerly the French island of Saint Domingue," the man confirmed. "Their religion is an old one, a fusion of the Catholic faith imposed first by the Spanish and then by the French, and the African belief system that is thought to have originated in the heart of the continent, in the country now known as the Congo."

"I'm not sure that I like where this is heading," said Sharp, his hackles rising at the very mention of the Papists.

"Baron Samedi, also known as Bawen Samdi or even Baron Saturday, so named because he draws his strength from the day between Good Friday and Easter Sunday when Jesus Christ was not yet reborn, is their Lord of the Cemetery. He guards the gateway to the underworld in that religion, and no soul can pass over, that does not first seek passage through him."

"Incredulous" laughed Clarkson, almost ready to throw the man from his host's house on his behalf.

"He is not entirely evil," continued their visitor. "He is the guardian of the ancestors, the gateway to ancestral knowledge and the pathway for the soul to meet up with them again in the afterlife. And most importantly, he is a protector of children – his wish is always that they grow up to have a long and fulfilling life, before they set their eyes on him, and can be called upon to deliver vengeance upon any and all who bring suffering upon their heads."

"So, you are saying," started Clarkson, trying hard to at least consider the man's ramblings as a genuine explanation for the ship's demise and the loss of their entire crew, "that this, 'Samedi' has somehow been summoned to wreak havoc aboard The Brothers, and to take the lives of all those who had a part in the capture and death of this boy?"

"Not just the boy," said the stranger, "I think it's more than that. I think it's every soul that was ever taken aboard that ship, for every life that was lost, for all the blood that was shed. I know not how, I can't say who or why, but it had something to do with the boy and the night of his disappearance. And maybe that boy and your boy are also related somehow, their appearances are so, so similar!"

"Yes, you said," muttered Clarkson. "So, you think that this boy was in some way related to Addae? A brother maybe, or a cousin perhaps? You say that the two looked identical? Could you have been mistaken in that assumption?"

"I don't think I can be", admitted the man. "I cannot forget his face, and your lad, Addae, he has the very same features, not just similar, but the same. They look the very same. Like twins. Like brothers."

"And what of the boat?" asked Sharp, determined to clear up all aspects of this curious tale. "What happened to The Brothers?"

"It was lost. At sea."

"How so?" asked Sharp, his countenance making it clear that he was not about to take this unnamed informant's word for it.

"It caught fire, in the bay, where it was at anchor," he coughed.

"Or was it set aflame?" It was Clarkson this time, and he suspected foul play. "It wouldn't be the first time that owners have scuppered their own ship to make good on an unprofitable venture. Let me ask you, friend, are you in the employ of the syndicate here? Did the Slavers place you on board in the Americas with this whole escapade in mind? To set tongues wagging about a curse and to see to it that an unprofitable voyage on an old ship came good in the end?"

"Believe what you will, but my word is true. The ship may well have been torched but not by my hand I can assure you, I never wanted to set foot aboard those timbers again and I never did. But two nights after I made it back onto dry land, I saw it light up the night sky and watched from the shore, as it burned through its keel and sank beneath the waves."

"Well, I think we've heard enough for one day," said Sharp, summoning his own authority in the shape of his burly butler to show their visitor to the door. "Thank you for at least telling us of Gardiner's fate, Mr..." It was an old trick, but it didn't work, and the stranger did not fall for it, but just smiled and taking his coat and hat from the insistent servant, took his leave of the two Abolitionists, and shortly afterwards, of the City of London itself. They had asked for a forwarding address and enquired how long he would be staying in London, which he dutifully supplied, but neither had any basis in truth. His promise to Doctor Gardiner was complete, and he had no intention to outstay his lukewarm welcome in the country of his birth.

-o-o-o-

The Sierra Leone Company was formally ratified in the legislature soon after the devastating Parliamentary defeat, but the experiment itself was already under way, and more than eleven hundred former slaves had already been returned to Africa on fifteen vessels, under the command of John Clarkson, the first Governor of the new colony.

The white couple and the black boy whom Granville Sharp had entrusted to their charge, boarded The Duke of Buccleuch at Gravesend on the edge of the Thames Estuary. A crew of seasoned mariners accompanied them, their prize, the many and varied woods of the African continent and the much sought after raw material of elephants teeth, or ivory as it was soon to be more commonly known. Captain McLean was the skipper on a ship belonging to the Anderson

Bros. of Philpott Lane, a trio whose previous ventures had frequently involved the purchase of slaves upon the Guinea Coast and so, both the Captain and the soon-to-be Governor were regularly at loggerheads debating and debasing each other's opinions on the matter.

Alexander Falconbridge had reluctantly agreed, at the behest of his learned friend and reluctant Chairman of the newly formed African Institution, to become the new Governor of the colony, a replacement for John Clarkson who was soon to retire from the post. He no longer went by the title of 'Doctor', hating its association with his days aboard the slaving vessels, and preferring to go by a simpler designation.

Nor was Mrs Falconbridge, his newly wed wife, a willing companion, but she had vowed to be a regular informant for the cause, via correspondence with her friends and family. She had never before been to sea and was but a young woman, unused to the ways of the world and the manners of mariners, though she had promised to do her best to act as guardian to the young boy, until such time as he was old enough to make his own way in the world.

The ship had skirted the coastline of Kent and made its way along England's southern shore to Portsmouth, where it would make its final stop to take on other passengers and goods, before heading out across the vast ocean to the mountainous shores of her new home. She was told to expect to see some wonderful sights, a bounteous country of jade forested hills and rich blue waters. The first port of call would be theirs – Bance Island - an eyot in a vast river, which could be reached only by a day's sailing upstream and the site of several troubles since its establishment as a British protectorate.

But all of that lay ahead of her, and a journey of several months' duration.

It was a pleasant day as she and Addae took to the deck to watch the ship push off from the busy Portsmouth quayside, an impressive array of warships amassed at its bustling docks, their guns at the ready and their bare masts and rigging bedecked in colourful flags. Addae's wide eyes were drinking in the view, his inquisitive face barely hiding his excitement at the prospect of his return to Africa and his homeland. They had discussed the matter already and she knew of his fears, mostly concerning the risk of being recaptured and put aboard another vessel bound for the colonies, though they had been assured that their new abode would be guarded by a militia who would protect them from all such incursions.

He had never mentioned if he had family and Anna-Marie had never wanted to ask him of them, worried that they too had been enslaved or had died during their capture or transportation. She had heard many of the terrible tales in all their gruesome detail from her husband, especially when he was worse the wear for drink, and she did not wish to torment the boy still further by reminding him of that pain.

So, as the ship's sails were lowered to the sound of yelling and bawling from the crew, they both sat in silent reflection, as the wind pushed the ship out of the harbour's protective grip and carried it away, past the low-lying Isle of Wight and out onto the open ocean.

"Are you scared?" she asked him, breaking the silence between them.

"Yes," he answered without hesitation.

"Don't you think we will be safe in the new colony?" she pressed on, looking to her young charge for some small comfort for herself.

This time he didn't answer so quickly, knowing what was in his heart, but not wanting to add to her obvious anxiety. In the end, he told the truth, for it would be impossible to lie. "No," he said, "it will not be safe there, nowhere on the coast is safe now. It was once, but that was many years ago, long before my grandparents time."

"Will there be any family for you there?" she asked him, using his words as a prompt for the question that she had longed to ask.

"No," he answered, equally certain. "I am not from that land. My family are from the heart of Africa, one day I hope to seek them out, those that are still free."

"Were many taken away by the white slavers?" she asked, a trace of sadness in her young voice.

"Many in my village were taken in raids," he said, "I remember them in my dreams. My brothers were taken, and my mother, but that was after. I was taken with my father; we were out fishing on the river when they came. My father was killed, he tried to protect me, but they were too strong for him, and he was hit by a long stick on the back of his head. He bled so much in the bottom of the canoe that I knew he was dead before they pulled us out for the fair."

"I'm sorry Addae," said Anna-Marie, tears welling in her eyes. "I truly am. But how do you know about your brothers and your mother?" It was then that his eyes locked with hers and he patted himself on the chest as if that would be answer enough. "In your heart?" she asked, understanding his gesture immediately. "You know in your heart?"

"Yes," he said defiantly. "Just like I know that my mother is still alive, but that both of my brothers are dead. My eldest brother, Kobe, he is dead, he died in the islands. My twin brother, Ebo, he died on the boat, but his light lives on inside me."

She did cry then, but turned her head away to hide her tears, for they were of no consequence.

She didn't speak again for some time afterwards, fearful that if she did, her chest would heave, and she would not be able to control the flow. The boy was old before his years, wise for a twelve-year-old, noble in his manners and in his speech. He would grow up to be a fine man, of that she had no doubt, if her savage countrymen did not get to him first. She prayed to a God that she no longer believed in, that the boy would never again fall foul of The Trade, that he would find a way to stay out of the slavers' clutches, that she and her husband could offer him protection in the years ahead. She would do her best to be a mother to him, but somehow she knew that she would fall short.

His mother would have been proud of him.

EPILOGUE

The ban on the Atlantic trade in human lives was finally passed into law on 25th March 1807, over twenty years after Clarkson's revelation astride his horse in Hertfordshire. It did not happen overnight and when it came, it only banned the traffic in African slaves that hitherto had been conducted under the British flag; it did not ban 'slavery'. A year after their first failure, in March 1792, the Bill was defeated again, albeit by a narrower margin, but a majority of 49 still stood resolutely against the Abolitionist cause. Four years later on 1st January 1796 another reading of a similar Bill was finally passed in the Commons by 151 votes to 132, but it was blocked by the House of Lords citing the excuse that it had come too late in the session to be afforded reasonable consideration. In 1799, the Slave Trade Regulation Act was finally passed to limit further overcrowding on slave ships and in 1804 another Bill was presented 'too late' to make its passage through the Lords.

It would be forty-three years after the 1791 defeat before the British Parliament would pass The Abolition of Slavery Act to finally abolish the practice of slavery in all of Britain's territories around the world, receiving its Royal Assent on 28th August 1834. In fact, it would be 72 years since the subject was first raised in the House of Commons by a Mr David Hartley, member for Hull, whose motion 'that the slave trade was contrary to the laws of God and to the rights of man", was first raised and defeated in 1776. In its three-hundred-and-fifty-year duration, an estimated 12.5 million Africans were captured and enslaved, of whom an estimated two million died in transportation via the dreaded middle passage. On emancipation in the British colonies, an estimated 800,000 slaves were freed from bondage, though few escaped from the cruelties of life that were endemic in those island communities.

In the end, it would take a mammoth sum of twenty million pounds – a full forty percent of the Treasury's annual income - to finally rid Britain of the curse of slavery, paid in compensation or reparations, to those members of British society who had held investments in The Trade, either as slave owners or in overseas plantations that were reliant on slave labour. As this was the final hurdle that stood in the way of full and complete abolition, it was an expense that the British government was forced to bear as it was necessary for *"compensating the Persons at present entitled to the Services of the Slaves to be manumitted and set free by virtue of this Act for the Loss of such Services."*

The US would follow suit in 1865, the Bill to abolish slavery in the United States passed on 31st January and ratified on 6th December in the 13th amendment which provided that; *"Neither slavery nor involuntary servitude, except as a punishment for crime whereof the party shall have been duly convicted, shall exist within the United States, or any place subject to their jurisdiction."*

The troubled history of Sierra Leone is well documented and will not be repeated here, needless to say that Granville Sharp's ambitious social experiment to repatriate the freed slaves of Nova Scotia and other cities, did not achieve its aims. Alexander Falconbridge was relieved of his office, as an alcoholic, a disease which would lead to his untimely death just a year later. Of the four hundred Africans and former 'orphans' on the streets of London, who were later joined by 1,196 ex-servicemen – who had fought on the side of the British in the war for independence - and their families from Nova Scotia, half may well have been dead within two years of their arrival, the victims of disease and fevers, induced by the harsh environment for which they were ill prepared. The first township was burnt to the ground after a dispute with a local chieftain at the end of 1789 and then, after being rebuilt, was again ransacked by an insurgent French fleet in 1794 after showing some initial promise of making a full recovery. Again, the colony rebounded with the support of the London based Directors and, after political pressure from Sharp, through Parliamentary grants and funds made available from Sharp's own personal estate. By 1798 the newly named Freetown had some three hundred houses, and the male children of local chieftains were being transported to England to receive an education in return for improved local relations between the settlers and the tribesmen.

In 1808 the settlement of Freetown became a Crown Colony, but its arbitrary borders were not always recognised by local tribesmen and many of the initial group of freed slaves, who were transported in its first five years, would not live to enjoy the utopian existence that Sharp had dreamed of - many continued to be picked off in local insurrections and skirmishes or were recaptured and enslaved once more. Britain had identified and banned The Trade in "recaptives" who formed themselves into a new tribe called the 'Kri'.

Thomas Clarkson died in 1846, after a life dedicated to the Abolitionist cause and the emancipation of the slaves, not just in Great Britain as after his success there in 1834, he also campaigned for an end to slavery across the Atlantic Ocean. Granville Sharp lived to see the Atlantic slave trade outlawed by the British Parliament in 1807, but died six years later in 1813, after a life dedicated to philanthropic struggles. His biographer, Prince Hoare should have the last word when he says; 'when to his arduous attainments and exertions are added the child-like mildness, simplicity, and humility of his character and the unceasing benevolence of his disposition, he must be ranked among those who have most zealously revered the 'example left to us' by our Divine Instructor, and who have most diligently, 'followed his steps'."

And of the 12.5 million Africans, stolen from their homes, their names lost to history, I leave the last word to the Methodist minister John Wesley, who did not live to see the "abhorrent" trade abolished – "O earth, O sea, cover not thou their blood."

AUTHOR'S NOTE

The Brothers is a work of fiction that is grounded in historical fact, much of which is drawn from Thomas Clarkson's own meticulous *History of the Abolition of the African Slave Trade*. In writing this book, I have often wondered if Thomas Clarkson really knew what he was taking on in 1787/88 and had he known then that it would take almost fifty years to bring an end to the blight of the African Slave Trade, would he have taken on the task. And had he been told then that it would take another fifty more, until the descendants of those first Africans would be able to call themselves 'free men' in the 'land of the free', I fear that he may have given up on his life's work as a nigh-on impossible task. Or that more than a century on from that long-awaited moment of emancipation, the world would still be fighting to prove that "Black Lives Matter" in the face of unrelenting bigotry at the hands of the very people who had vowed to protect them, then his heart may well have burst with the sheer and never-ending injustice of it.

Though The Brothers itself is a fictional ship and its voyage portrayed here is a fictional journey, a ship called Brothers was moored at Bristol and did ply its trade on the Guinea Coast. Captain Howlett was an infamous Captain, though not on board The Brothers, but many of the other characters included in the accounts of Bristol and Liverpool are real and their stories are recorded in the memoirs of both Thomas Clarkson and Granville Sharp.

The story of the abolition is based in fact, though I have taken some poetic license with the order of events and the names of the people involved, including the Bristol based society whose members made The

Trade their own and some of their prominent characters. There is no doubt that Thomas Clarkson really did travel the length and breadth of England in the years following 1787 and he did report having a 'message from God' on horseback in Wadesmill that put him on this track. He did rescue a Mr Sheriff from aboard a slave ship bound for Africa, though the ship's name was The Africa, and the captain had not yet boarded. Similarly, John Wesley, was indeed a Methodist minister and his speeches have been reproduced here in part, though some license has been taken with their timing, and the events of March 1788 are based in fact - the disturbance at the New Rooms actually happened, an event that Wesley did indeed assign to the works of Satan. The Doctors Gardiner, Falconbridge and Arnold are all real characters and the latter two did provide evidence to the Commission, Gardiner in fact dying on the coast of Guinea though his journal was reportedly buried with him. As for its contents, they are lost to history. The Parliamentary debates did take place as recorded and much of the dialogue is as it happened, though much shortened for the purpose of keeping the book to a reasonable length; for much of the dialogue I am indebted to the meticulous record keeping of Thomas Clarkson whose contemporary record provides an almost word for word account of all of the key confrontations in the chamber of the House of Commons. And I am afraid to say that William Wilberforce did indeed implement his 'bounty' as part of the Dolben Act in 1788 and from that point onwards, ship's captain's did receive a reward of £100 for successfully negotiating the middle passage with minimal loss of life amongst their stock of slaves – 2 dead out of every 100 was considered to be an acceptable ratio – and £50 to the surgeon. Finally, Addae is an imaginary character, though his plight was not – I hope that he made it back to his home, but I fear that he did not.

This book is self-published and though it has been thoroughly reviewed and edited there may yet be some typos. If you find any, please do email me at robertgderry@gmail.com so that I can edit the manuscript. Finally, a request. If you enjoyed this book, please consider leaving an honest review on Amazon.

And if you did enjoy it, please check out my previous novels – The Waterman – published by Austin Macauley Ltd. in 2021 and also available on Amazon in both paperback and eBook formats and The Burning, also available via KDP and Amazon.

ACKNOWLEDGEMENTS

Clarkson, T – *The History of the Abolition of the African Slave trade*, printed by CreateSpace, North Charleston, SCA, USA **

Richardson, D – *The Bristol Slave Traders: A collective portrait*, Bristol Branch of the Historical Association

Morgan, K – *John Wesley in Bristol*, Bristol Branch of the Historical Association

Coules, V – *The Trade, Bristol, and the Transatlantic Slave Trade*, Birlinn Ltd, Edinburgh, 2007

Hochschild, A – *Bury the Chains, The British Struggle to Abolish Slavery*, Pan Books, 2012

Gibson Wilson, E – *Thomas Clarkson, A Biography*, The MacMillan Press Ltd, 1989

Dresser, M – *Slavery Obscured, The Social History of the Slave Trade in Bristol*, Redcliffe Press Ltd

Jones, P – *Satan's Kingdom, Bristol, and the Transatlantic Slave Trade*, Past & Present Press, 2007

Ottabah Cugoano – *Thoughts and Sentiments on the Evils of Slavery*, Penguin, 1999, originally printed in London in 1787

Copley, E – *A History of Slavery and its Abolition*, published by the Sunday-School Union, Paternoster Row, London, 1836

Clarkson, T – *An Essay on the Impolicy of the African Slave Trade, in Two Parts*, Printed and sold by J.Phillips, George-Yard, Lombard Street, London, 1788 **

Hoare, P – *Memoirs of Granville Sharp*, Printed for Henry Colman & Co, London, 1820

Wesley, J – *Thoughts on Slavery*, original pamphlet printed in London, England **

Bailey, A – *African Voices of the Atlantic Slave Trade: Beyond the Silence and The Shame*, Beacon Press, Boston

Newton, J – *Thoughts Upon the African Slave Trade*, original pamphlet printed in London, England **

Newton, J – *Out of the Depths: An Autobiography of John Newton*, Kregel Publications, 2003

Falconbridge, AM – *Two Voyages to Sierra Leonne During the Years 1791/2/3*, original pamphlet printed in London, England.

Letters of the Late Ignatius Sancho, an African, printed by J Nichols and sold by C Dilly, London 1784

Marshall, P – *The Anti-Slave Trade Movement in Bristol*, issued by the Bristol Branch of the Historical Association, Bristol University, 1968

Eickelmann, C and Small, D - *The Mountravers Plantation* - https://seis.bristol.ac.uk/~emceee/

MacInnes, CM - *Bristol and the Slave Trade*, issued by the Bristol Branch of the Historical Association, Bristol University, 1968

Barker, K – *The Theatre Royal Bristol: The First Seventy Years*, printed by F.Bailey & Don Ltd, Dursley, Glos, 1969

Behrendt, SD – *The Captains in the British Slave Trade 1785-1807*

The memoirs of Captain Hugh Crow – *The Life and Times of a Slave Ship Captain*, Longman, Rees, Orme, Brown and Green and G. and J. Robinson, Liverpool, 1828

The Guinea Voyage, a Poem in Three Books, by James Field Stanfield, printed by J Robertson, London, 1807

Cursory remarks upon the Reverend Mr. Ramsay's Essay on the treatment and conversion of African slaves in the British sugar colonies, by a friend to the West India Colonies and their inhabitants (James Tobin), printed for G. and T. Wilkie, No.71 St Paul's Church Yard, London, 1785 **

Marcy, PT – *18th century views of Bristol and Bristolians*, issued by the Bristol Branch of the Historical Association, Bristol University, 1966

The Interesting Narrative of the Life of Olaudah Equiano, or Gustavus Vassa, The African, 1789 – The Gutenberg Project, 2005

Falconbridge, A – Account of the Slave Trade on the Coast of Africa, printed and sold by James Phillips, George Yard, Lombard Street, London, 1788

** contemporary pamphlets and accounts have been used as the basis for several conversations in this novel, the words spoken by Thomas Clarkson, Granville Sharp, William Wilberforce, James Tobin and others, having their basis in fact wherever possible, though much of the dialogue is a work of fiction, the sentiments are consistent.

Printed in Great Britain
by Amazon

29125328R00243